Dr. Susan Calvin is beginning her residency in psychiatry at Manhattan Hasbro teaching hospital, where a select group of patients is receiving the latest in diagnostic advancements—nanotechnology. Nanobots injected into the spinal fluid can locate and assess neural pathways and transmitters, unlocking and mapping the physiological workings of the human mind. The possibilities for such technology are almost endless.

Soon Susan begins to notice an ominous chain of events surrounding the patients, who begin exhibiting extreme behavior, from shocking violence to self-destructive tendencies. When she alerts her superiors, she is met with callous disregard by those who want to keep their project far from any controversy or scrutiny for the sake of their own agenda.

But what no one knows is that a technology that promised to improve life is now under the control of those who seek to spread only death. . . .

D0815997

Isaac Asimov's
I, Robot:
to protect

MICKEY ZUCKER REICHERT

A ROC BOOK

ROC

Published by New American Library, a division of
Penguin Group (USA) Inc., 375 Hudson Street,
New York, New York 10014, USA
Penguin Group (Canada), 90 Eglinton Avenue East, Suite 700, Toronto,
Ontario M4P 2Y3, Canada (a division of Pearson Penguin Canada Inc.)
Penguin Books Ltd., 80 Strand, London WC2R 0RL, England
Penguin Ireland, 25 St. Stephen's Green, Dublin 2,
Ireland (a division of Penguin Books Ltd.)
Penguin Group (Australia), 250 Camberwell Road, Camberwell, Victoria 3124,
Australia (a division of Pearson Australia Group Pty. Ltd.)
Penguin Books India Pvt. Ltd., 11 Community Centre, Panchsheel Park,
New Delhi - 110 017, India
Penguin Group (NZ), 67 Apollo Drive, Rosedale, Auckland 0632,
New Zealand (a division of Pearson New Zealand Ltd.)
Penguin Books (South Africa) (Pty.) Ltd., 24 Sturdee Avenue,
Rosebank, Johannesburg 2196, South Africa

Penguin Books Ltd., Registered Offices:
80 Strand, London WC2R 0RL, England

Published by Roc, an imprint of New American Library, a division of Penguin
Group (USA) Inc. Previously published in a Roc hardcover edition.

First Roc Mass Market Printing, December 2012
10 9 8 7 6 5 4 3 2 1

ALWAYS LEARNING   **PEARSON**

For Pat Rogers,
Chief Warrant Officer 3, U.S. Marine Corps (retired),
Sergeant NYPD (retired), a real hero

Acknowledgments

Editing and creation: Isaac, Janet, and Robyn Asimov, Marty Greenberg, Denise Little, Larry Segriff, and Susan Allison.

Inspiration: Koby Moore, Mark Moore, and Arianne.

Research: All the incredible professionals from Lightfighter (the expertise is theirs, the mistakes my own): Dorsai, 3P051, Sigsshooter, Casket, Naveronski, Borebrush, Dan Kemp, Renee, Ex11A, Murf214, Doctorrich, XGEP, Thekirk, Witch, Rob Frey, Firemission4mortars, Blackfox, CarlosDJackal, K_randomfactor, Mark LaRue, TimW, Mercy, Flynn, MrMurphy, KWG020, 3Humpalot, Eggroll, Fluffpuff, and especially Pat.

Also Sue Russell of Mayfair Lane and Mark Moore (again).

Those people who think they know everything are a great annoyance to those of us who do.

—Isaac Asimov

Chapter 1

July 2, 2035

Protestors mobbed the grassy swatches outside Manhattan Hasbro Hospital, their signs throwing checkered shadows in constant motion across the sidewalks. Among the hospital workers and mostly bewildered new interns, Susan Calvin headed grimly toward the entrance, already beginning to question her residency decision. Having graduated medical school at the top of her class, with impeccable references, she could have matched at any hospital, including the quieter and smaller private facilities upstate. Instead, she had returned to the bustling metropolis of her youth, to a massive facility at the cutting edge of technology and, also, the one closest to the father she missed and loved.

In the middle of the screaming and chanting demonstrators, someone lost his balance. The sudden jolting movement spread, wavelike, through the crowd, sending a young man staggering over the invisible perimeter onto the sidewalk and directly into Susan's path. For an instant, he stood, looking stunned and uncertain, clutching a sign reading DESIGNER BABIES ARE A SIN.

Instinctively, Susan caught his shoulder, steadying him. "Are you all right?"

For an instant, his dark eyes caught her pale blue

ones, and he seized the moment. "You're not planning to work here, are you?"

As he seemed to have regained his balance, Susan removed her hand, tossing back straight brown hair without a single wave. Though she had never worn makeup, and her familial slenderness robbed her of significant curves, she still displayed the natural beauty that often accompanies youth. "As a matter of fact, I am."

"Do you know," he said as he drifted from the sidewalk, "that Manhattan Hasbro *fashions* babies? That they create infants outside the womb and—"

Susan expected the protestor to couch his argument in eugenics, in the murkier science of choosing intelligence, gender, and height; but she suspected his actual concern lay with the classic religious arguments against artificial reproduction. She cut him short. "You mean . . . they help infertile couples conceive?"

Apparently, Susan had struck the proper nerve. The man's lips compressed into a grim line. "If God wanted them to have children, he would have blessed them with a pregnancy."

"Like the crack whore down the street who delivered her sixth baby into the toilet? Or the drunkard under the Verrazano who sold her infant daughter for a fifth of gin?"

Apparently unmoved, the protestor shrugged. "God works in mysterious ways."

"Yes," Susan agreed, shoving past him. "Like blessing us with the technology to 'fashion' babies." She rejoined the crowd funneling into the foyer.

Blocky, padded chairs in links of five filled most of the open area, with small wooden tables at the end of each grouping. Glass cases hung on the walls. Paintings done by children on the pediatrics ward filled one, while another held craft items with tasteful price tags attached. A third displayed a history of Hasbro toys: from ancient clunky-looking Mr. Potato Heads and antique

G.I. Joes, through the years of garish My Little Ponies and Transformers, then a slew of fly-by-night television- and movie-based creatures to the sleek, familiar characters and realistic, interactive animatronics of the day.

People slumped in some of the chairs, many sleeping, seemingly oblivious to the foot traffic peeling off in several directions around them. Susan Calvin followed an arrowed placard that read WELCOME, NEW RESIDENTS, winding her way through the chairs and passing the general patient updating area, an information desk, three cafeterias, five restrooms, and an in-house pharmacy before following another sign that took her down a long hallway filled with physicians' offices, an ethicist's station, and a legal wing.

An additional sign turned Calvin ninety degrees to an auditorium with the doors thrown wide. Tables in front of it held row after row of plastic name tags, interspersed with papers that presumably organized them in some logical fashion. A mass of mostly twentysomethings paused here, all in standard outfits of dress polos and pleated pants, the majority wearing tasteful khaki. Susan knew her blouse and canvas blues fit right in with the attire of the other interns. Murmurs suffused the group, occasionally split by a laugh or cough. As individuals grabbed their pins and headed into the auditorium, Susan gradually moved nearer to the tables.

Susan deliberately gravitated toward the leftmost table, assuming the name tags had been set up alphabetically. But, as she reached the tables, she found the papers divided them by specialty, and she had to edge toward the other end. Spotting PSYCHIATRY, she reached toward it, only to bump hands with a man already clutching his pin. She raised her head to apologize and met a pair of green eyes beneath prominent brows, and a generous straight nose, fine lips, and chiseled cheekbones. A mop of dark blond curls swept from his forehead.

Finding him unexpectedly attractive, Susan could not help smiling shyly before speaking. "Sorry about that."

The young man smiled back and acknowledged her with a nod. "No apology necessary. I'll take any excuse to hold hands with a pretty woman."

Susan's grin broadened, and she could feel warmth crawling across her cheeks. "How sweet."

"Remington Hawthorn." He pinned his name tag onto his dress polo; it contained his name and his residency program: NEUROSURGERY. "Harvard Medical, class of 'thirty-five. Kristy Honor Society. Nominated AOA."

Susan recognized the distinctions. Only the top ten percent of any medical school class got nominated for AOA, and only a third of those received the honor. Currently, Harvard was the second-ranked medical school in the country. She reached for her own tag, pinning it to her shirt. "Susan Calvin, Psychiatry."

Remington's grin wilted. Mumbling an excuse, he turned to leave.

Susan followed him only until they had moved out of the way of the interns behind them. He had switched off the charm in an instant, and Susan believed she knew why. Many surgeons saw the strictly medical fields, particularly the primary care specialties, as beneath them. Susan pursed her lips, irritation flaring, and caught his shoulder.

Remington turned to face her, his features bunching curiously.

"You didn't let me finish my introduction," Susan explained coolly. "Thomas Jefferson Medical." She named the one school that had consistently bested Harvard in the past decade. "Class of 'thirty-five. Hare Honor Society. Earned AOA."

Remington's brows inched upward. "Really?"

"Really." Susan studied him, waiting for the apology she deserved.

Other residents passed them, pouring into the auditorium.

"Forgive my directness." Remington seemed incapable of taking his eyes off Susan's name tag. At least, Susan hoped that was where his attention lay. Otherwise, he had fixed his gaze directly and fanatically on her left breast. "But why?"

"Why?"

"Why waste such incredible credentials on a specialty so . . . so . . ." Remington seemed incapable of finding an inoffensive term. "Well, unscientific?"

Susan spoke volumes with one crooked eyebrow. "Because I'm excellent at reading people, without the need to slice them open first. For example, I can tell you're an arrogant jerk who judges people on shallow criteria, then wonders why you get stuck with nothing but vapid bimbos." With that, she turned on her heel and headed into the auditorium.

A hand touched Susan's elbow, gently guiding her. She looked to her right, expecting Remington but finding a stranger. He had straight ginger hair, with a splash of freckles across his cheeks. His large-lipped mouth split into a grin, and his dark eyes appeared to be laughing. His name tag identified him as Kendall Stevens, also a psychiatry resident. "Calvin, you missed your calling."

Bewildered, she turned her attention to him.

"You should have been a urologist." His smile widened further, contagious. "Orchiectomies a specialty. I've never seen anyone castrate a man so quickly."

Susan's irritation receded in an instant as they slid past seated residents into a center row. "No one does surgical orchiectomies anymore. Not even for chronic prostatic cancer." She considered one remaining instance. "Not even for sexual predators. Drugs only."

Kendall passed an empty seat, taking the one beside it. "Tell me, Calvin—where do you get that tongue sharpened?"

Susan felt a hint of remorse. Her tendency to speak her mind had hindered her social life at times. That and her focus on her studies had severely limited dating. "Was I that hard on him?"

"A witch," Kendall confirmed. "With a capital *B*." He gestured to the empty seat, and Susan accepted it. As she sat, he planted both elbows on the armrest between them. "I'm just kidding. He deserved everything he got; most surgeons do."

Susan rolled her eyes. "Now who's stereotyping?"

"Me." Kendall turned to face the stage. "But it's based on truth. Surgeons act as if they have a lock on intelligence and competence. The rest of us are peons who exist only to perform their day-to-day scut work; obviously, if we had any talent, we'd be surgeons, too."

Until she started medical school, Susan had had no experience with physicians of any type. Her mother had died when Susan was in preschool, and she knew little about her father's job at U.S. Robots and Mechanical Men, Inc. When she asked questions, he always answered vaguely. *"What isn't restricted is dull. And actually, come to think of it, the confidential stuff is boring, too."* Then he would change the subject to her studies, her friends, her hopes and dreams. "All surgeons can't be like that."

Kendall shrugged. "All the ones I've met. And my dad's a hospital administrator, so I've met a bunch."

That caught Susan's attention. "Administrator? Here?"

"Here? Hell, no." Kendall feigned a dramatic shiver. "What a horrible thought."

Susan did not understand. She adored her father and would love working under him. Before she could reply, however, a slender middle-aged man took the podium at the front of the auditorium.

"Greetings, new residents." The nearly invisible microphone clipped to the pocket of his dress polo carried his voice evenly through the room.

A vague murmur rose from the audience, and the splendid acoustics carried that as well.

"My name is Brentwood Locke, and it's my job to begin your orientation to Manhattan Hasbro Hospital by explaining the three holy commandments."

Susan settled into her chair for a series of long-winded speeches. She glanced at the Vox on her left wrist. Currently, it displayed only the time: 8:03 a.m. With a few deft adjustments, she tuned it in on Brentwood Locke, bringing him into vivid focus on the screen. Looking around, she saw other residents doing the same thing. She double-checked to make sure the transmitter was turned off.

"The first thing you need to know is Manhattan Hasbro prides itself on being one of the most progressive hospitals in the country. We pioneered human manipulation of animal- and plant-based stem cells, created the passive ventilator, and have the largest in-vitro fetal diagnostic center in the world."

A spattering of polite applause followed the pronouncement.

"Which makes us a leading recipient of government and private research grants, but also the target of every kook with an agenda in the known world. As I'm sure you all noticed on your way in this morning, we always have a plethora of protestors."

Kendall leaned toward Susan. "A plethora of protestors," he repeated. "Is that like a gaggle of geese? A herd of horses? A pod of porpoises?"

Susan snorted.

Brentwood Locke continued. "Commandment number one: no engaging with protestors under any circumstances. Some of those people are rabid believers with agendas that might include violence. We don't want any of you harmed or killed, and we don't invite unnecessary controversy."

Susan sucked air through her teeth.

Kendall jerked his head toward her, then chuckled. "You castrated one of them, too, didn't you?"

"Shut up." Susan doubted anyone would fault her for a short conversation with a protestor before she learned the rules, but she did not need Kendall's blabbering her mistake all over the auditorium.

Locke was still speaking. "Commandment number two: We obey strict rules of confidentiality. It's fine to talk about patients with anyone who is involved in their care, including attendings in your specialty, consultants, other residents on your team, parents, guardians, spouses, designated spouse alternatives, and adult children of the patient. However, these conversations must not take place in areas where other people can overhear you, including occupied elevators." Locke said the last with enough emphasis to make it clear problems had already occurred in that last venue.

"If you speak about patients with your family and friends, you cannot say anything that could identify the patient. No last names, no clear descriptions, no occupational designations that might make it possible for anyone to guess the patient's identity. And, if someone such as . . . Lolinda Cosada," he said, naming a prominent movie star, "gets admitted for any reason, no specifics or details leave her room, even if they seem unimportant and unrelated to her treatment. Violation of confidentiality policy is grounds for dismissal and possibly legal action. Do you all understand?"

Mumbles swept through the audience again, along with a few clear affirmations.

"And, last but not least, stone tablet commandment number three is if you wind up involved with any medical studies, you do so with the explicit understanding that the lead researchers' word is law and no information leaves the hospital grounds. After years of arduous research and expensive grants, no scientist wants his results leaked, or his ideas stolen, before publication. If you violate number three, you will likely disappear off the face of the planet. And rightly so."

The directness of the speaker caught Susan by surprise, though she appreciated it.

Locke wound down his speech. "Now, if any of you here have any doubts about your ability to perform the necessary duties of a resident in such a facility, please step outside the auditorium now. We will find you another placement, no questions asked." He looked around the auditorium. "Anyone? Don't be shy. If you matched here, you graduated in the top half of your class. We will have no trouble placing you."

The rumble of conversation took over the silence, and every head moved about, seeking someone who did not belong. No one accepted Locke's offer. Susan supposed anyone who interviewed at Manhattan Hasbro already knew its reputation. She had chosen it more for location than anything else, but the cutting-edge research and facilities had seemed like a bonus.

"Thank you." Brentwood Locke stepped down from the podium.

A crisp young man, barely out of his twenties, took Locke's place. After a brief introduction, he proceeded to bore the residents with a thirty-minute presentation of the history of Manhattan Hasbro, from its inception as Manhattan Public through its long years of service and reconstruction, to the years when the current Hassenfeld CEO donated the money and had it renamed in honor of his company. Susan found her mind drifting, especially when her Vox display blinked to indicate a text message from her father.

Though she would have liked nothing better than to converse with John Calvin, Susan knew the moment she lost the thread of the history lesson, the speaker would say something she absolutely needed to know. Instead, she touched the Kwik-key sequence that indicated she was busy and would get back to him as soon as possible. Her father flashed a "^-luck," then an "ILuvU," and disappeared from the screen.

A skeletal elderly lady took her place at the podium next, detailing human resources issues such as salary and benefits. Both were as meager as everyone had warned her: slave labor in the name of learning, but only what Susan had expected. The woman discussed the no-more-than-every-sixth-night call the government currently mandated and the day off afterward if the resident did not log in a reasonable amount of sleep. The paging system programmed directly into the residents' Vox, and the hospital would supply a basic-level Vox to anyone who did not already own one. Susan doubted they would have to supply any. She could scarcely imagine a third- or fourth-year medical student who could have survived clinical rotations, with their barrage of questions, without a basic wrist computer.

Susan had seen the mechanization of supplies on her interview visit, but the woman at the podium explained them in more detail. When a patient entered the hospital, the system generated a series of cards, one for each staff member involved in the patient's care. She cautioned the residents to keep these cards safely in the pocket of their white coat or shirt. Anytime they needed supplies, they swiped the appropriate card through the slot of the machine, and it vended the required item, charging it to the proper bill.

The residents' shared call rooms, the correction of mistakes, the change of command, and all eleven forms of public transportation to the hospital were discussed. Manhattan Hasbro had three paging systems, in addition to direct calls to personal Vox. Nearly every bed also served as a monitor. All charting was electronic and could be accessed through the many stations and, with certain privacy installations, through portable palm-pross terminals. She ran through the various colors of codes and how to handle every one. The security systems seemed overbearing and Orwellian in their duplication and complexity, especially on the Obstetrics Unit.

Just when Susan wondered if her brain could absorb any more information, the woman finished.

A moment later, another man took the stage. He sported a face full of honest wrinkles and a head of thin white hair. He wore a pair of glasses balanced on a leathery nose. Either his age had caught up to his eye surgery or he had chosen not to risk it. Despite appearing ancient, he walked with a solid and deliberate tread and did not look debilitated in any way as he stepped to the podium.

"My name is Dr. Kevin Bainbridge, University of Pennsylvania, class of 1985. I'm sure you're all happy to know I'm your last speaker this morning."

Scattered murmurs and bits of applause followed.

Bainbridge cleared his throat, then spoke some of the most dreaded words in the English language: "When I was a boy . . ."

Susan dodged Kendall's gaze. If he so much as smiled, she would burst into laughter.

". . . just beginning my residency, things were much different, much harder."

Susan settled more comfortably into her seat, prepared for another long-winded speech, this one more self-serving.

"Our call schedule was one in two. That means, we were on call every other night, and there was no such thing as an 'after-call' day off."

Kendall leaned toward Calvin and stage-whispered in a gravelly, old-man parody, "And we liked it."

Calvin choked a laugh into a snort, biting her lips.

Oblivious, Bainbridge continued. "And we worried we were missing half the good cases by going home every other night. Some rotations, we had shifts that went twelve hours on, twelve hours off or twenty-four hours on, twenty-four hours off every day for a month. And we still worried we were missing half the good cases.

"We once calculated our pay at ninety-seven cents an

hour, working approximately one hundred to one hundred twenty hours per week. Then came a few high-profile cases of sleepy residents making foolish mistakes, and the system that had worked beautifully for a hundred years became obsolete overnight." Bainbridge sighed deeply, shaking his head. "There followed all the so-called humane residency laws that treat you all like grade school babies. Limited call, after-call days off, minimum wages." His head shaking grew more vigorous, as though the very idea of wanting mere sixty-hour weeks and expecting half a living wage made a person soft as bread dough.

"I want you all to realize how lucky you are compared to your teachers. We don't want to hear any complaining about hours or wages; you have it easy. We expect you to spend a significant amount of your home-time learning, reading, and studying journals. You will come to work up-to-date on diagnoses and treatments, prepared for difficult patients and conundrums, and ready for any emergency. From this moment forth, lives depend on your capability as medical professionals, on your ability to retrieve knowledge, on your every small decision.

"You had best not think of your off-time as downtime. The law demands you take this time for rest and to refresh your brain, to make sure you're not a danger to your patients, not for fun and games. It exists solely to make sure you come to work ready to perform your duties to the best of your abilities. If you attend a party, it had best be someone's birthday or retirement. If you find an alcoholic drink in your hand, think about how it will affect your performance, and your sleep, before downing it. Your years of residency are not the time to give birth, get unnecessarily ill, or entertain your hobbies. The next several years belong to Manhattan Hasbro and to your future patients, not to you. Whatever you do, think how it will improve your acumen and the lot of your patients. If it won't, don't do it."

Susan dared a glance at Kendall. He looked straight ahead, but his profile revealed a grin she could not currently handle. She turned her attention to her Vox, where Bainbridge was saying his thank-you and stepping down from the podium.

Susan typed a quick message to her father: "Hey D. Lss thn 1 hr & alrdy broke 1 crdnal rule. Only othr thng lrnt is dn't wnt wrk w/ ol doc Bainbridgc. Hpfully, he's pathologist or smthng. Luv S."

Brentwood Locke, the first man who had spoken, retook the podium. "And now, if you will all step out into the hallway, we will divide you by residency program. You will find someone holding a sign with your specialty, and that person will take you to your residency quarters and lockers."

The residents rose, turning toward the exit. In the conversational din, Kendall resumed his scratchy, mocking voice. "Patient records consisted of piles of parchment, which we scratched out of inkwells using turkey quills. We performed surgery by gaslight, using nothing but nitrous oxide. And, when we did these things, we worried about missing half the good cases."

Chapter 2

The psychiatry residents' office consisted of fifty cubbies, two-thirds of which contained medical bric-a-brac; a circular table that held three palm-pross computers; eight chairs; and lockers lining every wall. Taped to several of the lockers, Susan saw comics, silly drawings with cryptic jokes, photos, and small dangling toys. The new residents were called away in groups of five until only Susan, Kendall, and three others remained with the young man who had escorted them all to the office.

Susan studied their guide. He had a perfectly round head topped with a frizzy ball of dark blond hair. She doubted even the greasiest hair care products could tame it. His ears and lips stuck out prominently, making his nose look relatively small, and his cheeks were pudgy and flushed. Though not fat, his figure had a softness to it; his arms and legs were a bit short for his torso, and his hands were enormous. When he spoke, tiny bubbles pooled at the corners of his mouth.

"Hello, R-1s." He used the shorthand term for first-year residents. "My name is Clayton Slaubaugh. I'm the R-2 assigned to oversee you on the PIPU, the Pediatric Inpatient Psychiatry Unit."

"Pediatric *inpatient* psychiatry?" said a woman in an

incredulous tone. One of the two female interns Susan had not yet formally met, she had pixie-cut black hair, dark eyes, and a swarthy complexion. "I thought that had gone the way of ostomy bags and oxygen tents."

Clayton glanced at the Vox on his left wrist. "Are you Susan? Nevaeh? Or Sable?"

The woman bobbed her head, her face a long oval. "Sable Johnson, R-1. It's just we learned in medical school—"

Clayton interrupted, anticipating the question. "Pediatric inpatient psychiatry has become rare, but it's not defunct. We even have 'lifers,' kids who've been there so long, they might as well call it home." He looked around the table. "It's the most heartbreaking unit in all of psychiatry, which makes it the perfect place to start. That was my first rotation as an R-1, too." He hitched his chair toward the table. It caught on the rug, teetered, and fell backward, dumping Clayton to the floor.

Horrified, Susan leapt to her feet to assist. Kendall turned his head, as if to wipe something from his face, but Susan suspected he politely hid a smile. The other three R-1s simply stared in surprise.

Clayton scrambled awkwardly to his feet, tangling himself up with the chair's legs in the process.

Worried about getting caught in his thrashing, Susan stepped back.

It took inordinately long for Clayton to right the chair and place his bottom cautiously back into it. "Sorry about that," he said with a matter-of-factness that suggested he did such things all the time. "I'd like to get to know whom I'll be working with over the next month. Could you introduce yourselves, one by one, and tell me something special about you?" He looked toward Sable to begin.

She obliged. "As I said, my name's Sable Johnson. I graduated from the University of Hawaii, and I'm interested in psychiatry because my mother is schizophrenic."

Susan retook her own chair, between Kendall and Clayton.

Clayton nodded next at the male R-1 beside Sable. He had short, spiky brown hair, hazel eyes, and a slender figure. "I'm Monk Peterson. I graduated from Johns Hopkins at the age of twenty-three." Clayton made no comment, simply moving his gaze to the next woman.

She wore a dress polo, like the others, in plain khaki that matched her pants. A braided rope belt circled her tiny waist; and, unlike the others, she did not wear a Vox. "Nevaeh Gordon. Medical College of New York. I'm a vegan."

Really, Susan thought, *some people take "you are what you eat" a little too seriously.*

At a gesture from Clayton, Kendall piped up next. "I'm Kendall Stevens, graduate of New York University." He added, deliberately sounding like a personals ad, "I like dogs, long walks on the beach, and peace on earth."

The group chuckled. Then it was Susan's turn.

"Susan Calvin. Thomas Jefferson Medical." She racked her brain for some tidbit worthy of remaining permanently lodged in her colleagues' thoughts of her. "I also happen to like dogs, though I don't own one. I live with the perfect man," she said, then added conspiratorially, "my father."

Smiles wreathed every face.

"Thanks, everybody," Clayton said, rising. "Now we have to get your thumbprints established on the door lock and assign lockers and cubbies. Then, we're on to the on-call rooms to allow another group in here." He glanced at his Vox. "After that, it's a tour of the hospital, particularly the psychiatry areas, restrooms, cafeterias. And, finally, to the Pediatric Inpatient Psychiatry Unit, where Stony Lipschitz, our supervising R-3, is holding down the fort single-handedly until our arrival." He took a step toward the door, nearly tripping over the askew leg of his chair.

*   *   *

The tour of a cheery hospital with impressively up-to-date facilities ended with a descent into the basement that betrayed everything the new psychiatry residents had previously seen. Janitorial staff rolled massive equipment through bleak, gray hallways broken by unmarked doors, beyond which Susan Calvin could hear the whir and hum of machinery. At length, they turned down a quieter corridor, no less dreary, that ended in a thick metal door with an old-fashioned key lock below the handle.

Clayton Slaubaugh, R-2, stopped the interns in front of it, removing a key from his pocket. "It's an ugly part of the hospital, but necessary. The unit itself is far more upbeat, but the inpatient children need quiet isolation from the rest of the hospital. They're locked in for their own protection, and to prevent elopement, and the location keeps adults from wandering in where they don't belong." With that warning, he unlocked the door onto an empty hallway broken only by two doors and ending at another metal door with another key lock. "You will not be issued keys. Only the attending, the R-3, and certain members of the nursing staff carry them. To come and go, you will have to use the buzzers." He indicated a recessed intercom-type system.

Feeling extremely uncomfortable, Susan went silent as she looked around at the empty walls and listened to the echo of the door closing behind them. Even Kendall seemed to have nothing funny to say. As they passed the first doorway, Susan peeked inside to see an adult couple playing a board game with a girl who appeared to be about ten years old. The room across from it was empty. Clayton used the same key to unlock the second door, opening the way into the world of inpatient pediatric psychiatry.

The unit itself looked far brighter than the hallways leading to it, the walls painted a mellow blue with paper drawings and watercolors taped to them. A wall broke the area directly ahead into a large staff area on the right and a hallway on the left. Immediately to Susan's right, a door opened onto an enormous restroom; then a smaller area contained a medication room, where an orderly was placing items onto a snack cart. Directly to the left, Susan saw two doorways opening onto simply furnished bedrooms that each consisted mostly of a metal bed and shelving, all fastened securely to the walls and floors. Compared to the sleek, monitored beds in the rest of the hospital, these looked like ancient devices of torture.

After making certain the door closed and latched behind him, Clayton led the residents into the staffing area. A large nurse, a head taller than Susan, met them at the opening, nodded at Clayton, then stepped aside to allow them entrance. As the six resident physicians funneled through the opening, Susan noticed the nurse casually pushing a chair out of Clayton's way with her foot. Apparently, the clumsiness he had displayed in the psychiatry residents' office was not a fluke.

The staff area contained multiple tables, desks, chairs, and cabinets. Most of the level surfaces held computer consoles, some being accessed by staff members. Other than the cinder block partition that divided the staff area from the main hallway, the walls consisted of what appeared to be glass. Through it, Susan could see several more bedrooms swinging around the back of the unit, a closed white door marked SELF-AWARENESS ROOM, another restroom, and a large open area that currently held several children varying in age from elementary school to adolescence. Most sat on chairs and couches, watching an enormous television screen enclosed in a clear, unbreakable box. A few played games or sat talking in small groups. None returned her gaze. Apparently, what she had first mistaken for glass was actually a series of one-way mirrors.

A young man no older than thirty rose from his seat in front of one of the consoles. Tousled jet-black hair fell rakishly across his forehead, emphasizing eyes so strikingly blue, Susan assumed they were tinted. His nose jutted, perfectly straight, over a mouth that clearly smiled a lot. He had classic high cheekbones and a solid, undimpled chin. Though he was slender, his chest and arms revealed him as an athlete. Susan caught herself staring and swiftly looked away, only to notice every other R-1 studying him as intently.

"Stony Lipschitz," Clayton introduced, passing the key he had used to open the unit doors on to the R-3. "Our peerless leader."

"Hello," Stony said. Accepting the key, he dumped it into the pocket of his dress polo, along with a pack of laminated patient cards. "I'm the R-3 supervising PIPU this month." He spoke with just a hint of a lisp, which likely worsened with agitation. Susan winced at the irony of a lisper with so many *s*'s in his name. "Actually, I've been getting to know our patients the last three days. R-3s switch rotations a bit early so we're ready for the new R-1s and the patients don't completely lose continuity of care. Three days before you're finished, I'll train my replacement and move on to adult outpatients. But, for the rest of this month, you're stuck with me."

Clayton ran through a brief introduction, probably as much to refresh his own memory as to inform Stony. He pointed to each R-1 as he spoke his or her name. "Kendall Stevens, Monk Peterson, Sable Johnson, Susan Calvin, Nevach Gordon."

Stony paid close attention to Clayton's words and gestures, then nodded. "I think I have it, but I may ask once or twice more, if that's all right."

All of the R-1s bobbed their heads and mumbled their okays.

"The interesting thing about doctors is that no two treat patients exactly the same way." Stony retook his seat, leaned back against the desk, and gestured for the others to sit as well.

A wild scramble for the chairs sent Clayton dropping to the floor again. Stony smiled, as if at a private joke. "Clay, do you mind handling the patient work for a bit while I finish orienting the -1s?"

Clayton's round face turned pink, and he rose, brushing dirt from his pleated slacks. "Of course. No problem." He headed off toward the nurses.

Stony watched him pass beyond hearing range, then pulled his seat closer to the R-1s. "Ol' Clamhead's not a bad guy, though he doesn't have much grace, physically or socially."

Though Stony could surely tell the R-1s needed a moment to process the nickname, he did not miss a beat. "Every doctor finds his or her own niche. Some are sticklers for procedure and use the most cautious approach to every patient in every circumstance. Some are more liberal and experimental in their approaches. Others fall various places in between." He glanced around at each of them in turn, as if reading their futures. "You will wind up working with examples of each type of physician, and most of them will be excellent doctors in their own way. Despite protocols and studies, no two doctors approach a patient exactly the same way, and that's not a bad thing."

Stony leaned backward, against the desk again. "All of you will develop a style, and it might change over time. Some of the R-3s, and most of the attendings, believe their way is the only right way. I'm not one of them. I'm more of a hands-off leader. You can't learn responsibility, or to think for yourselves, if I'm always telling you what to do. These are your patients. If you want to try something different, go ahead. If it's outlandish, stupid, or dangerous, I guarantee the nurses will run to me before implementing it."

Susan saw her peers' heads bobbing in agreement and

found herself doing the same thing. With long-term patients, especially children, nurses often became every bit as attached and protective as the parents.

"You've probably heard the pediatric inpatient unit is the hardest psych unit, and it is. But it's also a great place to try new approaches. It takes a serious situation to land a child here, and conventional medicine has already failed them. You're unlikely to make things worse, and who knows? You might have a brilliant breakthrough that doctors with more rigid ideas have missed."

Stony looked around the group. "If you're uncomfortable with the sink-or-swim approach, Clamhead and I are here to help you with any problems or questions. Any. You're here to treat the patients. We're here to keep you, and the hospital, out of trouble. So, if you feel you need some backup, or just some advice from someone more experienced, come to Clammy or me."

Stony reached into a cubby and removed a baseball cap, which he held upside down by the bill. "He called me your peerless leader, but I'm just a resident, like you. Every day, we will round with the real man in charge, our attending physician. He will want to hear about your patients and their progress, and he's the one you have to impress. Tomorrow, he'll expect you to give a detailed presentation of each of your patients, so read your charts. After that, he'll just want to hear what's new and different. We were lucky enough to get assigned the head of Psychiatry himself, Dr. Kevin Bainbridge."

Susan's blood ran cold.

Monk spoke their realization aloud. "Isn't he the older man who talked to us in the auditorium?"

Kendall hauled out his gravelly old man Bainbridge imitation. "And by working only twelve-hour days, we missed half the good cases."

The R-1s snickered, and even Stony smiled broadly. "That's the one. He's a bit intense, but he's an excellent diagnostician." He tapped the Vox on his wrist. "He's

not a fan of devices, though. He prefers you try to mem-
orize every bit of medical knowledge and have it on the
tip of your tongue when he asks a question. But he's also
slow enough, you can usually sneak the answer off Vox
with a bit of distraction. Just be on time, don't try to slip
out early, look busy even when you're not, and you're
fine. He growls sometimes, but there's not a mean bone
in the old coot's body."

Stony shook the cap, then held it out toward Nevaeh.
"I've separated patients into reasonably balanced groups
of four. Whichever bunch you pick is yours."

Each of the R-1s took out a torn sheet of paper with
Stony's sloppy writing on it. Susan read hers:

1. Monterey Zdrazil: 12-yo white female: *traumatic mute* x 6 years
2. Dallas "Diesel" Moore: 10-yo black male: *psychotic depression, attention deficit hyperactivity,
   oppositional defiant disorder*
3. Sharicka Anson: 4-yo mixed female: *juvenile
   conduct disorder*
4. Starling Woodruff: 13-yo white female: *dementia* status post aneurysm repair

Susan stared at the paper, a strange mixture of emotions washing over her: excitement, fear, and uncertainty
blending into a cacophonous mix that held her spell-
bound. *My patients,* my *patients.* The awesome responsibility for those children lay in her inexperienced hands.
They deserved the best treatment she could devise, the
wisest decisions; yet Susan wondered what she could add
that previous doctors, more veteran and capable clini-
cians, had not already considered, discarded, or tried.

Doubts descended upon Susan an instant later. *What
if I make a mistake? What if I say the wrong thing and
further damage their delicate psyches? What if I take
away the only medication allowing them to function or*

add one that causes permanent harm? What if I kill someone?

Susan glanced at her companions. All of them stared at their own small pieces of paper, their expressions sober; and she imagined the same painful insecurities bombarded each of them. Doctors throughout history had contemplated their place in the world, had worried about these same issues, had realized the delicate balance of life, health, and sanity in those they served. Unlike those in other professions, doctors could not afford to have a bad day. A physician who got lazy might make a fatal mistake. Vox and other fast, portable computer links helped; but the human behind it still had to know enough to put the pieces together, to calculate the direction of thought, and to access the proper information.

No wonder John Calvin considered his work boring. No matter how skillfully a robot performed its job, no matter how magnificent its shape or precise its "fingers," no matter how much information filled its electronic circuitry, it was only as smart as the person who programmed it. At least, that was how Susan Calvin figured it. A computer might spit out the facts, but only a human could read the subtle signs that altered the course of consideration. One word, one small detail, one momentary thought could change what she chose to research and, therefore, the course of a human life forever.

Apparently recalling the overwhelming grandeur of that "first patient" moment, Stony waited a long time before speaking again. He held out his cap once more, this time with fresh pieces of torn paper. Wrapped in her thoughts, Susan had not even noticed him preparing them. "One of you has to take in-house call tonight," the R-3 said. "I've numbered the papers. Whoever gets 'one' is on tonight, 'two' tomorrow, et cetera. Clamhead gets night six by default."

Each of the R-1s drew a new piece of paper. Susan opened hers carefully to display the number one.

Chapter 3

Head whirling with the details of the unit and her on-call duties, Susan Calvin sought out a private corner to review patient charts and explore diagnoses and data. All of the residents on the Pediatric Inpatient Psychiatry Unit had stayed late preparing for the next morning's rounds. They had eaten dinner as a group, where Stony Lipschitz and Clayton Slaubaugh discussed helpful tips, tricks, and ideas for surviving the R-1 year. When the conversation turned to on-call suggestions, given that she had drawn the first night, Susan paid close attention.

And now, palm-pross in hand, she searched for the hidden charting room on the first floor that Stony had mentioned as a favorite on-call hideaway. She found it tucked away between an insulated staircase and the central processing area for information storage. She pushed open the door to reveal a room larger than she had expected. Modular shelving stood in rows, covered with labeled, opaque plastic boxes and well-worn textbooks that seemed to encompass every specialty. To her right, the area opened up into a cozy nook, with two overstuffed couches, three unmatched chairs, and a central table set at perfect height for palm-prosses. Apparently alone, Susan flopped down on one of the couches and placed her little portable on the table.

From her pocket, Susan pulled out the piece of paper with her patients' information. *What next?* She considered meeting the children first, before the information in their charts prejudiced her; but the idea seemed foolish. The children had lives and diagnoses that long preceded Susan's drawing their names from Stony's baseball cap. They did not just appear from thin air because she needed patients. Though children, they were not innocents, newborn. They had met more doctors in their short lives than most people did in a lifetime. They knew the ins and outs of Manhattan Hasbro Hospital in a way Susan might never understand. Her relationship with each child would surely vary, but they would sense her inexperience and unpreparedness quickly. *Better to be armed with knowledge and not need it than to cripple myself with ignorance.*

A shadow fell over Susan, then glided onward. Startled, Susan loosed a small noise and jerked her attention toward it. She had believed herself alone and had not heard the door open.

Apparently cued by her gasp, the one who had cast the shadow turned. He appeared to be about Susan's age and was tall enough to play professional basketball. Her father stood six feet eight, and the stranger would look him squarely in the eye. He wore blue hallway scrubs over a slender figure. Short brown hair outlined relatively nondescript features, with average-sized cheeks, nose, ears, and lips. Even his plain brown eyes did not stand out. He moved with a fluid grace that hinted of talent on the dance floor, in martial arts, or even gymnastics. "I'm sorry," he said. "I didn't mean to scare you."

Instinctively polite, Susan shook her head. "I wasn't scared. Just startled a bit. I was deep in thought." She rose and held out her hand. "Susan Calvin, R-1, Psychiatry."

He took her hand in a gentle but solid grip. They performed the standard brief shake and released. "N8-C. You can call me Nate."

"N8?" Susan repeated. She had heard some unusual names in recent years, but that one went even beyond the vast and accepted norm. *How soon till we're all just a series of random letters and numbers?*

"Eighth in the N-C model line."

Susan laughed; but, when Nate did not join her, she sobered quickly. "You're joking, right?"

Nate shook his head. "You do know I'm the resident robot, don't you?"

Susan chuckled again, alone. "Oh, come on. My father works for a robotics company. If mechanical men as humanoid as you existed, I'd be one of the first to know about it."

A light flashed through Nate's eyes. "Susan *Calvin*. Your father wouldn't be Dr. John Calvin, would he?"

Susan's grin disappeared in an instant. "How did you know that?"

Now, Nate finally did laugh. And Susan did not. "John Calvin's a legend at U.S. Robots and Mechanical Men. And, currently, USR's the only legal robotics company in America."

Susan could only stare. It did not surprise her to discover her brilliant father had made a náme for himself in his chosen field, nor that he had so belittled his achievements at home, she had come to believe he held a minor office position. What shocked her was the abrupt realization that she was talking to an actual robot she had so easily mistaken for human. Its answers did not seem stock or pat. It was clearly thinking, generating spontaneous conversation, and was physically and mentally indistinguishable from a human male.

This is a trick. It has to be a trick. Susan blinked her eyes in rapid succession, trying to make sense of the scene in front of her. She was tired, but she was definitely awake. "Come on, now, seriously. The joke's over."

Nate tipped his head, his features holding a perfect expression of confusion. "Joke?"

"You're not really a robot."

"I'm not?" The look of surprise Nate turned her was clearly supposed to appear feigned. "Then how come I have wires and coils inside instead of organs?"

"Do you?" Susan glanced back at her palm-pross. If she did not get to her research soon, it would be too late to meet any of her patients. She had no intention of rousing them from bed, even if the nurses would allow it. She knew from her M-4 rotations nurses often savagely protected their charges, especially children; and Stony had reinforced that belief when he stated the nurses would come to him before implementing an irregular order written by a new R-1. "I've obviously studied human anatomy, and I shook your hand. It's flesh. You have musculature, bone structure, blood vessels."

Nate examined his right arm as if for the first time. "Human stem cells coaxed into a dermal and muscular system grown over a skeleton of porous silicone plastic."

Susan had a scientific mind that did not make exceptions for hope, faith, and the paranormal. However, the science Nate described had concrete possibility, even if only in the future. She considered, lips pursed, hands clenching and unclenching. *How long could he have rehearsed this joke? How far would anyone take it?*

Nate rolled his eyes. "Ask your father." He headed back to work.

Susan intended to do so also, but she wanted more information first. "Wait, Nate. Let's say I believe you. Why are you here? What . . . exactly do you do?"

Nate turned back to face Susan again. "That depends on whom you ask." He smiled. "The USR believes my purpose is to demonstrate the usefulness, efficiency, and safety of robots, thereby opening the market for their products. To the hospital administrators, I'm a competent and thorough worker who draws no salary and never complains. To those physicians who know of my existence, aren't leery of me, and don't automatically despise all I stand for, I'm a proofreader, fact-checker, footnote-finder, hypothesis-tester, sounding board, source of ideas, and research assistant. To the Society for Humanity—"

Susan found herself interrupting. "The Society for . . . Humanity? That's a pretty ambitious title."

"It's a bipartisan political action group dedicated to 'rescuing' mankind from advanced intelligence, particularly the artificial type, and raising ethical challenges to several forms of robotic and medical technology. Surely you've seen them protesting outside?"

Susan could only nod. She had no idea the protestors had a particular name or united cause. "All those protestors are here because of . . . you?"

Nate pursed his lips, shook his head. "Not me particularly, no. Though not exactly a deep dark secret, my existence has not become common knowledge, either. And the SFH makes up only a small portion of that mob. Some of the other action groups have their own pet concerns: stem cells, prolongation of comatose life, assisted suicide." He shrugged. "That issue has protestors on both sides. Reproductive technologies of myriad kinds, in-vitro procedures, in-vivo fetal procedures, DNA-based diagnostics, reparation of disabilities, medication benefits versus side effects, appetite suppressants and stimulators in addition to fat-resistance therapies, cosmetic procedures . . . You name it, someone is vehemently for or against it. Manhattan Hasbro has had throngs of protestors since long before my creation. They've become such a normal and expected part of medicine, they don't even make the news without resorting to profound and extreme measures."

Susan suddenly understood the full significance of Manhattan Hasbro commandment number one—don't engage protestors in any fashion—and why Manhattan

Hasbro had entire wings devoted to legal matters and to ethical ones. *If this trend continues, lawyers and ethicists will soon outnumber doctors in the medical setting.*

Nate shrugged, still looking at Susan with an all-too-human expression. "The Society for Humanity would have me disassembled in an instant and my positronic brain erased. That's why I'm sent to the less populated areas of the hospital: record keeping, research, copyediting, and the like. I used to act as an orderly, but I don't get to do that very often anymore. And when I'm near the general public, I can't mention I'm robotic."

"You could do so much more," Susan realized aloud. The possibilities seemed endless. She could think of twelve grand ideas with only a moment to consider the matter.

Nate only nodded. "May I go now?"

"Of course." Susan waved a hand, feeling guilty for keeping him so long. She looked at her Vox, which currently read 8:08 p.m. Within the hour, the staff on the PIPU would be putting her patients to bed, not long enough to do significant research. She would have to wait until the morning to see them, but she could study their charts overnight, which already gave her a leg up on the other R-1s. They would have to come in early to prepare before rounds.

When Susan looked up from her wrist, Nate had already disappeared.

Susan sat for a moment in consideration. *Was that really a robot, or just a human male with knowledge of my family and an odd sense of humor?* She did not know for sure, but her instincts told her she had actually conversed with the highest level of artificial intelligence mankind could currently create. Yet, to believe her instincts meant her near-perfect father had misled her for years and that he had lied and hidden information. That thought seemed too heinous for serious contemplation.

Susan stared at her Vox, driven to call John Calvin

and straighten out the situation as swiftly and decisively as possible. In the end, logic won out over impatience. It made far more sense to wait for a face-to-face confrontation, where she could read his every expression and prevent him from disengaging until she had her answers.

For now, Susan Calvin returned her attention to her palm-pross and to her patients' diagnoses and histories, hoping no emergencies cropped up during the night. It seemed the one advantage of starting her residency on a chronic ward with numerous rigid protocols. She would, almost certainly, get a full and good night's sleep.

As Susan expected, the other R-1s came in early the following morning to cram their patients' charts before Dr. Bainbridge arrived for morning rounds. Later in the month, the chain of command would go in the opposite direction, but for now, the residents remained mostly silent as the nurses made tactful "suggestions" for changing orders and ways to handle patients they already knew well.

Having done her patient research the previous night, Susan found time to make brief visits to her charges. She began with Monterey Zdrazil, knocking on the child's door. As expected from a traumatic mute, Susan received no answer. She edged the door open a crack and peeked inside to make certain she had not caught the girl in an inconvenient stage of dress.

Skinny and chalky white, the twelve-year-old sat in bed, her back rigid against the headboard. She wore her brown hair short, hacked into a functional, masculine style. Dressed in a red T-shirt with a rainbow motif and faded blue jeans, she stared solemnly at the far wall, which was decorated with a collage of colorful get-well cards and children's drawings.

Uncertain how to approach such a child, Susan smiled

broadly. "Hey, Monterey!" Realizing she had just rhymed, she carried it further. "What do you say? How's your day?"

Monterey's hazel eyes rolled toward Susan, but she did not speak. That did not surprise Susan; the girl had not said a word in more than six years. The doctors had tried a myriad of medications and combinations, play therapy, group therapy, regression therapy, and others. Her single mother had subscribed to special diets, spinal manipulation, herbal remedies, and other desperate measures, all without result. Susan had not expected an instant breakthrough.

"I'm Dr. Susan Calvin. You're my very first patient, Monterey, which makes you extra special to me. If there's anything I can do to make you feel better, you just let me know, okay?"

Monterey only stared.

"Now," Susan continued, catching herself about to ask if Monterey would mind an examination. Susan realized she had best avoid phrasing things as questions that she planned to do anyway, in case the children answered "no." "I'm going to look you over a little bit. If you have a problem with that, let me know." Susan took her stethoscope off her neck and headed toward Monterey, who made no protest. The R-1 listened to the girl's heart, lungs, and abdomen, finding nothing amiss. A flashlight shined in the eyes revealed normal pupillary function. Reflexes responded appropriately, liver and spleen were the proper sizes, and Monterey was closing in on the fourth Tanner stage of pubertal development. Susan hoped someone had explained menstruation to her, because it would be coming soon.

Susan put her penlight back in her pocket and slung her stethoscope across her neck. "Great. You're a normal almost-teenager, except you don't sass your mother enough. If you're going to develop into a proper teen, you have to practice your sarcasm, eye rolling, and door slamming."

Susan thought she saw a ghost of a smile cross Monterey's face, but the girl did not speak.

Susan waved a dismissive hand. "Ah, don't worry. You'll get it. We all do." With that, she exited the room and headed to visit the second patient on her list.

She found Dallas Moore sitting in the common room with several other boys, watching a video on the enclosed screen. She recognized him at once, the only African-American in the group. He had close-cropped hair and pudgy cheeks. He looked younger than his ten years, notably short for his age, and as round as a basketball. Legs like tree trunks jutted from his shorts, the skin ashy dry and in need of lotion. He breathed loudly, almost snoring, though clearly wide-awake.

"Dallas Moore?" Susan asked.

The deep brown eyes darted toward her. "Call me Diesel."

"Diesel, okay." Susan remembered seeing the nickname on the sheet Stony Lipschitz had given her. "I'm Susan Calvin, your new doctor."

The boy nodded, clearly more interested in the television screen than in her. "Hopefully, I'll be out of here before you are."

Susan smiled. "That is precisely my plan. You mind if I examine you?"

"Here?"

Susan chuckled. "In your room. I can wait until after the movie, if you prefer."

"Thanks." Diesel's gaze went back to the screen.

Susan left him there and started looking for her other charges. She expected to find Sharicka first. The only preschooler in the mix, she ought to stand out jarringly. Instead, Susan found a girl standing in clear confusion, as if she had just awakened in an unfamiliar body in a strange location. She shuffled a few steps, stopped, and looked around with her brow furrowed. She went to take another step, staggered, and fell.

A nurse ran toward her, but Susan arrived first. "Here, let me help you." She took the girl's hands and gently helped her to her feet. "Are you all right?"

"I think so." The girl clung to Susan's arm, her fingers like ice cubes. "I get dizzy sometimes. And confused. But I'm all right now."

The description sounded familiar. "Would you happen to be Starling Woodruff?"

"Yep, that's me." The girl sounded shaken. "Would you mind helping me to my room?"

"Not at all," Susan said. "Which way?"

Starling pointed down the back corridor. Knowing the doors had patient names on the jambs, Susan headed in the indicated direction, reading as she went. She found Diesel's room, then, two doors down, Starling's.

"I'm Dr. Susan Calvin, Starling. I'm your new resident physician."

"Of course," Starling said. "First of the month." Her eyes narrowed. "Which month?"

"July." Susan helped Starling to her bed. "And it's the third. The first was a Sunday, and I got here too late to bother you yesterday." As Starling let go, the frigidness of her touch remained, engrained on Susan's flesh. "Your hands are really cold."

"They always are." Starling leaned her back against the wall. "Feet, too. I suppose you want to examine me?"

Susan closed the door. "If you don't mind."

Starling made a gesture to indicate she did not.

Susan performed a slightly more thorough exam on Starling, including a check of all four lower extremity pulses. She had just finished confirming Starling's cold feet when someone knocked on the door. Susan made sure Starling's body was appropriately covered before answering. "Yes?"

Kendall Stevens pushed the door open a crack. "Time for rounds, Calvin."

"Excuse me," Susan said to Starling. "Will you be all right now?"

"I'm fine." Starling rose carefully, walked to her shelf, and pulled down a Nancy Drew book. "I'll just sit here and read for a bit."

Susan headed out the door. "Do you want it open or closed?"

Starling nestled back on the bed, book in hand. "Open, please."

Susan left the door open, then trotted to the staffing room, where she could just see Kendall's back disappearing. As she rounded the corner, she noticed all of the R-1s sitting in chairs along with Clayton, the R-2. Stony perched on the edge of a desk, and Dr. Bainbridge sat on another, looking around the clustered group. The nurses hovered on the fringes, working and listening simultaneously.

Dr. Bainbridge addressed Stony. "Are they all here?"

"Yes, sir."

Bainbridge nodded briskly. "Let's start with . . ." His gaze wandered over the group and landed back on the R-3. "Which one took call last night?"

Susan's heart rate quickened.

"Susan Calvin." Stony gestured at her.

"All right, let's get to work." Susan suspected she was about to meet the side of Bainbridge that Stony had warned them about, the one that asked difficult questions and expected quick and well-considered answers. "Susan Calvin, present your first patient."

Chapter 4

Susan began with one of the patients she had actually examined. "Starling Woodruff is a thirteen-year-old white female with a history of odd behavior who has been on the Pediatric Inpatient Psychiatry Unit for almost two years."

"Odd behavior," Bainbridge interrupted. "Is that her diagnosis, Dr. Calvin? Odd Behavioral Disorder? Isn't that akin to diagnosing a child with a specific chromosomal deletion as having Funny-Looking Kid Syndrome?"

Irritation seized Susan, but she held her tongue. "Starling's official diagnosis is dementia, status post A-V fistula repair." She did not add she did not agree with the diagnosis. It would sound arrogant and ridiculous to contradict the numerous physicians who had treated her over the last two years. "Her symptoms consist mostly of memory lapses, particularly short-term, aimless wandering, lack of concentration, and confusion."

Nods suffused the group, residents and nurses included.

Susan continued, wanting to get out the entire history before letting the other shoe drop. Going first made things so much more difficult. She had to guess how much information Bainbridge wanted, enough so he fully understood the situation but not so much it made her look incapable of sifting out the pertinent from the history. The residents' reports at rounds might be the only knowledge Bainbridge would have of their patients.

"Starling underwent repair of a cerebral arteriovenous fistula in September of 2033. In the nearly two years since, she has developed worsening psychiatric problems, treated with various cholinesterase inhibitors. She is currently taking rivastigmine, which seems to help with memory and confusion, as well as sertraline for agitation and depressive symptoms. In addition to her psychiatric symptoms, she fatigues easily and has grown poorly for age, currently in the tenth percentile. She had previously been growing along the seventy-fifth percentile curve. On physical examination, she was pale, with remarkably cold extremities. Her pulse was thready. I could feel the liver edge, implying possible hepatomegaly, and I could hear a soft S4 gallop."

Susan looked at the nurses, several of whom had creased foreheads. Apparently, they had never noticed the extra heart sound, which did not surprise her. It was subtle, not something expected in psychiatry, and, even under normal circumstances, required significant training to hear.

Stony pursed his lips, head bobbing. "Nice catch."

Bainbridge looked from Stony to Susan. "Are you sure?"

"After rounds, I'll double-check it," Stony promised.

Bainbridge studied Susan. "What do you make of your findings, Susan?"

"Well . . ." Susan hesitated to speak. If what she believed was true, it would change the entire approach to the patient. "I don't believe Starling has dementia per se. I think she's actually suffering from congestive heart failure, a feature of which can be altered consciousness, especially in children."

The nurses murmured in the background. Bainbridge nodded slowly. "Does she have a history of some sort of congenital heart disease with reparative surgery? Hypoplastic left heart? Transposition?"

"No," Susan admitted. "But a child can develop congestive heart failure without a major defect."

Bainbridge tried another tack. "An ASD, perhaps? A suspicious murmur?"

"No," Susan admitted. "Prior to the A-V fistula repair, she was, apparently, perfectly normal."

Bainbridge continued to stare. "So, then, what would cause a child with a normal heart to develop congestive heart failure after a routine neurosurgical procedure?"

Susan found herself bridling under the scrutiny and stood up straighter to buoy her confidence. The child's life might depend on it. "Only one thing, sir. If the A-V fistula was not properly or fully repaired, it could cause a shunt that results in CHD."

The nurses responded with a collective drawing in of breath that added up to an actual gasp. The doctors turned to face them.

"What's wrong?" Bainbridge demanded.

The head nurse came forward. "Well, sir, the surgeon on Starling's case was none other than Dr. Sudhish Mandar. He's one of the greatest neurosurgeons in the world, and he personally signed off on Starling."

Bainbridge sucked in his lips, nodding. "Well, then."

Susan waited for his orders. It seemed impossible he would side with a first-year resident over a neurosurgeon with such stellar credentials, and she was not surprised when he did not.

Bainbridge patted Susan's shoulder. "It was a great theory, anyway. I like to see my charges thinking in new and different ways."

The smirks on the nurses' faces annoyed Susan. She supposed they saw the same thing the first of every month: fresh, new residents so convinced of their own brilliance, so eager to find the instant cure so many wiser heads had missed. She supposed nearly all came with the same familiar "brand-new" approaches and ideas. She could hardly blame them for doubting her. "Dr. Bainbridge, I don't think it would hurt anything to have Neurosurgery come down and reevaluate Starling. As far as I can tell by her chart, they haven't seen her in at least the last eighteen months."

Over Dr. Bainbridge's shoulder, Stony shook his head, an obvious warning to Susan not to pursue the matter further, at least not at the moment.

A tinge of purple rose to Bainbridge's wrinkled face, but his voice gave no sign of building rage. "Susan, when Dr. Sudhish Mandar signs off on something, it is off, finished, perfect."

Susan wondered why she had never even heard of this so-called best neurosurgeon in the world. They had neurosurgeons at Thomas Jefferson, in Philadelphia; and she had performed her neurosurgery rotation as a medical student. She had never once heard them mention Dr. Mandar. "Fine, sir. As I wasn't inside Starling's brain, I can't guess what they saw. However, I know pediatric congestive heart failure when I see it. Can I, at least, have a Cardiology consult?" No matter the cause of Starling's heart failure, the cardiology team ought to have the expertise to control it. Perhaps they could come up with a reason for the problem that did not reflect badly on the neurosurgery team.

Bainbridge looked at Stony, as if to say he pitied the R-3 having to deal with a difficult upstart.

Stony did not seem put out by Susan at all. "How about if I examine Starling after rounds? If I also see signs of CHD, then we'll consult Cardiology."

That seemed to satisfy Bainbridge, who flashed Susan a sincere smile and nodded broadly. Before he could call for information about the next patient, thunderous pounding echoed across the ward. It sounded as if an entire wall had collapsed. There followed a shout, then a loud string of the dirtiest swear words in the English language in the voice of a prepubescent male. Through the one-way glass, they could see Dallas "Diesel" Moore ripping children's artwork from the hallway walls and throwing the mangled papers at two nurses at his heels. Blood poured from his nose, gushing down the front of his shirt, but he paid it no heed.

"I hate you!" he screamed before disappearing around the corner, the nurses in tow. "I'm going to kill you! I'm going to kill you all!" He flung something in his hand that one of the nurses dodged.

Stony and several of the nurses excused themselves, darting out of the office toward the retreating figures.

"Whose patient is that?" Bainbridge demanded, watching Stony go.

Panic sparked in a few eyes. The other residents had had even less time than Susan to review and meet their patients. They might not know.

Susan rescued them. "He's mine, too, sir."

Diesel's shouts wafted to them, still mostly curses. The sound of objects hitting the walls rose over the din, as well as scuffling and the softer voices of the nurses, attempting to restrain and soothe him.

Susan tried to ignore the noise as she presented the boy. When she had met him earlier, he seemed so calm, so normal, she could scarcely believe she had seen the same child. "Dallas Moore, known as Diesel. He's a ten-year-old black male with morbid obesity, ADHD, oppositional defiant disorder, severe depression, and obsessive-compulsive tendencies, particularly in regard to food."

The thudding sounds ceased as someone apparently restrained Diesel, but the threats grew louder and more vicious. Susan heard someone say, "Get him into the Self-awareness Room."

Susan told the group, "He seemed quite normal this morning. I'm not sure what happened to him."

One of the nurses, a petite blonde, spoke up. "He broke into the med room and plundered the snack cart. Ashlynn confronted him, and he just went crazy."

Most of the nurses disappeared to the other side of the staffing area to watch through the one-way windows.

Another string of swear words rent the hallway; then came the sound of a large door closing. Silence followed until most of the nurses returned with Stony Lipschitz. Blood covered the front of the R-3's dress polo, the stethoscope around his neck, and the papers in his pocket.

Bainbridge looked alarmed. "What happened? You didn't have to hurt him, did you?"

Stony looked himself over. "It's nasal blood, sir. Apparently, when Diesel gets upset, the blood vessels in his nose burst. The more he fusses, the worse it gets, and he won't let anyone stop the bleeding until he's calmed down. In fact, he seems to delight in spreading it as far and wide as possible." Stony kept his hands away from his body. "Do you mind if I clean up?"

"Please do." Bainbridge flicked a hand dismissively. "In fact, why don't we all take a short break?" He looked at his Vox. "We'll reconvene in an hour, at nine fifteen. Does that work for everyone?"

A tangible wave of relief flooded through the residents as they realized they could continue studying and examining prior to presenting their patients. They scattered in an instant. Susan hesitated, watching a janitor appear to clean up the blood-splattered hallway and the torn hunks of paper scattered in Diesel's wake. She wondered what had come over him. She could scarcely imagine the stout, quiet little boy becoming a terror in an instant, as though he had swallowed Dr. Jekyll's potion. She wondered what it must be like to live with a child so volatile, to be his parents or, worse, his younger sibling.

Curious, Susan followed the blood trail to the massive white door reading SELF-AWARENESS ROOM in bold black letters. Two male nurses stood there, one peering through a small but thick polycarbonate window.

"May I see him?" Susan asked.

The nurse stepped aside wordlessly.

Susan leaned into the glass. Diesel stood near the door, bashing his head against the padded walls, leaving smears of blood and snot that betrayed his tears. He wore a T-shirt, cut in the latest triangular-sleeve style, and olive green sweats with the trendy T'chana label and its signature parrots. Short and round, he looked more like a bowling ball than a child, especially bouncing from wall to wall.

"I'm going in," Susan said, her hand on the knob before anyone could stop her.

"You can't—," one nurse started.

"It's not allowed," the other said simultaneously.

Susan pretended not to hear them, turning the handle and opening the door. It was heavy, thicker than she expected, and also covered with padding.

Diesel ignored Susan, banging his head repeatedly against the wall, nose blood splashing in surreal patterns each time he did so.

The door closed behind Susan. She could see one nurse watching them through the window, and she guessed it had less to do with curiosity and more with protocol. The rules, perhaps state or national law, demanded someone placed in isolation be watched every moment. Susan imagined the other nurse running for assistance. In the end, she doubted anyone would bother her. To do so would only agitate Diesel, and the purpose of the Self-awareness Room was to give him a safe place to vent and calm himself.

Susan approached the boy. "Diesel?"

"Leave me alone," Diesel growled. He stopped banging, grinding his head into the padding.

"Okay." Susan stepped back, then sat cross-legged on the floor. She retrieved a wad of tissues from her dress pants and laid them in a dense pile beside her. She also had some Slookies, hard sour candies; but she knew better than to offer them to an obese patient on a strict diet.

The blood from Diesel's nose dripped onto the floor beneath him in a steady patter, no longer squirting. Apparently, he had calmed a bit, at least enough to drop his blood pressure to a more normal level. She took that as a positive sign.

"What do you want?" Diesel said into the padding.

"Nothing." Susan tried to keep her voice absolutely neutral. She had no idea what might calm Diesel and what might provoke him into another wild tantrum. "What do *you* want?"

Diesel hesitated. He seemed as uncertain as she about how he felt like behaving next. "Got any tissues?"

"Right here." Susan patted the floor beside the piled tissues. "Come join me."

Diesel turned slowly, studying the situation as if he expected her to leap up and net him. Finally, he came over, picked up the tissues, and clamped them to his nose. Tears and blood streaked every part of his face.

Susan's training rushed to the fore. She should be wearing a gown and gloves and staying as far as possible from a biohazardous patient. It helped that she knew from his chart he did not carry hepatitis, HIV, or CIV; and she was legally vaccinated against everything contagious and known to science. "Sit," she said, not expecting him to obey. "Please."

To her surprise, Diesel sat. He kept the tissues clamped to his face with one hand, the other flat on the floor. He also sat cross-legged.

For several moments, they sat quietly on the floor together, neither saying a word. Susan kept her gaze from the window. Whether or not Diesel knew they were being watched, he did not need to be reminded of it. She let him speak first, knowing instinctively anything she said would only inflame him. Through the years, he had faced the inquisition whenever he acted in an irrational manner: *"Why did you do this? Are you insane? What were you thinking?"* She wondered what he might say if he had the opportunity to get in the first word.

"I'm a monster," Diesel said softly. "I hate myself, and I want to die."

And there's the depression part. Susan wished she had had more training. Her immediate thought was to disabuse him of such a terrible notion, to assure him he was a sweet boy with a problem, not a monster, that killing himself would only create more problems for all the many people who loved him. But she was sure he had heard it all before, and anything she said in this vein would only shut down a conversation that had just begun, one she suspected had the possibility of yielding important information. "Why do you say such a thing?"

"Because I am. And I do." Diesel hid behind the wad of tissue, not bothering to look at Susan.

That was useful. Now, Susan worried she had not only shut down the conversation, she had also left him believing she thought him a monster who ought to kill himself. *What made me think I could handle this?* Susan tried again. "Tell me more. What kind of monster are you?"

Diesel rolled an eye in Susan's general direction. "I'm a food-hogging monster. If I could, I'd eat Tokyo."

Susan could not help laughing. "What part of Tokyo?"

Diesel slipped into baby talk. "All of it. Da cakes. Da pies. Da can-dee." He paused. "Da bui-dings, da people, da can-dee."

"You said 'candy' twice."

Diesel managed a smile around the tissues. "That's my favorite."

Susan could not resist. She slipped a Slookie into his hand and whispered conspiratorially, "Careful how you put that in your mouth. And don't tell anyone I gave it to you."

Apparently, Diesel did know about the nurse observing because he peeked sideways at the object, then made a casual motion of moving the tissues and sneaking it into his mouth. "I'm hungry all the time, Dr. Susan. I'm hungry right after dinner. I'm hungry in my sleep. I'm hungry while I'm still eating."

Susan thought of all the psychiatry she knew about hunger. Most believed it a substitute for something missing, usually love. Nothing in Diesel's chart suggested inadequate parenting. He had a married mother and father, at least one of whom visited him at every opportunity. They had cooperated in every way with his therapy. They had two other children, an older boy and a younger girl, who seemed normal in every way. From his dress and vocabulary, it was apparent he did not lack for attention, money, or education.

"If I ever threw up, I think I'd be hungry doing it."

"Gross." Susan managed to chat even as she mulled the pertinent. "You've never thrown up?"

"I once broke into the freezer and ate three boxes of Popsicles, two things of ice cream, a cake, a loaf of French bread, and a package of shredded cheese in less than five minutes. They said I should be puking all over the place, but they couldn't even make me." Diesel seemed almost proud of the accomplishment. "I don't throw up."

Susan suspected if she had eaten all that, she would be in a coma. "Wow." She could think of nothing else to say.

Diesel loosed a raw, honest belly laugh so fun and contagious Susan could not help joining him.

She finally managed, "I'll bet you *could* eat Tokyo."

Diesel laughed again, and Susan realized she loved that sound. She bet people did silly things just to elicit it.

Having stopped his nosebleed, Diesel turned to wiping blood, snot, and tears from his face.

Susan could not help wondering if someone took

pleasure in Diesel's overeating. Perhaps he or she encouraged it, either intentionally or subconsciously. More than one person might be to blame. *Maybe even me.* She felt a sudden pang of guilt at having slipped him a candy. She wondered how many people had tried to win his trust that way and vowed she would never do so again. "So, how'd you get the nickname Diesel?"

Diesel actually smiled. "Football. I plow through the other line like an old-fashioned diesel truck or train."

"You're a lineman?" Susan guessed. She hoped her ignorance of football did not show too much. When she took her pediatrics rotation, she remembered one of the residents telling her the smartest thing a pediatrician could do was to keep up with the trends in gaming, music, and play. Nothing impressed a child more than a doctor who knew the hip shows, the names of the newest characters, or could keep up with him in a game of I-Star.

"Nose guard," Diesel said. "And center on offense. Right smack dab in the middle of the line."

Susan looked him over. Though notably short for his age, he was built like a tank. "So, I bet you love the Giants."

Diesel wrinkled his nose. "I like college. Longhorns."

"Texas?" Susan asked.

Diesel looked at her as if she had gone mad. "No, the *Pennsylvania* Longhorns."

"Pennsylvania?" Susan realized he was teasing her. "Funny." *Of course Texas, you moron.* "What do you like about them?"

"For one thing, they're good. Ten and oh last season. For another, they send a lot of guys to the pros. Especially quarterbacks."

Susan made a mental note to study up on football, especially the Longhorns. "You think you're calm enough to go back out there?"

Diesel sighed. "And apologize. Yeah, yeah. I know the drill."

"Good, because I have to get back to rounds." Susan looked around the room at the blood-splashed, padded walls. "And someone is going to have to clean up in here."

Diesel followed Susan's gaze as if noticing the mess for the first time. Only then, he studied himself. He looked as if he had gone ten rounds in an ultimate fighting ring.

Susan rose, walked to the door, and knocked politely. It swung open immediately.

"We're ready to come out," she announced to the waiting nurse, who gave her a gaze that spoke volumes. Susan had a feeling she was about to face a punishment worse than Diesel's own.

To her surprise, she did not care.

Chapter 5

When rounds restarted, they naturally focused on Diesel. More confident after their conversation, Susan started again. "Dallas 'Diesel' Moore is a ten-year-old black male who has been diagnosed with ADHD, oppositional defiant disorder, severe depression, obsessive-compulsive tendencies, and morbid obesity." As Susan glanced around the office, she could see the other residents looked more relaxed than they previously did. The hour off had given them more time to meet their patients and review the charts, while she had entombed herself with Diesel. Stony had changed into the blue corridor scrubs that served two purposes. First, they announced their lack of sterility, that the wearer was not headed for the operating room. Second, their bright color was a reminder not to wear them outside of the hospital.

Dr. Bainbridge studied Susan with a bemused expression. "You're about to tell us you don't agree with those diagnoses, aren't you, Susan?" He already had her pegged from her presentation of Starling Woodruff. Worse, he was right.

"Well, actually, sir . . ." Susan paused, uncertain how to continue. She had not expected to get to this point so quickly and had not fully organized her thoughts on the matter. "I think it's possible he has an undiagnosed syndrome, yes."

Stony leaned toward her. "What are you thinking?" Less jaded than Bainbridge, he actually seemed eager to hear her theories.

"Well . . ." Susan tried to work through her thoughts as she presented them. A well-reasoned argument would speak volumes over an educated guess. "Obesity has three main causes: familial, psychiatric, and physiological. The first one is the most common, and also the most treatable. The first and second types cover some ninety-eight percent of all cases of obesity."

"You think Diesel has the third," Bainbridge said predictably.

Susan did not wish to couch her ideas as speculation or intuition. Those would not fly in a scientific institution like Manhattan Hasbro. "I think there's a reasonable amount of evidence to come to that conclusion."

"Evidence." Bainbridge made a "come here" motion Susan took to mean he wanted more information, not for her to stand beside him.

"Neither his parents nor his siblings are obese. While there is some history of a maternal uncle who was, that's not strong evidence for familial obesity." Susan supposed she had not needed to present those details. That Diesel resided in the PIPU proved his previous physicians believed in a psychiatric basis for his problems, not familial or physiological. "Diesel hasn't responded to any of the standard antiobesity drugs." A plethora of those had emerged in the early part of the current decade, when medical research dollars had been restored after nearly two decades of attempts to balance the national and state budgets by channeling that money into medical care for the indigent. The anti-obesity drugs worked for anyone with even a modicum of self-control and the desire to attain a healthy weight.

Bainbridge made a more severe gesture, as if to get across to Susan they had a limited amount of time.

"Diesel was underweight until about age two and a half, when he developed hyperphagia and put on enormous amounts of weight quite suddenly. That's remarkably early for nearly all the psychiatric causes. He packed on the weight despite having ADHD, with an emphasis on the hyperactivity part in his case. He started walking very late. Intelligence testing reveals an enormous backward split between performance and verbal aptitude. Most children with learning problems do worse on the verbal parts, but Diesel has a profound vocabulary and the ability to use it. He has much more trouble with dexterity: drawing, writing, shoe tying. Also, he's short for both his age and his family history, with surprisingly long arms."

Monk Peterson blurted out, "Prader-Willi syndrome."

It was the obvious diagnosis. Though rare, it was still the most common obesity syndrome. Even at the turn of the twenty-first century, most children with Prader-Willi died before they reached adulthood. Driven to eat, they would choke to death, poison themselves with spoiled or uncooked foods, or rupture their stomachs. Those who survived all of those things frequently still died young of complications of obesity.

In the last twenty-five years, doctors discovered treating these children with human growth hormone, consistently locking up all food storage areas, and training the families and children from infancy could help delay the development of the deadly hyperphagia and even prevent the obesity in many cases.

"Is he intellectually disabled?" Clayton asked. "All children with Prader-Willi syndrome are."

Behind Bainbridge's back, Monk Peterson poked furiously at his Vox. "Not all. Ten to twenty percent have normal IQs, with severe learning disabilities."

Susan envied him the ability to use the Vox. With

Bainbridge's attention on her, she did not have the same luxury. "And a ten-point split between verbal and performance portions of the IQ test defines nonverbal learning disability. Diesel has a thirty-five point split. Severe."

Susan could see nurses whispering behind the other residents and knew they had something to say but did not have the temerity to interrupt an attending's rounds. She addressed them directly. "Has Diesel been tested?"

One of the nurses answered quickly. "Negative."

Monk punched more buttons. "Methylation or FISH?"

Everyone turned Monk a blank stare, and he casually hid his wrist behind his back.

"Methylation testing is a lot more accurate."

"It was the more accurate one," the nurse inserted. "The one that definitely ruled out the syndrome."

"Methylation, then," Monk asserted. "It's reportedly nearly ninety-six percent accurate."

That put Susan off a bit, though not entirely. She still believed she had read Diesel correctly. "There are other obesity syndromes and states. Prader-Willi is not the only one."

Directly behind Bainbridge, Monk still worked his Vox. "There's post-craniotomy syndrome, also known as secondary or acquired Prader-Willi syndrome. It occurs after removal of a craniopharyngioma from the brain."

As Diesel had not had brain surgery, Susan discarded the possibility. "There are also other congenital obesity syndromes." She desperately wished she had Monk's freedom, stuck with racking her brain from genetics class. "There's Bardet-Biedl syndrome, for instance." She hoped no one asked for specifics, as she could not recall them. "Hypothyroidism, hypercortisolism, leptin deficiency." Another thought filled her mind, a brief memory from a single class about rare syndromes. "I'd like permission to explore some of those possibilities."

Bainbridge stroked his chin. "I see no harm in that.

So long as you keep cost in mind. Start with the most inexpensive tests likely to yield the most results."

Susan had the perfect answer. "He's had borderline thyroid studies in the past, but it's only TSH and T4. I'd like to add free T4. Also, how about a vision screening? With a dark room, dilating drops, a cooperative patient, and a decent ophthalmoscope, I can do it myself."

Now, all attention in the room went to Susan.

Misunderstanding the staff's sudden interest in her, Susan added, "I believe he'll cooperate with me. He's not always in volcano mode."

Stony explained, "Susan, we're just wondering what an eye exam has to do with physiological obesity."

Susan had thought the connection obvious. "In Prader-Willi, the obesity is hypothalamic. The hypothalamus regulates food satiety and hunger, as well as body temperature, mood, thirst, vomiting, pain sensation, hormonal balance and secretion, and some other things I'm probably forgetting. Diesel has six obvious features of hypothalamic dysfunction." Susan ticked them off on her fingers. "Obesity, hyperphagia, serious mood disorder, short stature, inability to vomit, and high pain tolerance." She had learned about the last two just minutes earlier. He had directly told her about the vomiting. The high pain tolerance she deduced by his love of football and his positions, despite his squat figure.

"I'm with you so far," Stony said. "But still not making the vision connection."

Susan cleared her throat and looked around. Monk still furiously consulted his Vox, but he clearly had not yet found the thread of her logic. "Diesel has no history of head surgery or trauma to indicate he had damage to the hypothalamus. Monk mentioned craniopharyngioma."

As Susan drew attention to him, Monk swiftly dropped his arm.

"But, as he said, the tumor itself rarely causes these

kinds of problems. It's when the tumor gets irradiated or surgically removed that the hypothalamus becomes damaged. Since craniopharyngiomas are nearly always benign, they have no cancer markers to attack with immunotherapy; and we still have to remove them the old-fashioned, surgical way. So, we can obviously see what causes many of the problems in Prader-Willi syndrome, and post-craniotomy syndrome, is damage to the hypothalamus."

As Susan explained her theory, she began to realize she had previously jumped several steps. As she filled them in, she saw how she had lost her companions along the way. "So, if I assume Diesel has hypothalamic damage causing his symptoms, and it didn't come from surgery or head trauma, it has to be something he was born with, right?" She looked around at her fellow residents, the nurses, and Bainbridge. They all still seemed attentive to her. No one wore the "aha" expression of someone who had just figured out something that had previously eluded him.

"The hypothalamus forms during weeks four to six of embryonic development, the exact same time and place as the optic nerve."

Now, Susan saw a few heads begin to bob.

"Unlike the hypothalamus, which is deep inside the skull, we can actually view the optic nerve directly. We don't need an MRI or anything fancy. If he has abnormal optic nerves, it would indicate some sort of mishap in weeks four to six of fetal development and would help substantiate my hypothalamic obesity argument." The coup de grâce delivered, she looked around at her fellow residents.

Stony spoke first. "But if Diesel has abnormal development of the optic nerves, wouldn't he be blind? Or, at least, wear glasses?"

"I'm not sure," Susan admitted.

Monk launched into his Vox. Having edged behind Bainbridge, Nevaeh did the same.

Diesel's nurse, a large man with brown hair and a thick mustache, said, "I've often wondered if he didn't need glasses, but he won't cooperate with chart vision testing."

Susan still believed she could get Diesel to allow her to examine him.

Monk finally came back with an answer. "Congenital abnormalities of the optic nerve can result in blindness, decreased vision, loss of snippets of visual field, or even normal or near-normal vision."

Bainbridge nodded thoughtfully. "Definitely sounds worth pursuing vision screening and the free T4 level. We may also need to consider a growth hormone and cortisol stimulation test."

Susan smiled, appreciating his new faith in her. With a glance at his Vox, Stony tried to move things along. The longer rounds took, the less actual work got done. Susan knew from her experiences as a medical student that the first rounds of the month usually took much longer, as residents and the attending learned the new patients. Later, it would dwindle to things that had happened the previous day, changes in treatment plans, and discussion of new discharges and admissions. "Susan, do you have any patients without underlying undiagnosed medical problems requiring immediate attention?"

Susan laughed. "Two. Monterey Zdrazil." She stumbled over the last name. "Zzz-drah-zil."

"It's Zdrazil," one of the nurses corrected, pronouncing it "*Dra*y-zull."

Susan practiced the pronunciation. "Monterey *Dra*y-zull is a twelve-year-old white female with post-traumatic, hysterical mutism times six years."

"Six *years*?" Bainbridge could not help cutting in. "I've never heard of such a thing, at least not outside of a soap opera."

Susan could only nod. Her limited research the previous night had not gotten her far. Normally, mute children came in three varieties: deaf-mutes, selective mutes, and post-traumatic mutes. Monterey had spoken normally for the first six years of her life and had passed hearing tests in the newborn nursery and at school. Selective mutes, by definition, spoke when relaxed but refused to talk in anxiety-provoking situations, such as school.

By report, Monterey had not spoken a single word since a car accident six years ago, which put her clearly in the category of post-traumatic mute. However, she did not fit those criteria well, either. In most cases, post-traumatic mutes had serious head trauma affecting the midbrain area, and they recovered speech function gradually in days to weeks. Hysterical mutism fit her better, as she met the criteria of sudden onset after a stressful event and absence of a causal organic disease. However, Susan could not find any other cases of conversion reactions of any kind occurring before age ten.

"And it's definitely psychiatric this time," Susan said without a hint of doubt. "She's had the most complete workup for medical illnesses I've ever seen in my life. They've tried every antianxiety drug ever invented, including some so old we didn't learn about them in school. Her brain looks perfectly normal on MRI, even in the speech areas. On the other hand, the mutism started when she was involved in an auto accident that killed her father. No one knows exactly what happened, but she was firmly buckled into her booster and he . . . was not."

Stony's eyes glimmered. "So, what's your theory, Susan?"

Susan had nothing to add. "I agree with everyone else. She suffered a major trauma, and the mutism is a conversion reaction. Somehow, not speaking binds her anxiety and guards her against future pain. It's rare in children but not unheard of."

"So." Bainbridge sounded relieved the department

seemed to have this patient in hand. "What are we going to do with her?"

Susan sighed. Monterey was not the uncomplicated patient she initially seemed.

Nevaeh stepped into the fray for the first time since rounds began. "What about homeopathic treatments? She might benefit from acupuncture or something naturopathic."

Sensing another tirade from Dr. Bainbridge, Susan jumped in swiftly. "Monterey's mother shopped her from healer to healer. She's tried the whole gamut: faith, herbal teas, acupuncture, hypnotists, aminconmi, random ingredients of the Krebs cycle, indiscriminate megadoses of vitamins, Scientology, soul whisperers, psychics, you name it. When she started experimenting with toxic comas, child protective services stepped in and brought her here."

The tirade came from Nevaeh instead. "Lots of natural products work, with no impurities and fewer side effects."

Dr. Bainbridge's cheeks purpled. "Sure they do. Some of the most potent drugs in history were natural: digitalis from foxglove, aspirin from willow bark, curare, muscarinic mushrooms, rattlesnake venom. Unfortunately, they were also all deadly poisons, most even at low dosages."

Kendall could not help butting in. "I consider death a pretty significant side effect, even if it's the only one."

"Exactly." Dr. Bainbridge launched into what Susan had tried to avoid. "We eventually discarded all of them for safer and more effective alternatives; yet people still insist on self-medicating with arbitrary doses of unproven plant substances, believing them safer." He shook his head. "In the public mind, anecdotal 'evidence' and false promises trump science every time."

Stony gave Susan a pleading look. She alone could get the proceedings back on topic, by applying them to Monterey Zdrazil.

Trying to remain diplomatic, without antagonizing Bainbridge, Susan cut in. "The technique we're planning to use on Monterey isn't terribly scientific, either. We're trying to get permission for old-fashioned ECT."

That shut down the discussion.

Nevaeh finally broke the silence. "So, we're denigrating a few harmless herbal treatments; but we're perfectly fine with frying a child's brain?"

Stony's eyes went round as coins. Nostrils flared all around the group. No one spoke to an attending like that, short of another attending.

To Susan's surprise, Bainbridge did not fret over Nevaeh's verbal attack, though he did give Stony a significant look. Apparently, he expected the R-3 to lecture the R-1s on appropriate behavior after rounds. "So, it's perfectly fine to stab a child with pins and needles of no known benefit, fill her full of untested poisons, or bleed her with leeches; but using an effective, studied, painless technique is 'frying her brain'?"

Apparently realizing her mistake, Nevaeh tried to fade into the background. Her defense came from an unlikely place.

"In all fairness," Stony said, "ECT isn't harmless."

"I didn't say 'harmless,'" Bainbridge pointed out. "I said effective, studied, and painless. The decision is whether it's worth a bit of potential memory loss to regain a life for this child."

"Assuming it works," Stony said. "Otherwise, it's potential memory loss in a child for no gain at all."

Stony had had a bit more time to consider the situation, having come on service a few days earlier. "I'm not saying I'm for or against it in this case. Just that there is an argument for both sides."

Susan did not feel as neutral about the situation. "We've wasted six years already and tried everything else known to man, including much less tested and effective therapies. It's not as if Monterey is a busy mute

with an otherwise active life. She's one step from cata-
tonia, and she's only twelve years old. She's lost half her
life to this already. This obviously isn't going away by
itself. We have to do something, and ECT appears to be
all that's left." She glanced at Nevaeh. "At least all that's
logically left from a medical standpoint."

Bainbridge smiled. "Let's do it, then."

Stony shook his head, and Susan knew where he
had to go next. "We can't. There's a legal injunction
against us."

Bainbridge stared. "After trying everything else, her
mom's fighting this?"

"Not her mom. The Society for Humanity. The SFH."

Bainbridge groaned. "Those god-awful ignorant protestors?"

"They're defining it as torture and experimentation
on a little girl."

Bainbridge groaned louder. "So, what are we doing
about it?"

"Fighting it legally. Looking for precedent for using
ECT on a child."

"So, in the meantime, she languishes here."

"Apparently."

As there seemed nothing more to say about Monterey, Susan moved on. "My last patient is Sharicka Anson, a four-year-old female of mixed race with juvenile
conduct disorder."

Bainbridge held up a hand. "Did you say 'fourteen-
year-old'?"

"Four-year-old," Susan repeated.

"Four-year-old." Bainbridge shook his head. "Four?
As in baby?"

"Four, as in preschool. Definitely no baby." Susan
quoted from the chart, as she had yet to meet the child.
"Three purported attempts at murder, two of them on
the unit, and possibly more."

"At four years old." Bainbridge seemed incapable of

getting past that point. "What kind of history does she have?"

"Adopted as an infant into a doting, professional family. Met milestones shockingly early. Sat up at two months, talked at six months, put words together by twelve months, carried on full conversations with adults before the age of two years."

"That certainly doesn't sound like an environment ripe for abuse." Bainbridge shoved his glasses up his nose. "Though you never know."

"Never missed a well exam. Got all her vaccinations on time. No documented injuries or bruises. Proud parents bragged about her early accomplishments, chalked them up to a lot of attention and reading to her every night. No history of questionable visits to the ER. Two older siblings, both adopted, with no difficulties at home or school. Child protective services noted some hostility from the parents, but not until the third thorough investigation."

Kendall winced. "Which I imagine could make a saint turn hostile. Strangers with the authority of the state behind them grilling your children, your doctors, your school, your family and neighbors. Every little thing you've ever said or done scrutinized. Suspicions planted in the minds of all your acquaintances who figure CPS wouldn't be investigating for *no* reason." Kendall rolled his head. "That has to suck."

Susan had to agree. "Everything came out clean on investigation. No founded abuse."

Bainbridge only nodded thoughtfully. "Halfway into the 2030s, and people still want to believe all children are sugar and spice. Physical diseases, cancer, asthma, metabolic syndromes, those are sad accidents of fate. Anything that goes wrong mentally has to be the parents' fault."

Sable finally spoke up. "Doesn't heredity have the greatest influence on personality?"

"Bingo." Bainbridge jabbed a hand toward Sable. "There's no question babies come with a preformed personality. What do we know about the biological parents?"

Susan wished she had had time to dissect Sharicka's enormous chart. "I'm . . . not sure. I'll have to check on that."

Bainbridge looked around the nurses. "Anyone?"

For several moments, the nurses looked among one another until one finally spoke up. "Dr. Bainbridge, I don't mean to be obstructionist, but we're not sure about Sharicka's diagnosis." She glanced at her colleagues for support, and several of them gave strong nods of agreement. "She really is a darling little girl, and we think she might do fine in the right environment."

Susan could scarcely believe what she was hearing. The doctors' notes had clearly documented a long history of violent acts and an obsession with drowning and other forms of murder. "Didn't she attempt to drown another patient in the toilet?"

The nurse's pale cheeks acquired a reddish hue. "Well, yes. But we don't know exactly what happened there. We think the other child might have baited her into it."

Susan had read about the incident. Not only had Sharicka not denied being the aggressor, she had explained her intent to drown the other child with a smile plastered on her face. The other patient told a story of being lured to the bathroom with the promise of seeing a tiny alligator in the bowl. "And didn't she assault a staff member and beat her head against a window?"

The cheeks turned even more crimson. "I wasn't here when it happened, but the staff member quit soon after. She wasn't well liked, and we think the staff member exaggerated what happened. Other than those two incidents, which have other plausible explanations, she hasn't done anything bad here."

Bainbridge had a thoughtful smile on his lips. "Does that ring a bell for any of you?" He looked around the residents, brows inching upward.

It did for Susan. During the summer breaks between her years of medical school, she had worked at a veterans' psychiatric institution. She had met a patient there who had made her feel competent beyond her years. He had convinced her that she alone had broken through his desperation and loneliness, that only her brilliant diagnoses and soothing manner had worked for him. Later, she had learned about his borderline personality disorder and the ability these patients had to manipulate those around them, especially caretakers. The patient had won over every one of the nurses the same way, each believing his or her special manner and expertise had brought about remarkable changes in the patient. All of them had petitioned for extra favors, treats, or services for him.

Before Susan could speak, Nevaeh took a reasonable guess. "Schizophrenia?"

"Schizophrenia." Bainbridge fixed his gaze fanatically on Nevaeh. "In schizophrenia, it's the patients who have the delusions."

Everyone chuckled nervously at the obvious joke, which clearly insulted someone. Susan realized he aimed it at the nurses who defended criminal behavior, but they might see it as referring to the parents and alleged victims of Sharicka's antics. Susan gave the correct answer: "Antisocial personality disorder."

Bainbridge tapped his nose and pointed to Susan suddenly, like a game show host. "Definitely a personality disorder. Most likely antisocial type. Another possibility." He whirled abruptly, and Monk Peterson guiltily hid his arm behind his back. "You, there. The one named after a television character."

"Monk." The R-1 chewed his lip as he sorted through the information in his mind. "Um . . . fetal alcohol syndrome?" He waited tensely for a reaction.

"Is that a question? Or an answer?"

"Fetal alcohol syndrome," Monk said more confidently.

"Good thought." Bainbridge whirled back to Susan. "History of alcoholism in the mother?"

Susan shook her head. "Sharicka was adopted as an infant. Her parents gave up all social drinking when they first started trying to get pregnant, fifteen years ago. There's no alcohol in the house. Birth mother denied alcohol or drug use during the pregnancy, but nearly all of them do, whether or not it's true." Susan could understand a birth mother lying in order to ensure her child the best possible placement. "When I examine Sharicka, I'll watch for small palpebral fissures and indistinct philtrum."

"And flattened cheekbones," Monk added.

"And flattened cheekbones," Susan agreed. "But even without any of those features, she could still have all the behavioral and emotional disabilities. ARND." Susan carefully remembered the individual words of the acronym. "Alcohol-related neurodevelopmental . . ." It seemed as if it ought to have another letter.

"Disorder," Monk finished.

"So far," Susan said, "treatment has focused on controlling Sharicka's behaviors and getting her home, not on the cause of those behaviors."

Bainbridge gave Susan a stern look. "And, yet, the cause is important to know. Why, Susan Calvin?"

Susan was up to the task. "Because it can make a difference in our treatment, Dr. Bainbridge. Or explain our failures. For example, fetal alcohol and ARND still have no known effective treatment. Nevertheless, it's becoming far less frequent due to prevention, prenatal testing, and educational programs."

"Good." Bainbridge finally took his intensive focus completely off Susan. "Now, who would like to present his patients next?"

For the next two hours, the other residents described a fascinating parade of juvenile patients with diagnoses ranging from uncommon psychoses to exceptionally rare organic forms of dementia. Some were newly diagnosed and still being evaluated, while working treatments were still being sought for the more chronic patients.

Of the sixteen other patients, four had severe forms of schizophrenia, including one who was so catatonic that she had not moved or spoken in almost a year. Three had temper dysregulation disorder, previously called childhood bipolar syndrome, and another suffered from psychotic depression, as did Diesel. Two had brain damage from tumors, two from drug use, and one from serious trauma. Susan found the last three most interesting. A patient of Kendall's had terminal primary liver cancer. Sable had a patient with an uncontrollable epileptic syndrome that kept her so sleep-deprived that she had lost touch with the real world. The last was Monk's patient, a seven-year-old boy with an, as yet, inexplicable dementia.

Susan left rounds energized about helping her own patients as well as looking forward to the next day's rounds and finding out what her companions had done for theirs. She had a feeling she was in for a difficult, but fascinating, ride.

Chapter 6

The door to the Calvins' apartment swung open before Susan could insert the proper thumb into the scanner. John caught her up in an embrace on the threshold. His familiar, strong arms winched around her, and he rested his chin on the top of her head. "Hi, Susan. How was your . . . days?"

Susan chuckled. "Interesting in so many ways." She wriggled free. "And you might regret hugging me. They keep the unit hotter than I like, and the on-call shower sucks."

"You smell fine," John Calvin assured her, ushering her inside. He was slender to the point of gauntness, with the same pale blue eyes and straight brown hair as Susan, though he wore his short.

Susan stepped inside the main room and looked around at furnishings that now showed a hint of her decorating taste, as well as her father's. John had always kept things simple. Silver tubing framed myriad glass shelves holding everything from a stereo/television system to notebooks filled with his small, neat writings. The walls had held only black-and-white diplomas and a single color picture of the only woman he had ever loved: Amanda Calvin, Susan's mother. As a child, she had memorized every detail, every line, and she suspected her father had done the same. Since moving in, Susan had added a handful of tasteful paintings, with splashes of blues, greens, and reds.

John closed the door behind his daughter. "I have a casserole ready and waiting for you in the kitchen."

That intrigued Susan. Her father's casseroles were a mishmash of whatever remained in the refrigerator. Despite their experimental nature, they always wound up tasting at least reasonably good, if only because he had a keen eye when it came to shopping, especially for fruits and vegetables.

Susan walked through the den into the kitchen. She barely glanced at the familiar cupboards or the refrigerator/freezer, which still sported her childhood drawings clamped to the stainless-steel surface with animal-shaped Happeez. She took her usual seat and waited for her father to serve. He would have already eaten, she knew. Though kind and normal in so many ways, he had an oddity that used to bother her but no longer did. John Calvin preferred not to eat in front of other people, regardless of whether they shared the meal. Susan could still barely remember when they had eaten together as a family: her mother, her father, and herself. His neurosis had developed immediately after Amanda's death, and Susan wondered if it stemmed from that trauma as fully as Monterey's mutism did from the accident that had claimed her father.

It was one of the few images Susan still had of her mother, beaming as husband and daughter ate what she had made. Amanda had seemed to take great pride in her cooking and in her family's enjoyment of it, which might explain the origin of John's oddity. Perhaps he equated group meals with his beloved wife.

John placed a plate of steaming food, a glass of dark juice, and a fork in front of Susan, then took the seat directly across from her and leaned across the table. "So, tell me about Manhattan Hasbro."

Susan let the aroma of the food tease her nose. She had eaten breakfast and lunch in the hospital staff cafeteria, a good selection of institutional food. The casserole had an egg and vegetable smell, quichelike, and she could see chunks of carrot and ham. "I like it. The staff seems intelligent and competent, if a bit quirky. I like my R-3 a lot, and my R-2 is, at the least, entertaining. The patients have real problems that force me to think."

"Tell me all about them."

Susan shoveled food into her mouth. It had a unique taste, an odd combination of flavors that worked well together. She realized that might describe the hospital as well, but she had more than patients on her mind. Soon enough, she would spend hours on the palm-pross researching them. For now, she had questions only her father could answer. She looked directly at him. "I met Nate last night."

"Nate?" John Calvin's brow furrowed. "As in 'Nathan'?"

"As in N8-C." Susan studied her father's reaction.

John clearly tried to hide his surprise, but it leaked through his eyes.

"Nate says you're a legend at U.S. Robots and Mechanical Men."

"A legend?" John laughed. "What a silly thing for him to say."

"Is it?" Susan doubted anyone else would find it silly. "How come you never told me you worked with the actual robots?"

Even John's not-quite-casual shrug seemed uncomfortable beneath his daughter's scrutiny. "I didn't think it would interest you. It's boring stuff, really."

Susan put her fork aside and glared at her father.

"The bell's rung, Dad. You can't unring it." She took a swallow of juice to clear her palate. Like the casserole, it had a combination of tastes. She thought she recognized pomegranate and cranberry. "I now know you work directly with mechanical men who can pass for human." She quoted Nate verbatim, "'Human stem cells coaxed into a dermal and muscular system grown over a skeleton of porous silicone plastic.'"

John grumbled, "Nate talks too much."

"Just enough," Susan corrected. "And I intend to spend a lot more time with him, so don't try to feed me any bullshit."

Her father's brows shot up. "Surely, it doesn't taste that bad."

"What?" The sudden change of topic caught her off guard. Susan followed his gaze to the serving of casserole on her plate. "Funny. The food's fine, Dad. I'm just mad you convinced me you had an insignificant job for so many years we could have spent talking about miracles like Nate."

"It's not as interesting as it sounds."

The defense fell flat. "If it's even a tenth as interesting as it sounds, I'm fascinated."

John Calvin sighed. He had spent most of his life avoiding the topic he no longer could, and Susan could not help feeling cheated and angry. "What do you want to know?"

Susan picked up her fork. "Nate mentioned he had a 'positronic brain.' What does that mean?"

John kept his voice level, almost monotonic, as if trying to infuse the boredom he had hidden behind so many years. "It's kind of like a telephone switchboard on an atomic scale, with billons of possible connections compressed into a brain that can fit inside a human-sized skull."

Struck with a sudden realization, Susan chewed a bite of casserole. "You invented it, didn't you?"

"Good Lord, no! That would be my incredible friend, and college roommate, Dr. Lawrence Robertson."

"But you had a hand in it."

"A small one."

Susan suspected her father was still downplaying his role. "And you thought I would find this boring?"

"You were a child. How many little girls find robotic circuitry interesting?"

Susan ate more of her dinner. "I haven't been a little girl for quite a long time. I raved about algebra. I found physics, organic chemistry, and differential calculus exciting. Didn't that give you a clue I wasn't your average 'little girl'?"

"I never thought you were average, kitten. Not in any way."

Susan leaned toward him. "Then why did you lock me out of this incredible part of your life?"

John sat up, rigid. His blue eyes dodged hers. "Susan, if I talk to you about it now, will you let my reasons for waiting lie?"

Susan wanted it all but saw the prudence in waiting. The topic clearly agitated him; and, for now, the details of his projects interested her more than his excuses. "Fine. Tell me why robots that can pass for human, that can actually think, aren't everywhere. The world should be clamoring for them, fighting over every one USR can make as fast as you can make them."

John's head started bobbing, as if of its own accord. He clearly agreed with her, but he would not say so. "First, they're unbelievably expensive to build."

Susan shrugged. "All the more reason for popularity. All new technology is expensive. The price comes down as raw materials can be purchased in bulk, construction becomes more mechanized and widespread, and supply catches up to demand."

"But, mostly," John continued, as if Susan had never spoken, "it's the Frankenstein Complex."

Susan hesitated, fork halfway to her mouth. The word "complex" implied a medical diagnosis, but she had never come across this particular abnormality in any of her studies. "As in Victor Frankenstein's monster? From the Mary Shelley novel?"

"Exactly."

Exactly what? Susan tried to put the pieces together. "Some people . . . are afraid . . . thinking robots will become . . . uncontrollably destructive?"

John Calvin nodded, looking thoughtfully out the window. They lived on the tenth story, overlooking many similar apartment buildings. Walls were all he could see from his angle. "Basically. Too many people worry robots will destroy, dominate, or replace us."

Susan supposed it was not a wholly unreasonable fear, especially when it came to replacement. Already, most of the unskilled jobs had been given over to unintelligent machines. If positronic robots ever became cheaper, more reliable labor than humans, businesses would vie for their share.

"Think media, Susan, where your average person gets most of his or her information. How many movies have you seen where creatures with artificial intelligence set out to topple their human creators? Anything with superhuman, human, or near-human intelligence is presumed to eventually try to slaughter or enslave us, whether it's machine or organic, golem, android, or alien."

Susan had to agree. "Well, it definitely makes for better movies. It's hard to generate fear and excitement if the bug-eyed monsters come only to hug us. Surely that doesn't mean everyone—"

"Not everyone," John admitted. "But enough people in power do. Then we have to worry about general public perception, political groups, religious affiliates—"

It was Susan's turn to interrupt. "And the Society for Humanity."

John immediately stopped speaking. "You're full of surprise information today. How do you know about them?"

Susan chewed and swallowed completely, washing it down with juice. "They're a thorn in my side, too. In addition to being antirobot, they have an injunction against treating one of my patients. They're a powerful group with a megaton of cheek."

"Yeah." The word emerged strained.

When Susan examined her father closely, she thought she saw trembling fingers and moisture in his eyes. "Isn't there some way to make robots absolutely safe? Something in their programming?"

John's discomfort turned to a shaky smile. "There is. It's the reason USR has the only legal permit to manufacture robots, at least in the United States."

Now he had Susan's full attention. "What is it?"

"It's our patented Three Laws of Robotics. They're a fundamental part of every robot we manufacture, and we do not continue building or programming until it has become an integral part of them."

Susan had to know. "And the Three Laws are?"

John cleared his throat. She suspected he knew them forward and backward, that he could recite them in anagram form or even in his sleep. "Law Number One: 'A robot may not injure a human being, or, through inaction, allow a human being to come to harm.'"

Susan nodded with each word, trying to commit them to memory verbatim. This First Law, by itself, seemed like enough to keep the citizenry safe.

"Law Number Two: 'A robot must obey all orders given by human beings except where such orders would conflict with the First Law.'"

Susan could understand that one as well. It would keep the robots definitively subservient and ensure humans could not manipulate them into killing other humans.

"Law Number Three: 'A robot must protect its own existence as long as such protection does not conflict with the First or Second Law.'"

"Hmm." Susan grinned. "That last sounds like it protects your investment more than actually being necessary to keep humans safe."

"At face value, yes." John continued to stare out the window, as if accessing old memories better left buried. "But it can have important human applications. If, for example, a robot witnesses a murder or is asked to participate in a crime, this prevents the killer from ordering its robot witness to destroy itself."

It suddenly occurred to Susan that the Three Laws, though cautiously worded and direct, did have deeper implications well worth exploring. She wondered how humans would behave were they wholly governed by those same Three Laws. It might make an interesting psychological experiment. She finished the last of her casserole and juice. "Thanks for finally sharing. I'm looking forward to learning more and to talking to Nate now that I know his underlying . . ." She did not know what to call it. "Governance" seemed closest; but, given his near humanity, "religion" or "moral philosophy" seemed better. She settled for the obvious. "Laws. It'll be interesting to see how the need to abide by those makes him different from humans."

"Different?" John Calvin laughed. "Now you're psychoanalyzing robots? What's next, the bookshelves?"

Susan did not see the humor in it. "What happens, for example, when a robot is given conflicting commands? Or he's told to take a bath by someone who doesn't know an electrical appliance has fallen into the tub? That could put laws two and three into conflict." Several more potential problems came to her mind. "Let's say a robot impervious to temperature is in the Antarctic with a freezing and comatose human. Can he figure out the human's life is in danger from something that can't harm the robot? Or let's say he's ordered into a burning building, but he knows everyone inside is already dead? Law Number Three would force him to refuse."

John Calvin's expression gradually changed from one of tolerant humor to interest. "You've thought of everything."

A thrill of excitement swept through Susan. "Not nearly. There're thousands of possible scenarios."

"None of which have come up."

Susan added, "Yet. But when robots become an everyday commodity, they will, and probably quite frequently."

John did not seem convinced. "Maybe." He reached for Susan's dirty dishes and changed the subject. "Now, tell me about those fascinating patients."

Susan rose, shaking her head. "I will. I promise. But, first, I have to do some research on those fascinating patients, or I'm not going to make it through my fascinating residency." Walking into the main room, she snatched up her palm-pross. "By tomorrow, I have to know how to diagnose subtle abnormalities of the optic disk and their significance. Also, why a child with a normal heart might be in florid cardiac failure, how to treat chronic and resistant mutism, and what to do with a four-year-old homicidal maniac."

John Calvin called from the kitchen. "Wow. That does sound interesting." Dishes rattled. "We can talk when you're finished. Until then, I won't bug you."

It was a lie, and Susan knew it. At strategic times during the evening, he would interrupt her studies to ascertain her every comfort. She could count on an irresistible dessert at the least. For now, though, she took her palm-pross into her bedroom and began her search.

Susan Calvin met with the Moores immediately after rounds, in the room between two sets of locked doors installed especially for such meetings. She found them sitting in the plush mauve chairs provided for parental comfort. When the door opened, Mr. Moore rose, and a wan smile appeared on Mrs. Moore's face. They both appeared exhausted, the father's short, black hair speckled with gray and the mother's long and braided into permanent extensions.

Susan perched on the arm of a chair, meeting their gazes in turn. "I'm Susan Calvin, Dallas' new resident doctor."

They nodded, familiar with the monthly drill. They had met a parade of residents, though usually not this early in the month. Breakthroughs did not often come about this quickly.

Mrs. Moore sighed. "What did he do this time?"

Susan smiled reassuringly, though inwardly she cringed. She wondered what it must be like to have people constantly condemning one's beloved, if difficult, child. "Nothing we wouldn't expect from someone with his syndrome."

"Syndrome?" Mr. Moore repeated. A tall, well-muscled man, he leaned forward in his chair. "Are they calling depression a syndrome now?"

Susan explained her findings from earlier that morning. "Have you heard of Prader-Willi syndrome?"

The Moores nodded wearily. "A resident thought Dallas had it a few months ago. Tests showed he didn't."

"Right." Quailed by the intensity of the parental gazes, Susan wished she had a window on which to focus her attention. She had confronted families before, but always as a medical student observing residents or attendings. She had never held the spotlight, and it unnerved her. The parents hung on her every word, as they should. The future of their child currently rested on her diagnoses. "It's a rare chromosomal defect that causes, among other things, inadequate development of an area of the brain called the hypothalamus."

Susan paused to make sure she still had the parents on board. They stared at her with rapt attention, so she continued. "The hypothalamus is a control center of the brain. One of the many things it handles is hunger and satiety. People with Prader-Willi syndrome almost never feel full; and, even when they do, it's short-lived. Given free access to food, children with Prader-Willi syndrome will, quite literally, eat themselves to death."

The parents nodded. Mr. Moore cleared his throat. "Why are you telling us this? Dallas doesn't have Prader-Willi syndrome, does he?"

Susan nodded agreement. "Dallas has a far rarer syndrome. It's called the syndrome of optic nerve hypoplasia. For short, it's ONH." Such a diagnosis might devastate most parents, but Susan saw a hint of relief soften the tightness of Mr. Moore's features. Mrs. Moore almost smiled. Having a name for Diesel's behavior, a medical reason for the odd things he did, had to be liberating after the hell he must have put them through.

"Doctor," Mr. Moore said, "what does that mean?"

Susan tested a theory. "Was Dallas born in Texas? Perhaps Harris County?"

Both parents stared. Mrs. Moore finally stuttered out, "H-how did you know that?"

"I didn't," Susan admitted. "I just put the pieces together. It's not terribly uncommon to name a child after his place of birth. Also, of the cases of ONH, a high proportion of mothers spent the early weeks of pregnancy in Harris County, Texas."

"Harris County." Mrs. Moore was amazed. "It was Harris County, wasn't it, Jamal?"

"Houston," Mr. Moore replied. "That's in Harris County, all right. By the time he was born, we'd moved to Dallas." He frowned. "Why do they think Harris County has this problem? And what does it mean for our son?"

Susan had more information than answers. "The syndrome's so rare, no one has done any significant studies of it. I just happened to tap into one ophthalmologist in California who performed a survey, looking for a cause. He never actually found one, but he did find the uptick in patients who spent their early embryonic lives in Harris County. He believes something in the environment explains the defect. Mind you, most of the kids with ONH don't come from Texas. It's just a statistical thing.

"The upshot is Dallas has congenital abnormalities of his hypothalamus and optic nerves." Susan did not get deeper into the brain technicalities. Some people with the syndrome also had certain missing septa in the brain, but Dallas did not.

Mrs. Moore guessed, "He has trouble . . . seeing?"

"That's how it's usually detected," Susan said. "Hypoplasia is when things in the body don't develop to their full potential. Kids with ONH are often blind. Most have poorer than normal vision; but a few, like Dallas, have normal or nearly normal vision. His optic nerves are smaller and thinner than usual, but they work just fine. The best part is the damage is done before birth. So, we have no reason to believe Dallas' vision will get any worse."

Susan gave the Moores time to digest this information.

After several moments of dense silence, Mr. Moore finally spoke again, "So, how does this apply to Dallas?"

Susan anticipated the question. "As I said, ONH is nearly always diagnosed by ophthalmologists because of vision problems. Ophthalmologists know children with ONH often also have problems with the hypothalamus. The lucky ones with normal vision, like Dallas, fall through the cracks. They present with the hypothalamic symptoms first, and they become extremely difficult to diagnose." She hoped this would help the Moores understand why medical science had, thus far, failed them.

Mr. Moore still worked to grasp the greater significance of the syndrome. "So . . . Dallas' obsession with food is not obsessive-compulsive or oppositional. And his depression?"

Susan thought she had a reasonable understanding of the situation based on talking to Diesel and reading the charts and the nursing notes throughout his hospital stay. "Oh, he's depressed, all right. Deeply and severely. Among many other things, the hypothalamus regulates mood, and people with disturbances in hypothalamic function have *Moods*, with a capital *M*. Their highs are higher, their lows subbasement, their anger—"

"Volcanic," Mrs. Moore supplied.

"Yes." Susan felt certain they had experienced many of Diesel's explosions, probably since infancy. "Now, imagine you're hungry all the time, day and night. You're driven to eat. Tens of thousands of calories every day don't satisfy your belly because, no matter how full your gut, your brain keeps telling you to eat or die."

Mrs. Moore put her hands to her face. "Dallas feels like that?"

Susan did not answer, needing to continue her scenario until she made a specific point. "But you're constantly being told that taking food is greedy and disgusting, and that fat people are undisciplined slobs. But you *need* that food every bit as much as you need air. So you start to sneak it, to steal it, to hide it, which only brings down more anger and humiliation. Any moral child would come to believe himself"—she used Diesel's own words—"a monster. And hating oneself is the very definition of depression."

Mr. Moore sat in thoughtful silence, rocking ever so slightly. Tears formed in Mrs. Moore's eyes. "They told us he was just being . . . oppositional. Defiant. Fighting us for control."

Mrs. Moore's voice quavered. "One doctor said we didn't love him enough. That he ate to fill the void."

"Nonsense," Susan reassured them.

Mr. Moore turned entirely practical. "So, what do we do?"

Susan had a plan all worked out for them. "First, we get you hooked up with an endocrinologist. I'm willing to bet Dallas would benefit from growth hormone and thyroid hormone replacement. He may need testosterone to go through puberty; and, even then, I should warn you he will probably be infertile." Susan gave them time to process that information. Eventually, they would likely realize it did not matter. Given his severe lifelong problems with food, Diesel would never have the wherewithal to handle children of his own.

"Next, we hook you up with a security company that can go through your entire house and figure out how to secure any and all food-containing areas. You will need dependable locks on the freezer, refrigerator, garbage cans, and cabinets. Better yet, if you have an enclosed kitchen, lock the whole thing. We will have to work with the school as well and realize children with hypothalamic forms of obesity will take food wherever they can get it: stores, vending machines, other people's plates, floor sweepings, dog food bowls."

The Moores started talking at once, comparing memories of times when Diesel had raided places they never expected and had eaten items most people would never touch.

Susan let them converse. She had given them a whole new perspective on their son, and it would require them to turn their lives, and those of his siblings, upside down. Most people did not realize just how important and central a role food played in every social aspect of life until it became a problem.

When the Moores seemed ready, Susan continued. "Dallas will feel most secure when he has no personal access to food, when people he trusts fully control his access to it. If he tests the locks and finds them wanting, he will continue to work on them anxiously. If he tries and fails, he will become a much calmer person knowing his life, and his appetite, are controlled by a higher authority: his parents and doctors. We will make him up a diet and stick by it rigidly. Dallas must know he will be fed, at regular times and in predictable and consistent amounts. Food can never be used as reward or punishment, nor can it be present anywhere he is expected to concentrate."

"And when he does steal food again?" The mother's question left no doubt it would happen.

Susan shrugged. "We understand it's caused by biology, not disobedience. Talk about the incident in the context of keeping him safe and healthy rather than as a terrible or criminal act. You may need to involve other people: neighbors, his friends' parents, your church, and, of course, the school. Dallas may need a full-time aide to watch him if all of you together can't keep him safe."

Susan knew the parents needed time to process the vast amount of information she had dropped on them. "You can stay here as long as you want. When you're ready to leave, let the nurses know so they can unlock the doors. By then, you may have more questions. Don't hesitate to ask for me, Susan Calvin." She turned to leave, stopped by another question from Diesel's father.

"Dallas will come home soon?"

Susan turned back to face them again. "As soon as Endocrinology sees him, a dietitian writes a plan, and your home is secured. We will begin the transition immediately. When we change our approach to him, I believe he will respond quickly. In the meantime, we need to have your house and family fully prepared." With that, Susan headed out of the room and down the hallway, preparing for the rest of her day. During rounds, she had outlined her plans for Diesel, and the nurses had shown support. Susan had already spoken with Diesel, preparing him for the many changes. No longer would anyone berate his willpower or damn him for stealing food; those things would not work. From now on, they would become a team, working together to find ways to make his difficult life longer and better.

Mr. Moore called down the hallway. "One more thing, Dr. Calvin."

Hand on the locked door to the unit, Susan turned.

"We'll need someone to coordinate all his care, someone he knows and likes. Would you do that for us?"

Susan thought the job better handled by a general pediatrician, but she recognized the honor inherent in the question. She had found the answer so many others had missed, and they trusted her. Dallas was her first breakthrough, special for that as well as all his other issues. On a more selfish level, she realized she needed to know what happened to him from this point on. "I'd be thrilled," she replied.

Chapter 7

Susan chose to lunch alone, heading to the hidden charting room that had served as her on-call hideaway. She took her lunch and her palm-pross, dropping them on the central table in the cozy nook, but her real reason for coming was to find Nate. She sank into one of the unmatched chairs and opened her reusable lunch sack. Her father had packed her favorite: peanut butter on twelve-grain bread. She removed it from its container, took a bite, and chewed thoughtfully, studying the modular shelving, the well-worn textbooks, the computer-processing units, and the plastic storage boxes.

Susan had nearly finished her sandwich, her legs flopped over the arm of her chair, when Nate finally arrived, his tread light and his footsteps nearly silent on the tiled floor. When his gaze fell on her, he stopped, and a welcoming grin split his face. "Dr. Susan Calvin."

Susan sat up properly in her chair. "Robot N8-C."

"Call me Nate."

"Only if you call me Susan."

"Deal."

For the second time in two days, Susan studied the robot. He still looked like nothing other than a tall, male human. He might have gears inside, but they did not stutter and whir. If anything, he seemed more graceful, more easily gliding than most humans. "Nate, can you sit for a little while? Do you have some time to talk?"

"I do." Nate chose the chair catty-corner to Susan's.

It amazed her how human that action seemed. Most people would have selected the exact same spot, comfortably close for conversation but not violating any personal space. Nothing about him suggested mechanization. Had he not told her, had her father not confirmed it, she would never have known his true nature. "Would you answer a hypothetical question for me?"

Nate spread his hands and nodded, clearly trying to calculate a purpose that had not yet become obvious. "If you wish."

Susan leaned forward. "Let's say a fire broke out in a chemical factory with one man trapped inside. Based on the last-known location of the man, and the composition of the fire, he is certainly dead. You also know exposure to the particular heated chemicals involved would destroy your circuitry. You're told to go in and rescue the man. What do you do?"

Nate laughed. "Someone just learned about the Three Laws of Robotics."

Caught, Susan could only join the laughter. "Indeed. So, what do you do?"

"Hypothetically."

"Of course."

Nate sat back with a sigh of consideration. "It would greatly depend on the specifics of the situation. The Laws have a balance that can actually push Number Two ahead of Number One or Number Three ahead of Number Two in certain situations. It's not as black and white as the wording might, at first, seem."

Susan continued to smile. She had been right.

Nate went on. "If I knew for a fact the man inside was alone and dead, Law Number One no longer takes priority. The issue of a human coming to harm from my actions or inactivity becomes moot."

Susan nodded.

"Law Number Two commands me to obey all orders given by human beings. In your scenario, I've been ordered to rescue the man, presumably by a human being. If I know the man is dead, then the command becomes nonsensical; and, therefore, I am no longer obligated to follow it. In that case, Law Number Three comes into effect, and I must protect my own existence. So, assuming all the facts you and I presented, I would not enter the burning chemical factory."

Susan had surmised as much when she had discussed it with her father.

"However," Nate added, "if I had any reason to believe the man inside might still be alive, or another human being might be in danger, Law Number One would override all the others. With or without the command, I would do whatever I could to rescue those humans, even if it led to my own destruction."

Susan liked that she could predict Nate's actions, and she wished humans were that easy to read.

"Now let me add something to your scenario that might surprise you."

Susan became all ears. This, she had not anticipated. "All right."

"Let's say I heard meowing coming from that burning factory and saw a girl crying and calling for her Fluffy. Then, I would also go inside."

Susan paused in uncertainty. "To save a cat?"

"Yes."

Susan tried to guess the reason. "Because . . . if the cat survived . . . the man might . . . also—"

"No." Nate did not allow her to finish. "We're still assuming the man is definitely dead."

"The cat . . . ," Susan started, then stopped. "The cat

is not a human being. Law Number One says nothing about animals."

"True." Nate met Susan's gaze directly. His brown eyes looked placidly into hers, so very real, so human. "But the girl is. Losing her cat would harm her emotionally. And so, by Law Number One, I'm driven to save it at risk to my own existence."

Excitement thrilled through Susan, and she could do nothing more than stare. Instinctively, she had known the Three Laws of Robotics would not prove as solid and obvious as they originally seemed. However, she had not expected to discover such critical and expressive thinking from a robot. Her father had not given this positronic brain concept the credit it deserved. Clearly, robots did not just think and learn. Nate had applied logic to circumstances to account, not only for facts in evidence, but for complex human emotions. Susan knew more than a few living, breathing people with a lesser grasp of empathy than Nate. "Wow." She could think of nothing else to say.

Nate straightened his dress khakis, then ran a hand through his short hair. He had gestures and mannerisms that made him seem all the more alive. "Are we finished, Susan?"

Susan met Nate's gaze again, the remainder of her lunch forgotten. "Do you have a few more minutes?"

"A few." Nate remained in his chair. "Do you have more hypotheticals?"

Susan sighed and straightened her own clothing. "Actually, this is a real situation. I have a patient who had brain surgery performed by a man they call 'one of the greatest neurosurgeons in the world.' "

"Dr. Sudhish Mandar," Nate filled in.

Startled again, Susan managed only a "yes." Then, "Do you know him?"

"If you asked him, he'd say *the* greatest, not just one of a group at the top." Nate planted both arms on the armrests of his chair, gripping the ends in his hands. "You should know that, although I have read all those books"—he gestured vaguely toward the shelves—"I am not considered a medical expert."

Susan's attention followed Nate's motion. If he had read every book on those shelves, and retained even a quarter of it, he had as much knowledge as most physicians. "It's not a medical question. It's . . . moral."

"Moral? And you're asking me? Morality is a human construct."

Susan disagreed. The Three Laws inflicted an honor on the robot that humans might not appreciate, even if they recognized it. "Nevertheless, I'd like your opinion."

"Okay." Nate settled back into his chair.

"The neurosurgeon has declared the surgery a success and no longer looks after the patient. For months, she was believed to have dementia"—Susan looked up to see if she needed to define the word; Nate waved her on—"due to presurgical swelling of the brain because of the initial problem or damage to the brain tissue during the surgery."

Nate continued to nod his understanding.

Susan downplayed her role in the upcoming information. "Yesterday, we discovered this young girl's dementia is actually due to heart failure. The cardiologists put her on medicine to help control it, and her mental status is clearing."

Nate smiled. "That's good news. Right?"

"Well, yes." Susan gave a less than enthusiastic response. "Except they had to put her on very high doses of serious medications, and it's only helping to keep the problem in check. It's not a cure. My concern is the condition will soon overcome the medications, and, not only will the dementia return, but the heart failure will worsen."

"And she'll die?" Nate guessed.

"Eventually." Susan knew a young, strong body had

ways of compensating for congestive heart failure. Starling Woodruff's already had, or it would have been discovered sooner. "She can probably go home, but she can't live anything approaching a normal life until we fix the underlying problem causing the heart failure."

"Which is?" Nate prodded.

Susan shook her head. "We don't actually know. Heart failure occurs when the heart can no longer meet the metabolic demands of the body at normal venous pressure. A lot of things can cause it." A huge list ran through Susan's head. "Most of those have to do with the heart itself or the large vessels that pump blood to and from it. But the cardiologists have examined her heart and vessels with every scanner known to modern medicine. The heart's electrical systems and tissues, its valves and chambers are normal. The large vessels have no abnormalities. There's no big, honking tumor sitting in or near it."

"And the other causes?"

Susan's head did not stop moving. "Simple blood tests. She isn't anemic. Her endocrine system and kidneys function normally. Her blood pressure is fine."

"So the reason for her heart failure is?"

Susan still shook her head.

"You know, Dr. Susan Calvin. Don't you?"

Susan's head finally stopped moving. She bit her lower lip. "I believe I do."

"And?"

Everyone else, including the cardiologists and her own attending, had dismissed her idea; but nothing else made sense. She wondered what Nate would think, especially in light of his reading those books. "The initial abnormality in her brain is called an arteriovenous fistula. In Starling's case, it was congenital, meaning she had it at birth."

Nate nodded his understanding.

"Normally, blood with oxygen in it flows from arteries to capillaries. The capillaries give the oxygen to all the tissues of our bodies, and the now-deoxygenated blood flows into the veins and goes back to the heart, then to the lungs, for more oxygen. With an A-V fistula, the blood flows right from an artery into a vein, bypassing the capillaries."

Nate was clearly still following.

"Vein walls aren't meant for the high-pressure flow of arteries, so the vein wall stretches. Blood pools in the stretched area, making it bigger. If it's big enough, blood pressure falls. The heart has to pump harder to make up for it, and congestive heart failure can develop."

"So," Nate said carefully, "your concern is that the original A-V fistula wasn't fixed properly."

Susan cringed. Nate had summarized it perfectly. "And I, Psychiatry R-1 that I am, don't see how I'm going to convince the greatest neurosurgeon in the world he made an enormous mistake."

"Surgeons don't have high opinions of the nonsurgical specialties." It seemed more statement than question.

Susan could not forget her conversation with Kendall about that exact subject. "In general, that's true. The more specialized the surgeon, the less he respects the medical specialties. Unfortunately, many of them consider psychiatry the lowest form of medicine. And, of course, R-1s are the lowest form of doctor."

"Yet you are a doctor."

"Yes."

"And obviously a fine diagnostician."

Susan flushed. She had no idea how Nate would know such a thing. "I'm all right, but mostly unproven." She returned to her original question. "So here's my thing. If you were in my shoes, what would you do?"

Nate sucked air through his nose and let it slowly out his mouth. "In your position, I would have no choice but to act in Starling's best interests."

"Of course." It was the job of physicians always to act

in the best interest of any patient, regardless of age, situation, symptoms, or desires. "And it's clearly in Starling's best interests to find and treat the cause of her heart failure. The question is . . . how?"

Nate drummed his fingers on the end of the chair arm. "It seems to me you're in a better position to answer that. Are you sure the cause is a botched surgery?"

Susan doubted anything in medicine was a certainty. "Reasonably sure. If it's something else, it's an amazing coincidence; but amazing coincidences do occur."

"Can you prove it?"

Susan bit her lower lip in frustration. "I could, but not without doing tests I have no authority to order, ones that require a neurosurgeon's approval. It would also take a skilled neurosurgeon to reopen the skull and take another look."

"So . . . you need a neurosurgeon."

"Yes." Susan realized bringing in another neurosurgeon would cause more problems than facing the old one. She doubted any other neurosurgeon at Manhattan Hasbro would dare to second-guess Dr. Mandar's proficiency and decisions, and they would want to know his opinion first. "Someone has to talk to Dr. Mandar about taking another look inside Starling."

"Yes."

"Who?"

"Who indeed?" Though Nate spoke without emotion or accusation, Susan knew the answer. The cardiologists would only throw it back into her lap, and her attending refused to believe the great Sudhish Mandar could have made a mistake.

"Me," Susan said meekly.

Nate only bobbed his head, more in thought than answer.

Susan glanced up at the clock. It read twelve thirty; she needed to get back to her patients. Sweeping the

sandwich container into the bag with the rest of her un-
eaten lunch, she headed back toward the unit. "Wish me
luck."

"Luck," Nate said, rising from his chair and heading
back to his own work.

The unit phone felt like a lead weight in Susan Calvin's
hands as she punched in the Vox number for Dr. Sudhish Mandar and watched it enter the callback number.
She considered using her own Vox but imagined she had
a better chance of getting an answer if the neurosurgeon
knew for certain the call originated from a number inside the hospital.

To Susan's surprise, the callback came almost immediately. She picked up the receiver, her palms suddenly
slippery. She felt as if someone had dried her mouth with
a sponge and then shoved it, in a lump, down her throat.
"Hello?"

A male voice in a thick, subcontinental Indian accent
came through the receiver. "This is Dr. Mandar."

Dr. Mandar himself. Susan had expected a resident
or fellow, even a secretary or nurse to return the call for
him. "This is Dr. Susan Calvin. I'm an R-1 on inpatient
peds psychiatry. I have a patient—"

Anger tinged the voice. "You paged me during surgery!"

"What?" The word was startled from her.

"How dare you disturb the greatest neurosurgeon in
the world in the middle of a procedure. I'll have you
know—"

Susan quailed, and her thoughts muddled. On her M-4
surgery rotations, the attendings and residents had always
handed over their Vox to a nurse or unit clerk while they
scrubbed. In her experience, surgeons never answered
their own calls while performing an operation.

Dr. Mandar's voice got louder, shriller, and ever more enraged. "The tiniest interruption can mean the difference between life and death. Who do you think you are that you can bother me while I'm completing—"

Susan stopped listening. She could not bear the thought of abandoning Starling, not when she had screwed up her courage to face the self-proclaimed greatest neurosurgeon in the world. She waited only until Mandar took a breath to say in a voice edged with deadly calm, "You can't shout at me like this. I had no idea you would answer your phone in the middle of an operation. When you're ready to have a civil conversation, call me back." Decisively, she hung up the receiver.

Only then, tears stung Susan's eyes. She found herself trembling in every part, and that only fueled her anger. She doubted anyone had ever spoken to Sudhish Mandar like that, and she wondered how long it would take for the consequences to reach her, how long before she lost her residency at Manhattan Hasbro.

Worried someone might see her in such a state, Susan wiped the tears from her eyes and sought a distraction. She saw the younger children lining up to use the outside playground, including a heavyset biracial girl who could only be Sharicka Anson. The four-year-old wore a pink dress with embroidered flowers, her hair swept back into a curly ponytail. Through the one-way glass, Susan watched Sharicka reach forward and pinch the boy in front of her.

The boy whirled, snarling, "Cut it out!"

Eyes locked on the television, Sharicka appeared innocently startled by his sudden movement, and the boy slapped the larger girl behind her instead. The other girl screamed bloody murder.

The nurse dashed over, pulling the two children on either side of Sharicka out of line and scolding them. Susan could not hear her words, but her face looked angry. The two youngsters waved their arms and shouted in reply, loudly enough for Susan to catch most of the conversation.

"She pinched me. Really hard."

"I did not! He hit me for no reason!"

"She did, too."

"It really hurt," the girl said, sobbing.

Through it all, Sharicka remained focused on the television, appearing an oblivious spectator to the entire process. Susan suspected chaos broke out a lot in Sharicka's vicinity; yet, somehow, she never became directly involved in the matter. Susan made a mental note to watch the girl closely, starting immediately.

Susan grabbed up her palm-pross and moved to the head of the line. The July sun beamed down upon the rainbow-colored playground, with its plastic slides, ladders, and runways. The sandbox contained the airy, antibacterial sand that had replaced the grit and cat turds that had characterized Susan's own sandbox experiences growing up. A rideable ditch digger filled most of one corner, with pedals and levers for the children to dig in the sand.

A nurse unlocked the door. Susan went through first. The children followed, some pausing to blink in the direct sunlight and cautiously study their play area of choice. Others charged through the opening, heading pell-mell for the welcoming plastic structure, with its turrets, play bars, and tunnels.

Sharicka funneled through with the rest. Though she had surely played there many times, she scanned the equipment with a seasoned eye. Susan could almost hear the gears spinning in her little head as she marched to the tubes and ladders, climbed a slide, and rode down the plastic surface, bumping loudly against the sides. She seemed almost wooden in her play. She did not raise her arms to touch the wind, did not make "whee" noises, made no attempt to engage her caretakers or peers.

Susan feigned a complete lack of interest in the children, trying to look as if she were focused exclusively on her palm-pross and had only come outside to enjoy the beauty of the day. Sharicka went down the slide a second time, kicking and elbowing the sides but making no verbalizations. When she reached the bottom, she dug the toe of her shoe into a well-worn indentation in the recycled rubber. Soon, she became engrossed in it, scuffing at it with both feet while the boy at the top of the slide waited for her to move out of his way.

It soon became apparent Sharicka had no intention of clearing the path. Susan looked for the nurse and found her pushing a tall, silent girl in a swing, oblivious to the quiet drama unfolding at the slide. Susan did not interfere. She wanted to see what happened next.

"Sharicka, move," the boy called down to her.

Sharicka continued exploring the worn spot without looking up, though she had certainly heard him.

The boy's patience waned. "Sharicka, I'm coming down." With that, he started down the slide.

Sharicka did not budge. Susan saw her roll an eye in the boy's direction, but she did not step out of his way.

As he reached the bottom, the boy twisted sideways, hitting Sharicka in the side with his hip. Her knee came up as they fell, delivering a blow to his groin. As they tumbled over each other, he collapsed awkwardly to the ground, while she rolled a bit, then exaggerated it into a long, skidding movement that made it look as if she had sustained a heavy hit. She shrieked.

The nurse came running. "What happened?"

The surrounding kids started talking at once, describing the events of the last few moments from various angles. As Susan suspected, certain details became clear to the nurse. Sharicka had gone down the slide first. The boy had gone next and smashed into Sharicka. Therefore, it must be the boy's fault.

Neither Sharicka nor her victim added much to the discussion. She only smiled, seeming to revel in the lecture the boy got about slide safety and in the tender way he walked, and let the description of the events play out in her favor. She headed to the other end of the play structure and crawled into a tunnel.

For several minutes, play continued without a problem. Then a smiling wisp of a girl entered Sharicka's tunnel. Susan heard a thump. In an instant, the girl came out the other side, seemingly propelled and crying wildly. She had a red mark beneath her right eye that would surely bruise.

Again, the nurse came running over. "What happened?"

The weeping girl attempted to explain, but Susan could not understand a word of what she said. Sharicka poked her head out of the tunnel. "She tripped climbing over me."

"Whoops." The nurse swung the sobbing girl into her arms and carried her to the opposite side of the structure. "We can't have that." She turned her focus to consoling the girl, who buried her face in the nurse's chest.

Worried Sharicka would notice her watching, Susan turned her attention fully on her palm-pross for several moments, actually managing to type some documentation before she dared to look for the girl again. This time, she found Sharicka studying the sandbox. A boy sat alone in the middle, meticulously sculpting something Susan could not yet identify.

Relieved of her burden, the nurse took a seat on a bench on the opposite side of the playground. She rubbed her brow, looking harried and tired. The moment the nurse's bottom touched the seat, Sharicka ran over and hurled herself into the nurse's lap. Susan could not hear what she said, but the nurse laughed and hugged her tightly. They sat there for several minutes, talking, laughing, and embracing occasionally. Had Susan happened upon the same scene in a park outside of a psychiatric facility, she would have assumed them a loving mother and daughter team.

More telling for Susan, during the time Sharicka sat safely on the nurse's lap, the remainder of the children played without interruption. No one cried or shouted in pain. Nothing required refereeing. Not that anyone could mistake these for normal, happy children. They tended to play alone rather than in groups. Like toddlers, each engaged in his or her own activity, often despite the potential playmates less than a foot away doing much the same thing. Some chose one repetitive activity, such as the boy who did nothing but ride one slide from the moment he arrived until playtime ended. But all strife disappeared with Sharicka.

The quiet lulled even Susan, who managed to get some actual work done while Sharicka and the nurse interacted. The sounds of swings creaking, of children chasing one another through plastic tunnels, was so peaceful after the crying and screaming that had preceded it. The warm sun and natural light seemed a welcome change from stuffy corridors and low-energy bulbs.

Then, an anguished cry rent the air. Susan's gaze went instinctively to the nurse's lap rather than to the sound. Sharicka was no longer there. Susan then looked toward the sobbing child, the same girl Sharicka had kicked in the tunnel. The nurse confronted the child and a boy nearby. Sharicka appeared to have had no hand in the conflict; yet Susan suspected otherwise. It stirred memories of her M-4 psychiatry rotation. A resident she considered a fabulous teacher had once told her, when trying to find the conduct-disordered child in a family, not to ask which one is involved in the most conflicts but instead to ask which child is always on the scene when conflicts occur. A child with a problem on the conduct spectrum, whether simple ADHD or full-blown Conduct Disorder, can cause chaos merely by entering a room.

While the nurse dealt with the current problem, Susan watched as Sharicka took a seat on the excavator.

The boy in the middle of the sandbox had, by now, constructed a lavish series of roads, with hills and valleys, populating them with stone "cars" that ran around dry sand hills while he made motor noises. Susan watched, fascinated, as Sharicka's digging drew closer and closer to the boy's art. Soon enough, a new conflict would occur, with the boy screeching about his ruined work and Sharicka proclaiming it all a bizarre accident.

The glass door opened, and a unit clerk poked his head through it. "Dr. Calvin!"

Susan looked in his direction.

"There's a call for you."

That surprised Susan. Though accustomed to pages, she rarely received direct calls on the unit. If Stony, Clayton, or one of the nurses needed her, they used the Vox system. Only outsiders or consultants used the phone. *Consultants.* Abruptly, Susan remembered her interaction with Dr. Mandar, and her heart started pounding. *Oh, God. I'm fired.* She raced to the door.

The nurse stepped aside to let her through, then handed her the cordless.

Susan tried to sound professional. "This is Dr. Susan Calvin."

She recognized Mandar's voice at once. "Dr. Calvin, this is Dr. Mandar."

Susan's heart felt as if it were trying to slug its way out of her chest. When he did not continue, she took a deep breath and began. "I'm wondering if you remember a patient named Starling Woodruff. She's a thirteen-year-old white female on whom you performed an A-V fistula repair about two years ago."

Mandar made a wordless noise that spoke volumes. Apparently, he did not recall Starling's particulars, but he wanted Susan to continue.

"She's been on the psych unit ever since because of odd behavior they attributed to brain damage from the surgery."

Susan could almost feel Mandar's ire rising. "That's wrong. I have never damaged a brain with a fistula repair."

Susan remained composed. Starling's life depended on it. "I agree, Dr. Mandar. That was why I looked for other causes and discovered congestive heart failure."

There was silence from the other end. Dr. Sudhish Mandar was listening, raptly, to a psychiatry R-1.

"Which is not responding well to medical management. The source of the failure is clearly still present, but Cardiology can't find it. The only possible source, Dr. Mandar, is . . ."

"The original fistula," he filled in for her. "I'll be down this afternoon." In an instant, the line went dead.

The moment it did, all the excitement of the moment hit Susan at once. She sank down on the nearest couch, not even noticing she was still in the patient area and that the boy on the next cushion was Diesel Moore. She felt dizzy, faint, and her hand trembled as she clutched the phone in white-knuckled fingers.

Diesel stuck his moon face into hers. "Dr. Calvin? Are you all right?"

"I'm fine," she assured him, though her voice sounded far away.

Kendall seized Susan's arm and pulled her to her feet. Looping an arm around her back, he guided her toward the office. "Did I hear you say 'Dr. Mandar'?"

Susan went with him without bothering to wonder where. He could have guided her to a slaughterhouse, and she would not have noticed. "Yes. Dr. Mandar. He's coming down to see Starling."

Kendall's hand tensed on her arm. He did not speak again until he had taken her into the charting area and sat her down on a chair in front of one of the larger computer screens. "You talked Dr. Sudhish Mandar into coming down to see a patient?"

In an instant, all the residents in the staffing area,

Stony, Kendall, Monk, and Nevaeh, were at Susan's side, all talking at once.

On demand, Susan told them the story of her conversations with the hospital's greatest neurosurgeon. Monk clamped a hand to his mouth. Stony laughed. Nevaeh merely stared at her through widened eyes. Kendall nodded knowingly and spoke first. "I'd heard the way to gain surgeons' respect is to stand up to them. I've just never had the gall."

Stony slapped Susan on the back. "Apparently, Susan has enough gall for all of us."

"A whole bladder full," Kendall agreed, and the others laughed. "I once watched her decapitate a neurosurgery resident. Should have figured she could handle the most important one in the hospital."

Susan accepted the gibes good-naturedly, though she felt more nauseated than triumphant. She clutched her left upper abdomen. "At the moment, I think my gall-bladder has boulders."

Chapter 8

Susan spent the next hour spying on Sharicka Anson. So far, Susan had not spoken directly to the girl, nor had she introduced herself as the new resident. Once she did so, she would go on Sharicka's radar and lose the opportunity to silently observe. Susan appreciated it when Sharicka roamed the halls or settled into the main room with the other children, as it gave Susan the chance to watch more closely from behind the one-way glass of the staffing area.

Engrossed in watching Sharicka surreptitiously smear and rip posters and artwork on the walls in strategic places, Susan did not hear a newcomer enter the staffing area and walk up behind her.

"Well, if it isn't Dr. Susan Calvin, AOA."

Susan whirled to face Remington Hawthorn. He wore surgical greens and disposable covers on his shoes. He had the same emerald eyes she remembered, the chiseled cheekbones, his dark blond curls wild from the operating room hat. "Well, well, well. Dr. Remington Hawthorn, Neurosurgery." She played it cool. "About time you got here."

Remington glanced at his watch. "Less than two hours. That's pretty good."

"Two *years*," Susan corrected. "That girl has languished here because no one had the courage to face Sudhish Mandar."

"Except you," Remington pointed out. "You have more balls than an eight-peckered billy goat."

Susan bridled at the half-assed compliment. "And you have the manners of that billy goat." She passed him her palm-pross, with Starling's chart at the fore.

Remington set the palm-pross on the desktop, without looking at it. "I'm sorry, Susan. You're right. I made a huge mistake downstairs; you're as good a doctor as any of my colleagues."

"Damn right." Susan did not know or care if she spoke the truth. "Do they teach you condescension in your rotations, or are cads just drawn to surgical subspecialties?"

Remington gave the rhetorical question serious consideration before whispering conspiratorially, "Honestly, I think it's a bit of both."

Susan could not help smiling. Her anger dissipated.

"Give me a chance to prove I'm not as big a jerk as I seem."

"Fine." Susan reached for the palm-pross again, but Remington caught her hand. He did it with such ease and accuracy, he had clearly played sports in college.

"Over dinner. Tonight."

Startled, Susan stared. The media would have people believe men no longer competed with their women, that they did not discriminate against competence, intelligence, or strength. To judge by her own sparse dating experience, the media had it wrong. Susan was not beautiful in a flashy manner. She had thin, pale lips, and her blue-gray eyes could turn downright steely. She was too thin, like her father, with little in the way of curves. Nevertheless, she had balanced features, youth, and a reasonable amount of grace. At the residents' conference, she had felt an immediate attraction to Remington, one that his arrogance had destroyed. Now he seemed sincerely ready to make amends, and she saw no reason not to give him a second chance. "All right. When and where?"

Remington finally picked up the palm-press. "We can leave from here. I'll drop by when I'm finished."

Susan suspected she would complete her work before he did, if only because the hours of the operating room ruled his schedule. "What time do you usually get done?"

"Six thirtyish?" It came out more like a question than a statement, as if he could change the time if it did not work for Susan.

Susan knew she had no real power over Dr. Sudhish Mandar. Remington would finish when his attending gave him leave. "Can you meet me in the charting room?" She described the location of the first-floor hide-away. "It's a nice, quiet place to get some research done."

"Works for me." Remington saluted, then settled into the chair in front of the palm-press, acquainting himself with Starling Woodruff's history.

A thrill of excitement passed through Susan, but she played it cool. Snatching up an unused palm-press, she headed for the other side of the staffing area to docu-ment her observations on Sharicka Anson. If Reming-ton Hawthorn had any questions about Starling, she felt certain he would find her.

The charting room door opened at 6:43 p.m. Susan Calvin looked up from her conversation with Nate to a tall young man framed in the doorway. He wore pleated khakis with a green and white striped dress polo. A shower had softened and tamed his sandy hair so it hung down in loose ringlets. Despite his lean frame, she could not help noticing the masculine bulges of his arm muscles and chest. It took her a moment to recognize Remington.

Susan and Nate rose simultaneously to face the neurosurgery resident. With Nate beside him as comparison, Remington no longer seemed so tall. The robot had four or five inches on him. "Nate, this is Remington."

Remington stepped forward to shake Nate's hand. "Just call me Remy." He turned his gaze to Susan. "That goes for you, too, of course." His green eyes sparkled. They defined handsome all by themselves, even without the boyish curls and the perfect oval of his face.

Nate took Remington's hand. "Pleased to meet you."

"And you," Remington returned, but his gaze remained on Susan. He studied her with the same intensity she did him. "Are you ready to go?"

"I am." Susan had also showered in the psychiatry on-call room. Unlike surgeons, she did not routinely wear scrubs, so she had no change of clothing. Her work attire would have to do. "Where are we going?"

"Your favorite restaurant."

That surprised Susan. She wondered how he had found out such details about her so quickly. She had shared that sort of inane conversation with her fellow residents, but she doubted Remington had found the time to quiz them about her interests. "My favorite? How do you know which restaurant that is?"

Remington smiled and winked at Nate. "Actually, I was kind of hoping *you'd* know."

Nate chuckled.

Susan rolled her eyes but could not help grinning. "There's a little Chinese place a few blocks away." She had eaten there many times with her college friends and had gone several times on visits home from medical school.

Remington shrugged. "That's your favorite?"

"Well, yes. Short of—" Susan caught herself.

Remington persisted, "Short of what?"

"Nothing," Susan said. "It's my favorite."

Remington refused to let it go. "No, seriously. What's your real favorite?"

Susan sighed, not wishing to lie or create a problem where none existed. "A place that's far away and very expensive."

Nate studied Remington, brows rising slowly toward his hairline.

"Oh." Remington did not lose his smile. "Chinese it is."

"Chinese is perfect."

To Susan's surprise, he took her arm as they walked from the room. He called over his shoulder, "Nice meeting you, Nate."

"See you tomorrow," Susan called back, immediately wishing she had not. For now, Remington had no way of knowing what type of relationship she had with Nate. She did not want him worrying about competition.

Susan's words did not seem to bother Remington, however. He had a smooth self-assurance about him, the same that had put her off at the auditorium. She wondered whether she would come to adore it as a part of him or despise it absolutely. Only time would tell.

The decision to walk to the restaurant was so mutual, Susan could not decide who had initiated the suggestion. They just sort of did it, striding through the cooler evening air while electric trolleys whizzed past them. Other people had also chosen to walk, but Susan found her attention riveted on Remington. Using old-fashioned manners she would have believed dead, he walked on the street side of her, clasping her hand in strong fingers without a hint of sweat.

Susan enjoyed being with him in silence until they had nearly reached the restaurant. Then, suddenly, she found herself asking, "So, is Remington an old family name?"

"Nope, I'm the first." Remington gave her hand a gentle squeeze. "My dad is a gun collector. My twin brothers are Colt and Ruger. The family joke is that, when they named my sister, he was trying to decide between Uzi and AR-15."

Susan cringed. "Yuck. So, what's your sister's name?"

"Uzi."

Susan's cheeks turned scarlet. *Stupid*. She whipped her free hand to her mouth. "Oh, I'm sorry. I shouldn't have said that."

Remington shook his head, chuckling. "I'm kidding, Susan. My sister's name is Emily."

"Emily? Really?"

"Mom got to name any girls."

Susan relaxed. "Lucky Emily." Suddenly realizing the oblique insult, she added quickly, "Though I like Remington. It sounds . . ." She considered the right word.

Remington filled it in for her. "Arrogant? Jerky?"

Susan had caught on to his sense of humor. "I was going to say 'powerful.' But it is, obviously, the perfect name for a surgeon."

"I hear 'pretentious' more often than 'powerful.' That's why I've always gone by Remy. Colt's not so bad—kind of trendy. But I've always felt bad for Ruger."

Spotting the restaurant, Susan pointed. "There it is." They headed toward the Golden Chopstick.

"So, how many siblings do you have, Susan?"

"None." Growing up, Susan had appreciated being an only child, not having to share her father's attention with anyone. Aside from discussions of his work, he tended to involve her in everything, to speak to her like an adult. "My mother died when I was very young, and my father never remarried."

"Marriage isn't an ultimate prerequisite for children." Remington held open the door. The scent of food and sauces wafted through the opening, tantalizing. Susan realized just how hungry she was. They stepped inside.

"True," Susan admitted, "but I can't recall my father even dating after Mom died. He loved her with an all-consuming passion. He devoted himself wholly to his work and to me." As she spoke the words, Susan realized how odd they probably sounded to Remington. She had never thought much about her father's celibacy. As a child, it had seemed absolutely natural to remain wholly devoted to the memory of Amanda Calvin. "To him, she was the perfect woman. In his mind, no other woman could begin to measure up."

Remington nodded, lips pursed. "She must have been quite a woman."

Susan barely remembered her mother but gave the only answer she could. "She was."

The host waved the pair to an empty table. Susan took the seat facing the window, and Remington sat across from her. The table already had two plates and sets of chopsticks, as well as a pair of built-in menu screens. The host left them to seat the next group of guests.

Remington planted his elbows on his menu screen to lean toward Susan. "If you don't mind my asking, what happened to your mother?"

It was a sore spot, but the question and the questioner were innocent. "I don't exactly know, beyond that it was a car accident. Dad would rather have all his teeth pulled out without anesthetic than talk about it." Susan glanced at her menu screen.

Remington moved his arms to read his own menu. "And none of your relatives would tell you about it, either?"

For most of her life, Susan had simply assumed most families did not intermingle with distant relatives. "Neither of my parents had sisters or brothers. I only have one living grandparent, my father's mother." She flipped her hand over. "Susan. My namesake. She never raised the subject, and it was clearly so painful to my father that I would have felt disloyal bringing it up."

"Hmm." Remington studied the menu. "What do you suggest?"

For an instant, Susan thought he meant about her mother's death. Truthfully, she bore some of the blame for not knowing the details of the accident. She probably could have cornered Nana or pressed John Calvin until he told her. But the pain and discomfort the topic clearly inflicted on her father upset her, and she preferred not discussing it with anyone, including Remington Hawthorn. "Everything's good here."

Remington glanced around the packed restaurant. "That's obvious."

"The house lo mein's my favorite," Susan continued. "It has four meats, including shrimp."

"All right. House lo mein and . . ." Remington studied the menu again. "How about chicken broccoli?"

"Delicious." Susan liked the combination. "They make an excellent wonton soup, chock-full of Chinese vegetables and even some shrimp."

"Let me guess." Remington pressed his fingers to his temples in the manner of a psychic. "You like . . . shrimp."

"Very much," Susan admitted. "You're not allergic, are you?"

"Yes," Remington said. "Deathly. When I said we'd order the house lo mein, I was just hoping to test your ability to handle anaphylactic shock."

"Uh-oh," Susan said with mock seriousness.

"What?"

"When I okaycd the chicken broccoli, I was testing *your* ability to handle anaphylactic shock."

Remington laughed. "I'm a surgeon, remember? I'd skip the epinephrine or the wimpy antihistamines and steroids and go straight for the trachcostomy."

As their dinnerware consisted only of chopsticks, Susan hefted one. "What would you do? Poke me till I got a splinter? Tough to do a trach without at least a butter knife."

Remington reached into his pocket and dropped a handful of odds and ends to the tabletop, including a packaged scalpel blade, a tiny plastic suction tube, two nickels, and a cell-sized defibrillator. "I always travel prepared."

Susan shook her head, then rolled her eyes.

"When you work with attending surgeons, you have to be. If you don't have what they want the moment they want it, you have to weather disdain or, worse, a tantrum." Remington watched Susan closely. He seemed to be studying her features, and a slight smile crossed his face. He clearly liked what he saw. "But you must know that. You seem to have an incredible handle on how to get the most superior surgeons to do your bidding."

Before Remington could say another word, the server approached. "What can I get for you?"

Remington swept his gear back into his pockets. "We'd like two bowls of wonton soup to start. Dinner for two, with house lo mein and chicken broccoli." He looked at Susan to confirm she still wanted what they had discussed.

Susan nodded.

The server tapped the order into a cousin of the palm-pross. Their menu screens changed abruptly. "Anything to drink?"

Remington went silent and let Susan answer for herself. "Tap water, please."

"I'll have water, too, please. And a pot of green tea to share."

"All right." The server typed their drink order into his palm-pad, and their menu screens added another box.

Susan did not bother to look at her screen. From long experience, she knew it now contained a list of ingredients and calorie counts for the foods they had ordered. She had no allergies, and she wasn't worried about superfluous calories. Remington also did not bother to look. Susan suspected he never thought about such things, nor did he seem to need to.

Picking up where he'd left off, Remington said, "I

meant that, about getting surgeons to do your bidding. No one in the history of the universe has gotten the self-proclaimed 'greatest neurosurgeon' to apologize or admit a mistake. Starling was our last case of the day. We had to keep the OR open overtime."

Susan had no idea. When she had left the unit, Neurosurgery had not yet made a decision about Starling. Now, Remington had her absolute attention. "What did you find?"

"You tell me."

Susan knew. "An incompletely repaired A-V fistula."

Remington laughed. "You were right, and that only ratcheted up your celebrity among the neurosurgery crowd."

"I have . . . celebrity?"

The server arrived with the soup, placing a bowl and squared-off hard plastic spoon in front of each of them.

"Thank you," Susan said.

The wonton soup was exactly as Susan remembered it: clear, lightly salted broth with meat dumplings and vegetables, shreds of pork and two large shrimp. Remington picked up his spoon. "A couple of days to recover, and Starling's on her way home." He filled his spoon and sipped the hot soup carefully.

"Home?" Susan could scarcely believe it. "After nearly two years on the inpatient unit?" She took a taste of her own soup, reveling in the savory mix of flavors. "Just like that?"

Remington took some more soup. "Just like that. We're not a long-term unit, Susan. Open 'em up, fix 'em, send 'em home."

"Yeah." Susan could not help thinking Starling had lost nearly two years of her young life for nothing. Had someone only noticed the subtle signs of heart failure earlier, Starling could have spent the last year in school. She did not blame Dr. Sudhish Mandar. She suspected he had done nothing wrong, and Remington had simplified the problem. Likely, the A-V fistula had widened farther than it originally appeared, and the venous pooling problem occurred a short distance from the initial spot. "You know, twenty-two different residents and probably ten or eleven attending physicians missed the problem." It seemed the very definition of malpractice; yet no one appeared worried about that eventuality.

Remington kept eating, swallowing before he spoke. "It happens, Susan. More often than we want to believe. We think we know what's going on; we put the patient in the appropriate place; then we find out it's something entirely different. Psychiatrists aren't wired to look for circulatory defects, just as surgeons don't worry whether a patient loves or hates his mother before putting him under the knife."

Susan wondered if Remington had just subtly insulted her profession, then decided to let it go. "But twenty-two months of unnecessary hospitalization? Remy, to a child, that's a lifetime."

Remington put down his spoon to lean across the table toward Susan. "If you don't think to look for something, you generally don't find it. Everyone believed the psychiatric issues were primary until you heard that gallop rhythm. Whether it was there all those months or only appeared when you did, we'll never know. According to the chart, no one else heard it until you pointed it out. It's very subtle. Susan, if I hadn't known to listen for it, I probably wouldn't have heard it, either."

"The cardiologists heard it."

"It's their job to hear it. And they also had your notes to go by." Remington sat back but still did not touch his food again. "Medicine has come a long way in the last hundred years, but it's still an imperfect science that relies on human judgment." He smiled. "I think the first sci-fi medical scanners came along in the 1950s. Here we are, eighty-five years later, and we still can't take a hand-held device, run it around someone, and have it diagnose everything that ails him."

Susan sipped her soup thoughtfully while Remington talked, then said, "We do have devices that can read some things through the skin."

"Sure we do. Pulse oximeters are some fifty years old, and skin blood glucose monitors came along only a few decades later. Now, we can read a lot of things through skin using lights, magnets, vibrations, and lasers, but it's still only data, the levels of various chemicals and gases running through the blood. For diagnoses, we rely on human intuition, experience, knowledge, and intelligence. And, in my opinion, we always will. It takes thought to figure out things as amazingly complex as the human body, all the things that can possibly go wrong with it. No machine could ever do that."

Until a few days ago, Susan would have agreed wholeheartedly.

When she did not, Remington pressed. "Don't you agree?"

"Well," Susan finally said, "I don't think we'll ever have medical tricorders, lifeless devices that can make diagnoses about body parts they can't see or touch." Susan absentmindedly took more soup, chewed, and swallowed.

Remington prodded. "But . . ."

Susan did not disappoint him. "But . . . thinking robots could retain more information than any human. They could digest every medical textbook, every journal, and use that vast store of knowledge to examine patients and come up with appropriate diagnoses. They could use hearing and vision far superior to our own, memory storage areas we could only dream of, and unthinkable speed to do the jobs we take for granted every day."

Remington returned to his soup. "I don't see thinking robots happening any time soon. Maybe not ever."

Susan delivered the coup de grâce. "They already exist."

"What?"

"My father works with them. I'm telling you, they exist. And, tomorrow, I'll prove it."

Remington looked skeptical, but he did not challenge her. "How about tonight?"

Now it was Susan's turn to sputter out, "What?"

"If such a thing exists, I want to see it as soon as possible." Remington's green eyes sparkled. Clearly, the rush stemmed from interest rather than mistrust. "How far do we have to go?"

"Just to the hospital." Susan had no intention of spoiling the surprise by announcing that Remington had already met a thinking robot. She wanted him to get to know Nate as human before divulging the secret. She only hoped she could get Nate to play along. "I suppose tonight's fine. Just because I don't have call again doesn't mean I can't stay at the hospital all night, does it?"

Remington laughed. "I get it. How about tomorrow morning? Rounds start at eight o'clock, but I can meet you anytime before that."

Susan's rounds did not begin until nine a.m. Most of the psychiatry residents came in at eight o'clock to review patients ahead of time. She wondered how the neurosurgery residents managed to get in some work time before rounds and guessed they probably rounded first and saw patients afterward. "Let's make it seven o'clock. We'll meet the same place we did tonight."

"All right." Finished with his soup, Remington sat back.

Susan worked to catch up, concentrating on the food rather than on conversation.

Remington allowed her to finish before bringing up another subject. "I really would like to sincerely apologize for the way I treated you when we first met."

Susan pushed aside the soup bowl and gently dabbed her face with her napkin before returning it to her lap.

"You already apologized for that. I was under the assumption this dinner made up for it."

"Does it?" The tone of Remington's voice, the expression on his face, made it clear the answer mattered.

Susan did not dither. "Yes, of course. I wouldn't have agreed if it didn't. Now, should I apologize to you for, as Kendall Stevens put it, verbally castrating you in response?"

A slight red tinge touched the center of Remington's cheeks, but he smiled. "Please don't apologize for that. I liked it."

The server took the empty soup bowls and spoons, while Susan gave Remington an incredulous look. "You . . . like . . . being castrated?"

"*Verbally* castrated," Remington clarified. "I like that you stood up to me. Not many women would do that, especially not with such speed and accuracy. You'd have made a damn fine surgeon."

Susan's voice gained the flat tone of rising anger. "You're coming close to insulting me again."

"Sorry. I didn't mean that in a 'surgeons are better than internists' way. I meant it in a 'surgeons are dickheads' way."

"So . . . I'm a dickhead."

The neurosurgery resident buried his face in his palms and tried again. "I'm not saying you *are* a dickhead. Just that you'd make a good one. I'm trying to say you have . . ."

"Balls?" Susan inserted.

"I certainly hope not." Remington mocked being scandalized, his eyes as round as coins. He seemed to have conveniently forgotten that, on the PIPU, he had suggested she might have sixteen of those anatomical appendages. "How about chutzpah?"

Susan accepted that as inoffensive. "Chutzpah it is. I even like saying chutzpah." She emphasized the guttural "ch" as she repeated the word. "Chhhhhutzpah."

"Chutzpah is the only thing that impresses surgeons, and then only if it's backed up by competence. And that's what I like about you. You have both in spades."

It amazed Susan how quickly Remington had turned what started out as an insult into the ultimate compliment. "Are we back to the celebrity of getting the greatest neurosurgeon in the world to return my call? Because it wasn't that big a deal. All I did was demand he treat me with a little bit of respect."

"And therein lies the magic." Remington raised his hands as if preaching. "Most surgeons have this idea the world exists to serve them and that anyone beneath them should behave in a servile manner. And most do. So, when someone dares to stand up to them, they take notice. If it's backed up by ability, they respect. If it's all air, they attack. One false move, and you turn from equal to prey in an instant."

At that moment, the food arrived. The server placed their selections on the table, along with rice, glasses of water, teacups, and a pot of steaming tea.

"Most surgeons," Remington said, "are simple to understand." He ladled rice onto his plate, followed by dollops of chicken broccoli and house lo mein.

Susan took smaller portions of the same food. "Are *you* simple to understand?"

Remington only nodded until he swallowed a bite of food. "For the most part. I have a bit more insight into what I want for my future, though."

"Oh?" Susan pressed.

"I want a woman who can and will challenge me, not a young puppy whose only attributes are bleached-blond hair, round buttocks, and enormous breasts. I want to come home from work and share my day with a wife who not only has a life of her own, but can help me when I'm missing something that could save or lose a life."

Susan smirked. "You don't like breasts?"

"I'm a man. I love breasts, but they have to be attached to an intelligent woman for me to want a relationship." Remington ate some more. "So many of my older colleagues marry for nothing but looks and willingness to obey orders; and, at fifty-five, they have no problem trading their forty-year-old spouses for two twenty-year-old mistresses."

Susan had food in her mouth and, so, did not reply. She wondered if the same thing applied to female surgeons and supposed it did. Otherwise, he would have used the word "wives" instead of "spouses."

"They don't understand why their love life has gone stale, why they lost the excitement. So they try to find it in younger and younger men or women, never realizing what they actually seek is some emotional and intellectual stimulation, not kinkier sex."

Susan cut to the chase. "Are you asking me out on another date?"

Remington chewed thoughtfully. "I suppose I am. Was that a psychiatry trick?"

"Not really. I'm just good at recognizing a description of myself. Average looks, and too smart for her own good."

Remington dropped his chopsticks. "By whose description? I find you very attractive, and I believe I told you so when we first met."

Susan recalled. When their fingers had accidentally touched, he had said, *"I'll take any excuse to hold hands with a pretty woman."* "I thought that was just a line."

"Then I'll say it again." Remington took Susan's empty left hand and clasped it briefly in his right. His gaze found hers and held it, expressing all sincerity. "I find you very attractive, Dr. Susan Calvin."

Susan did not know what to say. She could feel her face warming uncomfortably. "Thanks, Remy. I don't imagine I have to tell you you're a handsome man."

Remington reclaimed his hand. "Of course not." He smiled broadly. "I'm a surgeon. I know I'm perfect."

Susan laughed and ate, trying for ladylike grace as she did so. The chopsticks didn't help.

Remington used his like a professional, handling individual grains of rice without difficulty. Susan wondered if that came from experience or naturally fine motor skills. She wondered if the decision to enter surgery had as much to do with hand dexterity as temperament.

"So, your father collects guns."

Mouth full, Remington only nodded.

"Does he go hunting?"

Remington swallowed. "Not often. He's more of a shooting range kind of guy. He spends more time reading about guns and cleaning those he has. I think he gets a kick out of taking them apart and reassembling them."

Susan liked that answer. She had always planned to have a home free of firearms. *One date, and I'm already thinking through a marriage to this guy.* Though it seemed premature, Susan knew her thoughts were normal. Surely most women in their late twenties considered the future whenever they dated. "Do you shoot?"

"I have." Remington studied Susan, clearly trying to read her opinion on the matter. "Could you imagine the jokes? A man named Remington never firing a . . ."

"Remington?"

"Yeah. I've hunted many times."

"Oh." Susan tried not to sound disappointed. She wondered if she could ever learn to live with a man who shot innocent animals for sport.

Chopsticks hovering, Remington continued to study Susan. "You didn't ask the follow-up question."

Susan had no idea what he meant. "Follow-up?"

"Have I ever shot anything?"

Susan put the ends of her chopsticks in her mouth to savor a few clinging grains of rice. "Well, I just assumed . . ."

"Never." Remington's gaze went distant. "I love

crouching in the tree stand, looking down on the forest. After a half hour or so, the animals come back. The birds sing in a way you never seem to hear when you're just hiking. They land on the stand itself and look right through you for bugs and crumbs. The squirrels chatter and play, without hiding on the far sides of the trees. The deer browse, nibbling at the trunk, at the greenery. This one's too small, that one's a doe, the other's a buck without enough points to bother shooting. Don't want to waste my tag on just anything. When a large buck does come along, it's never in quite the right position for a clear shot, you know?"

Susan could not help grinning. "I know. You're more of a deer watcher than a deer hunter."

"Besides, the report might scare away the even larger buck that might come along next." Remington smiled crookedly. "My dad says I'm hopeless." He returned to his food, finished his plate, and added a bit more of everything.

Still on her first serving, Susan gestured at the serving dishes. "Have as much as you like. I won't be able to eat seconds."

"I'm good now." Remington dexterously worked on his plate.

When the bill card arrived, Remington grabbed it, looked, and pulled a bank card from his wallet.

"Split it?" Susan suggested.

Never taking his eyes from the card, Remington frowned at her. "Not a chance. I asked you, remember?"

"But I picked the place."

"Yes." Remington finally looked at Susan. "And thank you. You're a cheap date."

"Why pay more than you have to for food this good?"

"For sure."

Remington fed the bill into the tableside pay slot. When the right amount flashed up, he inserted his bank card. The machine clicked, a green light came on, and the card returned. "Who'd have thought they'd find a new use for those ancient computer cards?"

Susan recalled her grandmother mentioning this, also during a restaurant payment. She had talked about a time when computers needed individual programmed cards just to work each step. She had once dropped a two hundred–card program that had taken months to write. From then on, she had painstakingly penciled page numbers on all her cards.

Of course, the restaurant cards were much sleeker and smaller than the old-time ones, which her grandmother described as the size of a three-by-nine-inch mailing envelope.

Remington rose. "Now, how do I get you home?"

"Just put me on the number seven tram, and I'll get right to the complex door." Susan also stood up. The mingled odors of sauces no longer enticed now that she felt comfortably full. The décor was simple: Chinese paper lanterns dangling over each table and stylized paintings of koi on the walls. "Which one do you take home?"

"The five." Remington put an arm across Susan's back to guide her safely to the door. "But I'm not going home yet. I want to check up on my last postsurgical patient."

Susan remembered. "Starling?"

"Yup."

Susan consulted her Vox as they passed through the door onto the now-dark street. "But it's after nine."

Remington shrugged. "That's the positive side of surgeons. We're dedicated."

Susan could scarcely deny it, at least when it came to Remington. "Clearly. But doesn't that defy the humane residency laws, the ones put in place to ensure we get sleep, food, and . . . a life? To make us safer doctors."

Remington shook his head. "The humane residency laws only define the hours they can make us work. We can volunteer extra if we wish, and I don't know a surgery resident who doesn't."

Susan got it. "So, anyone who follows the letter of the laws looks like a piker and suffers for it."

Remington shrugged. "I suppose. But I'll get home in time to sleep. I already ate, and I just finished a wonderful date."

"Wonderful?" Susan could not help smiling. She found herself edging toward him.

Remington swept her into an embrace. They kissed there on the street, just outside the Golden Chopstick, the taste of house lo mein and chicken broccoli still on both their lips. A tingle traversed Susan, and she found herself pressing closer to him. She had never felt both so comfortable and so wildly excited. She wondered if it would surprise or bother him to find out she was still a virgin.

As the kiss ended, Susan whispered into Remington's face. "Do me a favor." She did not wait for him to agree. "If you have the time, go to the charting room and say good night to Nate."

Remington stepped back, and Susan cursed herself for mentioning another man at that intimate moment. She silently berated herself, *No wonder I'm still a virgin.*

"Do you think he'll still be at the hospital? This late?"

Susan said cryptically, "I can virtually guarantee it."

Chapter 9

When Susan arrived at the first-floor charting room, she found Remington Hawthorn and N8-C sitting across from each other and engaged in spirited conversation.

Already dressed in his scrubs, Remington was speaking. ". . . it's intradural, intramedullary with decreased posterior column sensation, pain localized to two fingers' breadths over the lower spine, no correlation with time of day."

Nate did not hesitate. "Family history? Maybe . . ."

"Von Hippel-Lindau," they said together, then laughed. Spotting Susan, they went silent.

"Good morning," she said cheerily.

"Good morning, Susan," they replied, still simultaneously. Then, they looked at each other and laughed again.

Susan perched on the arm of Remington's chair. "You're scaring me."

"He's amazing," Remington admitted. "Makes me wonder how many thinking robots we already have on staff. Some of the guys I work with don't show any emotion at all."

"I'm the only humanoid robot at Hasbro," Nate said.

"I cost in the range of one hundred million dollars. And I do show emotions, when it's appropriate."

"So you figured it out on your own." Susan had not expected Remington to identify Nate so quickly. Nate had told her his status almost immediately, but he had recognized her name and knew she had the family robotics background to believe him. "And you know it's true?"

"Given our prior conversation at the restaurant, finding him here after ten p.m. yesterday and before seven a.m. today was a dead giveaway."

Nate smiled. "I'd like to point out you were also here after ten p.m. yesterday and before seven a.m. today."

Susan sucked in her lips, but she knew her eyes revealed her amusement.

"Well, yes," Remington admitted. "But I can't peel off the skin of my leg and reveal circuitry wrapped around my muscles, can I?"

Susan could not resist teasing, "Can you?" Nate had not given her the same amount of proof; she had not required it.

Remington reached for Susan's hand, caught it, and gave it a squeeze. "How about I prove it after our date on Friday?"

Susan could not recall making one. "Do we have a date on Friday?"

"I guess that's up to you."

Susan clasped Remington's fingers. "Friday, it is. How's Starling?"

"Great." Remington rose, released her hand, and looked at his Vox. "They moved her from intensive recovery to the regular unit this morning. I'd stop down today if you want to see her before she leaves."

"Today?" Susan could scarcely believe it. "You mean discharge? Home? Already?"

"I told you we're quick." Remington shrugged. "No reason to keep her." He tapped the Vox. "I have to go.

If I'm late for rounds, I'll get stuck with hole-drilling duty for a week."

Susan preferred not to know what that entailed. She waved as he rushed out the door, then turned to Nate. "What do you think?"

"Of Remy?"

"Yeah."

Nate did not spend long in consideration. "I like him."

"Me, too," Susan admitted. "What were you two doing when I came in?"

"Talking neurosurgery." Nate made a vague gesture toward the books. "You know, I was programmed to perform menial jobs: transporting patients, consent signing, cleanup, surgery prep, hand-holding, bed making."

"Really?" It seemed a ridiculous waste of his brilliance.

"Then, staff started worrying I'd take their places, lawyers speculated a malfunction might drive me berserk, and fear of more protests drove me into seclusion."

Susan glanced around the large room with its shelving, bric-a-brac, and old-fashioned textbooks. Since she had come here her first night on call, she had developed an appreciation for the quiet nook with its simple table, its clashing chairs, its comfortable couches. She could think of far worse prisons. "So, you . . . live here?" It seemed altogether the wrong verb for robotic existence. "All the time?"

"Here?" Nate made hand motions to indicate the room. "I'm not a vacuum cleaner stored in a closet, Susan. I spend time in the research tower, when I'm working on a project. I can move about freely within the hospital, if I choose. I just happen to like it here. It's quiet, so no one bothers me. It's full of computers and books, adjacent to the central processing area. The only people who come here are residents hiding from work, attendings, or other residents when they find a few moments to spare. And, of course, those few, like you and Remy, who know to look for me here."

Susan had not yet figured it out. "What exactly do you do here?" Then, recalling what he had told her previously of the differing expectations of U.S. Robotics, the hospital administrators, and certain members of the staff, she amended her question. "I mean, I know some of the doctors, mostly researchers, use you as a sounding board, a fact-checker, an assistant. But what do you do all day? What is your basic job?"

"Anything that doesn't involve patients. I spend most of my time on the computer, searching for charting errors, inconsistencies, mistakes, incomplete notes. Things like that. I transport inanimate objects such as bedding, pillows, and blankets from the laundry to the storage areas."

"What a waste."

Nate shrugged. "It leaves me lots of time outside my official duties. I have access to plenty of information. I started with the books and worked my way to the legitimate online medical sites." He indicated a palm-pross left on the room's only table. "Since I only have to read or hear things once, it's easy to stay current. So, when the research staff send articles for me to proofread or ask for help on their projects, I have no trouble assisting them."

Susan was surprised. "So I'm not the only doctor who visits you?"

Nate grinned. "Just the prettiest."

To Susan's surprise, she found herself blushing. "Sweet." She looked at her own Vox, though the time did not matter. The sooner she headed for the PIPU, the more she could contribute at rounds. "I have to go, now, too. But I'll come back when I can."

Nate waved a hand dismissively. "I'll be counting the hours till your return."

Amazing, Susan thought as she left. *He's even programmed for flirting and sarcasm.*

As Susan trotted toward the PIPU, she realized "programmed" was not the right word. As her father had described it, the positronic brain contained a network of circuitry as complex as the human brain. Nate might have started with some basic programs, the Three Laws of Robotics, for example, and the English language; but he had self-developed the remainder of his personality through thought, intention, and experience.

That latter realization would have floored Susan Calvin, had she not already discussed it with her father. The genius behind the invention had a name, Dr. Lawrence Robertson, the president of U.S. Robots and Mechanical Men, Inc. He had calculated the necessary data to create a spongy globe of platinum-iridium that replaced miles of relays and photocells and had ultimately become the positronic brain. Someday, Susan hoped, she would meet this supergenius.

Susan hurried to the locked PIPU door and buzzed for entrance. A familiar nurse's voice came over the intercom system. "Good morning, Dr. Calvin."

Susan waved in the general direction of the all-but-invisible camera. "Good morning, Saranne. May I come in?"

"On my way."

The clunky, old-fashioned system of the PIPU never ceased to confound Susan. It seemed foolish to retain a lock system that required a human to physically key through two heavy doors. Apartment buildings had had direct-wired buzzer systems serving dozens of stories since at least her grandmother's time, and cheap voice, print, or laser identification systems had existed for decades. The best explanation Susan had heard was that any push-button system would become liable to access by patients; coded entries required too-frequent maintenance for staff changes that would result in loss of patient confidentiality. The strong steel doors could withstand attacks that lighter electronic systems could not, and any attempt at tampering would become instantly obvious.

At the least, Susan had to admit the system had worked for longer than two centuries. And the ponderous, gloomy simplicity of it made the whole unit appear equally old.

Susan heard the lock click. The windowless door eased toward her. She caught the edge to help the nurse open it. Slender as a willow, and fine-boned, Saranne struggled with the enormous panel, just as any of the pediatric patients would. She had short blond hair in a feathered cut, china doll features, and pert blue eyes.

"Thank you," Susan said. She looked up and noticed the usually gray hallway now held a dozen brightly colored balloons. Several of the nurses and unit staff milled around the area, beneath a banner reading CONGRATULATIONS! Already trained to the rules, Susan scooted inside and let the door slam shut behind her. Saranne relocked it, placing the key in her flowered scrub-shirt pocket.

"Congratulations?" Susan glanced around the smiling group, bewildered. "Thank you. But what have I done to deserve all this?"

Murmurs swept the group, and Saranne slapped Susan's shoulder approvingly. "Discharge orders for Diesel Moore. Starling Woodruff off the service forever and about to go home from Neurosurgery!"

Someone else called out, "All in your first four days."

They came at Susan en masse.

"Congratulations, Doc."

The fuss embarrassed Susan. She had never liked being the center of attention. Smiling, bobbing her head, cautiously working her way to the unit door, she turned to face them all. "Thank you so much. I'll try my very best to live up to your expectations." She wanted to deflate the excitement, to remind them she had gotten lucky. Both patients had had hidden medical diagnoses that, once exposed, made their treatment so much easier. But doing so might denigrate the residents and attendings who had come before her, those who had not made those same medical diagnoses. She reached for the door handle, knowing she would find it locked.

A male nurse named Jordan unlocked the unit door, while the other staff discussed the dispensation of banner and balloons. They could not allow balloons on the unit for fear some patients might pop them to torment others who had phobias, nightmares, or delusions.

Susan headed for the charting area, surprised to receive smiles and applause from the remaining staff as well. She nodded at everyone she saw, then attempted to duck into the staffing area. Before she got there, a small child latched onto her leg.

Susan looked down to see Sharicka. She was not surprised to observe that someone had bent the balloon rule; Sharicka clutched the string of a crimson balloon filled with helium, and she enwrapped Susan's leg in a deathless embrace. "Dr. Thuzan!" she sang out, with just a hint of a lisp. "Sit with me. Pleeease."

Susan could not resist the childish tones and apparent sincerity. She sat in one of the plush chairs in the television room, ignoring the movie that seemed to have most of the patients mesmerized.

Sharicka climbed into Susan's lap, snuggling against her. "You never told me you were my doctor." She popped a thumb into her mouth, speaking around it. "I was scared I didn't have a doctor no more."

In her days observing the young girl, Susan had never seen her suck her thumb before. She wondered what it meant: Was it a conscious or unconscious action, a deliberate ruse, or expression of emotion? Did a four-year-old even have the mental connections and experience to play such intricate games with an adult? "You have a doctor, Sharicka," Susan said with proper adult reassurance. "I've just gotten so busy with other patients, I haven't had time to get to know you." She did not mention her silent observations. She did not want to cue Sharicka.

"I heared ya fixed 'em." Sharicka snuggled even closer. "I wants ya ta fix me, too."

The baby talk annoyed Susan. She had overheard Sharicka enough times to know she had a more than competent vocabulary.

"Can ya fix me?" Sharicka gazed into Susan's face with adoration, her eyes so sweet and dark, Susan could not help smiling.

"I don't know. I'd need your help, Sharicka."

The little girl's eyes transformed in that instant. Susan could not have explained the change in any logical or biological manner. It seemed as if the sockets sank to a slant as she watched them, and a bonfire smoldered, deep and unreachable. Those eyes speared through Susan like a physical weapon, painful, terrifying, inhuman. She shivered involuntarily.

Then, just as quickly, they reverted back to the same innocent child eyes Susan had melted for earlier. "I'll do whatever I gotta do, I pwomise. I'll take all my meds. I'll be gooder than good."

Susan tried to convince herself she had imagined the strange distortion in Sharicka's appearance. Nothing scientific could explain it, and she believed only in the real and earthly, the provable. Nevertheless, she wanted to get as far away from the child as possible. "That sounds wonderful, Sharicka." Susan half rose, sliding the girl toward the floor.

Sharicka drew up her feet, refusing to stand. "I want to stay here with you, Dr. Susan."

"I'm sorry," Susan said firmly, sliding the girl onto the couch cushion. "I have work to do, but I'll check on you later."

Sharicka allowed herself to be placed, though Susan thought she caught another glimpse of the strange light in her face, those weird demon eyes. Repulsed, Susan turned away and headed back toward the staffing room.

The instant Susan entered the staffing area, Kendall caught her arm and guided her to a far corner. "So," he said, "how was your date with the dreamy eunuch?"

Still focused on Sharicka, Susan was caught off guard. "What?"

"Your date," Kendall said impatiently. "With the handsome surgeon you castrated."

Susan finally got it. "I decided he was worthy, so I sewed 'em back on."

"Really?" Kendall sat, resting his elbow on the table, his chin in his hand. "A surgeon worthy of procreation? You'd better not tell his associates. They'll throw him out of his residency."

Susan knocked his arm away, and Kendall had to twitch backward to keep his chin from hitting the table. "Now who's being a jerk?"

"Me," Kendall admitted. "But at least I'm not pompous."

Susan wondered if Kendall reduced everything in his life to a joke.

Kendall changed the subject abruptly, speaking in low tones that did not carry. "Your brilliance is garnering some attention, Calvin."

Susan did not know exactly how to answer that. "I got lucky with a couple of patients. I don't understand why everyone's making such a circus out of it."

"Because it's the PIPU." Kendall looked around to make certain no one had drawn near enough to eavesdrop. Several of the other residents were in the room, reading palm-prosses or dictating notes. Monk Peterson looked at them several times, but no one else seemed to notice them. "Children aren't hospitalized in locked units unless it's absolutely necessary. These are the worst of the worst, the sickest of the sick. If they come here, they stay no less than a month, and it's more often for years. You sent home a lifer and a potential lifer in your first week. That's nothing shy of mind-blowing."

"I got lucky," Susan reiterated firmly, hoping she had just gotten the last word.

"You got brains," Kendall corrected. "And a skill with old-fashioned, low-tech observation. You used them. That has nothing to do with luck."

Susan shrugged. "I don't want to talk about it anymore. I just did what was best for my patients, and that's all any of us wants or tries to do."

Kendall would not let it go. "Yes, but you're the one who succeeded. I think that's great. The nurses love you. Dr. Bainbridge is proud to have you on his service; it makes him look good, too. But some of the other residents . . ."

Susan cringed, certain she did not want to hear what came next. "Our colleagues? What about them?"

"Some of them are jealous."

"They needn't be."

"But they are."

Susan glanced toward the residents again. They remained mostly in the same places. Only Monk looked away when she caught his eye. She saw a vague impression of a daggered glare before he returned his attention to his screen. "So, what do you want me to do about it? Deliberately mess up?"

Kendall chuckled. "Of course not. You should do exactly what you're doing, Calvin. Don't ever let other people's negative emotions stop you from going on to great things. I'm just warning you to be careful. Not everyone has your best interests at heart."

That's sad. She truly did not understand why others might wish her ill simply because she had done well. "That's crazy and petty and . . . just plain . . . stupid."

"Yes, it is," Kendall agreed wholeheartedly. "And who understands that better than psychiatry residents?"

Susan flushed. She did not understand it. Perhaps Remington had a point; she did not belong in psychiatry if she found herself flummoxed by something others saw as basic human nature. Yet, even as the thought arose, she found herself intrigued by the reaction Kendall had described. She wanted, in fact needed, to comprehend it; and that only proved she had chosen the right career path. "Why do you suppose they would feel that way?"

Kendall sat, placing both hands loosely in his lap. "If you'll pardon my psychoanalyzing our colleagues, it's not that uncommon a reaction for people whose self-esteem derives from being the smartest person in the room. When they get dethroned, they feel uncomfortable and displaced, and it's not unnatural to harbor anger against a usurper."

Susan wondered why it never bothered her. She had always felt awed and safe in the presence of genius. *Perhaps because my father is one, and he tells me Mother was, too. To me, it's normal.* "Kendall, how come I don't threaten you?"

Again, Kendall looked around the office, leaning toward Susan and lowering his voice even further. "If you started getting all the laughs, you might. I needed a tutor to make it through college calculus. I graduated in the middle of my medical school class. My sense of worth doesn't stem from being the smartest person in the room. It comes from cracking jokes. You're not terribly funny, so you're no threat to me."

Susan vowed not to kid around during rounds. She did not need anyone else disliking her.

"And there's a personality factor, too. Some people feel secure about their self-worth, regardless of the situation. People like Stony. And I don't think there's a jealous bone in Clamhead's body." He laughed, adding, "The way he flops around, I sometimes wonder if there're any kinds of bones in his body."

Susan chuckled, knowing Kendall meant it good-naturedly. Somehow, it was all right for them to make fun of Clayton Slaubaugh, so long as no one outside the "family" did so.

"In fact," Kendall said, "to show you how little concerned I am about your showing me up, I'm hoping you can help me with a patient."

Susan looked through the glass. The nurses had wheeled out the medicine cart, and Sharicka stood near it, looking over the tiny paper cups. The little girl always drew Susan's attention. "I'm happy to help anyone. Just don't expect something preternaturally brilliant. I can put things together and make some intuitive leaps, but I don't have a photographic memory."

"It's about Connor Marchik."

Susan could not help wincing. The fifteen-year-old boy had primary hepatic carcinoma, refractory to every form of treatment. Genetic markers, personally targeted medications, blood cell therapies, monoclonal antibodies, radiation, and even multiple cocktails of tried and true chemotherapy drugs had proven useless against it. Every week, the oncologists came down with a new attempt at decreasing the tumor load, something to prolong Connor's life a bit longer. The boy had built a wall around himself that kept everyone, at times even his parents, at bay. Like a badger, he remained perpetually angry, attacking when someone tried to tempt him from his cave.

Susan bit her lower lip and shook her head hopelessly. "Believe me, Kendall. I have nothing the oncologists haven't already tried."

Kendall rolled his eyes. "Even the nurses don't think you're God."

Susan lowered her head and looked up at Kendall, trying to appear appropriately chastened.

"I'm not asking you to cure his cancer. I just wonder if you have a thought about how to draw him out."

Susan started to speak but only sighed. She tried

again. "Connor has every right to be angry; the universe or God or Mother Earth or whatever theology you ascribe to has treated him incredibly unfairly."

"Agreed." Kendall gave her a searching look. "Aside from that whole, rambling, politically correct 'theology' thing. But no one should spend his last years in a fog of impenetrable rage, especially when he has so few of them in the first place."

Susan knew Kendall had a point. She could argue Connor ought to be allowed to act any way he wished to in his last months, but it seemed foolish. Connor's anger had a reasonable explanation, but that did not mean he necessarily enjoyed it or wanted to spend the rest of his life enmeshed in it. "Nothing like jokes to cheer a person. And you clearly have a million of them."

Kendall shook his head. "I've tried humor. I've gotten a rare smile, but he still chases me out of the room."

"That rare smile is probably more than most people have managed."

Kendall ran both hands through his hair, until it stuck up in ruddy spikes. "Maybe, but it's not enough. It might win him over in time, but time is something he doesn't have enough of."

"Yes." Susan watched Sharicka wander away from the medicine cart to sit in a plush chair and watch television. The well-cushioned chair made her look like a pudgy doll in its recesses. She no longer carried the balloon, instead clutching a stuffed monkey that looked worn and well loved. She placed the plushie in her lap, facing it toward the screen. "What does Connor do all day?"

"He lies in bed with a palm-pross on his chest. That's about it. Day in and day out, just sitting or lying in various positions and sucking in passive entertainment."

"What kind of passive entertainment?"

"Sports. Cartoons," Kendall said. "I've noticed manga, and he does keep a stuffed animal in his bed. I'm not sure what it is; he won't let me close enough to see it.

It's battered, though. He's either had it a long time, or it takes the brunt of his anger."

Susan had no special tricks up her sleeve. "Would you mind if I looked in on him this morning? It might give me some ideas."

Kendall made a broad, dismissive gesture. "Be my guest. I'm not proud. Anything you can do to make things better is all right by me." He winked at Susan. "If you can make me the hero this time, so much the better."

Susan gave him a single, strong nod. "I'll try my best." She resisted the urge to tease him. To even jokingly suggest he did not have the stuff to become a champion meant vaunting her successes even further.

Susan headed out of the room to check on her patients before rounds. Diesel had an early-morning counseling session with his parents, a dietitian, an endocrinologist, and a social worker, preparing him for discharge. He could wait until after rounds. She headed for Monterey's room, more in dutiful obligation than any hope she might accomplish anything. After a short visit, she intended to check on Connor Marchik.

Susan had barely exited the staffing area when an alarm bell shrilled through the corridor and over every PIPU Vox, directing them to the PIPU patient lounge. Silver light flashed around the television area, where a nurse named Alicia performed the Heimlich maneuver on Kamaria Natchez, a refractory schizophrenic patient of Nevaeh's. Kamaria's face had turned bluish, and she clutched wildly at her throat while the nurse drove both fists into her abdomen.

The children had scattered. A few watched curiously, including Sharicka Anson, who stood on her chair for a better view. Most bolted to their rooms, terrified either of the events or of getting blamed for them. A few cowered behind the furniture. Nurses came running, but Susan reached Kamaria and Alicia first. As the nurse was properly performing the technique, Susan did not attempt to take over. She merely stood by, waiting for Alicia to request assistance or for the situation to change.

It did, and swiftly. Kamaria went suddenly limp in Alicia's arms. The nurse looked hopefully at Susan.

"Lay her down," Susan said calmly. "On the floor. You need to clear her airway."

Alicia did so. Kamaria sprawled onto the floor, fingers and face turning a duskier shade of sapphire. Placing a hand behind her neck, Alicia tipped Kamaria's head backward to fully open her airway. Kneeling at Kamaria's side, Susan asked, "What happened?"

"She had just taken her meds when she started choking."

Kamaria gasped. A rubbery, vibrating sound emerged, but no air.

Susan looked into the girl's mouth and thought she saw something red. She reached in with a finger and swept carefully, concerned she might drive the object deeper into Kamaria's throat. Something clung to her finger as she removed it, a floppy piece of red balloon.

Kamaria huffed in another explosive breath. This time, the welcome, rushing sound of air went with it. The bluishness receded from her face almost immediately, and her eyes fluttered open. She breathed quickly, deeply, hyperventilating. Susan and Alicia helped her to the couch.

Susan put the piece of balloon into her pocket, then turned her attention to Sharicka.

The little girl met Susan's gaze steadily, without a hint of guilt or discomfort, a slight smile playing across her lips. The whole incident had clearly amused her.

Susan could not help shivering. This was no accident. Instinctively, she knew she would find no other traces of what had once been Sharicka's balloon except, perhaps, the string tucked away among the child's belongings until Sharicka could find another cruel use for it.

By now, a crowd of nurses, aides, and residents had gathered. Kamaria's face returned to normal, and she managed a hoarse "Thank you."

Applause followed, from the staff and the other patients. Trying to downplay her role, Susan moved away and applauded Alicia and Kamaria along with the others. Monk's expression looked pained. Nevaeh rolled her eyes. Sable clapped with the others, but she kept her gaze downcast. Only Kendall and Stony seemed truly happy for the rescue and Alicia's and Susan's quick reactions.

Leaving Alicia to explain what had happened, Susan hurried off to visit Monterey. The young teen sat in her bed with her earbuds in, listening to whatever music she had recorded on her Vox. Susan waved from the doorway but got no response. It would do little good to talk to Monterey. The girl could not hear her and would not answer even if she could.

Susan saw the irony in the situation. She would finish quickly and move on to Connor Marchik, trying to reach Kendall's patient when she could not even reach one of her own. Monterey truly seemed like the ultimate hopeless case, and Susan understood why her doctors wished to resort to desperate measures. She had more difficulty comprehending the motives of the Society for Humanity. Did those protestors truly prefer that the girl live out her remaining decades in a psychiatric institute rather than undergo a process that might give her a chance at a completely normal life? Electroconvulsive therapy had its drawbacks, of course, but how could anything be worse than counting the hours and days till death in utter silence?

Susan thought back to the years when cancer therapy was as much of a crapshoot as refractory mental illness. Then, bone marrow transplant offered the possibility of a cure for otherwise certain death. It had required massive doses of radiation and/or chemotherapy to destroy all of the patient's fast-growing cells, then an infusion of nondiseased bone marrow, usually from a donor. Patients frequently died of overwhelming infection, bleeding, graft failure, relapse, organ failures, or graft versus host disease. Even when it worked, the patients felt lousy for months, and full recovery often took years. Survival rates varied from disease to disease but averaged about fifty percent, assuming the cancer itself did not recur.

Nevertheless, people with otherwise fatal diseases would choose the procedure, willing to risk immediate death for a possible cure rather than the slower, certain lethality of the initial illness. In contrast, mortality from ECT was exceptionally rare. The worst common complication was memory loss, most often mild. In the extremely unlikely event Monterey became wholly amnestic, it still seemed preferable to the existence she currently suffered.

Susan performed her obligatory greeting. "Good morning, Monterey." She paused, hoping for some sign the girl had heard her.

But Monterey only stared back, blinking occasionally, her face expressionless.

Susan tried her best. "If you want me to stay and keep bugging you, do nothing. If you want me to leave, wave."

Monterey kept studying Susan in silence. Then, to Susan's surprise, the girl raised a hand and moved it feebly. A ghost of a smile touched her features.

Susan froze for an instant. Then, true to her promise, she turned on her heel and left the room. Her heart pounded. Monterey had not spoken; but she had communicated, even if only to send Susan away. When it came to Monterey, Susan would relish even those tiny victories.

Having interacted with her two remaining patients, however superficially, Susan felt free to visit Connor Marchik. She stood outside the room for several moments, taking deep, calming breaths and loosing them slowly. She knew she was entering a lion's den and promised herself that, whatever he said, she would not take it personally. Having fully prepared herself, she walked into Connor's room, grumbling loudly. "This sucks. Everything sucks."

Connor looked up from the palm-pross balanced on his thighs. He had dark, uncombed hair that tousled in every direction, sunken blue eyes, and long bony cheeks. A hint of downy hair fuzzed the area between his nose and upper lip, and a few hairs clung to his chin.

Arms crossed over her chest, Susan glanced in his direction, then snarled, "What are you looking at?"

Connor seemed shell-shocked. Since he had transferred to the PIPU, no one had ever spoken to him that way. Susan supposed they all plastered on fake smiles, trying to sweet-talk him from the depths of his raging depression. Images flashed across the palm-pross, and Susan recognized them as characters in the newest display case in the Manhattan Hasbro Hospital lobby. The grimy stuffed animal on his pillow vaguely resembled one of the main critter characters. He finally managed to speak. "Who the hell are you?" Though hostile, his tone sounded practically neutral compared to her own.

Susan maintained her stance, half-turned away, arms across her chest. "I'm Dr. Susan Calvin, and I wish I were dead."

Connor growled, "No, you don't."

"I do. I'd trade places with you in a second."

"Bullshit."

Susan turned fully toward him. "You've got it made. Lying around all day doing whatever you want to do, watching whatever you want to watch, until the day you die."

"Which could be tomorrow."

"Or two years. Or three years." Susan turned him a sullen look. "Or maybe some brilliant scientist will discover a cure, and you'll have the bad luck to live seventy more years."

"Yeah, right." Connor returned his attention to the palm-pross. "I've been hearing that 'future cure' shit for years." Sarcasm deepened his voice. "Be happy. Nobody knows for sure when it's his time to go." He snorted. "Well, I fucking know. I've got a few more fucking months at best, and I don't want to spend them skipping around rainbows with dancing ponies, okay?"

Susan shrugged. "Yeah? Then why go on at all? Why not end it all now?"

She had Connor's full attention again. "What?"

Susan let her arms drop to her sides. "Your room seemed like the perfect place to commit suicide. I have enough pills to share." She pulled the Slookies from her pocket. From across the room, they could pass for drugs.

Connor shut the palm-pross. "Hey! You can't kill yourself here."

Susan drifted toward him. "Why not? You don't give a shit about anyone else, so I knew you wouldn't try to stop me."

Connor looked distinctly uneasy. Susan hoped she had not overplayed her gambit. "What's so bad about your life, anyways? I heard you fixed Starling. And Diesel."

"Yeah. And now everyone expects miracles. I can't do anything for Monterey . . . or for you." Susan shook her head angrily. "I can't stand the pressure anymore. Better to end it all now." She shook the candies in her hand and raised them to her lips.

"Don't do it!" Connor shouted.

Susan froze, then slowly turned her head toward him. She wrinkled her brow, as if in confusion. "Why not? Life blows."

"Yeah, it does," Connor agreed. "But what if you're the one who's supposed to find the cure for me? Or for Monterey? Or, if not for either of us, for someone just as desperate next month?"

"Are you saying what I do or don't do affects . . .

other people?" Susan spoke as if she had come to a great epiphany.

"Of course . . . it . . ." Connor caught on. "You bitch."

Susan dumped the candy back into her pocket. "That's *Dr. Susan* Bitch. Now, don't you think it's about time to stop torturing everyone around you just because your life sucks?"

"I'm dying."

"Get over it. And yourself." Susan refused to show any sympathy. "We're all dying at our own speed. You're neither the oldest nor the youngest person to die. Do you know how many people would pay good money to have a couple years' warning? Most of us crawl into our deathbeds worrying about trivia, never knowing we won't wake up in the morning. We leave a million things undone. At least, you can tie up all your loose ends."

"I'm fifteen," Connor reminded her. "My ends are all pretty tight."

Susan chuckled.

"You're not supposed to laugh at a dying kid."

"Well, no wonder you're so spittin' mad. No one laughs at your jokes."

Though tempted to continue while she had him listening, Susan knew when she had said enough. She had given Connor something to think about. Lecturing him about how he affected his family, his doctors, and his friends would only form a wedge, losing all the ground she had gained. With teenagers, often the less said, the better. "Dr. Susan Bitch," she repeated. "And don't you forget it." With that, she turned and left the room.

Chapter 10

Susan caught up with Kendall in the staffing area preparing for rounds. "I saw your patient."

Without taking his eyes from the palm-pross on the table, Kendall said, "Charmer, isn't he?"

"Yes," Susan said with none of Kendall's sarcasm. "I like him."

Kendall met her gaze, his dark brown eyes lacking their usual sparkle of humor. "Seriously? Connor Marchik and neurosurgeons." The light went on. "I get it. You're one of those women who enjoys abuse."

"Nope. You know me better than that. I'm way more sadistic than masochistic." She reminded him, "I'm the evil, castrating bitch."

"Witch." Kendall remembered his own words. "With a capital *B*." Seeing the other residents heading to join them for rounds, he returned to the subject at hand. "Any tips for reaching Connor?"

Susan looked through the one-way glass. Activity in the common room appeared to have returned to normal. Even Sharicka sprawled lazily across a couch, fiddling with the stuffed monkey, for the moment satisfied with the morning's excitement. "Call up the original reruns of the manga series *Ganuto Hiro*, and spend a night watching them. If it has an accompanying collector card or figures game, you might want to invest in it."

"Okay." Kendall did not seem impressed. "We're going for common ground here, I assume."

"Of course."

"I did once engage him in a conversation about the Giants. He has a pennant on the wall." Kendall sighed. "But it didn't hold his attention long. We were right back to biting my head off within a few minutes."

Susan stated matter-of-factly, "That might work better during football season."

"Assuming he survives the summer."

Susan gave Kendall a weary look. "You'll do better treating him like an intelligent young adult rather than a dying kid."

"He *is* a dying kid. That's why he's here."

"He's a dying young adult, and he's irritated that everyone's acting like he's a pathetic fragment of shattered porcelain."

Kendall closed the palm-pross. "I didn't think I was doing that. I tried joking around with him."

"Did you tell him any jokes about . . . death?"

Kendall's expression crumpled, as though he believed Susan had gone stark raving mad. "Of course not. I'm not an insensitive boob."

"Look," Susan said, "Connor doesn't have time for pussyfooting. He wants a doctor who'll give it to him straight. Someone he can trust to always tell the truth, even if the news is bad."

"For example . . . ?"

"What would you say if he asked why he's stuck on the PIPU?"

"Well . . . um . . ."

"Wrong!"

Kendall screwed up his freckled face. "Wrong? I haven't even said anything yet."

"You said, 'Well . . . um . . . ,' which means you're

thinking of a delicate answer. Connor doesn't want a thought-mangled fantasy world; he wants the straight truth."

"All right." Kendall turned his focus fully on Susan. "What would you say to him?"

Susan did not hesitate. "You're stuck here because you're acting like an ass."

Kendall stared. "Susan, I might be wrong about this; you are the child psychiatry messiah and all. But I was under the impression that insulting and swearing at dying children is frowned upon in polite society."

"This isn't polite society," Susan insisted. "It's the hospital. Life and death aren't polite topics."

"But swearing at a child?"

"He's not a child. He's a teenager. Most teens go through a stage when they feel the need to swear as much as possible, at least among themselves. It's like they have to roll the words around their mouths a few thousand times before they pack them away in preparation for responsible adulthood."

Kendall studied Susan with a look of dubious hope. "So I should be direct, even to the point of swearing?"

"Yup."

"Research *Ganuto Hiro* in the hope of a conversation, or even a game?"

"Yup."

"What else?"

"The kid—"

"Young man," Kendall reminded her.

Susan smiled. "The young man's a virgin with about two months to live, right?"

Kendall's expression grew downright uncomfortable. "Ye-eah."

"So, he has cancer, not plague. He's not contagious. He should be out there finding a sympathetic girl and humping her till his liver dissolves to a toxic puddle of goo."

"Susan!" Dr. Bainbridge's voice cut over the conversation.

Startled silent, Susan clutched her chest, worried her heart might have stopped. She whirled, expecting to find him right behind her.

Bainbridge waved at her from a row of tables away. Apparently, he had not overheard the conversation; he had merely shouted her name to get her attention.

A shiver of relief traversed Susan, and she could hear Kendall chuckling at her back. She hurried toward the attending, meeting him halfway. "Yes, sir?" she asked timidly, still worried he might have heard something untoward.

Bainbridge spoke in a booming voice the other occupants of the staffing area could not help overhearing, including the nurses, desk clerks, and the other residents. "I've been approached by Goldman and Peters."

Susan had heard of them. Lead researchers at Manhattan Hasbro, Ari Goldman and Cody Peters authored an enormous number of articles in the *American Journal of Psychiatry*, *Psychiatry*, and *Psychiatric Annals*. She knew they had discovered two forms of schizophrenia, helped uncover a genetic defect in a common familial form of bipolar illness, and paved the way for a new class of antipsychotics, now in common use.

Bainbridge lowered his voice a bit. "They're working on a fresh project and need the help of a psychiatry resident."

Although she knew any resident would serve as the low man on the totem pole, the doer of all "scut" work, at least the name of said resident would appear on any research paper that came out of the experiment. Listed last, of course, but still an amazing feat for any R-1. Susan's heart rate quickened again. If Bainbridge had recommended her, he had granted her a remarkable opportunity; but she also realized the older residents might consider it a grave insult. Stony and Clayton deserved it far more than she did.

"They asked specifically for you, Susan."

The objections died in her throat. Susan could hardly suggest others if the researchers had requested her by name. "Me, sir?" Surprise sent her voice an octave higher. She cleared her throat. "They asked for me?"

"They asked for you," Bainbridge confirmed. "Apparently, word of your competence has spread." He seemed personally proud, as if his invaluable training had created her and the choice was a personal compliment.

"That's a great honor," Susan said.

"Yes," Bainbridge agreed proudly. "I told them they could have you, as long as it doesn't affect your work here. I figured with only two patients, and no impending admissions, you could accomplish both. Assuming you want to work with them, of course." He looked so hopeful, Susan could not imagine saying no.

"I . . . ," Susan started. She looked around to find all her colleagues staring, awaiting her words. "Do you know what their project entails?"

"No idea," Bainbridge admitted. "But they're the leading researchers here. Working with Goldman and Peters is a rare honor. It's sure to be something brilliant."

Susan had already figured that. She tried to find the words that would leave the way open without insulting the researchers or Bainbridge, or further inciting her fellow residents. "I'm very pleased, of course. But I want to be absolutely sure it won't interfere with my responsibilities on the unit. Would you mind if I visited with them sometime and held the decision until afterward?"

"Room 713. Seventh floor, Hassenfeld Research Tower. You're excused from rounds to head up there now."

Susan accepted the invitation, from curiosity and from the need to escape the scrutiny. She had no intention of deliberately failing, or refusing an invaluable opportunity, just to appease people jealous of her good fortune. She had always followed the responsible course in the past, and she intended to do so the remainder of her life. "Thank you, sir. My patients are stable, with nothing new to report." With that, she headed off the unit, accompanied by a key-carrying nurse who wished her well at the outer door.

Susan had never been to the research towers. Few residents ever got the opportunity to participate, and those who did were nearly always chief residents, who dedicated an extra year to learning and teaching. The elevator doors opened to the mingled odors of cleaners, cedar chips, and the distinctive musk of rats. Through the years, researchers had genetically modified the rodents to approximate nearly every human disease state. Also, few protestors worried about the humane treatment of rats the way they did for primates, dogs, cats, and other cuter critters.

The cinder block walls of the older research towers barely resembled the patient areas, where paintings covered every wall and glass-encased craft projects and collectible toys filled every alcove. Here, the furnishings remained sparse, the rooms containing solid lab tables and light metal chairs that moved easily through the confines as needed.

Susan stopped in front of room 713. Labeled PSYCHIATRY LABORATORY, it gave no hint of the stunning brilliance inside, looking no different from any other room on the floor. Through the leaded glass window, Susan caught a glimpse of a desk covered with papers and a spattering of chairs, but she would have had to crane her neck to see the entire room. Not wishing to get caught bobbing around like a spy, she knocked.

"Come in," a friendly voice called.

Susan opened the door. The smells of rubbing alcohol and burnt paper wafted through the crack. Pushing the door all the way open, she entered, letting it spring closed behind her.

Room 713 closely resembled all the other research facilities on the seventh floor. Four large desks, pushed together, filled most of the room, with several metal chairs left in various locations around them. A solitary wooden desk sat in a corner, apart from the others. A man sat on a plush rolling office chair in front of it. He had coarse brown hair that rose and fell across the top of his head like waves. Horizontal lines scored his forehead, and he chewed savagely on the end of an eraser.

At the opposite end of the room, a tall, skinny man held a burning piece of paper over one of the laboratory desks. He looked up, smiling, as Susan entered. He had unkempt auburn hair, a matching mustache, and a long, crooked nose.

As the man watched her, Susan focused on the flames creeping ever closer to his fingers. "Your fingers," she finally called out, just as the fire reached them.

The younger man leapt to his feet, dropping the paper, where it burned to ash on the tabletop. The other man finally looked up as well, still apparently oblivious to his companion's distress. "Can we help you?"

Susan stepped forward to greet him. Before she could speak, the skinny man said, "Don't be absurd, Ari. That's Susan Calvin. Don't you notice the resemblance?"

Now the older man's face split into a grin as well. "Susan Calvin." He rose and held out a hand. "Pleased to meet you."

Susan hurried to clasp the hand of the man who must be Dr. Ari Goldman. She did not want to leave him standing long with his fingers in midair. He had a firm, dry handshake she attempted to emulate. "Yes, I'm Susan." She tried to make sense of the taller man's comment. "Have you met my father?"

"Many times," Ari said, his voice as gruff as his appearance. "When there's a robot study to be done, we get it. That's why we chose you to help us. Figured you'd have the knowledge and the interest."

Susan loosed a pent-up breath she did not even realize she had been holding. She appreciated they had not selected her solely because of her success with two patients. At some point, though, she would have to tell them she had developed an interest in robots only since meeting Nate and she knew very little about her father's business.

"That's Ari Goldman." The tall man took over for his partner, who had neglected the introductions. "So, of course, I'm Cody Peters."

"Of course." Susan had seen only their names, never their pictures. "You've worked together for many years. Your names top an insane number of articles."

Cody laughed. "Insane, indeed. Twenty years now, and he's driven me there more than a few times."

Ari's brows rose. "*I* have driven *you*? You're the one burning crappy data rather than just tossing it into the recycler."

Cody Peters continued to smile but gave no other reply. Susan could already tell that, of the two, he would have the more irritating mannerisms. He was probably also the more fun. He walked over to one of the laboratory desks, produced a key, and opened a vault with it. He pulled out a test tube with a thick, greenish liquid and held it up to the light for all to see.

While he did that, Ari turned his attention to a door Susan had assumed was a closet. As he opened it, she could see a small room. A human figure stepped through, one she recognized immediately.

"Nate!"

Nate's head swiveled toward her, and he grinned. "Susan!"

Still holding the test tube, Cody looked over at the pair. "Well, well, well. You already know each other. That ruins the surprise."

"Of course they know each other," Ari grumbled. "Why wouldn't they? Her father probably put him together, piece by piece, in their living room."

Susan laughed. "Nate and I met here, at the hospital. My father has never been very open with me about his work." That needed to come out before the researchers expected her to act like an authority on robotics.

Nate added, "And she's been either fascinated with me or in love with me ever since. She visits me a lot downstairs." He smiled to show her he was only kidding. "And I like it."

Ari ignored the teasing to explain. "Nate hasn't gotten to show off his paces much, but we find him invaluable. We're not the only ones, either. If people could get past their silly prejudices, we'd have a whole robot workforce and a lot to show for it."

Cody cleared his throat, still hefting the test tube. "Do you know what this is?"

Ari gave Cody a quizzical look. "Of course I know what it is. It's—"

Cody interrupted. "Not you, you moron. I'm talking to Susan."

Ari scowled.

"Oh." Susan glanced at Nate from the corner of her eye, hoping he could help her. When he did not, she admitted, "I have absolutely no idea."

"It's greenish liquid," Cody announced.

Ari gave him another look.

Susan played along. "I can see that. I'm just wondering what's in that greenish liquid." She figured he must want her to guess. "Is it some sort of infectious bacteria? A fungus, perhaps?"

"Not even close." Cody lowered the tube, placed it back into its vault, and relocked it. "I'll give you a hint. It's worth ten million dollars a vial."

Susan still had no idea. "Um . . . designer narcotics? Liquid fame?"

Ari had tired of the game. "Say 'diamondoid nanorobots.'"

Susan wasn't wholly sure she could. "Diamondoid nanorobots."

Cody snorted with enthusiasm. "We have a winner. Diamondoid nanorobots, the newest treatment for refractory mental illnesses."

Susan could only stare. "Are you saying that greenish liquid contains itty-bitty robots?"

"Itty-bitty robots," Cody confirmed, "with the ability to police chemicals and neurological connections. Injected into the spine, they scatter through the brain, recording electrical pulses and interplay, finding aberrant neural pathways, testing circulating blood and cerebrospinal fluid components, measuring quantities and locations of neurotransmitters. After a week or so, we remove the nanorobots and have them analyzed by computers. That allows us to directly target individual therapy for psychopathology refractory to standard treatments."

Susan could only stare. If this was true, science had taken a gigantic leap just since she had graduated medical school two months earlier. "Really?" She wished she had had a much closer look at the greenish liquid.

"Theoretically," Ari said before Cody could reply. "It's passed the preclinical trials, at least as much as we can test it given the current . . . political climate. And when I say 'political,' I mean 'stupid.'"

Though she had never directly participated in a research study, Susan knew the preclinical phase involved laboratory testing on nonliving objects and animals, when possible.

Cody shrugged. "As you can see, Ari doesn't have much patience for the animal rights crowd."

Ari corrected him. "I don't have much patience for radicals of any stripe, left or right. On the one hand, we have zealots committing murder under a pro-*life* banner. Pro-*life*? Please. On the other, we have nutcases breaking into labs, destroying decades of research on medications that could save thousands of lives, in order to throw animals into the wild, where they promptly die of predation, starvation, and hypothermia in the name of 'saving' them."

"So let me guess," Susan said. "The preclinical trials did not include much animal testing."

Cody winced, clearly concerned Susan's innocent question would trigger another tirade. He answered quickly, before Ari could. "Enough to get us to Phase One, which was all we needed." He said it sternly, as if to remind his fellow researcher. "USR really didn't want to risk losing ten million dollars in investments in the brains of pigs and chimps, so it worked out just fine for everyone."

Susan longed to study the greenish liquid again. Logically, she knew she would not see the actual robots; anything on a nanometer level required a microscope. Yet, just knowing the substance contained swarms of mechanical beings programmed to assist humanity intrigued her.

"Fine," Ari grumbled, "until the so-called Society for Humanity gets wind of it. They'll ring this place so tightly, we'll need helicopters just to get to work."

Susan looked at Nate, who smiled back at her. He had remained so quiet, she had nearly forgotten he was there. "Are they really that organized?"

Ari only snorted. Cody gave her a wide-eyed look. "You, of all people, should know. If not for the SFH, we'd have eighty Nates in this place instead of old-fashioned candy stripers and nursing aides. Medical students and residents could focus solely on patients and studies, with robots to do their scut work. Medical mistakes would become so rare, we'd forget the words 'iatrogenic' . . ."

Cody cringed.

". . . and 'malpractice.'"

"Quit swearing!"

Susan laughed.

Ari grunted. "Don't get too comfortable with the joking. When it comes to research, we're both dead serious."

Cody shrugged, bobbing his head from side to side.

It was a deliberately contradictory gesture, and Susan had to suppress a smile. "I'm just honored to work with such renowned . . . and serious researchers." She added "serious" for Ari's benefit. "I suppose I get the honor of writing down your observations?"

The researchers exchanged looks. Cody addressed the question. "Actually, Nate can do all that. We want you to review charts and help us select patients. Also, you'll be doing the lumbar punctures. When it comes to penetrating the cerebrospinal fluid," he confessed, "we're a bit rusty."

The idea enticed her. Some residents despised procedures, whereas others relished them and could not get enough. Susan fell somewhere in the middle. Psychiatry did not have a lot of hands-on opportunities, and Susan liked the thought of getting in some practice. Here, being fresh out of medical school helped. She had done her share of lumbar punctures, withdrawing the fluid to check for imbalances, disease markers, cells, and infections on medical rotations. "Understandable." She hoped her tone made it clear she had no problem with the request. "Timewise, I'll still be able to handle my ward duties, right?"

"Right," Cody confirmed, though Susan doubted he had given it much thought. A common failing of doctors was to grossly overestimate residents' time and the comparative importance of their own pet projects.

Susan found her gaze gliding back to the lockbox holding the precious liquid she would soon inject into a patient's spinal fluid. *Nanorobots.* It seemed the stuff of science fiction. If the experiment worked, she could think of so many uses: identifying cancer cells and, eventually, selectively obliterating them; assisting or enhancing white blood cells in patients with immune system problems; finding imbalances in every cell of the human body. Her mind boggled at the possibilities, limited only by human imagination and programming skills. *Nanorobots*. Susan made a mental note to corner her father and make him tell her everything he knew about robotics.

Chapter 11

Susan downplayed the Goldman and Peters study, not wishing to create more distance between herself and her envious colleagues. She used techniques well learned from her father to make the whole thing sound more like tedious busywork than the chance to become a part of research history. That her part was relatively small made it easier.

Susan found herself dreading the obligatory meeting with Sharicka Anson's parents. She had nothing truly positive to report. In fact, nothing had changed. Susan had not even experimented with the little girl's medications, as previous physicians already had her on a maximized regimen. Susan also doubted any of those drugs truly mattered. Sharicka had no interest in or intention of changing.

Keyed through one of the doors, Susan headed toward the conference rooms that branched off the hallway between the two sets of locked doors. Only one was occupied. A tall, slender man paced around the table, while a woman sat with her face buried in her hands. As she entered, the man took a seat directly beside the woman. His thinning hair had turned mostly gray, with only a sprinkling of his original jet-black locks. He had soft green-gray eyes that seemed older than his years and a face the same perfect oval as Remington's. As Susan entered, the woman looked up. She had longish brown hair that would have seemed dyed if not for the smattering of white hairs in the very front. She had a long narrow face, pale eyes, and generous lips.

"Hello," Susan said. "You must be the Ansons."

The man nodded wearily. "Doctors Elliot and Lucianne Anson. And you must be Sharicka's new resident."

"Dr. Susan Calvin," she said, taking a seat directly across from Sharicka's parents.

"Let me guess," the mother said, with just a hint of venom. "Sharicka is a sweet little girl, and you can't imagine she's capable of the heinous acts we accuse her of. You'd take her home, if you could."

Susan swallowed hard. She wondered how many people had spoken those words. "To the contrary, Doctors Anson. I've witnessed more than enough of Sharicka's deliberate cruelty to thank God she's not my daughter."

The parents' faces brightened, and their full attention went to Susan.

It seemed the height of bad parenting for them to take pleasure in someone saying terrible things about their child, yet Susan understood their relief. Sharicka had probably terrorized them, and their family, until it shook their parental instincts to their core. Social workers, nurses, and even some physicians who ought to know better fell easy victims to Sharicka's superficial charms. It was so much easier to blame the parents than to believe a child capable of such evil. Susan remembered what she had told Kendall about putting the cards on the table. Sharicka's parents needed the truth.

"Sharicka has what we call juvenile conduct disorder."

The parents nodded. They had heard the term applied before.

"Do you know what that means?"

Elliot cleared his throat. "We have a reasonable understanding. I have my PhD in social work. My wife's is in childhood special education."

Susan had not known those details. "So you have a professional understanding of the term?" She did not wish to offend them by over- or underexplaining.

Lucianne shook her head. "We have experience with a lot of childhood disabilities, but neither of us has specific psychiatric knowledge. We've looked it up, but the books at the parental level seem too cautious and nonspecific. The technical journals go over our heads. What is the long-term prognosis for Sharicka? We're sick to death of pussyfooting."

Susan took them at their word. "Conduct disorder in children is rarely diagnosed because it's considered a permanent label. It's reserved for the most intractable cases."

As the parents did not seem put off by that revelation, Susan continued. "About five percent of children get the ADHD diagnosis at some point in their lives, and about a third of those carry it into adulthood. Of the five percent with ADHD, about twenty percent are diagnosed as also having oppositional defiant disorder or ODD." She pronounced each letter separately. "About half of those with ODD go on to have serious adult psychopathology. When it comes to conduct disorder, however, it's one hundred percent. That's why psychiatrists hesitate to ever place that diagnosis on a child, particularly before the teen years." She allowed that revelation a moment to sink in. "The younger the individual is when conduct disorder is diagnosed, the worse the prognosis."

Lucianne nodded repeatedly before finally speaking. "So Sharicka's prognosis is poor."

"Yes," Susan admitted. "May I be brutally honest?"

"Please," the father said quickly.

Susan wondered just how offensive her words would sound. "I would never 'give up' on a child, especially one so young. However, given her current level of treatment and response, I worry about Sharicka. Until she decides to cooperate with her treatment, and the right combination of medications is found, it's only a matter of time before she kills someone, probably before the age of eighteen."

The mother stiffened but showed no other signs of agitation. "Depends on how you define 'kill.'"

Susan did not understand. "What do you mean?"

Though the mother had raised the issue, the father explained. "We noticed from a very young age that Sharicka had a cruel streak. She has two older, nonbiological siblings, whom we also adopted; and we also had younger children in our home through foster care. It started as constant tears and bickering. Then, our oldest began locking his bedroom door at night or crawling into our bed with a score of sudden fears. Mysterious wounds and bruises on the fosters brought us into the spotlight."

A light sparked in the mother's eyes, actual anger. "We had fostered for longer than a decade, without ever using any type of physical discipline. We actually published a book on firm but gentle child rearing. We were considered experts. Then, suddenly, we were being accused of abuse. Us!"

Elliot hushed his wife with a wave. The topic, and the rage it sparked, had probably not served them well in the past. "It was Lucianne's mother who noticed it first, Sharicka's grandmother. She had always loved all our children unconditionally, but she admitted one night to disliking Sharicka because 'that little girl is just mean.'"

Lucianne took up the story again, "So we started watching Sharicka, and my mother was right. Wherever we took her, someone got hurt. Playgrounds were the worst, especially if they had solid plastic crawling tunnels, where the insides were essentially invisible. She had no compunction about harming strangers. She seemed to target older children, whose parents found it difficult to become irate about the behavior of a toddler, even when it hurt their own child. Some of the fathers came down hard on their own kids instead of us."

Mean. Susan became stuck on the word. It was short, simple, and vividly descriptive of Sharicka Anson. "She's quite smart for her age, isn't she?"

"Brilliant." Lucianne managed a wry smile. "We used to take such great pride in that; but now it seems her downfall, because she's capable of plans far more cunning than her age would suggest."

Elliot added, "She's also subtle. If someone announced they needed to use the restroom, or simply headed there, she would zip in first and slam the door in their face. Didn't matter if she was inconveniencing an adult or a not-fully-potty-trained child. We noticed urine in peculiar places: people's laundry, around the refrigerator, on one of the kids' rugs. At first, we blamed the dog."

The parents looked at each other and winced before he continued. "But the problem went on long after she beat the dog to death. She was three years old."

Tears filled Lucianne's eyes. "We all loved that dog. Even Sharicka, we thought. She can disappear in a heartbeat. By the time we found her behind the garage, the deed was nearly done. It was the first time we ever spanked her; it's hard to argue that capital punishment might teach violence to someone who just slaughtered a beloved pet. Sharicka hollered bloody murder. She never could tell us why she did it, never showed a hint of remorse. And the misplaced urination continued."

Elliot clearly wanted to end the discussion, but not without making a few more important points. "Once, we got an incident report from the day care center that our current foster child, just learning to walk, had tumbled down a flight of concrete steps. It was weeks before one of the young women finally told us Sharicka had offered to help her brother down the stairs, then shoved him. The worker claimed the reason she didn't tell us was because she thought we had a bias against Sharicka, and this moron of a girl felt all Sharicka needed was 'someone to love her.' "

Lucianne fairly growled. "What an ungodly, offensive thing to say. No one, *no one*, could have loved that little girl more than we did. She is our daughter, and we have stood by her through things most parents could never comprehend."

Her husband took her arm, squeezing warningly. Clearly, this was a familiar tirade that could result only in wasted emotion. Rehashing past offenses would not help the current situation. "Lucianne . . ."

The father continued, finally getting to the issue that had raised the sudden outpouring of information. "After killing the dog, Sharicka developed an obsession with death, constantly asking questions about it. What was it like? What happened afterward? What kinds of things could kill people? After a visit to Florida, she focused on drowning. I guess it shouldn't have surprised us when Sharicka nearly succeeded in drowning her older sister in a bucket of water."

Susan's nostrils flared. "How old was this sister?" She had not known about this incident.

Now, Lucianne's eyes blurred completely. She rose from her seat, unconsciously, and started to pace.

"Misty is nine. She took Sharicka for a walk, trying to be a good big sister. Sharicka seemed absolutely thrilled. Usually, her older siblings don't have a lot to do with her." The father watched his wife walk; but, as she made no move to stop him, he went on. "After a bit, I thought I'd better check on them. I found them at a neighbor's house, and I heard splashing. Then I caught up to them. Sharicka was holding her sister's head in a bucket of water. Misty was thrashing wildly, but Sharicka is stronger than she seems, and . . ." Now, tears filled his eyes, too. "I stopped it immediately, but Misty fell unconscious . . . and . . . and . . ." He started sobbing too hard to continue speaking.

Lucianne stopped, placed her hands firmly on the back of her chair, and finished for him. "You've heard of near drowning, I presume."

Susan nodded, fingers knotting of their own accord. Technically, anyone who survived at least twenty-four hours after submersion was considered a near drowning, even if he expired at twenty-six hours. "She survived?" Susan asked hopefully.

The mother bit her lip. "It was touch and go. Three months in the hospital, now in physical therapy. She's not the same clever, sweet girl who gallantly offered to take her little sister for a walk."

Elliot finally found his voice again. "Misty remembers nothing. I'd probably be in jail right now if Sharicka hadn't admitted to everything. Proudly, I might add." He shook his head. "I think most people still secretly believe I tried to kill my daughter and Sharicka just took the blame to save me.

"Sharicka was admitted here then, but they only kept her two weeks. Said she was a model patient, and they used the word 'alleged' a lot, especially when it came to the near drowning." The father shook his head. "On the drive home from discharge, she punched and kicked her older brother, flung toys at us, went into a swearing fit, kicked the back of my seat until I nearly crashed the car, and refused to stay in her booster. We managed to get her off to bed, then ourselves. We were awakened at three a.m. to anguished screams from her brother. When we ran downstairs, she was standing over his bed hitting him with a baseball bat. We brought her back immediately."

Susan guessed, "And she's been here since."

"No." Lucianne retook her seat. "She stayed another two weeks. Then, they sent her to a so-called professional foster home, where she attempted to strangle a thirteen-year-old autistic child."

Susan remembered reading about that. She also saw places in the chart where physicians had recorded an extremely abbreviated version of Sharicka's home-based crimes, always preceded by "her adoptive parents report. . . ." The near drowning seemed easy enough to check on, had anyone bothered. Susan made a mental note to do so. "What do you know about Sharicka's birth parents?"

The parents exchanged looks filled with meaning. Elliott explained. "Recently, we hired a private detective and learned that little of the information the adoption agency gave us was true, and they withheld a lot."

Lucianne opened a large purse and removed a manila envelope. "Sharicka's biological father is serving a life sentence for murder. Her birth mother has a long criminal record, too, mostly for identity thefts, drugs, brawling, and credit card fraud."

Susan nodded thoughtfully. Many articles demonstrated that diagnoses of dangerous social deviancy tended to run in families. Workers in the social field played up the environmental role, that children raised with abuse tended to become socio- or psychopathic. However, adoption and foster studies showed no less of a trend in biological children of dangerous criminals brought up in positive environments. Clearly, psychopathology could be inherited, an unsettling fact often downplayed.

So caught up in her thoughts, Susan would have missed the next utterance had it not fully captured her attention.

"You can see it in her eyes."

The parents spoke simultaneously, clearly unrehearsed. She had never seen two people so honestly, so innocently stunned by what the other had said.

"You noticed it, too?" Lucianne asked her husband.

"Can't miss it," Elliot replied. "Though I thought maybe I was seeing things. The eyes of a—" He caught himself, flushed, and turned to Susan. "You must think we're crazy."

Susan knew some relief of her own. "I don't like to use the word 'crazy,' for obvious reasons. But, no. I truly think you're good parents doing your best with a child hardwired for . . ." "Evil" came to mind, but Susan discarded it as extremely unprofessional. "Sociopathy," she finished. She had to confess her observations. "I saw those eyes. I know exactly what you're talking about, and I'm glad I'm not the only one who noticed them."

Lucianne breathed a loud sigh. "So it's not all in my head?"

Elliot reassured her. "Not unless we share the same head."

Susan suppressed a shiver and changed the subject, "So, what can I do for you? What do you want to accomplish during this hospitalization?"

The parents exchanged another look. This, they had clearly discussed in detail. "Can you fix her?" the father asked softly. "Is there any medication, any therapy that can turn Sharicka into a normal child?"

Susan knew no one could do such a thing. "Not normal, no. No more than we could regrow an amputated leg. There are some things medical science still can't cure. We can only attempt to control it with therapy, medication, accommodations, and training. Most importantly, she has to want help."

Lucianne spoke so softly, Susan had to strain to hear her. "What do you recommend?"

Susan could read the mother's eyes nearly as well as the child's, though they appeared so much different. In Lucianne's she read pain, love, desperation, and uncertainty as clearly as a billboard. This was a woman in agony, forced to choose between her love for one child and the safety of her others. Despite all that had happened, she still prized all of her children. Susan started to speak, but Elliot interrupted.

"Please don't say, 'It's not my decision; it's yours.' Or, if you must do that, at least educate us enough to make a choice."

Lucianne spoke before Susan could. "So far, the doctors just seem to want to get her controlled enough that we'll take her home, deal with any consequences, and see what happens. Meanwhile, we want some guarantee that, if we take her home, she won't just make our lives miserable until she's finally old enough and strong enough to kill us. Can we work toward that?"

Susan sighed. "The problem is medicine isn't an exact science, especially psychiatry. It makes sense that the last medical frontier would be the human brain. There are no guarantees; and, even if you gave us a list of what you could and could not tolerate, we have no treatments that would specifically control those exact problems." Susan's own words sparked realization. "If we could, everyone would use those medications, and we could selectively eliminate all negative behaviors and habits in everyone."

Lucianne dropped her face into her hands. Her husband gave his full attention to Susan. "Understood, Dr. Calvin. We're not asking for absolutes; better odds will do."

Susan could not help smiling. Despite the seriousness of the discussion, the words were a small attempt at humor. The significance of her next words, however, dispelled all amusement. "Doctors Anson, there is no doubt psychopathology is hardwired. There are definite, proven defects in the chemical makeup of the brain, the neurological response of the brain to certain stimuli, and underactivity of important portions of the brain related to such things as impulse control, empathy, and higher function, such as love and caring. Unfortunately, those abnormalities vary from psychopath to psychopath."

"Psychopath?" Lucianne raised her hands, fingers spread. "No one's called Sharicka that before."

Susan did not want to get deeply into semantics. Psychiatrists, psychologists, and laypeople had argued for years, but the word psychopath still did not exist in the seventh edition of the *Diagnostic and Statistical Manual of Mental Disorders*, also called DSM-VII. "It's essentially the lay term for antisocial personality disorder. And ASPD can't be officially diagnosed before age eighteen. A major criterion for diagnosing ASPD is that the patient has been diagnosed with conduct disorder prior to the age of fifteen, so it's only a matter of time." Susan dismissed the explanation with an erasing movement of her hand. "My point is that, at four years old, Sharicka already meets the definition for ASPD, other than age. If she were over the age of eighteen, she'd be in prison."

Susan paused, awaiting more questions. When they did not come, she finished, "The younger the age the antisocial behaviors start, the more likely it stems from genetic causes, not environmental. Also, the more refractory it will be to treatment and the worse the extent of the illness. A personality ingrained from the moment the egg met the sperm is a lot less amenable to treatment than one developed because of a single traumatic incident—or even because of years of abuse." As she spoke the words, Susan felt a sudden jolt of realization. *I've just described the difference between Sharicka and Monterey and definitively stated Monterey should prove a much simpler cure.*

Susan wondered if she had just placed the parents in the position of having to defend their child from a verbal assault. As they had said, they did still love Sharicka.

But the Ansons simply mused over the words, lips tightly pursed. Finally, Elliot spoke carefully, gauging his wife's reaction to every word. "I do not think it's fair to subject Rylan and Misty to that, not after all Misty has already suffered."

Lucianne nodded wearily.

The father flicked his gaze to Susan. "Is it possible you would support us in finding long-term institutional care for Sharicka? We would still visit her, of course, and attend any meetings you thought necessary. We just wouldn't support placing her back into our home, unless some miraculous new treatment was found."

Miraculous new treatment. Those words sparked another thought. *Nanorobots for refractory psychiatric patients.* Susan shook the thought away. They had not even injected the first adult patient. Goldman and Peters would surely need some significant, positive, and safe results before daring to try them out on one so young. But at least the idea brought some hope. "Anyone who would fault you for that decision doesn't understand the situation. Your children have a right to feel safe in their own home."

Sharicka's father managed a crooked smile. "Thank you. It means a lot just having someone in our corner."

"It's easy to judge only on the superficial. It takes a lot more time and work to truly understand." Susan could not help adding, "And don't completely discount the possibility of that miracle."

Chapter 12

In the first-floor charting room, Susan sprawled across a floral-patterned chair, her legs flopped over the armrest. Engaged in the conversation, Nate relaxed in the navy blue chair across from Susan's. The table between them held two palm-prosses, the one she had been using to type in notes about her meeting with Sharicka Anson's parents and the one Nate had been using to proofread the day's endocrinology entries. Currently, both lay closed as they talked about Monterey.

"Okay," Susan said. "We've established we're a normal six-year-old girl safely buckled into our car booster. In the front, Daddy is driving. For some reason, he has his seat belt undone."

"Why?"

"That's what we're trying to establish. The car won't start without his belt buckled, so we have to assume it was buckled at one time."

"So he unbuckled it."

"Yes."

"Why?"

Susan wondered if Nate was deliberately playing stupid to try her patience. "Why indeed? That's still the million-dollar question." She heaved a slow, deep sigh.

"We know from history he's either an excellent father or is just remembered that way to honor his memory. For now, let's assume it's true. That presumes he kept his seat belt buckled until some point when he unbuckled it." Worried Nate might insert another "why" and she would have to strangle him, Susan continued. "And about that same time, the car was involved in a deadly crash. The two events are clearly connected."

Fatal crashes had become much less frequent in the last decade since the outfitting of vehicles with sensors, monitors, alarms, and internal navigation systems. However, many people still drove older cars or overrode systems that became as much nuisance as help. The current airbag designs were safer for children at the expense of adults, except around the driver's seat. Cars no longer started without a driver breath analysis, all seat belts in place, and a fingerprint key, so she had no reason to believe Monterey's father had been drunk or high or medically incapacitated. At the least, those would have shown up on the black box.

Nate finally did something more than question. "I think we can discard the possibility that the father unbuckled because he anticipated the crash. Unless we have reason to believe he intended to kill both himself and his daughter?"

Susan shook her head. By all reports, father and daughter had shared an intense bond. He adored her, and the feeling was mutual. Monterey's extreme reaction to his death confirmed that description. "Now, a conversion reaction is the involuntary loss of a bodily function, such as speech, that has no biological explanation." Nate nodded matter-of-factly as Susan continued. "If we dissect a conversion reaction, there is always logic at its core. Often, it's a strange logic, but logic nonetheless."

Nate sat up straighter. "Now you're getting into the realm of primary and secondary gain."

Susan stiffened at his use of medical terminology, then

laughed. "I keep forgetting you've read all those medical texts and edited thousands of charts. Sometimes I lose track of the fact that I'm not discussing this with my usual sounding board, my dad."

"I'll take that as a compliment," Nate said. "Your dad's a brilliant man."

Susan could only agree. She had a great respect, as well as affection, for her father. "Primary gain: Not speaking somehow lessens her anxiety about either the crash itself or the loss of her father. Secondary gain: Admission to the hospital and focus on her muteness allow her to avoid mourning her father, talking about the details of the crash, and gains her the full attention of mother and staff."

"How does not speaking decrease anxiety?"

Though simple and obvious, the words sent Susan's thoughts in another direction. Her own mind distorted the question to how not eating with others/never dating would decrease anxiety. She sat bolt upright. "Oh, my God! My dad's having a conversion reaction."

Nate stared. No one outside of Susan's head could have followed that conversational leap. "What?"

"Sorry. I just had an epiphany about something that's made me curious for about twenty years now."

Nate guessed, "There's overlap between Monterey's case and your father's?"

Susan nodded. "I'll deal with that later. With him." The realization opened her to a new line of thought. "Nate, there's the obvious. If Monterey can't talk, she doesn't have to relive the accident verbally. She doesn't have to talk about her father. But what if there's more? What if words coming out of her mouth caused the accident in the first place?"

"Voice feature to change the radio station? Perhaps the sudden switch startled him?"

Susan felt certain that was not the answer. "Something that caused her father to unbuckle his seat belt, as well as distracting him. Something like . . ."

Nate caught on quickly. "A request for something beyond his normal reach."

"A dropped toy or some food, perhaps." The logic seemed infallible. "She has something important to her. Playfully or accidentally, she tosses it into the front seat area. She asks for it back. Dad unbuckles and is reaching for it, loses sight of the road for a moment, and the crash happens."

Nate continued the thread. "Monterey blames herself and can't process the emotions of an event this traumatic. So she expresses the psychological conflict through mutism."

Susan nodded broadly. "And it would also explain something I've noticed in the chart but didn't give much credence to."

Nate waited patiently this time.

"I've noticed there's a difference in what her female nurses chart compared to the males. In the males' notes, she's nearly comatose, while the females document some episodes of nonverbal communication. I've experienced that myself, while the resident who had her before me, Aiken Mallory, could not get her to respond to him in any way."

Nate drew himself up to his full height. "Why don't they just assign her female doctors and nurses?"

"Patterns are always easier to see in hindsight, and you have to make the assumption first. I'm going to suggest all female nurses for Monterey at rounds tomorrow." Susan looked Nate over carefully, and another idea came to mind. "And I'm going to suggest a visit to meet you."

"Me?" Nate clearly did not follow again. "What good would that do? According to you, I'm indistinguishable from a regular, boring male."

Susan smiled broadly. "Except for one very important difference."

Nate guessed, "My circuitry?"

"You can't die in a car crash."

*   *   *

Susan Calvin broached the subject with her father over a dinner of stew that she ate alone as they talked. "Dad, I used to love the big family meals with Mom."

John dodged her gaze. "I thought we were talking about what you did at work."

"We are," Susan assured him around a mouthful of whole grain roll. "I have a patient who hasn't spoken since the car accident that killed her father. And a father who hasn't dated or eaten since the car accident that killed his wife."

"I eat," John protested.

"Not that I've seen. Not for years."

John shrugged. He reached across the table, snagged a carrot from Susan's stew, and took a bite. "Happy?"

Susan rolled her eyes.

John chewed and swallowed before explaining. "It's not that I can't eat with people anymore. It's just that food doesn't taste right since the accident, and I never know if something's going to hit me the wrong way while I'm with a friend or an important client. Why spend a fortune on gourmet cooking that tastes like cardboard or plastic or dish soap? Eating in groups also makes me think of your mother, and that makes me sad. Grief is entirely normal."

"Grief is normal," Susan confirmed. "But it's not supposed to keep people from participating in normal life experiences forever. Don't you think that, after twenty years, you should have gotten over it enough to do something as ordinary as eating in public?"

John put down the remaining piece of carrot. "Susan, it's not a matter of 'getting over it.' I've come to grips with losing your mother; but the damage the accident did to my neurological system is not reparable. My sense of taste is permanently haywire, and I'm not that great at smelling, either."

Susan could only stare. "The . . . accident? You mean, you were *there*?"

Now it was John's turn to stare. "Of course I was there. I was driving. Don't you remember, Susan?"

Susan dropped her fork to sit in contemplative silence. She had just spent five minutes excoriating her father for refusing to accept the past when she had just as intently attempted to make it disappear. She tried to force her mind back to her preschool years, but she had created so many walls, diversions, and U-turns, she found it difficult to find her way.

"For a brief period, you were an orphan. You lived with Nana for months. If not for several miracles of modern science, I wouldn't be here."

That brought back a glimmer of memory. Susan recalled spending time alone with Nana in her cramped apartment in the Bronx. Sunlight streamed through her bedroom window every morning, waking her, and Nana had seemed as happy and welcome as the bright sun most of the time. Sometimes, though, Susan could hear her grandmother sobbing in the deepest part of the night. The mere thought made Susan shudder. She wanted to close it away, to never think of it again. *My God, I'm as bad as Dad and Monterey.*

"Susan, my life choices, silly as they might seem, don't harm anyone. They don't cripple me from doing any of the things in life I wish or need to do."

Susan had to agree. What differentiated a conversion reaction that required hospitalization from a mild neurosis was exactly what John had described. Unlike Susan's deliberate forgetting or John's secluded eating, Monterey's refusal to communicate made her activities of daily living impossible. "But what about dating?"

"What about dating?"

"Why don't you?"

"How do you know I don't?"

That stopped Susan cold. "You're seeing someone?"

John smiled crookedly. "No. I didn't date while I raised you. I made the choice to dedicate myself fully to that task, putting it above all others. How do you know what I did or didn't do while you were at school?"

I don't, Susan realized. "I guess I believed you would have mentioned it. I told you about my boyfriends." They had already talked about her first date with Remington.

"When are you seeing Remy again?"

"Dinner tomorrow night." Susan refused to be distracted. "But we're talking about you."

John tried again. "Surely, you don't expect your father to discuss his sex life with you?"

Susan did not flinch. "You can tell me about nights out and girlfriends without going into those kinds of details."

John sighed and rose from the table. He started to pace farther into the kitchen, his back to Susan. "Fine, I don't date. And don't get any ideas, Susan. I don't have any desire to do so. If that ever changes, I promise I'll let you know. For now, I like to believe that Amanda was my soul mate." He turned back to face her.

So long as it did not make him unhappy, Susan could not condemn the mind-set. He clearly had no more interest in a second wife than she did in a second mother. "I guess that would make me the child of true love. The perfect kid."

John grinned. "You always have been, in my eyes."

Susan believed him. Whenever she made a mistake, he had always corrected her in a way that made it seem she had figured it out herself. She could not remember his ever raising his voice to her. As much as he had believed in her, she had believed in him. He was a treasure, a gem of a father.

Susan realized she had allowed this saint of a father to distract her from the point once again. "Thanks, Dad."

"For what?" A hitch had entered John Calvin's voice.

"For talking about the accident. I know how much it hurts. . . ."

John turned away again. He was clearly struggling to be gallant. "Had I realized . . . that avoiding the subject . . . had left you with . . ."

Susan helped him, "Some misconceptions? That's not your fault; it's mine. I guess I just didn't want to think about how close I came to losing both of you." She contemplated what a child's mind could make of such a tragedy. "My preschool thoughts made you invincible. As I matured, I guess I just whisked you completely out of the memory. Safe and sound." That realization forced Susan to look at the comparisons in a new light. "You know, Dad, I was comparing you with my patient and thought understanding you might help me to help her. Now, I realize I'm more like her. Except she got a front-row seat to her catastrophe."

John seemed to have gotten hold of his emotions. From the back, Susan could tell he was wiping his eyes, but his voice became steady. "You never stopped speaking."

"No." Susan kept her own voice steady, trying to match her father's courage. "But I did use at least one unhealthy defense mechanism, a bit of repression. Nothing too terrible. My patient, on the other hand, is somatosizing her anxiety."

John turned around to stare at his daughter. "Are you speaking English?"

Susan chuckled. "Freudian English, such as it is. She's channeling her anxiety into physical symptoms."

"How do you fix that?"

"Other doctors have tried all the usual stuff: Certain medications can help, as can properly pointing out the psychological nature of the symptoms."

As the subject got further from Amanda Calvin, John drifted back to the table. "You mean, letting the patient know that you know she's faking?"

"Faking?" Susan frowned. "There's a huge difference between a malingerer and a hysteric. In fact, you have to specifically rule out faking before you can make the diagnosis of a hysterical conversion reaction."

"Really?" John sat, truly interested.

"Really. You also have to rule out an actual medical condition."

John put it all together, his brow crinkled in uncertainty. "So, there's no physical cause, but your patient actually can't talk. It's not something she's doing on purpose."

"Correct. And that's how it's explained to a person with a conversion reaction. With support, that's usually enough for a gradual full recovery."

John made a noise of interested understanding. "But it's not working in this case?"

"Apparently not. She's six years mute."

"Hmm." John studied his daughter. "So what brilliant ideas do you have to fix her?"

Susan appreciated she had no obligation to disabuse her father of the genius notion. Fathers were supposed to believe wholeheartedly in their daughters' intelligence. "I think it's time for her to confront the details of the accident. Not as a six-year-old in the preoperational stage of thought but as a twelve-year-old in the operational stage."

John guessed, "Freud again?"

Susan smiled. "Jean Piaget, this time. In the preoperational stage, a child acts in the realm of magical thinking. Everything revolves around her. My patient truly believes she directly caused the accident that killed her father, apparently because of something she said."

"Hence the silence?"

Susan nodded. "But if we can advance her to the operational stage and allow her to relive the situation as the twelve-year-old, near adult she currently is . . ." She let her father finish.

"She might come to realize she did not cause the accident, thus lessening her anxiety."

"Right." Susan frowned. "Except for one problem."

"Which is?"

"I think something she said *did* cause the accident."

John reeled backward a bit. "That does complicate the matter."

"I'm still hoping, if we can get her to look at the situation in a more mature way, she may at least realize she is not entirely to blame. Multiple decisions and events came together to cause that accident. That might be enough to snap her out of the conversion reaction so we can start some effective psychotherapy for the guilt." Susan ran through some considerations that had come to her in the charting room. "If we can at least get her to realize her words aren't literally toxic, we may open the way for effective treatment."

"And how do you propose to do that?"

"I'm working something out with Nate."

"Nate?" John's face fairly split open with obvious joy. "I'm so glad you're finding an effective use for him. If it works, don't keep it secret."

"All right." Now that she had completely dispelled the sorrow she had forced on him by asking questions about her mother's death, Susan attempted to cheer him even further. "Nate and I are working on another project together. A research project with Ari Goldman and Cody Peters involving nanorobot technology."

The grin disappeared as abruptly as it had come. "You're on the nanorobot project?"

"Uh-huh. Cool, isn't it?"

John Calvin's fingers threaded through one another in obvious discomfort. "It's a great project, but . . ."

Susan waited for him to finish the thought. When he did not, she prodded. "But what? It seems amazing."

"Amazing," John repeated, with little of Susan's enthusiasm. "Yes, but a bit . . . dangerous."

Susan supposed injecting anything into the cerebro-spinal fluid brought the risk of injury or infection. Anytime particles were introduced directly into circulatory fluids, the risk of thromboses, sludging, and rejection arose. She felt certain the researchers had considered all of those risks and decreased them as much as the experiment allowed. She looked at her father, the concern in his eyes, the worried creases in his face, and realized he had meant something quite different with his warning. "Dangerous? In what way?"

"The Society for Humanity."

Susan almost laughed. *He's concerned about those protestors?*

"They may seem harmless, but they can mount a startling offense when pushed."

Susan did not doubt him. "They have a legal injunction against treating the patient we've been talking about. I know they're serious and organized. But dangerous?"

"Dangerous." John stressed the word. "If they feel pushed, they will stoop to murder. The same way a few of the most rabid and fanatical of the antiabortionists slaughtered doctors in the late twentieth century. The way the Weather Underground attempted to blow up government buildings with the workers still in them. People wholly committed to a single agenda do not always act in a rational fashion."

Susan appreciated that pharmaceutical abortions had taken doctors wholly out of the crosshairs. Now, people who needed the procedure could order the necessary preparations from the privacy of their own computers. They shipped in unmarked packages, and those who disagreed with the process had no central location to protest. "Assuming they even know about the study—"

"They'll know."

"They're not going to target the equivalent of a janitor. Killing the person who does the scut work isn't going to postpone the project for a second."

"But if you're in the room when they go after the others, they'll kill you, too."

Susan could scarcely believe the discussion had gone this far. "Dad, you're being ridiculous. Goldman and Peters have done about a thousand studies, including, according to them, all of the medical ones involving the use of robotics. They're a common target of protestors; I'll give you that. But no one has tried to murder them."

"Yet."

The qualifier seemed unnecessary. "Fine, 'yet.' Just like I haven't sprouted a tail . . . yet." Susan studied her father's face, waiting for the realization of how ridiculous he sounded, watching for the wrinkles to smooth. "Dad?"

Gradually, John Calvin's features returned to normal, and he even managed a tight smile. "Perhaps I am going overboard. Just promise me you'll be careful."

It seemed to mean so much to him, Susan could hardly refuse. "I promise."

Chapter 13

A casual aura accompanied Friday rounds, as most of the residents looked forward to their first chance at substantial downtime. On the weekend, everyone would come in early to stabilize patients and have a short rounds. Then only the on-call resident would remain, Clayton on Saturday and Susan on Sunday. Susan did not mind. The six-day call rotation would mean she worked next Saturday as well, but that would open up her next six weekends. She had always preferred to get the hard stuff out of the way early rather than have it hovering overhead.

Aside from the occasional personal tirade, Dr. Kevin Bainbridge demanded orderly rounds. On Monday, Susan had presented her patients first simply because she had taken call that night. Since then, Bainbridge continued to have the residents present their patients in the same order: Susan, then Kendall, Sable, Monk, and Nevaeh last. It seemed more than coincidence that they always tended to run out of time when Nevaeh started talking about some outlandish fad diet or described some new article in *Holistic You*.

To Susan's surprise, Bainbridge was not nearly as rigid as she had expected. He had no difficulty accepting alternative forms of medicine, so long as the person who presented it brought concrete evidence of scientific testing and results rather than testimonials or half-baked theories or anecdotal stories. Now that Susan had demonstrated two successes, he seemed willing to listen to anything she wished to try, which boded well for the odd request she intended to make.

Busy with her morning work, Susan had not had a chance to talk with Kendall. As they gathered for rounds, he flashed her a thumbs-up, followed by a jerk of his hand toward Connor Marchik's room.

Susan smiled back at Kendall.

The moment Susan arrived, Bainbridge waved for her to begin, and she obliged. "Starling Woodruff was discharged yesterday from the Neurosurgery service."

On the outskirts of rounds, several smiling nurses bobbed their heads.

Susan continued. "Diesel Moore will go home today with outpatient follow-up in two weeks." She looked directly at Bainbridge. "I'd like permission to take one of my other patients off the unit."

A spattering of applause followed the question, which startled Susan. Bainbridge gave the nurses a sour look from beneath his glasses. "This is rounds, not a performance."

The grins disappeared, and red tinged several cheeks. One of the older nurses spoke for the rest. "We're sorry, Doctor. It's just that Dr. Calvin met with Sharicka's parents yesterday. They've been reluctant to take their daughter on a home visit, and we're just happy she's talked them into it. It would be wonderful to discharge the poor little girl."

"Discharge!" The word was startled from Susan, and she spoke it too loud. "To juvie or Mars?"

It was the first inappropriate thing Susan had exclaimed at rounds, and it resulted in utter silence. She thought it best to apologize before anyone else found his tongue. "I'm sorry, sir. It's just that I can't believe anyone could speak casually about discharging Sharicka Anson. Especially the day after she attempted another murder."

The nurses all started talking at once, but the upshot seemed to be they had no idea of the incident to which Susan referred. "Don't you all remember the Heimlich Alicia had to perform on Kamaria Natchez?"

The silence continued, but all eyes rested directly on Susan now. One voice came through the crowd. "You're blaming that on a four-year-old?"

Susan reached into her pocket, pulled out the piece of red balloon, and dropped it on the desktop. "That's the culprit. Shortly before Kamaria choked, I saw Sharicka hovering around the medicine cups. Shortly before that, she was skipping around the unit with a red balloon." Susan spread her hands to signify the conclusion was obvious.

The owner of the single voice stepped forward, a nurse named Shaden. "That's pretty circumstantial evidence."

Susan could not deny it. "Yes. But when I put it together with this"—she hefted her palm-pross, then set it down for all to see—"the hospital records of one Misty Anson, Sharicka's sister, I get the full story. Misty spent months in the PICU after a near drowning Sharicka confessed to."

Shaden had become Sharicka's staunch defender. "I think her father put her up to that."

Kendall entered the fray. "Drowning her sister?"

Shaden gave him a disgusted look. "Admitting to the crime. He knew they wouldn't jail a little girl, so he asked her to cop to it."

Susan rolled her eyes. "You think a father deliberately tried to drown one of his daughters, then got the other committed to a long-term, locked psychiatry unit."

"Why not?"

"Because it doesn't make any sense."

Shaden had a theory. "Let's say the father was trying to force the first daughter to do something by submerging her. It got out of hand. When he realized he had almost killed her, he blamed Sharicka."

Susan pretended to accept the premise for the purpose of demonstrating its ludicrous aspects. "So he chooses to 'submerge' her in a bucket in broad daylight in a neighbor's yard? Then he calls 911. Within five minutes, he has an alternative story and has trained Sharicka to comply with it."

"It's not impossible."

Susan added to the coincidences, hoping the theory would grow so unwieldy, it toppled for everyone in the room at once. "Another time, he beat their son with a bat at three a.m., got the boy to blame it on his little sister, and also got Sharicka to take the blame for that?"

Shaden shrugged. "It's certainly more believable than a four-year-old dragging her older, bigger sister to a neighbor's house to deliberately drown her. An abusive father might turn on any or all of his children. Perhaps they were so afraid of more beatings, they went along with his story."

Susan did not get into the fact that no other injuries appeared on the Ansons' other children or on Sharicka herself. Other than the young fosters, no reports of abuse had come from that household before or since that time. She had more than enough ammunition. "And the strangling of an autistic child in the therapeutic foster home?"

Shaden's protests came slower and less vehemently. "We have only the foster mother's word on that."

"Mmm." Susan accepted his explanation. "And the incident in the bathroom with one of our kids? And the staff member? And Kamaria?" Susan looked at each of the nurses in turn. "Poor Sharicka. She's just a magnet for getting blamed for other people's attempted murders. Six times by seven different accusers. What blind bad luck."

Out of arguments, Shaden could only say, "She's four years old, and a sweeter child you couldn't find."

Susan wanted to complete Shaden's sentence with "In all the levels of hell," but she doubted Bainbridge would appreciate the humor.

Dr. Bainbridge took over. "I realize this is a pediatrics unit, but we shouldn't lose professionalism in our compassion. I'm giving everyone who works on this unit an assignment: Write a one-page paper on how a person with antisocial personality disorder uses 'charm and wit' to manipulate others. It's a hallmark of the condition."

Shaden had no choice but to step back, although he did add one piece. "You can't diagnose antisocial in children."

Dr. Bainbridge did not argue the point. "Which is odd, because the diagnosis requires that the symptoms start in childhood." He looked around the nursing staff, most of whom appeared either chastened or ready to explode. No one liked being chided by a superior, especially about something that aroused such strong feelings. "Antisocials have an uncanny feel for social situations and an extraordinary ability to manipulate people's emotions. Anyone in psychiatry who denies falling prey to one at some point has either never treated one or is a bald-faced liar."

"With all due respect, Dr. Bainbridge." This time, one of the female nurses took Sharicka's side. "She's four years old. How much can she even know about influencing adults?"

Another of the nurses laughed. "Clearly, Calida, you don't have any children. When my daughter was four, she had her father and grandparents wrapped around her little finger. There is nothing in the world more capable of manipulation than a preschool child."

Bainbridge made a gesture that implied he had proven his case.

Susan had heard enough about Sharicka Anson. For now, she appreciated that she had not managed to run into the girl on her first day. Had she not become focused on Starling's A-V malformation and Diesel's syndrome, she might have gotten snared by Sharicka's superficial charm. Instead, she had had the opportunity to watch the child in secret, which had allowed her to see things she otherwise would have missed. To know Sharicka was to watch her actions without preconceived notions or personal interaction.

Susan returned the conversation to its long-lost starting point. "If no one objects, I'd like to try assigning only female nurses to Monterey Zdrazil for a while. Presumably because of some issue with her father, she seems to respond better to women."

Several of the nurses nodded silently. No one seemed to take umbrage, and one even added, "I'd noticed that myself."

Susan continued. "And I'd like permission to take her off the unit." It was an odd request. Usually, taking a child from the PIPU was a prerogative reserved for parents and guardians.

Bainbridge rested his buttocks against a desk. "Where do you plan to take her?"

"I'd like to commandeer one of those car-gurneys they use on the peds unit and take Monterey to visit the resident robot."

Whispers suffused the group, but they all waited for Bainbridge's response. The attending's face bunched in confusion. "The resident robot? I thought they dismantled that thing."

The idea rankled. "No, *sir*! What a horrible thought."

Susan's vehement answer drew curious looks, but Bainbridge took it in stride.

"I'm not saying they should. Just that I hadn't heard

'boo' about it for years. People objected, they took it out of commission, and it disappeared."

"He's still working," Susan announced, unable to use the gender-neutral pronoun on someone as obviously male and sentient as Nate. "And, since Monterey lost her father, I thought it might help for her to get to know a man who's not mortal." There was more to her plan, but she did not want to elaborate on it yet. She did not want to raise hopes until she felt more confident it would work.

Monk added his piece. "Far be it from me to question a doctor with your history of success, but doesn't it seem a bit ironic to take a virtual robot and bring it to visit . . . well, a literal robot?"

Several of the nurses bobbed their heads in agreement.

Susan had anticipated people clambering all over her to learn about the robot in their midst, so Monk's line of questioning took her by surprise. She answered lamely, "Why not? Nothing else has worked."

Bainbridge hopped up onto the desk. "Why not, indeed? Make it happen." He glanced at his Vox. "And as we seem to have wasted a perfectly good fifteen minutes, you're excused to upstairs. I promised you to Goldman and Peters."

"Thank you." Susan glanced around but had nothing to gather. The researchers would have their own palm-prosses upstairs. Without another word, she headed out of the staffing room.

The procedure room in the research towers was a cold, sterile white. Rarely used, it appeared brand-new, the countertops clean and flawless, the steel taps and cupboard handles gleaming. Payton Flowers swayed on the sheeted table, watching Susan's every move, his manner definitively odd. His parents and sister sat in plastic chairs along the wall. A towel was wrapped around Susan's equipment, its bright orange color signifying its successful passage through the purifier.

Susan knew from his chart that Payton was thirty-five years old. His short blond hair lay neatly combed, his nails properly clipped, and his face freshly shaven. He wore a standard hospital gown, which brought to mind one of Kendall's quips: *"The only garb in the world that's rated G in the front and X in the back."* Despite his cleanliness, the patient gave off an aura that set every nerve jangling. Susan could not explain it. She felt unsafe, hunted, as if the patient might leap from the table at any moment to chew out her throat. Payton Flowers seemed to radiate some sort of ions that told her, in no uncertain terms, to go away. Although she relished her part in the project, she wanted to be anywhere other than where she was.

Susan addressed Payton directly. "Good morning, Mr. Flowers. Do you know what brought you here today?"

Payton studied her like a snake examines prey. She almost expected his tongue to flick out, forked and testing. "I walked." His speech emerged pressured, separated into strange bursts, oddly enunciated, and a bit slurred. "Ninety-three billion miles."

Susan glanced at the parents, who squirmed. They, too, would have preferred being elsewhere.

"Oh." Susan tried to sound interested rather than repulsed. "Where did you come from?"

Payton spat out, "Da sun!"

Because of his bizarre pronunciation, it took Susan a moment to make sense of the words. She suppressed the urge to correct his science; it seemed absurd to point out that the average distance from the Earth to the sun was only ninety-three *million* miles. "I see." Susan could think of nothing more significant to say. Obviously, Payton Flowers was in no condition to give consent to anything. "Well, thank you for coming." She turned her attention to the family. "I assume you have guardianship."

The mother gave a weary nod. She looked elderly, frail, and tired. Her eyes sank darkly into her wrinkled face. "We do. I know it's hard to tell now, but Payton was his high school valedictorian and a talented basketball player, too. He had an A average in prelaw when he decided he could fly off the roof of his dorm."

"I'm so sorry," Susan said. She could think of nothing else. She knew about schizophrenia, how it came out of nowhere, striking young adults with a madness most people could scarcely comprehend. "I wish I could have met him then." She could imagine the call that had come from Payton's college, the desperate rush to the hospital, the certainty that illegal drugs had played a role. The parents had probably fought a losing battle to jaded hospital staff far more accustomed to experimentation than a sudden break with reality. Then would have come the clean toxicology screen, the hallucinations, delusions, and a diagnosis that left the parents wondering why they had so fervently prayed against drugs. Rehab might work for those; schizophrenia was forever.

There followed years of promising medications, lost to ineffectiveness or intolerable side effects. Some schizophrenics preferred the disease to the medications, and forcing treatment on someone required a criminal history most schizophrenics did not have.

Mrs. Flowers seemed to read Susan's mind. "We try to keep him on his meds, but he gets so miserable. Even when he's on them, he's not . . ."

"Normal," Mr. Flowers inserted in a slow, raspy voice. He said nothing more, almost as if conserving syllables.

"Not himself," Mrs. Flowers asserted.

Susan commiserated with a problem that existed for as long as effective treatment. "When they're lucid, they notice only the side effects. It's hard to remember the side effects are the price for lucidity."

"Yes," Mrs. Flowers said, and the sister nodded enthusiastically.

Susan opened a lower cupboard to retrieve a palm-pross containing the consent information. "Before you sign this, I need to go over it with you." She held it directly in front of the sitting group, while Payton's gaze rolled around the examination room. As she turned her back to him, Susan could feel sharp prickles along her spine, her mind creating imaginary gouges and bites.

Susan had gone over the consent form earlier and summarized it for her patient's guardians. "Basically, it states this is an experimental procedure with limited prior testing. We have just entered the human experimental stages." She lowered the palm-pross to look the mother directly in the eyes. "In fact, Payton is our first patient."

"Understood," the woman said.

"If you choose to sign this consent, I will be injecting radioactively tagged diamondoid nanorobots into Payton's cerebrospinal fluid at the level of the lower spine." Susan tapped a finger on a diagram of the human circulatory system. "These will travel through the spinal fluid and into the brain itself." She traced a pathway from the lumbar area, along the back, to the skull. "Theoretically, these nanorobots have no biologically active ingredients, so rejection should not be an issue. Also, their diamondoid coating should not be capable of stimulating an immune reaction or actual infection." Susan looked up to make certain the parents were following her explanation.

The sister's head was bobbing. Dad crossed his arms on his chest. Mom studied the screen.

"The nanorobots will be left in place for two weeks, during which time they will gather information about the chemical and neurological processes occurring in Payton's brain. At that point, we will remove the nanorobots via another lumbar puncture. We will then insert them into a special computer, which will help us target appropriate therapies to assist with Payton's mental health issues. In this case, schizophrenia."

Susan could hear herself adopting the neutral voice common to all doctors while explaining a complicated procedure to laymen. "Risks include discomfort during the lumbar punctures and the possible introduction of bacteria or viruses, which I will minimize with sterile procedure. As we discussed, the nanorobots should not theoretically cause either rejection or foreign body reaction, but a small risk still exists for either of these. As with any procedure, minimal but possible risks include death, debilitation, or worsening of the problem."

The mother laughed nervously. "You certainly do cover all the bases."

It seemed ludicrous to Susan, too; but aggressive lawyers always spurred greater caution, sometimes to a ridiculous extreme. Manufacturers even plastered warnings on their boxes such as CAUTION: HOT WHEN HEATED. "Do you have any questions?"

The mother shook her head, but Payton's sister piped right in. "What's to prevent these nanobots from escaping into the rest of his body? What if they get loose . . . into the food supply or something?"

Susan appreciated the question. It meant at least one member of the family had a full understanding of her explanation. "There's a semipermeable system of endothelial cells in the brain that separates the cerebrospinal fluid from the circulatory system. We call it the blood brain barrier. Most of the time, its job is to keep dangerous things out of the brain: bacteria, foreign substances, body hormones, dyes, most medications. In fact, it's what makes brain infections both rare and hard to treat; most antibiotics can't cross it, either. These nanorobots were manufactured with the blood brain barrier in mind. They're too large to slip through, completely fat-insoluble so they can't diffuse through, and also highly charged. Radiation can break down the blood brain barrier, so their tags are deeply inserted." Susan knew she had gotten too technical. "In other words, it's not possible for these nanorobots to get out of the patient's brain except by lumbar puncture."

The parents sat silently, but the daughter had one more question. "And when you remove them, how do you know you got them all?"

"Good question." The sister clearly was paying attention. "When we perform the second lumbar puncture, we use a small magnetic device to draw the nanorobots. Another device keys onto the radioactive markers to ensure we don't leave anything behind. If any of the nanos get stuck, we only need to reposition your brother in such a way as to free it. On his side, his back, standing. I'll make sure they're all in the right place before performing the lumbar puncture. Even if one did get left behind, it's inert. It would simply flow around with the cerebrospinal fluid, taking in data forever."

Susan could only imagine the reactions at USR to having one of their ten-thousand-dollar robots lost in a schizophrenic brain for a lifetime. For the patient, however, it would not prove a danger.

Finally, the mother found a question. "What about the radiation?"

Susan reassured her. "It's just a tag and deeply buried in the nanorobots. It won't affect your son directly." She handed the palm-pross to Mrs. Flowers.

The woman stared at the screen, rereading everything Susan had elaborated. She seemed reluctant to sign. "Dr. Calvin, there's a chance this could kill Payton, right? Or he could develop a brain infection that might make things even worse than they are now."

Susan dared not lie, even to pacify a worried mother. During her M-4 pediatrics rotation, she had watched a panicked mother beg absolutes from a tenderhearted resident. The routine nature of the surgery gave the resident leeway to say the chance of death was as close to zero percent as anything ever got. The procedure had gone fine, but an atypical sensitivity reaction to the anesthesia had resulted in a massive heart attack that killed the patient. It was the kind of thing no one could have foreseen, but the parents felt betrayed, and the resident had slid into a deep depression. "A very small chance, yes. Unfortunately, nothing in life is wholly without risk, and an experimental procedure is more dangerous than, say, eating a meal in a fast food restaurant or taking a shower. Yet people do die of those things, too."

Susan had no intention of talking this family into the procedure. If they refused, Goldman and Peters would simply find another desperate patient. Schizophrenia affected one percent of the world's population. Current procedures cured nearly fifty percent, and all but about five percent of the chronic patients responded at least tolerably well to some form of medication. That still left a million and a half possible replacements for Payton Flowers.

When the mother still did not sign, her daughter stepped in. "Ma, how many times have you secretly wished the fall from the roof had killed Payton? At least then we could remember him as the bright, generous boy he had been until that day. The horror of the last few years wouldn't clutter and cloud those memories."

Mrs. Flowers jerked toward her daughter, an appalled look on her face. "I've never said that."

"No," the daughter concurred. "But you've thought it. We've all thought it."

The mostly silent father nodded.

"You've thought it, too?" Mrs. Flowers choked out. Tears turned her eyes shiny.

Susan stepped in. "It's a perfectly normal reaction. People who don't live with mental illness day in and day out can't understand the agony. It's why most mental illnesses have a standard ten percent suicide rate, and that's with all our modern forms of treatment. A recent survey of the inmates of a top psychiatry inpatient hospital found that eighty-six percent of them would trade their current diagnoses for terminal cancer." She had read it in *Psychiatry* only the previous month.

Susan had meant the words to console the mother, to make her feel less guilty for the thoughts her daughter had elicited. Instead, the two women sobbed in each other's arms.

The father grabbed the palm-pross and signed his name with a flourishing finger. Clearly the practical one in the family, he rose from his seat. "Now, Doc, how would you like me to hold him?"

Chapter 14

Susan Calvin did not return to the PIPU until well into the afternoon. Keyed through the doors, she rushed onto the unit to receive glares from most of the staff. Uncertain what she might have done, she ignored them and headed for the staffing area to read the nurses' notes on her patients. If anything had happened that day, someone should have keyboarded it into permanent history.

Sharicka's day seemed to have consisted mostly of begging for human helicopter and horsey rides, though one note documented a near flood in the girls' bathroom that was traced back to the girl. Apparently, Sharicka had "accidentally" left a wadded towel in the sink and the tap wide open. At least, this time, no alternative possibilities for the crime had been postulated. It seemed like a step in the right direction for the manipulated nursing staff.

Sable looked up from a palm-pross to give Susan a squint-eyed look that baffled her. Ignoring her, Susan glanced over Monterey's notes, but the hostility stayed with her. She had never had a problem with Sable before. Monterey's nursing notes contained nothing of interest. The girl remained uncommunicative, verbally and mostly nonverbally as well. The only new mention concerned a car-shaped gurney that had arrived from the pediatrics unit.

Susan had just decided to talk to Sable when Kendall entered the staffing area and plopped down heavily in a chair beside her. "Howdy, stranger. Thanks for joining us."

Susan looked over him to where Sable had been sitting, but the female R-1 had gone. "Is that why everyone's giving me the evil eye?"

Kendall crossed his feet on the desk and ran a hand through his hair until it stood up in red spikes. "I think it still irritates the nurses you made them look bad in front of Bainbridge."

Susan had not considered that. "I didn't mean—"

Kendall forestalled her with a raised hand. "No, that's true, but it's not the reason for the evil eye. There were two new admissions. At least one of them definitely should have been yours; you've only got two patients. I snagged one."

"Don't tell me." Susan thought she had it figured. "Sable got the other one."

"Yup. And it's a doozy. Teenager. Burned her brains out on amphetamines. Nothing left but a kicking, biting, cursing handful of crazy."

Susan winced. "Maybe she would give me—"

"Too late. She's been assigned. If Sable lets you have her, she'll look lazy in Bainbridge's eyes."

"Yeah." Susan did not know what to do. "Well, I'm sorry. I didn't mean to be gone so long. It's not like we went out for lunch or anything." Her own words reminded her she had not eaten since breakfast. *Should have grabbed something on the way down here. Now it's too late.* "I'm not up there playing games. First, I had to convince a patient's family . . ."

Again, Kendall stopped Susan. "You're not going to win any sympathy by complaining about a project we would all give an eyeball to be a part of."

Frustrated, Susan turned argumentative. "I'm not trying to win sympathy."

"Sorry. I could have worded that better. We're not angry; at least I'm not. It's more a matter of . . . abject jealousy."

Susan got it. She just didn't like it. "I see. Good things are happening to me, so that's a reason to hate me?"

"Sure it is."

It was not the response Susan expected.

Kendall smiled, and his dark eyes sparkled. "Not a particularly good one, but a reason."

Susan snorted. She was tired of pussyfooting around everyone's insecurities.

"Lighten up." Kendall uncrossed his ankles and prodded Susan with a toe. "When you chose psychiatry, you knew the kind of colleagues you'd have."

Susan froze. She did not know psychiatry had a type. "You mean, not arrogant and jerky?"

"That's surgeons," Kendall reminded her. "We're quirky."

"Quirky?" Susan had no idea what he meant.

Kendall sat up suddenly. "You really don't know the reputation of people who go into psychiatry?"

Susan shook her head. When she had chosen her profession, she had selected the one she had found most interesting during her M-3 and M-4 years. She supposed the residents and attendings she had worked with, the practices she had drawn, and the particular patients who came to her during that month had as much to do with her decision as anything. She did have a keen interest in the human mind, communication of every sort, and in the challenge of the most complex organ in the human body. There was more yet to discover about the brain than all the other living systems put together.

Kendall enlightened her. "It's supposedly the first choice for residents who worry they might be crazy or, at least, have trouble with social dealings and want to understand the reasons why."

Susan started to reply, then stopped.

Kendall glanced around, then shifted toward Susan and lowered his voice. "Think about it. Clamhead's socially a mess. Nevaeh's . . . obvious. Monk never had a chance to be a kid, and Sable's mother has schizophrenia, which is inherited."

Suddenly, Susan understood something that had troubled her earlier. "That's why Monk tries so hard and dislikes me so much. He's used to being the little brainiac."

Kendall raised his brows knowingly. "Two, three years makes a huge difference at eight. Not so much at twenty-three, especially when you're getting compared to other highly intelligent people instead of common folk."

Susan had to ask, "What about us, Kendall?"

"Well," Kendall said, clearly taking the challenge seriously, "I sublimate my lack of social skills with humor. And you're working through some . . . parental issue."

An unconscious squeak snuck out of Susan's mouth. "How could you possibly know that?"

"What?" Kendall looked truly surprised. "You mean I'm right? You have parental issues? I just guessed that because you mentioned your father on our first day. The perfect man, remember?"

"My mother died when I was three. I was considered too young to attend the funeral, and my father and I never talked things out. Until yesterday."

Kendall pursed his lips and nodded. "I . . . am amazing."

"Yes, you are." Susan would have liked to chat longer, but the workday had nearly ended. She still needed to handle Monterey. "Now, if you'll excuse me, I have a patient to take off the unit. I have my Vox, if anyone needs me, and I'll take any admission, even if it means I have to stay into on-call time."

Kendall threw her a satirical but friendly salute.

*   *   *

Though made for younger children, the car-gurney fit Monterey well enough. If she felt silly, she gave no sign of it, or anything else. She allowed Susan to pull her through the corridors in silence, barely looking around her, showing no emotion whatsoever. The locked, austere hallways yielded to brighter, art-lined walls filled with bustling patients, workers, and families; but Monterey gave no indication she noticed any difference.

Apparently alerted by the rattle and creak of the gurney, as well as the movement of the knob, Nate met them at the door to the charting room. He greeted Monterey with a smile and a short bow. "Hello. You must be Monterey."

Monterey stared at Nate, saying nothing.

Susan shut the door behind them, then threw a quick glance around the room to be sure they were alone. She could not forget the lecture on patient confidentiality, especially when it came to mental illnesses and other conditions with stigmata. Only then, Susan continued the introduction. "Monterey, Nate. Nate, Monterey."

Nate's grin grew broader. "How do you do?"

Monterey kept staring.

Nate's smile wilted. "She's afraid of me."

Susan wondered what Nate saw. Nothing in Monterey's body language gave away any emotion. "How do you know?"

"The eyes." Nate stepped aside to give Susan the same vantage he had. "She doesn't want to know me. She's scared."

Susan imagined she could see a hint of fear in Monterey's hazel eyes. She hunched down, forcing the girl to meet her gaze. "Monterey, Nate's not a man. He's a robot and a very good friend."

Monterey's attention flicked immediately to Nate. Susan had never seen any part of the child move that fast.

The girl studied the robot, the discomfort disappearing, replaced by confusion and uncertainty. She clearly did not believe it.

"Show her," Susan said softly.

Nate dropped his bottom down on the closest chair, flopped a leg over the gurney, and peeled back a thick layer of skin to reveal circuitry tangled over a framework of realistic muscles.

Monterey reached out a curious hand.

Susan held her breath as the girl traced the wires, tapped her fingers against the muscle tissue, and stared in awe. Susan had never seen Monterey deliberately reach out to anything.

Swiftly, Nate withdrew his leg and replaced the flap of skin. Susan heard a step right outside the door. The knob turned, and the door eased open to reveal Remington Hawthorn.

Quietly, Susan motioned him inside. Monterey's gaze went toward him, and the fear that had wholly vanished reappeared.

It's not Nate who scares her; it's men in general. Why? Susan's thoughts immediately went to a history of molestation, and she hated herself for it. She had grown weary of that as the explanation for all things bad. By all reports, Monterey and her father had shared a close and happy relationship. Her problems had begun the day he died. *Maybe she's not afraid* of *men . . . but* for *men.* Susan tried to take the thought further. *She's afraid that men . . . die.* It did not feel quite right. Although psychiatric illness hinged on irrational thought, it usually followed a logical path. *She's afraid that . . . if she bonds with a man, he will die.* That made more sense to Susan. It had the proper quality of childhood "magical thinking," that the world revolved around them and they caused events to happen.

"Do you want me to leave?" Remington asked quietly.

Susan shook her head and motioned him to a distant

couch. She did not want a human male to interfere with the rapport she hoped to create between Monterey and Nate. She also had not realized how long it had taken her to create the situation. If Remington had come, all of the other psychiatry residents had left for the day, except for Nevaeh, who was on call.

"Nate, can you sit here?" Susan indicated the front of the car-shaped gurney. The vehicle had only one seat, which the flick of a latch and a pull could turn into a classical gurney; but Nate could perch easily on the support structure for the pulling handle.

Nate did as she asked. It placed him with his back to Monterey, which Susan hoped simulated a car. She had not initially intended to force Monterey to actually relive the trauma, but the idea seemed suddenly sound. Classical therapies had not worked. Forcing her to relive the unpleasantness seemed unlikely to make things any worse, and it might just work. Monterey's mother had already tried hypnosis; but, even with drug enhancement, that had proven unsuccessful. However, Susan intended to use the little information that had come out of the session to help her set up the current situation.

"You're driving to Six Flags," Susan informed Nate.

Nate grasped a pretend steering wheel and made appropriate motions, which impressed Susan. Surely, the robot had never actually driven a motor vehicle. Given the enormous number of choices in public transportation, most humans in cities this populated never bothered to learn. Monterey's father had clung to his car and delighted in any opportunity to join the traffic.

"It's a 'twenty-eight Toyota, I believe."

Monterey's eyes pinched, and she shook her head ever so slightly.

Susan bit back a smile. Apparently, the girl intended to play the game. She tried again. "A 'twenty-nine Toyota. Blue."

A light flickered in Monterey's eyes as she, apparently, fully realized what Susan intended. They widened slightly, and her pupils dilated. Her fingers tightened on the sides of the gurney.

Susan considered aborting the trial, then thought better of it. Monterey had probably suffered the shock of reliving the event many times in her head, as well as with physicians and quacks. Susan doubted she could startle the girl any worse than electroconvulsive therapy. This time, Susan had one thing no one else had: Nate. She only hoped she could interpret Monterey's thoughts and actions correctly and would make the right decisions to improve rather than worsen Monterey's condition.

Susan leaned forward to whisper Monterey's father's nickname for her into Nate's ear, along with some vague instructions.

Nate nodded, readjusted his clothing, then retook the driving position. "So, Rey-rey, which ride do you want to go on first?"

Monterey stiffened ever so slightly at the mention of her nickname.

Nate turned his head to look at Monterey briefly.

Instantly, the girl's breathing quickened almost to a gasp. Her mouth opened, but no words emerged.

Nate turned back to face the imaginary windshield. "How about some cotton candy, Rey-rey?"

The moment Nate returned his focus forward, Monterey relaxed visibly. She looked down, into her lap, saying nothing.

Susan glanced toward Remington, who smiled encouragingly. He had taken a seat well behind the car-shaped gurney, where Monterey could not see him without turning. She showed no sign of doing that.

"Rey-rey?" Nate twisted his head to look at Monterey again. "Cotton candy?"

Again, Susan saw the sudden change in Monterey. Her breathing quickened, her pupils opened, and a sheen of sweat appeared below her nose and across her brow. Suddenly, she raised a hand and pointed decisively toward the front of the car.

Obediently, Nate returned his gaze in the direction she had indicated.

The nonverbal communication with a male impressed Susan, and the subtext seemed obvious. Clearly, Monterey worried that the man driving the car, the father substitute, would lose focus and have an accident. Yet, Susan realized, there was more to her reaction. Her responses seemed too extreme for someone who usually kept all expression and communication hidden. There was more to it than fear. Susan knew she was seeing something else, another emotion she could not yet recognize. *Think, Susan. Think.*

Nate continued fake-driving, and Monterey's face returned to neutral. The robot turned his attention to Susan, silently requesting more direction.

Susan ran through her mind, trying to remember what seemed out of place. *A dipping of the body, almost hiding. Shifting gaze.* She gave Nate a subtle thumbs-up to indicate he should continue as he had started.

Nate cleared his throat. "Rey-rey, if you're not going to talk to me, how will I know where to take you?" Again, he turned. "This is our special day."

Susan watched Monterey as closely as she dared. Again, she saw the fear reaction written plainly on her face and also the hunching into her seat, as if she wished to disappear. Her gaze shifted, and she again jabbed a finger forward.

Guilt, of course. Susan believed she had plucked the micro-expression from the overwhelming concern for safety. *Monterey's not worried for her own life; she survived the accident. She's worried for Nate. And feeling guilty for killing her father.* That fit in with Susan's previous discussions with Nate and John Calvin. The affliction spoke for itself. There was no doubt about it anymore. *She definitely said something that caused her father to take his eyes from the road.*

The same possibilities presented themselves to Susan as before, the only two things a six-year-old might request in a moving car that a parent might indulge: food or a toy. Susan tweaked her memory by attempting to recall all of Monterey's nursing notes. She was certain the girl had never shown any aversion toward food, not even the pickiness that usually afflicted young school-aged children. There had been a recent incident regarding a toy. *A missing stuffed animal.* Monterey had gone as frantic as a mute child can until one of the nurses found it wadded under a sofa cushion in the patients' lounge. *What was it?* Susan tried to remember without success. The nurses had referred to it only as Bobo. *Bobo.* A different memory found itself lodged in Susan's mind, one of Sharicka watching television with an unfamiliar plush monkey that looked worn and well loved. *Bobo.*

Susan sprang forward, keeping her voice calm. "Nate, Monterey dropped her stuffed monkey. Its name is Bobo. You don't want to drive for an hour with a bored child, do you?"

Nate played along. "Definitely not. Where is Bobo?"

Susan planted her gaze on Monterey. The girl's nostrils flared, her brows drew together, and her upper lip rose. Susan could see an artery in her neck pulsating so wildly it seemed to vibrate. Monterey had gone beyond fear to welling terror. "It's in the passenger seat, just out of your reach. You're going to have to unbuckle to get it."

"Right." Nate pantomimed releasing a seat belt and started leaning toward the passenger seat.

Abruptly, Monterey dove forward, catching Nate's neck with both arms and squeezing with such violence that Susan took a step forward before remembering Nate did not need to breathe. A low humming sound seemed to come from nowhere. It took Susan a moment to realize it originated from Monterey's throat.

Unable to move without first dislodging the girl, Nate rolled his gaze to Susan.

Susan tried to make sense of the noise emanating from Monterey. Gradually, she pieced it together as a deep, guttural "no" repeated so rapidly in succession it became a constant sound.

Suddenly, Monterey screamed. The sound was raw agony, a depthless, primal howl from some forgotten ancestral memory. Susan's blood froze in her veins. Remington leapt to his feet, Nate went still, and Susan rushed toward Monterey. Before she reached the girl, another scream ripped from Monterey's throat, then another. Worried she would bring the entire building running, Susan enwrapped the child as well as she could from beside the gurney and spoke in the calmest voice she could muster. "It's all right. He's a robot. He can't die, Monterey. He . . . can't . . . die."

It was not wholly truth. Otherwise, there would be no need for the Third Law of Robotics: "A robot must protect its own existence as long as such protection does not conflict with the First and Second Laws." But Monterey could not know that.

Nate spoke in a muffled voice. "If I could die, it might be by strangulation."

The screaming stopped. Slowly, Monterey's arms slipped from Nate's neck. She grasped Susan into a hug so fierce that she had no trouble lifting the child from the gurney and placing her on the floor. "It's all right, Monterey. Everything will be okay."

Monterey heaved with great sobs. Susan's dress polo absorbed the tears, and she could feel the warm moisture seeping through to her chest. She grasped the girl more tightly, afraid to let go.

Nate stepped away from the gurney, readjusting his collar. Remington watched Susan and Monterey, not daring to break the near silence that followed those heartrending screams.

Susan gave man and robot uncertain looks. Clearly, things had changed for Monterey, but whether for better or worse remained to be seen. One thing seemed certain. To make Monterey well, they needed to address the burden of guilt she carried. In her heart and mind, she believed she and Bobo had killed her father, and Susan would have to disabuse her of that notion.

"Thank you," Susan mouthed silently to Nate.

The robot only shrugged and smiled.

Chapter 15

By the time Susan got Monterey Zdrazil resettled in her room, the gurney returned to Pediatrics, and finally took herself back to the charting room, it was almost nine p.m. She found Nate and Remington seated in plush chairs, chatting amicably. Both of them looked up as she entered.

"I'm so sorry," Susan said before either of them could speak. "Nate, I put you in a difficult position."

Nate waved off the apology. "Sometimes I think you're the one forgetting I'm a robot. I was built to serve mankind and the physicians at Manhattan Hasbro in particular."

Susan had not thought about those things, and the reminder might have made her smile had she not felt so guilty about how she had treated Remington. "Remy, I imagine I'm the worst date you've ever had."

The neurosurgery resident rose. His green eyes sparkled in the shadow of his sandy curls, and a smile split his face to show the perfect, white line of teeth. She had always found him handsome, but never more so than at that moment. "Believe it or not, I've had worse. And I'd rather not go there, if you don't mind."

Susan laughed. "If they're worse than this, I'm sure I don't want to know the details."

Remington's smile broadened. "I enjoyed watching you work your magic. You're an aggressive doctor, a risk taker. I like that."

Susan nodded, unconsciously psychoanalyzing her boyfriend. Surgeons had a reputation for leaping in without fully assessing a situation, changing strategies on the fly, and making enormous changes swiftly, for good or ill. It reminded her of a classic joke about four physicians duck hunting. The psychiatrist studies the creature flying over, thinking it looks like a duck but trying to determine if it really *feels* like a duck. The internist notes the beak, webbed feet, and feathers are consistent with the creature probably being diagnosed as a duck. Then the surgeon catches sight of the creature and immediately shoots it down. He turns to the pathologist and says, "Go over there and find out what that was."

Susan could understand where a surgeon might find her approach to Monterey commendable, even while her fellow psychiatrists were horrified. The effects of what she had inflicted upon the girl might not fully manifest for weeks. Now that the excitement had waned, exhaustion crushed down on Susan. She glanced at her Vox. It felt unbearably rude to postpone the date when Remington had waited so long.

But the neurosurgery resident had tuned in to Susan's mood. "It's getting late, and we both could use our sleep. What's on your agenda for the weekend?"

Susan considered, then groaned. "Rounds in the morning. Should be finished by ten, but I'm supposed to inject two study patients after that. Sunday, I'm on call."

Remington nodded, sighing. His schedule would prove every bit as busy as hers. "No problem. I don't know who's on Sunday for neurosurg, but whoever it is will jump at a chance to switch with me. That should get us on the same rotation schedule." He stroked his chin and a few wisps of blond hair clinging there. "By law, they have to give us Monday off. What say we get up at the crack of noon and go skating at the mall?"

Susan brightened. She was a decent skater, and the hectic residency schedule had made exercising nearly impossible. "Perfect."

They entered each other's vital information into Vox, v-in-v as it had come to be called. Then Remington opened his arms, and they hugged tightly, almost viciously, and kissed until Susan felt flushed with desire.

Discreetly Nate turned away, feigning interest in one of the nearby portables; but a grin wreathed the robot's face.

By the time Saturday morning rounds finished, Monterey had not yet awakened. Susan gave a brief description of her efforts the previous night and promised to check on her patient when she finished her work for Goldman and Peters that afternoon.

When Susan entered the sterile room, she found her supplies bundled on the counter and her patient sitting regally on the examining table. The woman wore a purple silk pants suit and a matching cape trimmed with white faux fur. A tiara, garish with rhinestones, perched upon her head. She had wrinkles etched deeply into her face and watery blue eyes that still seemed full of life. Her hair was cut short, completely white with age. She might have appeared like anyone's great-grandmother if not for the costume, better suited to a preschool girl.

The chair beside the examination table held a weary-looking, thin man with a full head of gray hair. He wore a black suit with a white shirt and wide, striped tie, the likes of which Susan had seen only in old pictures, videos, and books. He clutched a palm-pross in his hands.

Susan had read the chart and knew the story. The

woman was Valerie Aldrich, the man her husband, John. She carried the diagnosis of non-Alzheimer's dementia with fixed delusions. Three years ago, she had gotten the idea pinned into her mind that she was a princess, and nothing could dislodge it, including therapy and medications. She had surprisingly few other issues. She could still do crossword puzzles and basic mathematics, could answer historical questions, and knew loved ones and friends by name. All of her issues ballooned out from this one, rigid delusion. Her insistence on living it at all times, however, interfered intolerably with her activities of daily living.

Poor John Aldrich spent nearly every moment of his life catering to the delusion. It was his job to play the part of her butler, to indulge her desires, and to explain to everyone around them why she acted the way she did. He kept her home as much as possible, so as not to have to involve strangers and workers in the charade; but the difficulty of corralling someone who believed herself royalty had taken its toll.

Susan made a formal curtsy. "Good morning, Your Highness."

Princess Valerie nodded her head ever so slightly to acknowledge the gesture. She wore a pretty smile. John breathed a sigh of happy relief.

Susan moved on to the husband, explaining the procedure as she had to the family of Payton Flowers. Unlike them, John Aldrich did not pause a moment before signing, though he did explain. "I love her, Dr. Calvin. We've been married fifty-four years, and she's also been the sweetest woman in the world. This"—he made a subtle gesture to indicate insanity—"isn't right; it isn't her. I . . . just want my wife back."

Valerie gave him a withering look. "John, we're not here to talk about your marital problems. We're here to treat the princess' headaches."

John gave Susan a look she understood. He had given

his wife a story that would make her more cooperative with the procedure.

Susan played along. "Your Highness, I'm Dr. Calvin. I'm here to administer the . . . headache treatment. It will require you to lie still and me to put a needle in your back. Can you handle that, or would you like me to call in some helpers?"

Valerie's expression demonstrated nothing but serious contemplation. "My butler, John, shall assist you. No one else is necessary. Commoners and servants should not see their princess compromised."

John gave Susan a secret thumbs-up, and she winked at him behind Valerie's back. After tending to her delusion for three years, he had become adept at manipulating her into accepting situations that might have caused problems in the past. Had he not come up with the proper story, it would probably have taken multiple assistants and involved a lot of outraged screaming to get the "princess" to submit to a spinal tap.

To Susan's surprise, the third patient to receive an injection of diamondoid nanorobots turned out to be the simplest stick of all. Fifty-six-year-old Neal Fontaina had suffered from refractory catatonic schizophrenia for thirty-three years. Early on, he had gone into a stupor that left him utterly immobilized, and that had become his natural state. Medications released him for differing periods of time, but they always stopped working after a few weeks or months. For the last half year, nothing could bring him out of the cataleptic state, so he lay in the hospital, fed intravenously, on a bed that kept him in perpetual motion to prevent bed sores and muscle contractures.

Neal's regular doctor had signed the consent form; he had no one else to do it. Whatever family he might once have had had either died or abandoned him to the whims of the medical community. It seemed unlikely that even the information the nanorobots brought could help him. In his last lucid moments, Neal had signed a paper agreeing to any therapy that had a chance of helping him, stating anything was preferable to his current state, even death itself.

Susan could not help marveling at the desperation that had brought these patients into the study. Medical science had advanced so far, it seemed no one should ever have to suffer again. She had never before stopped to consider the randomness of the universe and the study of it. Often the most deadly diseases found simple cures or controls, while things well understood and financially supported continued to defy the best minds any laboratory could gather. Pancreatic cancer, once a death sentence, was now cured with ablative therapy and autotransfusion of islet cells. Gene therapy had put an end to the complications of several hereditary conditions that had once uniformly slaughtered children. Yet mankind still suffered from the common cold, from heart attacks, from strokes.

The human mind remained the next great frontier. Despite a multitude of new medications and procedures, mental illness lagged behind the other scourges of humanity. Addressing the obesity crisis had first taken a wholesale change in dietary habits and exercise before studies targeting the proper genes and hormones allowed the creation of breakthrough medications. Yet children with hypothalamic obesity, like Dallas Moore, still suffered from a wholly mind-based hunger current therapies could not begin to quell. In addition to addressing pancreatic cancer, islet cell transplants had put an end to most complications of diabetes, but depression continued to claim its many victims. People still debated the ethics of fetal diagnosis, but researchers had quit seeking cures and treatments for anencephaly, trisomies, ring chromosomes, and serious inborn errors of metabolism. Why bother to fix body-wide problems piecemeal when it was so easy to prevent them in the first place?

It all seemed so random, so unfair. Doctors from a hundred years earlier would gape to discover tuberculosis now had a cure, while a simple strep throat, once always responsive to basic penicillin, could be a death sentence depending on the type and resistances.

Neal Fontaina had come to Susan on a wheeled gurney, left in the treatment room by a bored orderly who stepped outside the room and waited for Susan to finish. Now she studied the patient without bothering to speak. He lay in a comfortable position, his legs straight, his arms at his sides, and his gaze fixed on the ceiling. If not for the steady rise and fall of his chest, he could have passed for a mannequin.

Sighing, Susan turned to the counter to prepare her materials.

Someone knocked at the door.

"Come on in," Susan hollered.

The door eased open to reveal Remington Hawthorn. He wore his street clothes, a pair of black T'chana jeans, a triangle-sleeved T-shirt that advertised a local band, and the blocky sandals that passed for the latest style. "Just me. Finished rounds and figured I'd see what you're up to with this study." He stepped into the room and closed the door behind him. "Need any help?"

Susan smiled. "Neal Fontaina, this is Dr. Remy Hawthorn. Remy, this is Neal Fontaina."

The patient gave no response. He did not move a muscle.

Susan explained, "He's catatonic."

That being self-evident, Remington only nodded. "So I see." He looked closer. "In fact, I believe we've met. A bit of direct motor strip electrical stimulation." He looked directly at Susan. "Didn't work, obviously. What do you have that I don't?"

Susan grinned. "About ten million dollars' worth of nanorobotics." She walked over to her sterile bundle. "We inject them into the CSF, they float around for a couple of weeks, we take them back out, and they give us information about every neurotransmitter that might be circulating improperly, any connection that might be misfiring."

"In other words," Remington said facetiously as he leaned casually against the gurney, "you're trying to put me out of a job."

Susan did not see it. "Actually, just the opposite. If we isolate something direct and physical, we'll give it to you skull-crackers to fix."

Remington worked the gurney controls and tugged the blankets to get Neal onto his side and positioned for a lumbar puncture. "Nanorobots, huh? Sounds like sci-fi. Do they really work?"

Susan could not answer that question yet. "We'll find out, won't we?" She carefully unwrapped her bright orange parcel, keeping the contents sterile. "They come from the same company that made Nate, and I'm suitably impressed with him." She appreciated Remington's assistance. "Thanks for your help. I was wondering how to get a catatonic into the proper position."

Remington kept moving Neal. "I just assumed you're going through the spine, since you're alone. You're not injecting straight into the ventricles or anything."

Susan gave Remington a withering look. "Don't they always send a first-year psychiatry resident to drill a hole through the skull and access central brain areas?"

"Lumbar puncture it is." Remington continued to joke. "You have nanorobots. I thought maybe you had personal lasers or something."

"We're not injecting tiny Nates. Something this small consists only of the most basic components. Think of them as the robot equivalent of a virus. You can only program in a single, easy function, like assessing the brain milieu."

"Milieu," Remington repeated. "Meeeee-leeeee-uh. What a great word." He lifted one of Neal's arms, and it remained in position, floating a few inches above the body. "Hey, look at this. Classic waxy inflexibility. I've read about it but never actually seen it."

Susan could not help staring as well. Before the significant effectiveness of schizophrenic medications, such sights had probably seemed commonplace to psychiatry residents. "No playing with the patient's disabilities," Susan chided. "It's undignified."

"For him? Or me?" Dutifully, Remington tucked in the arm. He wheeled the patient over to Susan, placing the gurney bed perfectly for the light and position of the tools.

Susan suddenly realized how much that small act enhanced her task. In the past, she had always adjusted the light to the patient, which required either a sterile handle or her ungloving and regloving. Also, she tended to carry the tools to the work site, which sometimes placed them in awkward positions around and on the patient. Naturally, such things would be second nature to a surgeon, but Susan appreciated Remington nonetheless. "Thanks. This is going to be the easiest one yet." She looked at him thoughtfully. "Do you want to do it?"

A light flashed in Remington's eyes. Clearly, he enjoyed working with his hands. The medical students destined to become surgeons usually did volunteer for procedures first.

Abruptly, Susan wished she had not asked. Remington got to perform such things all the time, while she rarely did. While he was, therefore, less likely to make a mistake, she needed the practice more than he did.

Remington started toward her, then stopped himself. Apparently, he read her hesitation as easily as she had his eagerness. "Nah. I'd rather backseat drive."

I think I love him. Susan tried not to smile too broadly. "Seriously, don't hesitate to make suggestions. You have a lot more experience."

Remington studied her features, as if to determine

whether she meant her words. Many a man had lost his beloved only by following her directions to the letter. *I don't need anything for my birthday this year, darling, so don't waste your money.* Or, *Tell me the God's honest truth; do I look fat in this?* "Fine. But, remember. If you slap me, you'll have to resterilize."

To Susan's surprise, Remington did know a couple of tricks that made the process safer and more productive, logical things one could learn only from peers or experience. Though swifter than any of her previous procedures, this one also went more smoothly. She supposed having no family members looking over her shoulder helped, and the stillness of the patient added to the ease of it; but she liked to think having Remington around had something to do with it as well. Other than his one snap judgment prior to Orientation, he had displayed nothing but common sense. He demonstrated competence in his own field, without bragging, and could support her in hers without competing or worrying about who acquired more professionalism or success. *Slow down, Susan,* she reminded herself. *We've only had one date.*

Susan bundled up the supplies. "Now, all I have to do is hand the patient back to his orderly, and I'm finished here."

It occurred to Susan they could make up for last night's date immediately and not have to wait for Monday. Neither of them could stay out late, but they could at least grab a meal together before resting up for the next day's call. Then, she remembered she still had Monterey to deal with, and the whole thing came crashing down. *A neurosurgery resident courting a psychiatry resident who is also working on an important research project.* She shook her head. *We're doomed.*

It was as if Remington had read her mind. "I'd walk you to your public transportation, but I still have a few postsurgicals to watch. How's Monterey?"

Susan wheeled Neal to the door, opened it, and

pushed him out into the hallway. The orderly jumped to his feet. "Finished?"

"He's all yours." Susan stepped back into the procedure room with Remington. "Still asleep when I came up here. I have to go back and check on her."

"I'm curious to know what happened. Text me when you know something, and I'll try to run into you Sunday for the longer version." Without allowing Susan to reply, he caught her into an embrace and kissed her fully on the mouth.

Stunned for an instant, Susan quickly found herself kissing him back, eagerly. She wrapped her arms around him. He felt solid, muscular, safe. She liked the feel of him, the slight but distinct aroma of him, and the taste of his lips.

As swiftly as he had started, Remington withdrew and headed for the door. Susan watched him leave in silence, enjoying the view of his slim body, even in scrubs.

Susan hurried to Monterey's room, only to find the bed empty. She hesitated, uncertain what to think. The girl rarely left her room, and then usually only at someone's request. Susan turned around to look elsewhere and bumped into an older nurse, named Jasmine, at the door. "Where's Monterey?"

The nurse put an index finger to her lips in a plea for silence. She grabbed Susan's arm and walked her quietly to the common room. Three boys played a spirited game of Sorry! at one of the tables. The remainder of the furniture held mostly female patients watching an animated movie on the well-protected screen. Monterey sprawled in a plush chair. Sharicka lounged on her lap, her gaze locked on the screen, a thumb in her mouth.

Jasmine gestured Susan to the charting room, and the

R-1 followed. A pair of nurses sat chatting at the farther end of the room, and Nevaeh worked on a palm-pross. Otherwise, no one occupied the room. "They've been like that for the last hour and a half," Jasmine explained. "Monterey came out of her room all by herself to watch the film. Sharicka guided her to the chair, holding her hand and jabbering on about how wonderful it is to see her walking around. Sharicka told Monterey you're the best doctor ever and they're both lucky to have you. Then, she told Monterey to promise to work really hard to go home and she would do the same."

Susan wished she could share Jasmine's excitement but managed only a wan smile. She could not help wondering what Sharicka was up to.

Jasmine clearly noticed Susan's hesitation. "You don't believe me, do you?"

"I believe you." Susan tried to repair the rift. "I do. I'm just worried about Sharicka's real intentions."

Jasmine sighed. "That little girl can't do anything to please you, can she?"

Susan had to admit, when it came to Sharicka, she always assumed the worst. "How does Monterey feel about the situation? How do we know she's comfortable?"

Jasmine made a broad gesture. "Ask her yourself. See what happens."

Susan saw no reason not to take the challenge. She had specifically come to reassess Monterey. Without another word, she left the charting room and headed toward the girls.

Both looked appropriately enraptured by the movie, one Susan did not immediately recognize but which had the timeless hallmarks of popular young girls' shows: a young, beautiful princess, a friendly dragon, and a hyperactive squirrel. Susan had to step up directly beside them before either bothered to spare her a glance.

Sharicka's face opened in a smile that certainly

looked sincere. "Dr. Susan! You fixed her." She jumped out of Monterey's lap to give Susan a hug. Her hands seemed so small and warm against Susan's sides, and she smelled faintly of urine. "If you can fix Monterey, you can fix anyone. Even"—she turned her face up to Susan—"me?"

Sharicka had never looked so innocent to Susan, like a small, lost child in a world where children never belong. She gave Sharicka a squeeze but did not lower her guard. Susan spoke softly. Only Monterey might overhear them, and she seemed focused on the movie. "Sharicka, I can't fix people. I can only guide them to fix themselves."

"I want to fix myself." Sharicka's voice and eyes matched perfectly, all sincerity. "I don't want to live in the hospital forever. Please, Dr. Susan, help me."

A doctor made of stone could not ignore that plea. Though she wanted more than anything to go home, Susan took Sharicka's hand. "Let's talk about this in your room."

Sharicka pursed her lips, glanced at the television screen, then nodded. She touched Monterey's arm gently. "I have to go talk to Dr. Susan now. I'll be back, okay?"

Monterey looked at Sharicka and nodded. Then she turned her attention to Susan. "Nate," she said.

Susan stiffened. Had she really just heard Monterey speak spontaneously?

Sharicka confirmed it. "She spoke!" Though she said it with emphasis, the four-year-old kept her voice appropriately low.

Susan paused, needing to choose between breakthroughs. She put a gentle hand on top of Sharicka's head. "Can you give me a couple of minutes, Sharicka? I'll meet you in your room."

Susan anticipated a battle of some sort. Even regular children did not take well to losing a favored adult's attention to another child. Children with mental illnesses often craved it with such ferocity that they went to bold extremes, even if it led to punishment or parental consternation. Susan shook aside her train of thought to concentrate on Monterey. "I'm sorry for the interruption, Monterey. What were you saying?"

"Nate," Monterey repeated in a hoarse, raspy voice.

Susan's mind raced. She could put the idea together without too much difficulty. Monterey wanted to assure herself that Nate was all right. Perhaps she wished to thank him, or berate him, or maybe just to see him again. She could suggest these possibilities one by one and allow Monterey to choose, but she went a different direction with it. "Nate. Okay. What about Nate?"

"Nate," Monterey said, with more emphasis. "Nate."

Susan shook her head, refusing to make it easy. Monterey would have to work for this one. "I don't understand. I hear you saying 'Nate.' Of course, I know who Nate is, but you're going to have to use a complete sentence for me to know what you want."

Monterey closed her mouth tightly.

Susan did not allow herself to wince, to blink, to show any sign it mattered to her whether Monterey succeeded or not. Children had a tendency to turn deliberately oppositional when they felt they deserved something an adult refused to give them. The less something bothered the adult, the less likely the child would indulge in it.

Monterey started again. "Can I visit him again?"

Susan tried to remain neutral, but she could not keep her nostrils from flaring in surprise. She did not know what she had expected; perhaps for Monterey to speak like some sort of partially coherent movie monster. *Want see Nate.* "Sure you can. Anytime you want, and I'm here, I'll try to make time to take you to him. It can't be in the middle of rounds or while I'm examining another patient, but I'll do my best to open my schedule for you." Susan hoped Nate's duties would mesh as well. She felt certain he would make time to assist her with Monterey if at all possible.

Monterey nodded and returned her gaze to the television. Apparently, the conversation was finished.

Susan wanted to draw it out, to ask a few questions and try to get Monterey talking but decided against it. Not only did she have Sharicka to handle, but she did not want to rush Monterey. If she pushed too hard too quickly, she might drive the girl back into silence. Susan knew she would have plenty of free time at the hospital while on call for the entire next day. She would have to deal with any new admissions or crises, but she would otherwise have open time to catch up on charting, work with the patients, and chat with the nurses. She touched Monterey's shoulder to get her attention. "How does tomorrow sound?"

Monterey nodded, and Susan accepted that as reasonable communication. Turning, she headed toward Sharicka Anson's room. After almost a week of observing the youngest patient on the PIPU, they would finally have their first significant conversation.

Chapter 16

When Susan arrived at Sharicka's room, she found the girl sitting on her neatly made bed. She wore her wavy hair in a thick ponytail, oiled and pulled back from her plump brown face. The dark eyes looked larger than Susan remembered, almost pleading, and the demonic sparkle had left them completely. For the first time, she truly looked like a little girl to Susan, a four-year-old with issues even most adults could not handle.

Susan stepped inside and closed the door behind her. "What can I do for you, Sharicka?"

The girl looked up suddenly. Her hands lay in her lap, worrying at each other. "Fix me," she said without a hint of the childish lisp she had used the first time she had spoken to Susan. Her eyes developed a glaze Susan did not, at first, recognize as welling tears.

As the room had no chairs, Susan sat beside Sharicka on the bed. "I don't know what you mean, Sharicka. Tell me."

The words tumbled out; and, with them, the tears. "I miss my mommy and daddy. I miss Rylan. And Misty." She sobbed. "I want to go home."

Susan did not know what to say. For the first time since she had come on service, she believed Sharicka actually spoke the truth. The instinct to gather the child into her arms and hold her while she cried was strong, but Susan resisted it. "Sharicka, you tried to kill Misty." She said nothing more, leaving the ball in the child's court. The seriousness of Sharicka's intentions would come through in how openly she spoke about the crime.

"I know," Sharicka said, so softly Susan had to strain to hear. "I don't know why I do things like that."

Susan did not accept that explanation. "If you're going to get better, you're going to have to dig deeper than that. You do bad things, Sharicka. Horrible things."

"Yes." The girl continued to sob. "I did horrible things. I hurt Misty."

"Why? What are you thinking when you do these things?"

Sharicka finally got specific. "I was wondering . . . what it's like to drown. I wanted to see." She shook her head, probably tapped out for descriptions given her young age.

Although it did not make sense from her worldview, Susan gave Sharicka credit for trying. "Didn't you think that if you killed your sister, you would no longer have a sister?"

"No." Sharicka gazed at Susan through the tears. "I just wanted to see . . . what would happen. I didn't . . ." She clearly struggled to find the right words, and Susan had to remind herself the girl was not yet five years old. "I didn't . . . think . . ." She changed her tack. "When I'm not on my meds, I don't think that far ahead."

Susan shook her head. "You're on your meds here, Sharicka. Yet you put a piece of balloon in a peer's cup. You hit people. You even attacked a member of the staff."

Sharicka pursed her lips. For an instant, Susan thought the demon light would reappear in her eyes. Instead, she rose and gestured for Susan to do the same.

Susan stood up.

Sharicka grabbed a corner of her mattress, lifted it, then groped beneath it. She brought out a small jar that had once held fish food and handed it to Susan. She kept her head down as she did so.

Susan held the plastic jar up to the light to reveal white mush that probably represented wet pills and several bits and pieces of capsules. She stared at it, stunned. Psychiatric patients had been known to hide or spit out their meds for as long as these medications existed. She could scarcely believe this could still happen. "You haven't been taking your pills?"

"Not always, no." Sharicka raised her head. Her eyes still appeared normal, aside from the tears. "I'm showing you because I'm going to take them now. Always."

Susan put the jar into her pocket. "Always?"

"Always," Sharicka said firmly. "Always always."

Susan realized Sharicka had a point. If she was lying, trying to manipulate Susan, she did not have to reveal such a secret. If Sharicka had not shown her the bottle, Susan and the nurses would never have known. "Why now? What's changed?"

Sharicka grimaced; at least it appeared that way to Susan. A moment later, she recognized it as a smile. "When I heard you fixed Diesel and Starling, I thought you might help me, too."

Susan remembered. "When the nurses prepared them for discharge, you asked me to 'fix' you. But you didn't mean it then, did you?"

Sharicka hesitated. For an instant, Susan thought she saw something less than innocent cross her features. "I . . . did, but I wasn't on my meds. Since then, I've swallowed them every day. Then, you got Monterey to talk." She shook her head, her gaze distant. "Anyone who can get Monterey to talk is amazing. If you could fix her, you could fix anyone." Now her lips clearly bowed upward. "Even me."

Susan met Sharicka's gaze. She could feel her gut recoiling as she anticipated the demonic sparkle, the evil expression. This time, it did not come. Susan saw only a little girl with an advanced vocabulary and real insight. For the first time, she could see Sharicka the way the nurses saw her: a little girl with massive problems who needed her help.

Susan sighed. She knew better than to get drawn in by a manipulative patient. "Sharicka, I didn't fix anyone. Those others . . . wanted to get better. They just didn't know how. All I did was guide them in the right direction."

"Guide me," Sharicka said.

"The hard work is yours," Susan continued. "Staying on your meds is a great start, but it doesn't end there. You have to want to change. You have to think before you act, to consider the effect of your actions on other people before you gratify your own curiosity. You have to consider other people's safety, other people's feelings, and truly understand them." Susan shook her head, wondering why she took the time to explain things a psychopath could never really comprehend. She switched to something she knew they could. "You have to know right from wrong. And choose right."

"I do." Sharicka sat back on the bed. "I know I did bad things, and they were wrong. I wanted to do things, and I just did them. By the time I realized they were bad, they were already done." Sharicka gestured feebly, as if having trouble putting her point into words. "The meds give me time to think. I still want to do stuff, but I have a chance to think about it before I do it. Like, right now, I want to kick you in the leg. Without meds, I'd kick you. Now, I can think it would hurt you, so I don't kick you."

Susan appreciated that. "You wouldn't want me to kick you."

"No," Sharicka said with great sincerity. "And I won't kick you, either. It would hurt."

"Yes." The conversation seemed to have come to a natural conclusion.

"Can you watch me?" Sharicka said. "I won't do any bad things. I'll take all my meds." Childish desperation touched her tone. "I want to go home."

After the conversation Susan had had with the Ansons, she wondered whether they would ever take Sharicka home again. *What's different this time? What can I tell them has truly changed? What guarantees do I have?* Susan had no answers to her questions, but one thing seemed clear. This time, Susan believed, Sharicka really did plan to get better. Whether the attempt proved successful was another matter.

Susan marched resolutely down the sidewalk to the hospital entry, ignoring the signs and shouted slogans of the protestors. The summer sun beamed down upon them, striking brilliant glimmers from some of the metallic lettering. Susan wondered idly if they purposely chose reflective material to catch the eye of hospital workers and passersby. If so, it worked only if the intent was to cause temporary blindness.

Susan had once asked Stony Lipschitz why the staff did not have pass-protected, private doors. Stony had reminded her that all of the many entrances and exits from the hospital were monitored; and, as long as the protestors remained peaceful and did not block the sidewalks, they had a right to make their voices heard. Preventing protestors from clotting smaller, more enclosed staff entries required enormous amounts of security, maintenance and repair of the scanners had become prohibitively expensive, and hospital clientele had complained that, when the staff "sneaked" into the building, the protestors turned their venom on the patients and their already overstressed families instead.

Susan had nearly reached the entrance when a hand

seized the sleeve of her dress polo and a voice hissed into her ear, "Dr. Calvin?"

Susan glanced sideways at a man in his thirties with spiky light brown hair, the style a throwback to his parents' youth. He had a narrow face, a prominent Adam's apple, and an odd, predatory look in his pale eyes. "Yes?" Assuming him a patient's relative, Susan spared him a moment.

"Get out while you can."

His words seemed nonsensical. "What?"

"The cyborg experiment, Dr. Calvin. Get out while you can."

Susan tried to disengage politely. "I have no clue what you're talking about." She attempted to walk around him.

But the man stepped directly into her path. "Goldman and Peters and USR. They're tricking you. They're creating cyborgs from mental patients."

Susan had no idea how this man knew about the nanorobot experiment, but she remembered the first-day admonitions about talking to protestors and revealing details of experiments, as well as her father's overstated but understandable concerns about the Society for Humanity. Worried this could spark into something violent, Susan moved forcefully leftward. "You're way off base. Our only goal as doctors is to help the sick and injured become healthy again. Nothing else."

The man moved with Susan, but she managed a quick spin that opened the way, then ran into the sanctity of the building.

Just what I need this morning. Morons leaping to horrific conclusions from bits of misinformation. Susan already battled a tough mood. The excitement of her first week had waned, and she desperately wanted some time to herself. She had returned to Manhattan to spend time with her father; yet she had barely managed a significant conversation. She had the best boyfriend of her life, and she had already broken their second date. She drew some solace from realizing Remington understood and shared the rigors of her schedule. *I love my chosen life; I just need some time off.* Susan knew she would get her wish tomorrow, but only after she had dedicated another full day and night to Manhattan Hasbro.

Rounds went swiftly, as even Dr. Bainbridge had Sunday plans. Susan finished out the morning with the little tasks that would keep the patients on par until the new week started. Things coasted on the weekends. No new treatments or approaches were considered; no procedures or meetings that could wait until Monday were conducted. Once the morning frivolities ended, the unit worked on autopilot and the nurses would not bother Susan with details unless they affected her own patients.

Monterey's current nurse, Saranne, caught Susan daydreaming at a palm-pross. "Monterey is asking for you."

Susan sat up. "Asking? As in . . . asking?"

Saranne smiled. "As in speaking your name with a question mark at the end."

Susan nodded. "Well, I can hardly pass that up, can I?"

"You cannot," Saranne agreed, gesturing toward the staffing room exit. "She's at the door to her room."

Susan found the girl exactly where Saranne had said, surprised to find Sharicka standing beside her. "Dr. Susan," the younger girl said, "Monterey wants to see Nate again. Can I go with you?"

Susan forestalled Sharicka with a raised hand. "If Monterey wants something, she will have to ask me herself." She turned her gaze directly on Monterey, her brows rising in slow increments.

Monterey was up to the challenge. "I want to see Nate again."

Susan noted with satisfaction she had used a full sentence, and it surprised and pleased her when Monterey continued.

"You promised you would take me today."

"I did." Susan could barely contain her joy. *Monterey is talking.* The realization of another success filled her with more warm pride than she expected. She tried to remain professional but could not help remembering how long Monterey had suffered, how little hope anyone had had for her until Susan had come on service. The idea she might save Sharicka as well overwhelmed her. *Pride goeth before a fall,* Susan reminded herself, but she could not shake the feeling of satisfaction that assailed her. *I'm great at this. I really am.* "And I will. Can you walk this time?"

Monterey nodded vigorously.

Sharicka looked longingly at Susan. She seemed afraid to open her mouth again.

Susan had already set things up with Nate the previous evening, and he had promised to make himself available in the charting room. She felt certain he would not mind adding another child. "Of course you may come with us. As long as your nurse gives us permission."

"He will! He will!" Sharicka said excitedly.

Susan knew she was right. Shaden had already proven himself the young girl's staunchest supporter. "All right, then. You two get ready. I'll let the nurses know where we're going, get Shaden's permission, and meet you here at"—Susan looked at her Vox—"exactly eleven oh eight hours."

Sharicka got into the game, examining her bare arm with the same intensity Susan had her Vox. "Should we sinkonize?"

Impressed a four-year-old could come so close to correctly pronouncing "synchronize," Susan rewarded her efforts by joining in. She consulted her Vox again. "It's exactly eleven oh five and forty seconds."

"Check." Sharicka pretended to fine-tune a Vox, though such was unnecessary as they all self-adjusted to the world clock. She must have gotten the whole synchronicity routine from an old show or movie.

Monterey giggled at the interaction.

Susan turned and marched off, trying to appear as competent as an old-time spy whose very life might depend on how well she "sinkonized" with her partners.

When they came back together, Saranne keyed the three through the massive, confining doors of the PIPU and out into the main portion of the hospital. The girls remained silent as they walked with Susan, focused on anything and everything. Sharicka paid so much attention to the key locks that old fears resurfaced and Susan worried the little girl might attempt escape. She made a vow to keep a close eye on the child, to never once let Sharicka out of her sight or beyond a few steps. She felt certain she could outrun the chunky preschooler, so long as she did not give Sharicka too large a head start.

Both girls studied the walls of the regular part of the hospital, nudging each other and pointing to some of the more colorful or unusual paintings. People flowed through the corridors singly or in small groups, discussing everything from family members to duties, from hopes to sadness, from lunch to vomit. Gurneys rumbled past with clipped IV lines and personal charting screens that appeared blank to anyone who might glance at them from the hallway and required passwords to read. At last, the three arrived at the charting room. Susan had discussed bringing Monterey back sometime this late morning or early afternoon, and Nate had promised to do his best to be there when they arrived.

When Susan opened the door, N8-C was sitting in one of the plush chairs tapping away at a palm-press. As they entered, he looked up and smiled. Susan wondered idly if he found the softer chairs more comfortable or if he simply emulated the things he saw humans do. The very thought struck her as odd. Usually, she found herself forgetting his origins, thinking of him as just another colleague/friend, like Kendall or Stony. "Good morning, Nate," she called as she ushered her charges inside and closed the door.

Nate rose to meet them. "Good morning, Susan. Good morning, Monterey." He gave Sharicka a quizzical look. "Hello, little girl I've never met."

Sharicka dashed forward, took his hand, and shook it. "I'm Sharicka. Nice to meet you, Nate."

Monterey waited until Sharicka had finished before sliding in and capturing Nate in an embrace.

Nate hugged Monterey back, but his gaze found Susan.

Susan just smiled and waited.

Monterey held on longer than would be considered appropriate in most situations, and Sharicka nudged the other girl's arm with an elbow. "Let go, now. You don't want to break him."

Nate's closeness muffled Monterey's response. "Can't break him. He's a robot; he can't die."

Susan felt a smidgen of guilt for her deceit, but she had no intention of correcting the misconception she had started. If believing Nate indestructible spurred Monterey to talk, Susan would not disabuse her of the notion.

Monterey finally pulled away. "Thank you," she said.

Nate merely smiled. "For the hug? I give those away to anyone who wants them."

Sharicka cut in. "She means for fixing her. For helping her start talking again."

Susan realized Sharicka might become a problem for Monterey. Like a well-meaning older sister who did all the talking for a toddler, she might delay Monterey's verbal development.

"Is that what you mean, Monterey?" Nate asked.

Monterey nodded briskly.

Nate dropped to crouch at her level. "Because I didn't do anything, really. You fixed yourself, Monterey. We just reminded you of your problem, and you worked through it."

Susan could not take her gaze from the interaction, though she could feel Sharicka staring directly at her.

"I wanted to see you again," Monterey explained. "Can you . . . take me to a park, sometime? With . . . Mommy?"

Susan considered Monterey's words, expressing so much more than they said. Her use of the term "Mommy" instead of "Mom" or "Mother" or the trendier "Mym" that came from shortening "my mom" in text messages suggested she operated at a level far younger than her actual age. She had stopped speaking, and mostly inter- acting, at six. Passive exposure to movies, maturation of her brain and body, and the conversations from her mother and the medical staff would probably help her catch up quickly. But, for now, it made sense she might befriend a precocious four-year-old rather than another preteen. It also confirmed that her issues stemmed from her feelings about her father and their relationship to the accident.

Nate shook his head. "I'm sorry, Monterey, but I'm not allowed outside the hospital."

The look on Monterey's face showed more than dis- appointment. She looked scandalized. "Why not?"

Nate sighed. His gaze trickled upward from Monterey to Susan. "I'm not human, Monterey."

"I know that."

Susan thought she detected some defensive anger. This was not going to go well.

"I'm a tool, created to perform a service, like an MRI scanner. My work is inside the hospital. I'm not comfort- able outside; and, worse, people are not comfortable with me."

"I am."

Nate grinned. "And I'm so glad you are."

Susan intervened. It was easy to forget Nate had no

actual training when it came to handling children or psychiatric cases. "Monterey, visiting Nate is a special reward you'll get when you work hard at getting back to a normal life. We need to work on your relationship with your mother."

Monterey froze in place. Sharicka stared at her, as if hypnotized by what the older girl might do next. Susan suspected she might actually lapse back into silence or, perhaps, fling an explosive temper tantrum. It surprised Susan to realize that she preferred the latter. In Monterey's case, it seemed the healthier response.

But Monterey only turned Susan a partially suppressed smile. "I have to learn to sass her and slam doors?"

Susan could not help laughing as the words of their first meeting came back to haunt her. "You *were* listening." That boded well. If Monterey had not completely shut out the world during her extended silences, she might have matured mentally during her six years of self-imposed isolation.

The girls spent the next hour romping with Nate and plying him with questions. The interaction amazed Susan, even though she knew how much like a normal human Nate generally acted. He could easily have passed for their uncle, tirelessly providing them with horseback rides, startling them with a sudden ankle-grab that sent them tumbling, or allowing them to catch their breath in the crook of his all-too-human lap. Had Susan not kept reminding herself, she would have forgotten he had no childhood of his own, that he never aged, that he had no precedent on which to base his play and answers other than what he had read or watched. According to her father, the programming for positronic brains was minimal, a language chip, the Three Laws, and a basic idea of primary function. All else came to Nate from personal learning.

The hour ended too soon for everyone. Susan had a

scheduled meeting with Goldman and Peters, and she wanted to make sure she handled any potential issues on the PIPU before she left. Better to address things that might never need her input than to leave them festering and risk getting called away. "All right. Fun time's over. We need to get back to the unit."

The girls made loud, disappointed noises.

Susan explained without apology. "Nate needs to go back to work, so he doesn't get in trouble." She suspected assisting a doctor with two psychiatric patients counted as part of his job, but the girls did not need to know that. An hour of playtime with two unrelated youngsters was enough for any adult. "And we need to get back to the unit before your nurses and parents start worrying I kidnapped you."

"No one will miss me," Sharicka said, almost proudly. "I could stay all day."

Susan ushered the girls toward the door. "That won't work for the rest of us." She opened the door and gestured them through it, watching Sharicka closely, still worried the child might try to break for freedom. Without taking her eyes from the girl, she threw a friendly wave back over her shoulder toward Nate. She would get together with him later to compare notes; but, for now, she dared not remove her gaze from Sharicka.

Monterey fairly skipped the whole way back, though she lapsed into silence. Sharicka took the same dense interest in everything she had on the way to Nate. She studied the details of the walls and floors, the locks and keys, with a fanaticism that bothered Susan, though she could not quite say why. In the end, both of the girls hugged and thanked her, then trotted off together to the television room.

When the nurses pressed her, Susan had to admit the whole affair had gone off well.

*   *   *

When Susan arrived at room 713 on the seventh floor of Hassenfeld Research Tower, she found Ari Goldman pacing furiously between the metal desks and his own, clutching a pencil in his hand, the eraser savagely chewed. The willowy Cody Peters sat in one of the chairs, head clamped beneath his long arms. They both looked up as Susan entered, and Ari stopped in his tracks. "He's not here," he grumped.

Susan let the door spring closed behind her with a faint whoosh. Having no idea what Ari meant, she glanced at Cody, whose presence was obvious. "Who's not here?" Alarm trickled through her. *Is he upset about Nate? Was he supposed to be here instead of cavorting with my patients?*

Cody's answer put her mind at ease for a moment. "Payton Flowers. Our first subject."

Discomfort flared anew. "The schizophrenic patient?" Susan remembered his parents' anguish at losing their brilliant future attorney to madness. She knew every subject had a check-in routine, but she did not know all the details. Goldman and Peters involved her as much as possible but tried to accommodate her ward schedule as well.

Cody explained, "He was supposed to be here an hour ago. We called his family. They don't know where he's gone, either. He took off during the night, apparently."

Susan could feel her heart hammering in her chest. A man with schizophrenia wandering off was not usually a frightening or terrifying event. People with psychoses who took their medicines as prescribed posed no threat, and even those who skipped doses or went undiagnosed rarely caused problems that required concern. The media played up those one-in-a-hundred-thousand cases where a patient with paranoid schizophrenia murdered someone he mistook for the devil.

Ari explained, "If something bad happens to him, or

anyone around him, we'll have a hell of a time keeping the study quiet. And once it's out, everyone will blame the nanorobots rather than the disease."

Susan could not argue. Once someone posted an accusation, no matter how false or corrupted, others with an agenda would cling to it even after its debunking. Cody shook his head, turned his gaze to Susan, and rolled his eyes. "Nothing bad is going to happen just because a man who happens to have schizophrenia decides to lose himself for a day or two."

Ari growled something wordless. He cleared his throat and spoke again. "Why did it have to be *our* man with schizophrenia? We should have admitted him for the week."

Cody heaved a deep sigh. "Were you planning to pay for weeklong hospital stays for all our study patients out of your own pocket? Or do you have some magic words to allow them to stay for free?" He shook his head. "And how many of our patients would willingly allow us to coop them up? Would you hold them against their will?"

Ari had no answers. He continued to grumble to himself but did not speak aloud again.

Uncertain what to say, Susan shuffled her feet. She could understand Ari's concerns. Although Cody made sense and spoke the truth, she could not throw off a vague feeling of dread. Her thoughts went back to the protestor. He had known about the study and her role in it, which meant the study was not wholly secret. She could not imagine him snatching a grown man from his bed, but coincidences did not sit well in those circumstances. "Is there anything I can do?"

Cody winced and glanced at Ari. He clearly did not want to speak of anything negative with his partner already in a snit. "We had another patient for you to inject, but he backed out. We're scraping the bottom of the barrel for possible replacements. Do you have any suggestions?"

Susan shrugged. "I'm the wrong person to ask. It's my

first rotation, and I'm on the PIPU. I'm only working with children."

Ari said softly, "We're cleared for children."

That surprised Susan. She had little knowledge of research, but she had always heard safety and efficacy had to be proven on adults before the administration allowed children to participate.

Cody nodded. "Special exemption for time and need." He did not go into details, which relieved Susan. She did not need to hear a recitation of hundreds of rules governing medical research. These two knew them backward and forward. If they said children could participate, it was the truth.

"Hmm." Susan considered the possibilities. "Let me think about it for a bit, and I'll get back to you."

"Sooner is better than later," Ari said. "The quicker we finish and get the data out there, the less chance the SFH has to interfere."

Susan would have liked to wait until she found Ari Goldman in a better mood, but she realized not speaking now would make it look as if she had hidden something later. "You should know I got accosted on the way into work this morning. Nothing violent or dangerous, but this man knew enough about the study to call it"—she tried to remember his exact words—"'making cyborgs from mental patients.' And he warned me to 'get out.'"

Now, even Cody's smile vanished. "Did he say why? Did he threaten anything?"

"No," Susan said. "They trained us to ignore protestors, and I disengaged as quickly as I could."

"Good job," Cody said, arousing a pang of guilt. Susan could not help remembering her first day and the conversation she had held with one of those protestors. She shook away the thought with the knowledge that the conversation had had nothing to do with robots or research. At the time, she did not even know the study existed.

Ari's frown deepened. It seemed to permanently score his aging features. "Making cyborgs from mental patients. Now I've heard everything."

"Oh, I'm sure I could say a few things you haven't heard yet," Cody teased his partner, running a hand through his unkempt hair and leaving it mostly standing on end.

Ari ignored the taller, leaner man. "But wouldn't it be cool if we had that technology?"

Cody shrugged. "We do, depending on how you define 'cyborg.' There are people with functioning, robotic limbs with neural connections."

Ari dismissed him with a brusque wave. "I mean mental cyborgs. Positronic brains in human bodies. Toss out the old, malfunctioning head and replace it with working wire coils that can think and learn."

The thought seemed chilling to Susan, and Cody must have had a similar instinct. "Don't say that where the Society for Humanity can hear you. They'd have a field day." He rolled his gaze toward Susan again, indicating with a glance not to take certain musings of Dr. Ari Goldman seriously. "Isn't it the intellect that makes the man? I mean, somewhere, there are freezers full of cryogenically frozen heads waiting for replacement bodies."

"Where?"

"I don't know. I thought I read that somewhere."

Ari defended his idea. "I'm not really suggesting we toss some human's thinker into the garbage and put Nate's in. I'm just saying we might replace a section of brain, say after an accident or stroke, with positronic circuitry. If we can map the brain down to the molecular level, perhaps we could replace a misfiring synapse or two and cure all mental illnesses." He gave Cody a pointed look that probably passed for return humor. "Maybe even your arachnophobia."

"Hey! That's a carefully guarded secret."

Both men looked at Susan, who made a zipper motion across her lips.

The casual speculation convinced Susan her encounter with the protestor would neither get her banned from the study nor essentially killed, as Dr. Bainbridge had suggested in his initial lecture to all of the incoming residents. "If you don't need me for anything today, I'm going back to the PIPU."

Ari waved a gruff good-bye. Cody shrugged. "Without Payton Flowers, or the newest patient, your schedule has completely opened. We'll call you if anything else comes up."

That suited Susan just fine. She turned to leave.

"Oh," Ari added, "I'm serious about letting us know if you find another subject. Someone desperate with nothing to lose."

"Desperate with nothing to lose." The phrase hung with Susan long after she left Hassenfeld Research Tower and headed back toward the unit. She could see how that phrase would make people worry about becoming a part of the study, but she also knew anything new and different required such a warning. In some ways, it harmed the research process, because medications and procedures that might help people in mild circumstances seldom got tested. In other ways, it helped, because it ensured that any new medication or procedure had to work on even the most extreme cases to get notice and approval.

Susan realized if they had asked her the first day for patient suggestions, Monterey would probably have nanorobots circulating through her cerebrospinal fluid right now. The breakthrough with Nate had made even the controversial electroconvulsive therapy unnecessary. She wondered how the protestors would feel when the hospital and mother gave up the battle. Would they use Monterey's improvement without ECT as an I-told-you-so victory for their agenda, or would the loss of a rallying point disappoint them? Would they savor their win and head for home, or would they channel their energy into a new cause, energized by their success?

Susan shook those thoughts aside. She had no real interest in the political aspects of medicine, other than simple curiosity. Her job was to see the patients, diagnose them, and make them better, to ease the burden on the children and parents in her charge. The journalists, protestors, and politicians could go to hell for all she cared. They mostly just got in the way of the practice of competent, proper medicine.

As Susan trotted down toward the bowels of the hospital, she studied her Vox to make certain she had not missed any pages or messages. Only one flashed up on the screen, a shorthand from her father wishing her a quiet, peaceful day. Susan smiled at the sentiment, touching the Kwik-key sequence to relay an "All's well" in return. In fact, thus far, the powers that be seemed determined to keep her world quiet.

By the time Susan arrived on the PIPU, however, her streak appeared to have ended. As Saranne keyed her through the first of the doors, she said softly, "The Ansons are here."

Susan did not know whether to smile or grimace, so she simply nodded. She appreciated that the Doctors Anson had not given up on their wayward daughter, or her caretakers; but the poor family had surely suffered enough. "Please tell me Shaden's not pressuring them for discharge."

"Not discharge," Saranne assured her. "Just a simple home visit."

Though it pained her to do so, Susan gave the suggestion serious consideration. When she had brought up the possibility of institutional care at rounds the previous week, the nurses, Stony and Clayton, and even Dr. Bainbridge had laughed. Few enough places accepted any patient for lifelong care, and none would consider a child, especially one so young, particularly a female. That had led to a discussion about inpatient psychiatry protocol, reasonable expectations, and ultimate objectives.

Susan had always understood that the eventual goal for every patient was discharge to home as quickly as possible. No one wanted to stay in the hospital longer than necessary. The intrusiveness, exposure to super-bugs, and 24/7 noise were bad enough; but most patients could envision their bank accounts emptying as the hours ticked past. Third-party payers, especially the government, allowed set amounts of hospitalization time for specific diagnoses. Keeping patients longer required a ream of paperwork that brought every administrator, from the charge nurse to the CEO, down on the doctors' heads. Inquiries often seemed more like inquisitions. Denials occurred frequently, forcing the choice between premature discharge and personal payment, which few people could afford.

Patients such as Sharicka made life especially difficult for physicians. Unlike most of the other PIPU patients, she had no evidence of psychosis or dementia. Personality disorders, even the antisocial type, were not justified diagnoses for inpatient therapy. Her youth further hampered them, as they could not even officially use the ASPD designation until she reached the age of majority.

They had to settle for ADHD, ODD, and conduct disorder, none of which sufficed for inpatient care, especially long term. Sharicka had serious and permanent issues; weeks, months, even years on the PIPU could not change her underlying problem. The treatment for her, and other children on the conduct disorder spectrum, was to medicate them to some tolerable baseline of comportment, teach the parents behavioral modification techniques, and wait for the future. Concern for imminent criminal actions was not excuse enough to interfere with anyone's freedom, especially a child's, whether with prison, an institution, or long-standing hospitalization.

Susan finally understood why the PIPU staff had discharged Sharicka to a therapeutic foster home after her first couple of weeks on the unit. Ultimately, everything the care team did had to bring, or at least attempt to bring, each patient one step nearer to discharge. So far, the Ansons' insurance company had proven reasonable, but Sharicka only had to go a week or two without a violent incident for them to refuse further payment. It seemed inevitable given that Sharicka did seem truly determined to change this time. All too soon, Susan would have no choice but to discharge her, if not to her parents, then to another foster home.

Susan realized that refusing any type of visitation, then dropping Sharicka on the Ansons the day of her discharge did not serve anyone's best interests. The purpose of home visits was to ease the patient back into everyday life as well as prepare the family for the future in gradually increasing increments. A single overnight would also reward Sharicka for trying and, with any luck, rekindle the hope her family had all but lost. "Does Sharicka even want a home visit?"

"She's practically pleading."

Susan walked down the hallway with Saranne, pausing to glance in the open doorway where Sharicka snuggled on her mother's lap, her father hovering like a guard dog. He looked up as doctor and nurse walked by and gestured silently to Susan.

Susan held up a finger and nodded to indicate she would return shortly, then continued to the second massive iron door with Saranne. The nurse unlocked it, and they walked onto the unit and straight into the staffing area. Saranne could barely wait to ask, "What do you think?"

Susan found herself nodding quietly for too long. From the corner of her eye, she saw Shaden coming to join the conversation. "I . . . think . . . ," Susan started without a clue as to how she intended to complete the sentence, ". . . it might be . . . possible."

Shaden jumped right in, easily guessing the topic of the conversation. "She hasn't done anything wrong in a while, Dr. Calvin."

Susan wondered if Shaden even remembered that, earlier the same week, Sharicka had put a piece of a latex balloon into another child's medication cup.

"Since she started taking her meds faithfully, she's been so different."

Susan had to admit Shaden made a good point. Sharicka did seem to have made a miraculous change in the last couple of days. "Maybe we should demand a full week of positive behavior before we inflict her on the world."

"It's just a home visit," Saranne reminded Susan. "It's routine. Most kids start those a week after they're admitted."

"Besides," Shaden added, "the Ansons are going away next weekend. It's today, or they have to wait two weeks."

The nurses seemed so earnest and eager, and both had excellent reputations on the unit. Susan sighed. "I do believe Sharicka is making an honest effort. But do you really think she's ready?"

Shaden made an important point. "If she were on some of the older antipsychotics, no. They can take weeks or months to really work. But she's on hefty doses of Antoladol and Vilyon."

Susan knew the second-generation neurotransmitter stabilizers did act quickly. Some psychiatrists started at subtherapeutic doses and worked their way up slowly, but Sharicka was already at the maximum dose for her size. Her previous R-1 had raised it, not knowing that Sharicka had been hiding her medications. "You're sure she's swallowing them?"

Shaden could have taken that as an insult. It implied,

and quite rightly, the nurses had not acted thoroughly and properly in the past. Providers assumed people took their medication; and, under most circumstances, would not bother to check. It was a patient's prerogative not to fill a prescription or take a medication, even one he required to live. But an underage mental patient in a locked unit ought to have better than usual attention paid to such details. "Sharicka is taking great pains to prove to us the meds are going down her throat."

Susan doubted she wanted the specifics. "I'll talk to the Ansons," she promised, "but I'm not going to push them. If they decide they can't handle her, we wait at least a week before presenting the possibility again."

Shaden bobbed his head, clearly finding the conditions reasonable. "I'd like to come with you."

Susan bit her lower lip. She was not the sort of person to squash conflicting opinions, and he was Sharicka's most frequent caretaker. Although he had a soft spot for the girl that did not always seem logical, he was a competent professional with far more PIPU experience than she. The Ansons had run into people like Shaden many times. They would understand his point of view. Just maybe, Shaden would learn to value theirs as well. "All right. When do you want to do it?"

Shaden smiled. "They've had a solid forty minutes together. How about now?"

"Now suits me fine." Susan swallowed her misgivings, turned toward the door, and they headed for the conference room together.

Chapter 17

Saranne handled unlocking the metal door and escorting Sharicka back to the ward, while Susan and Shaden remained with the Ansons. They looked different to Susan somehow: less morose, more animated and alive. Lucianne's eyes had a faintly hopeful glimmer, and Elliot's face bore just a hint of a smile. He stepped forward, his hand outstretched. "Good afternoon, Dr. Calvin." He took her hand and shook it, nodding at the nurse as he did so. "Shaden."

"Good afternoon, Dr. Anson," Shaden replied respectfully.

Susan addressed the mother, still sitting on the chair where Sharicka had recently perched in her lap. "Hello, Dr. Anson."

Susan shut the door as the others took seats around the table; then she joined them. The couple sat together, doctor and nurse across from them. Lucianne spoke first, "Sharicka says you 'fixed' her. I hope she doesn't mean . . ."

They all chuckled, though somewhat uneasily. The idea had to flash through more minds than just Susan's that Sharicka should never bear children. It chilled her to even consider the cruelties someone like Sharicka could inflict on a helpless infant. "Sharicka will always be Sharicka," Susan said. "I'm concerned we're all prematurely optimistic, but I have to admit she does seem to have become honestly committed to improving her life and the lives of those around her."

Shaden nodded vigorously. "She credits Dr. Calvin with inspiring her to do her best. She's taking her medications like clockwork, and she hasn't acted impulsively in days. She's even made some real friends among the other patients."

Though Susan could not deny the truth of those statements, she wished Shaden would tone down his rhetoric. The Ansons had seen the many cycles of Sharicka, and they knew better than to pin their hopes on a few days of cooperation—or so she hoped. She had read enough books, had studied enough couples and parents, to know human emotions lived in the moment. She had seen mothers in supermarkets ready to fricassee their young one moment and buying them ice cream the next. Nature had endowed children with the ability to bring out the best and worst in adults from moment to moment, and love tended to drive humans to illogical faith and actions.

Lucianne sucked in a deep breath, releasing it gradually through pursed lips. "You say she's committed to improving her life. But, given her"—she glanced at Shaden, then back to Susan—"her diagnosis, is that even possible? Can she even understand morality? The difference between right and wrong?"

"All sociopaths understand the difference between right and wrong, especially ones as intelligent and well-raised as Sharicka," Susan replied. "I'll bet she could recite the rules of your household, and the reasons for them, in her sleep. What they lack is empathy, compassion, guilt, remorse."

Susan took the discussion into the realm of Lucianne's understanding, childhood special education. "You know how children with a nonverbal learning disability rely on spoken words and explanations? They can't intuitively grasp nonverbal communication. They don't 'get' tone of voice, figures of speech, gestures, personal space, facial expressions, humor, and so forth?"

Lucianne and Elliot both nodded, and the mother added, "If you catch it early, those things can be taught with repetition, verbal explanations, physical outlines, and behavioral rewards. It works for higher-functioning autistics, too."

Susan appreciated that they had not only followed her example but improved upon it. "If you start young enough, you can internalize the lessons to the point where at least some of those skills can seem almost normal. Kids with NLD can eventually use idioms correctly. They may not tell jokes, but they know one when they hear it and laugh in the appropriate places. Their own faces may be expressionless, but they learn to recognize other people's moods by rote."

"Right." Lucianne cocked her head in consideration. Color formed in her cheeks and gradually spread to light her entire face. "Are you suggesting we might be able to teach Sharicka . . . remorse and compassion?"

Susan did not know. Historically, the success rate for treating people with sociopathy was abysmal. However, that had changed in the last few years with the creation of the second-generation neurotransmitter stabilizers. Since antisocial personality disorder could not technically be diagnosed before age eighteen, the literature about treating children for it was nonexistent. She wondered if they had just stumbled upon a brand-new treatment for juvenile conduct disorders. "I'm not sure," she admitted. "Until now, Sharicka hadn't shown any insight into her problem. Now that she acknowledges it, and has expressed and acted upon the intention to change, I think we might have a chance."

Elliot laced his fingers on the tabletop. "She does

seem . . . different," he admitted. "More like . . . our
Sharicka. The one who used to fall asleep watching a
movie in my lap. The one who loved 'hangaburs' and
'pockasickles' for dinner and begged for just one more
story at night."

Lucianne smiled at the memory. For the first time
since Susan had met her, she looked like a typical mother
misty-eyed over a child's scribbled drawing of her. "Do
you think . . . now that she's really taking her medication . . . ?"

Susan felt torn. "I think . . . she is really trying, yes."

"She loves your family," Shaden cut in.

Susan did not like his phraseology. It made it sound
as if Sharicka stood apart, that they had never really accepted her as a full-fledged member. "She loves *her* family," Susan corrected. "I'm sure she always has, but she
had more difficulty expressing it off her meds. Now, she
talks about you . . . wistfully. She wants to go home." Susan realized just how differently her conversation was
going with the Ansons this time, and felt awkwardly balanced on a swaying tightrope. She wanted to encourage
them to look at the situation more positively; success
never came out of a defeatist attitude. However, she did
not want to get their hopes so high that they dropped all
caution. Sharicka was still a very sick little girl.

The father scratched his beardless chin. "Dr. Calvin,
it sounds as though you're saying you . . . fixed Sharicka."

Susan shook her head. "I didn't do anything but observe her. Sharicka heard I had helped some other patients, and it inspired her. She's making changes all on
her own, and I think that's a good sign."

The mother looked from her husband to Susan and
back again. She glanced briefly at Shaden before returning her attention to Susan. "Some people don't believe
there's anything wrong with Sharicka. She's good at . . .
making people think she's"—she turned her gaze to her

husband, as if seeking his assistance—"misunderstood. When, actually, she's . . . sneaky. And frequently mean."

Shaden frowned. Susan touched his leg warningly under the table, and he did not speak aloud.

"You know me better than that, Dr. Anson." Susan tried to fully capture the mother's attention. She had eyes so pale they seemed almost colorless, a steely gray with just a hint of blue. "Sharicka has a serious psychiatric condition. However, she is four years old, and we can't keep her in the hospital indefinitely."

"We talked about an institution," Lucianne reminded her.

Susan knew the Ansons liked her because she had never downplayed the significance of Sharicka's illness the way most providers did, and she had never questioned their integrity or intentions toward their daughter. Suddenly, Susan felt like a traitor. "I've looked into that. There's not a single institution in the country that will take a child under the age of thirteen." She tried to dodge Lucianne's stare. "There's no possible way we can keep her here for a year, let alone nine years. At some point, we have to release Sharicka to a family. She's your daughter, first and foremost, but we would all understand if you decided yours was not the right home for her."

Lucianne followed Susan's gaze, refusing escape. "You can't possibly be talking discharge."

"Not in the next week or two," Susan said quickly. "But it's time to start thinking about it." She felt confident the Ansons had already discussed the possibilities and had come to at least a superficial decision.

"What happens if we refuse to take her?"

Elliot replied before Susan could. "She becomes someone else's problem."

"Foster care," Shaden said. "And, eventually, adoption."

Lucianne's jaw drooped until it all but touched her

chest. She snorted suddenly, bringing her lips back together. "Downplaying all of her issues, no doubt. They'll foist her on some unwitting, well-meaning family and tell them not to worry. Love will conquer all."

Susan could not deny it. Sharicka knew how to win hearts, how to present her best side, how to manipulate even trained psychiatric nurses. Most social workers would be putty in her hands.

"She's best off with us," Elliot Anson said firmly. "We loved her, unconditionally, before we knew what she would become. We love her even now. We'll always love her." His eyes blurred as he clearly fought back tears. "I doubt anyone else will have the time to form a bond that strong before she does something hateful to them. Bouncing around foster and adoptive houses can't possibly be in Sharicka's best interests, let alone anyone else's." He put his arm around Lucianne, who also looked on the verge of tears. "She's trying, Luci. We have to reward that effort."

"How?" the mother asked, with clear suspicion.

Susan broached the subject cautiously. "We were thinking maybe . . . a home visit?"

"You mean an overnight?" The mother still did not sound convinced, but she also did not refuse outright.

Elliot was nodding. Clearly, he would prove easier to convince. "There's a limit to the damage a four-year-old has the strength to do, especially under the watchful eye of two wary parents in a childproofed home."

His wife turned on him. "She was under the watchful eye of two parents in a childproofed home when she almost drowned Misty."

"That was before we knew what she was capable of. They were outside alone, without us. We won't let that happen again."

Susan allowed the discussion to evolve, not daring to add anything to it. For the first time, she found herself secretly siding with Sharicka, hoping the Ansons decided to take her home, to give her this one small chance. However, Susan also realized they knew Sharicka better than she ever could. She tried to imagine something demonic taking over her kind and gentle father. If he had murdered her mother, could she have ever taken him back into her home? She supposed she could if the demons were vanquished. *But are Sharicka's demons vanquished? How could we ever know for sure?*

"Can we stop her?" The mother sighed deeply. "I love my daughters, Dr. Calvin. Both of them."

Shaden held inordinately still, but Susan nodded broadly. "It's hard to do what's best for both of them."

"I'll stay right with her," the father promised. "She can't do anything bad with me glued to her side."

Susan could see Lucianne wavering. It soon became clear, however, that as Susan studied her, she studied Susan. Finally, she spoke. "Dr. Calvin, I trust you. What do you think we should do?"

It was exactly the question Susan did not want to field. She had been trained to avoid it, to firmly state that such a decision belonged solely to the family. "I . . . understand your hesitation. It's completely logical and makes perfect sense." Susan had little choice but to play both sides. "On the other hand, that you've decided not to terminate your parental rights to Sharicka means you still have hope for her. If we believe she's trying, and I know I do, then home visits are the necessary first step toward working her back into the family. We could wait another week. Maybe even two." Susan raised a hand, palm up, and finally deliberately braved Lucianne's eyes, now blue-gray pools of water. "Much longer than that, we're going to get serious resistance from your insurance company."

Apparently, the parents' honest angst was not lost on Shaden. His tone turned as gentle as Susan had ever heard it, especially when forced to defend Sharicka. "Doctors Anson, in my years of experience, I find that insurance companies are more open to time extensions if they see you trying. If you bring Sharicka for a home visit, they'll be more likely to bargain. If it goes well, that's wonderful. If not, it will give us ammunition to use against them if they try to deny your coverage."

The mother bobbed her head ever so slightly. "So you think we should take her home . . . today?"

Susan did not feel wholly comfortable with that. "I'm saying I think either decision is reasonable and defensible."

The mother made an irritated noise, still trying to pin down Susan. "If she were your daughter, would you take her home? Yes or no?"

Cornered at last, Susan could do nothing but speak the truth. "I like to think I would, Dr. Anson. But, as I've said several different ways, I don't think a right decision and a wrong one exist here. There are only intuition and faith."

Nothing remained to be said, and the father took over the conversation. "Give us a few minutes to talk about it, and we'll give you our answer before we leave."

Relieved, Susan rose. She preferred to let the parents make their own decision. Following her cue, Shaden also stood up, and the two left the room. Susan knocked on the locked door. Saranne's face appeared in the window; then the door whisked open, and the two came through it. Saranne locked it behind them.

Sharicka was there, too. She jerked at Susan's hem. "What'd they say? Am I going home?"

Susan took Sharicka's sticky hand and led her back to her room. Once there, she released the girl, who hopped up onto her bed. Susan closed the door behind them. "Sharicka, home visits aren't easy things to arrange. They have to work into everyone's schedules: both parents', yours, your brother's, your sister's, the nurses', mine. Everyone's."

Sharicka tried to guess. "So, I'm not going home?"

The look of sheer disappointment on her face twisted at Susan's heartstrings.

Susan clung to professionalism to harden her stance. "I don't know yet, Sharicka. We'll know soon, but I want you to understand something."

Sharicka did not allow Susan to finish. "I know. I know. I have to be good."

"You have to be on your best behavior, or there might not be another home visit for a very long time. You have to take all your medicine and listen to what your parents tell you."

The months that had passed without a step beyond the playground or the unit had to show Sharicka the seriousness of Susan's words. "I will. I promise. I'm going to be good from now on. You'll see."

Susan did not want to build up false hopes. "No one is good all the time, Sharicka. We don't expect perfection." Susan did not want the child abandoning all principles after a minor slipup. "But you must treat others with kindness and respect. A bad word, a stolen cookie—those things can be overlooked, as long as you apologize and are truly sorry. But you cannot, under any circumstances, hurt a human being or an animal, Sharicka. Those are not mistakes; those are deliberately evil actions."

"No hurting people or animals," Sharicka repeated, legs swinging. "I won't do that."

Before Susan could say another word, Shaden burst into the room. "Guess what, Sharicka?"

Sharicka sprang to the floor and clutched her hands to her little chest. "I'm going home?"

"You're going home," Shaden confirmed, not bothering to contain his excitement. "It's just a home visit, but it's a start."

"I'm going home!" Sharicka danced around the room with the unselfconsciousness only children can muster. "I'm going home!" She rushed past Susan and Shaden. "I have to tell Monty! I'm going home!"

"Monty?" Shaden said, then laughed. "She must mean Monterey."

Susan had assumed that. She had heard Monterey's mother call her Rey-rey and Monny, but she had never heard Monty before. Since Monterey still seemed to enjoy playing with Sharicka, she must not entirely despise the nickname. "Do you think we're doing the right thing?"

Susan did not expect an answer, but Shaden gave her one. "I'm sure of it, Dr. Calvin." He put a friendly arm across her shoulder. "At some point, you have to trust that even a mentally ill child is a child, and love really will make the difference."

Love. Susan bit her bottom lip. *Is Sharicka even capable of it?* She tried not to think too hard about it. If Sharicka was not, there was no hope at all for the girl or her family.

The day finished smoothly, without new admissions or emergencies, and Susan even managed to get a reasonable amount of sleep that night in the on-call room she shared with three other psychiatry residents serving other units. Their snuffles, snores, and Vox calls proved a nuisance, but she did not begrudge them. At least she did not have to go traipsing off to the Emergency Room or to a unit as each of them did at least once during the night.

Susan's turn came at a little after six a.m. Her Vox buzzed to life, startling her from a vivid dream involving a million-dollar bet and a billiards table. Only after she had confidently laid down the bet did she remember she had no particular skill at the game or the money to gamble on it. Susan sat up and tapped the Vox before it could start making noises that might awaken her fellow residents. She looked at the display. Unsurprisingly, the call had originated from the PIPU.

Susan clambered off her cot, straightened her white overnight scrubs, and ran a hand through her hair. Quietly, she threaded her way through the darkened room, turned the knob, and stepped out into the hallway. She pulled the door shut behind her before making the return call across Vox.

It was picked up immediately. "Dr. Calvin?" Usually, the unit clerk answered with the fictitious unit number of the PIPU they used to hide its purpose and location for confidentiality reasons. This time, someone had clearly stood by the phone, waiting for her call.

"This is Susan Calvin, R-1. How can I help you?"

"It's Justin, Dr. Calvin." It was one of the night nurses, an older man with white hair and a complexion still scarred by adolescent acne. "Sharicka's back. The police brought her. It's . . . not good."

Susan saw no reason to discuss the situation over Vox. Her heart rate shot up, and she could feel an uncomfortable tingling in her chest. "I'll be right there." She ended the call, running toward the PIPU without worrying about her morning toilet. She dashed through the mostly empty hallways, taking a corner too fast and nearly slamming into an empty gurney. In less than four minutes, she was ringing the entry button and pounding on the locked PIPU door.

It was opened almost immediately. Susan found herself in the usually empty hallway between the locked doors, now filled with people. Two uniformed police officers stood with four of the night nurses. There was no sign of Sharicka, or any other patient.

Susan did not care that she interrupted at least two separate discussions. "I'm Dr. Calvin. What happened?" Dread crept up her spine, and a sudden wash of ice overcame every part of her. She had to focus to remain in control.

Both policemen turned to look at Susan. "Are you the guardian of one Sharicka Anson?"

Susan saw no reason to launch into technicalities. The Ansons remained Sharicka's parents and guardians, but the hospital currently had physical jurisdiction over the child. In crisis situations, only judges and physicians could take over instant custody of a minor. Susan had learned that during her pediatrics rotation, when an abusive parent had insisted on taking his daughter home and the clinic had had to call for law enforcement backup. "I am. What has she done?"

The other cop said, "She killed someone, Dr. Calvin."

Susan found herself unable to breathe. Light-headedness swam down on her before she forced her chest to expand and the air to flow inside. For the first time in her life, she had to focus on the act, had to remind herself to inhale and exhale. "Who?" she finally managed, her voice a squeak.

"A girl named Misty, ma'am." A blatter of noise over the policeman's radio made Susan jump. "Her sister, apparently. Stabbed her multiple times with a butter knife."

Susan wished she did not have to concentrate so hard on breathing. She found herself unable to speak, unable to harbor coherent thought. She could only stand there, speechless, and attempt to process the words spoken in her general direction.

"Then she went after her brother. Stabbed him a few times before her father wrestled her to the ground."

Susan knew she had to say something. "Where . . . is the family?"

"They're in the ER," the officer explained. "The boy's being admitted, and the father's getting patched up. They said to bring her here." He added firmly, "If you plan to send her anywhere else, you need to contact us first."

Susan nodded. She had no idea what would happen next. Clearly, they had caught Sharicka in the act, but the police had brought her back to Manhattan Hasbro rather than to a jail or a juvenile facility. She supposed the law would not allow a minor to remain in adult detention, and she had never heard of a serious crime committed by anyone under the age of twelve. A locked psychiatry unit familiar with Sharicka's history, in a tertiary hospital setting, might well prove the safest place to keep her for all involved.

Susan addressed the nurses. "Get Sharicka out of anything with blood on it."

A small woman named Rietta said, "They're doing that right now. Bagging up the bloody clothes for the police." She tipped her head toward the officers.

Susan continued. "Make sure she gets and swallows her morning meds immediately. Keep her in the Self-awareness Room until I've had a chance to talk to her."

Susan looked at the officers. "We'll have those clothes out to you in a moment. If you need anything else, let us know."

The policeman who had done most of the talking addressed Susan once more. "We may need to question her again. Obviously, she can't leave town."

Susan raised and lowered her head once, firmly. "She may not even get to leave her room." Her vision grew blurry, and she rubbed her eyes, surprised to find them moist. The moment she realized she had started crying, a rush of emotions assaulted her. Agony clawed at her guts. Guilt rushed down on her. *I told them to take her home; I wanted them to do it.* Rage accompanied it. *She tricked me, too.* Seized by the sudden urge to tear Sharicka's head off, she bit down on her lip until she tasted blood.

The officers thanked everyone in the room, then walked to the outer door, where Rietta let them out with a key.

Susan waited for Rietta to return and let her onto the unit. She did not want to meet with Sharicka. Not ever. The idea of looking into those demonic eyes, of facing that childish smirk, made her crazy. She realized how lucky Sharicka was that the Ansons had adopted her.

Her biological parents had a history of impulsive, negative behaviors. By now, they would have chopped her into pieces small enough to fit through a sieve.

Susan tried not to dwell on that thought too long. Sharicka just might be the youngest conduct-disordered child in history, but she was certainly not the only one. The Ansons were highly intelligent and educated people with a well-above-average understanding of normal and abnormal child behavior. What happened to the children with conduct disorder raised by parents who had little or no education, who probably had psychopathology of their own? Might that explain the inexplicable: parents who murdered or abandoned their children? It all seemed just too terrible to contemplate.

Yet Susan had no choice but to contemplate one thing. The Ansons had suffered a trauma so horrible, most people could not imagine such a thing. It must have happened in the wee hours of the morning. The father had promised to glue himself to her, but even he had to sleep. Likely, Sharicka had chosen the only weapon she could find. Anything obviously lethal would have been well hidden. The Ansons had worked so hard for their family, had suffered the long anguish of infertility, had been put through the wringer to adopt, had raised their three beloved children through crisis after crisis. Now, one was dead, another would need permanent psychiatric care, and the last was hospitalized with potentially life-threatening injuries. And the cause of all the recent trauma awaited Susan in the so-called Self-awareness Room.

For one horribly selfish moment, Susan wished the whole thing had happened just two hours later. Rounds would have finished, and she would have gone home for the entire day. She could have dined and skated with Remington, none the wiser, and taken up the cause on Tuesday. Despising herself for the bare thought, she abandoned it instantly. She knew the Ansons did not have that luxury. The incident had happened on Susan's watch, had occurred because the family had faith, not in Sharicka, but in Susan's ability to evaluate Sharicka. Now, Susan realized, she was not the hero the nurses had once heralded with balloons. She had made the worst mistake of all, and it had cost at least one child her life.

Susan wondered if she could ever sleep again, could ever trust her own judgment. Her own words cycled through her mind until she could no longer stand to hear them: *"If we believe she's trying, and I know I do, then home visits are the necessary first step toward working her back into the family."* What have I done? A picture of Lucianne Anson filled her mind's eye, her face open in uncertainty and hope. *"Dr. Calvin, I trust you."* Why? Why did she have to put her faith in me?

As she stepped onto the unit, Susan's feet felt like lead. She heard the door clang shut behind her, so loud, so final, and the noise echoed through the subdued confines of the PIPU. Most of the nurses were in the charting area, nearly all of the patients asleep. That accounted for the quiet hush that seemed so out of place on a unit where children regularly shrieked and threw tantrums. She dragged herself to the Self-awareness Room. A nurse named Hanniah stood outside of it, looking through the window.

"What's she doing?" Susan asked.

"Nothing." Hanniah did not look away. "Just sitting there, picking her nose."

Susan peeked through the window. As if sensing the new presence, Sharicka slowly raised her head. A slight smile played across her lips, and she met her resident doctor gaze for gaze. Susan felt like a hunted animal beneath that killer stare. The idea of going into the room with Sharicka seemed madness. *She's a four-year-old child,* Susan reminded herself. *She's barely half my size and currently without a weapon.* Susan knew, logically, Sharicka could not harm her. She took a deep breath, then loosed it slowly before announcing, "I'm going in."

Unlike when she had decided to confront Diesel Moore, the nurse made no protest. She stepped aside and allowed Susan to open the door.

Susan tried to look nonchalant as she did so, strode into the padded room, and allowed the door to close and latch behind her. Seated on the floor, Sharicka glanced up at the doctor, looking for all the world like an innocent four-year-old child. "Hi, Dr. Susan."

It seemed ludicrous to simply return the greeting, but Susan could think of nothing better to do. "Hi."

Sharicka wiped her fingers on the clean clothes she had changed into on the ward. She wore a pair of black sweatpants and a Craft-a-Critter T-shirt. "How's Rylan doing?" She posed the question with the casualness of a sister asking after the health of a brother with the flu. The query seemed strangely genuine.

Susan found it difficult to look at the girl. "I don't know."

"How's Misty?"

"She's dead, Sharicka. You know that."

"Can I see her?"

Susan looked away. Was it actually possible Sharicka did not understand the finality of death? "Never again. She's dead."

"Can I see her in her coffin?"

The question seemed so odd, so unutterably antisocial and wrong. Susan looked sharply at Sharicka.

The girl's expression did not compute. Susan read curiosity and a faint hint of pleasure.

"You can't see her, Sharicka. Not ever. You killed her."

"I'm a murderer." Sharicka rolled the word in her mouth, as if testing it.

Susan did not indulge the recognition. She did not want Sharicka to identify herself with evil, to view the act as an accomplishment. "Why, Sharicka? Why did you do it?"

Sharicka could no longer hold back the smile. It slipped past her guard to light her entire face. The dark eyes went cold, and even the sockets seemed to shift right before Susan's eyes. "We all have to die sometime."

Susan could not stand to look at Sharicka for another second. Rising silently, she left the room and told the waiting nurse, "She can go to her room now." She wanted to put the child into a straitjacket right out of an early-twentieth-century movie. The death penalty had existed for people like Sharicka, the homicidally incurable, those most despicable and desperate. *Desperate.* The word clung to Susan's memory. Activating her Vox, she zipped off a bitter text to Doctors Goldman and Peters: "Found stdy pt."

Susan managed a quick shower and change before rounds, discovering two messages on her Vox when she finished. The first came from Ari Goldman, requesting the details of the study patient. She typed in some basic information about Sharicka in reply, then moved on to the second. This one came from Remington: "B L8. E! Boy stb/chke by 4yo? Dad?"

Susan groaned. The E! meant an emergency. If Rylan Anson needed the on-call neurosurgeon, he had sustained serious spinal or head wounds. Susan would need to explain Sharicka and clear poor Dr. Anson. The last thing he needed was to fall under a cloud of suspicion while he rushed to save the last of his children.

Susan went to the staffing room, hoping to find at least one of the other psychiatry residents. To her relief, Kendall sat in a chair, leaning so far back, its headrest was braced against the table. She walked over to him, and he sat up quickly. "Good morning, Calvin. How was your night?"

Susan shook her head. "Quiet until about two hours ago when I had to deal with the police."

"I heard." Kendall leaned forward. When the nursing

shift started, it was the sole topic of conversation. "So, Sharicka murdered her siblings on a home visit."

"The brother's still alive. I need to go down and see him. Can you cover for me at rounds?"

Kendall stared. "I just got here. I'm supposed to sum up what happened all day yesterday?"

Susan did not want to waste time bandying words. "Nothing happened all day yesterday, except little things documented on the charts. As far as my patients, Monterey is talking more, and you know about Sharicka."

"I only know what the nurses are saying," Kendall reminded Susan. "I have no idea why or what you plan to do about it." He gave her a smile that, somehow, did not seem patronizing. "Besides, I think the great Susan Calvin should own up to her first mistake."

Susan realized Kendall made a good point. "It's hardly my first mistake, but it's definitely my most horrific." Guilt clamped down on her again, and she closed her eyes to keep from succumbing fully to it. "I should never have asked them for a home visit."

She heard the scrape of Kendall's chair, then felt his arms wrap around her and the warmth of his body against hers. "I was just kidding. I'm always kidding. It's not your fault."

Susan fully lost her composure, bursting into tears and clamping her arms tightly around Kendall. "I'm sorry. I'm so sorry." The force of the crying jag prevented more words, and she collapsed against him.

Kendall held Susan, saying nothing, lightly stroking her hair with the patience of a father. "It's not your fault. You didn't know. No one could have known."

Kendall had to say it; but, to Susan's conscience, it was all lies. They had had more than enough warnings. It was not even the first time Sharicka had assaulted Misty. She had tried to kill her sister before. She had done so many terrible things and had proven herself manipulative and deadly dangerous. Somehow, Susan had allowed herself to believe a four-year-old would not have the wherewithal to kill, not under the watchful eye of educated, professional, and wary parents.

But even educated, professional, wary parents have to sleep. And the beast within Sharicka, apparently, never did, a charming four-year-old genius with a penchant for murder. Susan sobbed out, "I shouldn't have suggested it. I shouldn't have approved it. I shouldn't have allowed it."

Kendall cradled Susan's head. "Hindsight is telescopic."

"But I knew what she was. What she could do. I knew she was manipulating the nursing staff. Why did I let her manipulate me, too?"

"Because you're human?" Kendall's grip never wavered. "And she's four years old. She's a cute little bundle of baby fat. . . ."

"And homicidal fury, Kendall. What does a four-year-old have to be that angry about?"

"Angry?" Kendall's voice revealed confusion. "I've never seen Sharicka angry, and I don't think she's lashing out in some kind of seething fury. She's colder. Calculating. It's as if she's . . ."

"Possessed?" Susan tried.

"Do you believe in that?"

"No." Susan found her faith in science wavering for the first time ever. "Do you?"

"No," Kendall said without hesitation. "Just because we can't explain everything yet doesn't mean everything doesn't have a logical explanation. I mean, so far, everything in history that people once attributed to supernatural phenomenon has been thoroughly and utterly disproven or explained."

Susan did not argue. She was absolutely grounded in science. "Four years old, Kendall."

"Almost five," he reminded her. "And not the youngest killer in the world."

That caught Susan off her guard. She finally pulled

away far enough to look into his face. "Who's the youngest?"

"Who knows? In every state in the union, probably in every country in the world, kids under the age of seven are automatically presumed not responsible for their criminal acts, including murder. We just throw a few meds at them, send them home, and wait until they kill someone else, when they're old enough to prosecute."

Susan wondered why Kendall knew that. And she did not. Likely, he had done some research since learning about Sharicka's night. "What's the youngest you've heard of?"

Kendall obliged. "Well, we have the Kelby Cross gun containment law because a two-year-old shot his sister."

Susan knew that well-publicized case. "That was accidental. I'm talking about a deliberate act."

Kendall reached across her to consult his palm-pross. He tapped a few buttons, then studied the screen. "In 2001, an Illinois three-year-old bashed in the skull of a two-year-old and injured a three-week-old left in his care."

"Who would leave babies in the care of another baby?"

Kendall shrugged. "That's not the point, is it?"

Susan supposed not. She had asked about children with a penchant for murder, not about irresponsible parents.

Kendall continued to consult the palm-pross. "In 2021, a three-year-old in Detroit fatally shot his drunk father while the father was beating the boy's mother. A four-year-old girl in India snatched and killed three infants in separate incidents just last year. In 1986, a five-year-old shoved a three-year-old off a Miami Beach balcony and, when the younger boy grabbed onto a ledge, the older boy pried his fingers loose and dropped him five stories to his death. There have been at least three recent cases where kids, usually in groups of two or three, between the ages of three and six, brutally murdered infants or toddlers."

It seemed insane to take solace in ghastly crimes, but it did help Susan to bring reality back to the fore. Sharicka was not possessed by some demonic entity; she was betrayed by some terrible defect in her brain. With any luck, the nanorobots could find it because, clearly, current treatments held out no hope for her at all.

By the time Susan fully regained her composure and Kendall returned to his work, the other residents had arrived. Soon afterward, Dr. Bainbridge came for rounds. They all looked so alert, clean, and well rested to Susan, who felt like she had aged a decade in the last few hours. She joined them reluctantly. The nurses may have talked to some of the residents, but they would leave Susan to break the news to the attending doctor.

Dr. Bainbridge swept in with all the authority in the universe. "Good morning, Doctors." He looked around the assembled group, surely noticing the somber faces. "Judging by looks alone, I'd say Dr. Calvin took call yesterday."

Stony Lipschitz stepped in to rescue Susan. "She's had rather a bad morning, sir."

The grin wilted from Bainbridge's face. "Why wasn't I called?"

The R-3 continued to take the heat. "I just found out about it myself an hour ago. It didn't seem worth bothering you for that little bit of time."

Susan had delayed calling her superiors until she had a reasonable grasp of the situation. She had also been taught not to bother sleeping people unless there was something they could do. Seeing no reason to prolong the agony, she explained, "Sharicka Anson went on a home visit yesterday. In the wee morning hours, she attacked her siblings, killing one and badly wounding the other. The police escorted her back here."

Bainbridge listened intently without interrupting as

Susan described the situation. When she finished, he stroked his chin thoughtfully. "So, I guess we can all see now why Susan came down so hard on a four-year-old when others mentioned discharge." He looked around at the nurses intently. "Now does everyone understand the manipulativeness that characterizes the antisocial mind?"

Susan would not let her detractors take all the heat, though she did wish Shaden's shift had not ended hours earlier. "I'm afraid she manipulated me, too, Dr. Bainbridge. I'm the one who okayed the home visit and suggested it to her parents."

Dr. Bainbridge nodded thoughtfully. "Master manipulators, antisocials. As I have said before, the psychiatric worker does not exist who has not fallen prey to one at some point." He shook his head, now staring directly at Susan. In an uncharacteristic action, he walked to her and put a fatherly arm across her shoulders. "It's not your fault, Susan. She's four years old, and the rules say we have to give children second and third and fourth and fifth chances. Had you asked my opinion, I would have done nothing different. We knew she was dangerous, and her parents knew it, too; yet we all believed that even if she did something bad, an adult could stop her.

"It's not your fault," Dr. Bainbridge repeated, "but for a long time it's going to feel as if it is. If you find it taking over your life, let me know immediately and we'll arrange some counseling. Sometimes big mistakes have small consequences. And sometimes small mistakes have big ones. You can't let chance rule your life."

Susan glanced around at her peers. All of them wore solemn and sympathetic looks. They might harbor other grudges against her; but, at this time, they stood unanimous in support of her. "I'll be all right," she said. "But I'd like permission to leave rounds early to talk to the Ansons. I'm not sure Neurosurgery has much of a clue about juvenile conduct disorder, and I'm already getting the sense they blame the father. This family doesn't need any more trauma."

Bainbridge nodded agreement. "Go," he said. "We'll call you if we need anything more from you."

"Thank you," Susan said with all the gratitude in the world. She raced toward the operating room waiting area, where she knew she would find the Ansons. She only hoped they would still be willing to see her.

Chapter 18

The surgical waiting room had brilliant aqua walls, a multicolored rug, comfortable chairs, and surrealistic paintings teeming with colored swirls and odd-ball shapes. The Ansons were alone, the mother sobbing in her seat and the father pacing wildly, his left hand and right wrist covered in fresh bandages.

The father stopped moving the instant he spotted Susan. "Dr. Calvin." His voice emerged in a neutral tone. It was less a greeting than an acknowledgment.

Lucianne Anson's head jerked up. She stood and faced Susan.

Susan did not wait for her to speak or make her feelings or intentions clear. Tossing her palm-pross gently on a chair, she caught Sharicka's mother into an embrace. The woman stiffened, then collapsed against her. Warm tears dribbled across Susan's neck.

"I'm sorry," Susan whispered. "I'm so very sorry." She could think of nothing else to say.

Elliot appeared beside them. "Do you know anything about Rylan's condition?"

Susan could only shake her head. "Not yet." She did not say anything about Sharicka. She did not know if telling them the child was safe would soothe or infuriate them.

Before she could say anything more, the father spoke in anguished tones. "It's all my fault. She behaved so well all evening, I guess I let my guard down. After she fell asleep, I figured we were good till early morning."

The mother pulled away from Susan long enough to say, "It's not your fault, Elliot." She added forcefully, at least partially for Susan's benefit, "It's not anyone's fault. It's . . . her brain. It's just not right." She dissolved into tears again.

Elliot Anson eased his wife off Susan. "I just thought . . . I guess I figured . . ." He did not need to finish the sentence.

Susan shook her head. "Stop blaming yourself, Dr. Anson." She wished she could take her own advice. Despite the mother's effort to absolve her, Susan only felt guiltier. She had suggested the visit. She had encouraged them, even when Lucianne Anson had voiced serious doubts. She was the one with the medical knowledge, the one who should have known better.

Susan forced herself to continue. "No one could believe a child Sharicka's age was capable of doing so much harm so quickly. I have to believe people like Sharicka inspired the stories of demonic possession, that they explain the occasional infanticide in ancient cultures. Medical confidentiality is strict, especially when it comes to both mental illnesses and children. Juvenile conduct disorder is rare, and the extreme nature of Sharicka's case is exceptionally so. I believe other patients this young, this severe, exist; but there is little to no available information about them." Susan hoped she had made both of her cases: that the cause of Sharicka's problem was a brain abnormality no one could have seen or prevented and that the degree of her violence went beyond what anyone could have predicted.

Lucianne Anson pulled free from her husband. "Would you think less of us if we . . . never took her home again?"

Susan could barely believe any other option existed, even in the minds of loving parents. "Of course not. Are you wanting to terminate your parental rights?"

The parents exchanged glances. They had clearly discussed this topic thoroughly as they waited for news of Rylan's condition. Elliot detailed their conclusions. "Sharicka belongs in permanent residential care, where trained professionals can watch her twenty-four/seven; but you've told us that can't happen because of her age. We're worried if we terminate our rights, she'll wind up in someone else's home."

Lucianne blurted out, "And kill someone else's children, too."

Susan wanted to tell them such a thing would not happen, could not happen; but she had a grim and terrible feeling they were right. Kendall's words came back to haunt her: *In every state in the union, probably in every country in the world, kids under the age of seven are automatically presumed not responsible for their criminal acts, including murder. We just throw a few meds at them, send them home, and wait until they kill someone else, when they're old enough to prosecute.*

Elliot cringed. "Believe it or not, we will always love Sharicka. She's our daughter. But, if Rylan . . . if Rylan . . ." Now, tears dripped down his face. He could scarcely squeeze out the words.

Susan wished she could help him, but she did not know what he intended to say.

"If Rylan survives, it would be torture for him to have her in our home. We love our son as well, and he is innocent."

Susan could see their point. If the Ansons terminated their parental rights, Sharicka would become a ward of the state. She would spend a significant amount of time in the PIPU. All too soon, however, the horror of the moment would fade and people would start to rationalize the murder. They would say the Ansons orchestrated it or abused Sharicka so badly she had to lash out. Someone else would suggest that Misty and Rylan had ganged up to mercilessly torment their little sister until she could stand it no longer. Others would sincerely believe that a preschooler had no capacity for evil, that a girl so young simply had no ability to understand the consequences of her actions. Eventually, Sharicka would learn to manipulate the system, to "remember" nonexistent abuses, to say whatever gained her the compassion she had no capacity to experience herself.

Well-intentioned social workers would foist Sharicka into multiple foster placements, where she would leave havoc and a wake of bodies behind her. The Ansons had an impossible decision. Regardless of their innocence, a cloud of suspicion would always follow them, regardless of whether they chose to terminate their parental rights. Protecting their only remaining son might mean damning so many other children and destroying other families.

Susan reached for her palm-pross. "I have one new option to offer you, still in the research stage."

The Doctors Anson fixed their gazes on her, clearly interested.

Susan explained the nanorobot study, first superficially, then in more depth. Whether they chose to try it or not, at least the conversation allowed them to take a break from worrying about Rylan. When Susan finished her explanation, the parents did not even bother to discuss it.

"We'll do it," the mother said.

The father nodded.

The absolute desperation of both of their replies did not escape Susan. They would have agreed to almost anything. They had nothing to lose, and neither did Sharicka.

Susan gave Elliot Anson the palm-pross to sign, and he did so awkwardly because of the bandages but without any hesitation. Lucianne affixed her name below his. As the mother wrote, Susan noticed movement from the corner of her eye. When she turned to face the entrance, she found Remington Hawthorn coming toward them.

Leaving the palm-pross with the Ansons, Susan darted over to meet him, took his arm firmly, and escorted him away from the waiting room.

Remington looked at her dazedly as he found himself walking opposite the direction he had intended. "Susan. What are you doing here?"

"Talking to a patient's family. I presume you're doing the same."

Remington caught on immediately. "The alleged four-year-old murderer is a patient of yours."

Susan nodded forcefully. "And there's no 'alleged' to it. She's fascinated by what she did, and it's not her first attempt."

Remington's brows shot up. "A four-year-old *serial* killer?"

The thought chilled Susan to her marrow. "Attempted serial killer. So far, she's only completed one murder, though it's not for lack of trying." Susan realized the imaginative array of Sharicka's attempts did not bode well for the future: drowning, stabbing, strangulation, and the choking hazard added to a child's drink. When Sharicka discovered guns, there would be no telling what might happen.

"I'm glad you told me," Remington said, sounding more perplexed than pleased. "It changes my feelings about the family, which will probably affect my approach when I tell them Rylan will likely make a full recovery."

"Oh, thank God." Susan spoke before she had a chance to consider her words. "I don't think they could handle any more bad news."

Remington studied Susan as if seeing her for the first time. "You're positive the four-year-old really did this . . . and of her own volition. That she's not under the influence of . . ."

Susan understood his hesitation and doubt. It had become predictable. "Her father is not manipulating her into taking the blame, nor into taking these actions. She's a very sick little girl."

Remington sighed. "I have to admit I would have expected deeper cuts had an adult inflicted them, even with something as blunt as a butter knife." He glanced past Susan, and she appreciated that he accepted her authority without further questioning. If she said a four-year-old caused the trauma, he would no longer cast suspicion on the father. "I'd love to give you a full report, but why repeat myself? Let's let the worried parents off the hook."

Susan nodded, then gestured to indicate Remington should go first. He did so, and she followed him back into the waiting room.

Dr. Elliot Anson had returned to his pacing; but, the instant Remington entered the doorway, he grabbed a seat beside his wife. "How's Rylan?" Both parents turned agonized gazes onto the neurosurgery resident. Seeing their raw and honest expressions, Susan wondered how anyone could suspect them of harming any of their children.

Remington crouched in front of the parents. "Most of his wounds were superficial, but one managed to penetrate the spine. It tore a hole in the dura, the membrane covering the spinal cord, and caused what we call a traumatic herniation."

Susan held her breath. She did not know enough about neurosurgery to guess the long-term effects. Herniations of the brain nearly always proved fatal. She did not know if there was any connection between spinal cord and brain herniation. Then she remembered Remington had told her Rylan would probably make a full recovery, and her concern slowly dissipated. *Do neuro-*

surgeons mean "full recovery" the same way nonsur-
geons do?

Gently, Remington extracted Susan's palm-pross from the mother's hand and tapped in a connection to a diagram of the spinal cord. "Right here." He pointed to the thoracic area of the back. "The dura got torn, which allowed the spinal cord to slip out of its canal. That caused him to have what we call a Brown-Sequard phenonmenon, usually caused by damage to one side of the spinal cord. Rylan had weakness on the right side of his body and lost pain and temperature sensation on the left."

The parents only stared, listening intently. They had become accustomed to bad news when it involved their children.

Remington continued to explain. "In the OR, we were able to restore the herniated spinal cord to its correct position, and we patched the dural defect. He's in Recovery now, and neurological tests are essentially normal. He still has slight weakness of the muscles on the right, but he did just get out of surgery." Remington rose, smiling. "We expect a full recovery."

The parents seemed stunned. "Full?" Lucianne Anson rose, clutching her hands together at the level of her chin. "As in . . . normal?"

Remington's grin broadened. He looked tired, yet his face still managed to light up in a way that made his features seem perfect to Susan. "As in normal. Exactly how he was before the incident, aside from some scars." He glanced over at Susan. "At least physically. I think counseling, though, is probably in order."

The Doctors Anson caught each other and practically danced around the room with glee. "Counseling, yes," the father boomed. "We'll all need it." He hugged Lucianne tighter. "Our son is going to be all right."

Susan breathed a sigh of relief. The situation was so ugly, it seemed weird to find joy in it. Yet things could have turned out even worse.

The Ansons disengaged. Lucianne lurched over to catch Remington into an embrace. For an instant, he stiffened in surprise, then caught her in his arms.

"Thank you," she sobbed. "Thank you so much, Doctor."

Remington glanced at Susan, clearly uncertain how to handle his sudden predicament. "Don't thank me, ma'am. I only made the diagnosis and assisted the surgery. My attending, Dr. Arlington, is the one who saved your son's neurological system."

Elliot Anson gave Remington a careful pat on the back, while his wife still clung. "We'll thank him, too, when we can. We appreciate what all of you have done for Rylan . . . and for us."

Remington waited until the mother had released him before speaking again. "The Recovery Room is through the door, to the right, and down the hallway. Do you have any questions about the surgery?"

"Can we see him now?" the father asked.

Remington pointed. "When you get to Recovery, the nurses will take you to him. They should be able to answer all your basic questions, and they can call Dr. Arlington." He added firmly, "I'm finished for the day."

"Thank you." The father walked past them and out the door.

The mother grasped and squeezed Remington's hand one more time as she passed. "Thank you."

"Just doing my job," Remington said to her retreating back.

The instant they disappeared, he caught Susan into an embrace. "So, about that day on the town? You get any sleep?"

"Quite a bit, actually," Susan said, still eager to spend the rest of the day with Remington. She would understand if he canceled their date again, but she hoped he would not.

"Great!" he said with clear enthusiasm. "I caught a

shower in the on-call quarters, but if I smell too much like the OR, I can take another one."

Susan had her nose pressed against his scrubs. While he did carry the chemical odor of anesthesia and cleansers, they did not bother her. "You smell fine. Just get some street clothes on, and we're gone. Every extra moment we stay is just one more chance for someone to ask us a question or get us caught up with another patient."

Remington gave her a look that said everything. "I don't care if my own grandmother needs a subarachnoid evacuation. Once I'm past those doors, I'm not coming back till tomorrow."

Susan laughed. "I'm not waiting until we're outside." Using one finger, she made a show of muting her Vox. "See you at the main exit in ten minutes."

"Or less," Remington promised, dashing off into surgeons' territory.

Susan went in the opposite direction, determined to let nothing stop her from reaching the front exit unmolested.

Remington took Susan's hand as they stepped out into sunshine and damp late-morning air. Birds whistled at one another from the branches of trees planted in clumps at regular intervals along the sidewalk. She could still remember when the decision was made to add regular greenery to the city blocks in the hope of straining carbon dioxide, heat, and pollutants from the air. Many of the trees had died; but the city had diligently replanted until the living trees finally outnumbered the lampposts along the streets. Insightful city planners had chosen small, hardy varieties, planted them in groups to shade one another and capture rainfall, and placed them in elevated beds to form a barrier to runoff salts. Porous paving materials helped guide the roots but still supplied them with water, and cracked sidewalks had become a rarity.

Songbirds flitted through these poor excuses for makeshift forest, their nests perched high in the branches and protected from would-be meddlers by wrought-iron fences surrounding the trunks. Gaily painted bat houses hung from the limbs to help keep the insect population in check by night and day; the creatures' "protected" status made it a crime to harm them or disturb their boxes.

People whisked along the sidewalks, while glide-buses, trams, and occasional cars whooshed past them on the city streets. Whenever she walked in the city, Susan believed she could sense the slight vibrations of the subground u-ways and elevated e-rails, although her father and others insisted these things were undetectable and only someone with an overactive imagination could feel them.

Remington released Susan's hand and consulted his Vox. He punched a few keys. "If you're still keen on skating, we can take the fifteen bus, the eight tram, or . . ."

In no hurry, and enjoying the feel of sun and wind, Susan interrupted. "Let's walk."

"Walk?" Remington's brows inched upward. It would take them most of the morning. He shrugged. "Walk, it is. But after a day and night on call, I might not have the energy left to skate once we get there."

Skating had seemed like a good idea at the time, but a new idea had crept insidiously into Susan's mind, planted by several conversations and the research project. "That's all right. I'd kind of like to sightsee, do some window-shopping, and there's a building not too far from the mall I want to discover."

"Oh?" Remington took her arm. "Any particular building? Or just your generic hunk of concrete with windows?"

Susan smiled. "I'd like to check out USR, U.S. Robots and Mechanical Men. My dad's worked there since as long as I can remember. Now I'm researching a product for them, and I realized I've never seen it. Not ever."

Remington accepted that explanation with barely a nod as they continued their walk.

Susan looked at him. "Can you say the same? I mean, have you ever been to the place your dad works?"

"Well, my dad co-owned the supermarket down the block from our house, so I've been there a couple"—he paused dramatically—"hundred thousand times. But I'll bet a lot of people whose parents work in factories and labs have no idea what those places look like." He added quickly, as if concerned he might have offended her, "Not that I'd mind seeing the USR building. I'll bet it's amazing. It ought to have flashing neon signs and animatronic entryways."

Susan laughed. "More likely it's a drab, half-hidden, gray nothing of a building. You know what Nate said; they don't want to draw attention to themselves in any way that anyone could construe as negative." As that did not exactly make it a fabulous destination, she also felt the need to tack on something. "Though I'd still like to see it."

"Then it's settled. A walking tour through the city, followed by a glimpse into the world of USR and your father." Remington spoke with genuine enthusiasm, for which Susan gave him credit. "Sounds like the perfect day."

Susan squeezed his hand, wondering if he had any idea how much she appreciated his openness to unusual ideas and trying to find the words to tell him without sounding syrupy. A glide-bus pulled up to a nearby stop with a faint hiss of electric brakes. From the corner of her eye, she saw a man racing awkwardly to catch it as the waiting passengers funneled inside.

As the man flashed past, Susan took a closer look. In his midthirties, he had wildly unkempt blond hair that trailed him in tangles and several days' growth of beard. Oddly familiar, he wore dirty blue jeans with multiple patches and a long trench coat that seemed inappropriate for the summer weather. Perhaps he had started out early, with the morning chill still in the air. Then, as he brushed past her and onto the bus, Susan felt herself repulsed, wanting to move as far away from him as possible. That clinched his identity in her mind: Payton Flowers, the schizophrenic she had injected with nanorobots, the man for whom Goldman and Peters had practically put out a bounty when he had not shown up for his last appointment.

Without time for explanation, Susan grabbed Remington's arm and half dragged him toward the bus door. Payton was disappearing inside; and, as there was no one behind him, Susan worried the doors would close before she could catch him. "Come on!"

Though surely surprised, Remington ran with Susan. They reached the door in two bounding steps, and Susan managed to stomp a foot onto the platform, activating the mechanical sensor, just as the doors started closing. The doors froze in place, then eased fully open. Susan staggered in, pulling Remington behind her. He waved raggedly at the driver. Someday, Susan supposed, the glide-buses would become fully automated, obviating the need for direct human guidance. In that moment, she understood why people might feel threatened by positronic robots like Nate.

Payton Flowers took a seat near the front. The one opposite him was already occupied, so Susan kept walking down the aisle until she finally found a fully open seat, three rows farther on. She deliberately avoided the back of the bus. Since all public transport had become essentially free, covered by taxes, certain types of people had a habit of climbing aboard and spending the day staring out the windows. So long as they remained relatively quiet, and self-confined to the back of the bus, most of the drivers tolerated them and left them to their own devices. Susan wondered if Payton might have spent the last few days or weeks among them, which could explain why he had disappeared so completely.

Susan gestured for Remington to take the window seat. She wanted to keep herself free to slip up to Payton Flowers and try to talk to him en route. If impossible, at least she would be able to keep her eye on him so they could debark at the same stop.

Remington swung into the seat, and Susan sat down beside him. The bus glided smoothly back into traffic. The moment it moved, their seat belts clicked into place around them, automatically adjusting to fit snugly over their waists and chests. "You women really are fickle, aren't you? What happened to our leisurely, sightseeing stroll in the fresh air?"

Susan took her eyes from her patient to fix them on Remington. She could not help grinning at the comment. "I'm so sorry. I'm not usually . . . insane."

"I'll be the judge of that," Remington said with not-wholly-mock seriousness. "What happened?"

"One of our study patients went AWOL. Goldman and Peters have been going mad trying to find him. I saw him getting on the bus, and I didn't want to lose him." Susan tapped the laboratory number into her Vox and sent off a quick text: "Found P.F. 15 bus. Advise."

Remington stretched to peek around Susan. "Is it the shabby one in the coat?"

Susan nodded. "His name's Payton." For discretionary reasons, she did not divulge his last name.

Remington continued to peer past her. "How crazy is he?"

Susan winced. Psychiatrists were generally not enamored of the "c" word. "You know I can't say. Confidentiality."

"Yeah." Remington surely understood, but he did not seem happy with the reply. "But I like to know a little bit about a guy when I'm stuck on a bus with him and he's wearing a trench coat in July."

Susan dismissed Remington's concerns. "Just because he's a psych patient doesn't make him dangerous."

Remington sat back, though clearly still uneasy. "Susan, one of your patients, age four, tried to murder one of my patients. She did murder his sister. You want to come up with something more comforting than 'just because he's a psych patient doesn't make him dangerous'?"

Susan had little to offer. While not the most dangerous of psychiatric diagnoses—antisocial personalities such as Sharicka had that sewn up—schizophrenia did make its victims unpredictable and, sometimes, dangerous. She could not forget Payton's answers to her questions about how and why he had come to the procedure room: *"I walked. Ninety-three billion miles. From da sun."* Susan shrugged. "As long as we're just following him and don't confront him, we shouldn't incite any problems."

Remington grunted. "No way a paranoid schizophrenic would lash out at people following him, right?"

Susan tried not to reveal that Remington had inadvertently discovered the correct diagnosis. "Well . . ."

"And you wouldn't actually try to talk to him, that is, confront him, would you?"

As that had been Susan's plan, she could hardly deny it. A buzz from her Vox rescued her from a reply. It was the lab: "StA wth. Wll gt prmssn frm fmly fr cops."

"Doesn't look like I'll have to. Goldman and Peters are contacting the family. They should be able to get permission for intervention by law enforcement."

Remington glanced around Susan again. "Good." He craned farther. "Where's he going?"

Susan turned her attention to Payton Flowers. The man had risen from his seat, heading toward the front of the bus.

The resident physicians watched him approach the bus driver, talk for a moment, then flip the edge of his coat. Even from a dozen seats back, Susan could see the driver of the bus grow visibly pale. He punched the intercom button. "Passengers, please remain calm."

No words in the English language could have had a more opposite effect. Though no one left his seat, all of the passengers visibly stiffened, including a woman who had appeared so deeply asleep she sprawled partway into the aisle, held in place by her seat belt.

"If we all stay in our seats and don't panic, we'll be fine."

Susan's heart rate tripled. She found herself leaning on Remington, who put a steadying arm around her.

The driver continued, his voice tremulous and edged with fear. Clearly, he was trying to control it, but it would not wholly obey him. "This man has a bomb and has threatened to set it off if anyone leaves their seat."

A bomb? Susan's first thought was to deny it. Things like that did not happen on glide-buses in downtown Manhattan. Then, her thoughts scattered in several directions. *This can't be real. This can't be happening. Why would Payton Flowers want to blow us up? Why would anyone hijack a glide-bus; it wouldn't have the power to make it out of the state, let alone the country.* Then, one thought shattered all the others. *We're going to die!*

All around her, Susan could hear the faint click of Vox messages being sent. Likely, some of them had locked into Emergency mode. Others were probably sending love notes to friends, children, parents, and spouses. Surely, the police would pinpoint them before Payton could do anything stupid.

Pinpoint us and what? Make sure we explode somewhere less populated? Susan looked at Remington. His Vox glowed red. He, at least, had put his Vox into Emergency mode. The police computers could lock onto it and, probably, several others on the crowded bus. *I know this guy. I should be able to do something no one else can.*

Yet, Susan realized, she barely knew him. She had done little more than punch a needle into his back, hardly the starting point for a friendship. She considered texting her father but discarded it. He already knew how much she loved him. She would do better focusing on how to fix this situation, dredging her brain for some way to handle a raging, unmedicated schizophrenic that only a psychiatrist would know.

A psychiatrist, Susan realized, *would inject him with an emergency dose of antipsychotics.* That information did little to help. She did not carry around spare doses of hospital medications, let alone a needle. *If I did,* she decided, *it would contain a potent and fast-acting anesthesia.* She punched another message to Goldman and Peters: "E! P.F. w/bomb. Hijack! Advise." She had no idea what they could tell her that would make any difference, but it seemed worth trying. They might know how to contact Payton's regular psychiatrist.

Remington whispered, "If you distract him, I'll grab him."

"No!" Susan returned in a forceful whisper. "It's not like he has a gun or something you could take from him. He'd just detonate the bomb and kill us all."

Remington's jaw set. "We have to do something."

Susan could hardly argue. The only other option was to sit back and leave their fate to a psychotic, assuming no one else tried anything stupid and got them all killed first. "Patients with hallucinations and delusions may not see things as they are."

Remington's gaze seemed to bore through her, as if trying to read the point behind her words. "Are you saying he might not act or react in a rational fashion? Because that seems rather obvious under the circumstances."

Susan could see how he might interpret her words

that way. "I mean he may believe he has a bomb, but it
might be something . . . harmless."

"In which case, I can jump him."

"In which case," Susan corrected, "you don't need to
jump him."

The buzz of the lab's reply joined a cacophony of Vox
noises: "StA clm, quiet. Sndng hlp."

Remington peered over the heads of the people in
front of him. "That's real fear in the driver's voice and
face. If it's not a bomb, it's a good facsimile."

"Yeah." Before Susan could say anything further, the
driver came on again.

"Everyone, I must remind you to remain in your seats
for the safety of us all."

Susan had not seen anyone attempt to stand, but it did
not hurt to remind people.

"Also, the gentleman has asked that you shut down
all electronics, remain silent, and . . ."

Payton said something Susan could not make out.

"And stop talking about him." The driver fairly
screeched the words, as if realizing how ludicrous they
sounded but certain choosing others might get him
killed. Remington had an excellent point. The person
sitting closest to Payton Flowers, the one who should
know, was clearly convinced the device beneath his
trench coat was actively explosive. He added pleadingly,
"Please do as he says."

Susan pursed her lips. To most of the other passengers, his plea probably sounded bizarre. Anyone who
knew schizophrenics, however, could understand the
concern. In a situation such as this one, it only made
sense people would talk about the person holding them
hostage, but Payton's concern more likely stemmed from
the intense and overpowering delusion that people always talked about him, perhaps even that computers and
television broadcasted his thoughts and actions to the
world. Dutifully, she silenced her Vox. Others must have

done the same, because the buzzing and clicking disappeared into an eerie, fear-filled hush.

The bus sped along its usual route, different only in that it made no stops. Susan watched out the window as the people at the proper bus stops pressed forward. When the vehicle showed no signs of slowing, most leapt backward for fear of getting hit. Some shouted, waved fists or middle fingers, or stared bewilderedly after the speeding bus.

Reality squeezed in on Susan in the moment "bomb" moved from a word to a concept. Her heart pounded in her chest. A lump formed in her throat, and all oxygen seemed to have left the air. Remington caught her hand and squeezed it. Susan clamped her fingers around his palm as if her life depended on it. Now she wished they had sat farther back in the bus. Maybe they could duck behind the seat back in front of them and it would shield them from some of the blast.

Remington whispered so softly even Susan could barely hear him, "Talk to him."

It was the first suggestion that made sense to Susan. She was a psychiatrist. In theory, she should know how to speak to irrational people, to calm their hysteria. Her own education undid her, however. If Payton suffered from almost any neurosis, she might have found the right words, the right phrases. She could reason with a histrionic, with a narcissist, even with an antisocial. Though the latter might play manipulative games, he would not detonate the bomb, at least not until he had induced the optimal amount of panic, terror, and uncertainty to feed his thrill. With a schizophrenic, however, no rational approach existed. One had to feed into the correct hallucination, the right delusion; and she had no way to know which one, if any, might delay and which might send him over the edge.

In other circumstances, Susan might have shouted out his name. Her knowledge would surprise a man without psychosis, might inflame enough curiosity to make him pause and listen. But a man like Payton, suffering from a thought-broadcasting, persecutory delusion, would simply see Susan as a mind-reading threat. Just discovering someone on the bus had knowledge about him might drive him to destroy her and everyone around her. Susan had never felt so helpless in her life.

I have to try something, don't I? The answer seemed obvious; and, yet, so far, simple obedience had served its purpose. So long as no one did anything threatening, Payton seemed content to leave things as they were. It felt foolish to rock the boat until something changed, until the danger intensified and it no longer mattered whether her actions might actually enrage rather than soothe him. "Logic won't work," Susan hissed back directly into Remington's ear. Even the obvious realization that Payton Flowers would die along with his hostages would not help in this situation. He might not care. He could have already decided to kill himself and just wanted to do it in a grand fashion. Or, perhaps, he believed himself invincible.

Forcing herself to try to think like a wholly irrational human being made Susan's head ache. She rubbed her temples and tried not to focus on how it all came down to Payton Flowers and whatever hallucinations and delusions assailed him at the moment. To him, the passengers might all be demons on their way to hell, aliens plotting to devour humanity, a clicking lot of locusts hell-bent on destroying the world's food supply. Dislodging schizophrenic delusions never happened with words or rational proof. One could remove a schizophrenic's normal kidney, put it in his hand, and still not convince him it was not infested by rats. A thousand mirrors could not disabuse him of the notion that he had green hair or purple eyes.

But the idea of sitting back and passively dying did not work for Susan any more than for Remington. Once she discarded the possibility of overwhelming or bargaining with a florid psychotic, her mind turned to escape. The driver controlled the windows and doors, and Susan had already seen several people attempting to loosen or break windows without success.

The bus lurched to a stop. Through the window beyond Remington, Susan could see the familiar, broad outline of the Turtle Bay Mall, their original destination. They had pulled into a bus stop, so no one outside of the vehicle seemed perturbed. From the corner of her eye, she thought she could see the red, white, and blue strobing lights of at least one police car. She was glad they had had the good sense not to alarm the bomber with sirens.

Everyone had fallen utterly silent, so the driver's voice over the speaker sounded particularly loud. Several people stiffened, including Susan, who felt a wash of cold fear slide down her spine. "The gentleman has asked that I open all the doors. If you debark in an orderly fashion, and no one tries anything foolish, he has promised not to detonate the bomb until we're all safely off the bus." As if to prove his words, the seat belt buckles clicked off and the belts glided away.

Seized by a sudden urge to be the first one out, Susan forced herself to stand slowly and remain in place. She could imagine the passengers trampling one another in a sudden panicked rush. For the first time since Payton Flowers had taken control, she dared to hope they might actually survive.

The doors eased open. Passengers flowed into the aisle so quickly Susan barely had time to blink. She tried to muscle her way into the crowd heading toward the front, but Remington held her back. "This way." He ducked beneath their seat.

Though confused by his action, Susan followed. They squirmed back two rows, then practically fell into the empty stairwell of the middle set of doors and out into the street. *The street, the blessed street.* Susan wanted to kiss it, but Remington grabbed her arm and hauled her toward the curb, onto the sidewalk, then made a mad dash toward the looming skyscrapers.

Susan could not help going with him. He pulled her along at a sprinter's pace, dodging the dazed people waiting at the bus stop, hurling her around trees and nearly sending her careening into a bench. She wanted to tell him to slow down, but she couldn't catch her breath. Then, suddenly, she was tossed to the sidewalk and he flung himself on top of her.

Noise thundered through Susan's ears, so loud it caused physical pain and fully deafened her. The ground seemed to buck and shake, as if the entire world had come apart. Heat washed over her, and her lungs refused to function. She struggled for breath, found it, and sucked in several acrid lungfuls. Her hearing returned abruptly in the form of strangers screaming. Remington rolled off her. "Are you all right?"

Susan wiped liquid from her cheek and discovered blood on her hand. She probed her face, without finding a source, while she took in the scene around her. Everything had changed. People ran, shrieking, in all directions. Only hunks of twisted metal remained from the shelter that had once housed the bus station. Where the glide-bus had parked, she saw only a scorched outline. Two police cars were clearly visible behind it, their windshields shattered and their front ends bashed in. People staggered up from the sidewalk, some moaning, others tottering, a few walking in crazed circles.

"Payton," Susan said, the single name carrying all the necessary information.

Remington helped her stand. His jeans showed myriad holes with burnt edges, and a shard of thin metal jutted from his profusely bleeding shoulder. "I think," he said carefully, "we can conclude the bomb"—he looked Susan over—"was real."

Susan stood there a moment contemplating the scene. Then, through no intention of her own, she started laughing. It seemed strange and out of place, yet the perfect reaction to Remington's understatement. It was an expression of joy amid depthless sorrow and fear. *We're alive!* She took Remington's injured arm. "You're bleeding."

"You, too." Remington dabbed at her face.

Susan brushed away his ministrations. "I think it's your blood on me, too." She reached for his arm. "Let me take care of that."

"There are people hurt a lot worse than I am." Remington started to turn away, but Susan grabbed him.

"You're worthless to anyone if you bleed to death." She indicated he should sit, which he did on the sidewalk. "If you severed your brachial artery, and I won't know till I remove this thing, you're first on the triage list."

Susan went to work, trying to imagine herself on call in the ER rather than on a city street, seeking normalcy in a situation that contained none. Soon enough, she could start assessing the injured and possibly the dying around her, but not until she assured herself she would not have to do so alone.

Chapter 19

Under strict orders not to show her face on the PIPU for two full weeks, Susan Calvin sat in her bed, her palm-pross balanced on her lap. Sunlight from the bedroom window cast a glare across the screen that she ignored as she poured through Payton Flowers' history. As far as she could tell, he had never done a violent thing in the whole of his brief life, at least prior to blowing up a bus in downtown Manhattan.

Susan sat back, frustrated. She felt fine, but hobbled by the ordered recovery, though she understood the purpose of it. She knew Remington was at least as eager to return to work as she was.

It took a special kind of workaholic to worry for every moment away, the kind who had had it drummed into his head for years that doing so meant "missing all the best cases." Dr. Bainbridge and his ilk, she realized, had affected her, and Remington, more than she had initially understood.

Susan sat back, frustrated. Payton's actions made no logical sense, but that should not have bothered her per se. It was the very hallmark of schizophrenia to act irrationally. *Irrationally, not totally rabbit-ass, over-the-moon crazy.* Susan relived racing from the bus, still half convinced the bomb strapped to Payton Flowers might consist of cardboard and bare-ended wires. She felt Remington hurl her to the ground and throw his body over hers, the explosion that deafened her and quaked the ground, the raw terror that followed. She shook away those memories. She had spent the previous day focused on them, dissecting them in detail. It was already time to move on.

So now Susan found herself hopelessly intent on solving the mystery of Payton Flowers. He was not the first schizophrenic to commit murder. Once every few years the psychosis took over someone and he lashed out at a friend or acquaintance, or even a stranger mistaken for the devil or a monster or the one responsible for broadcasting his thoughts to the world. Susan had never personally heard of a schizophrenic mass murderer. Though some surely existed, that was more the realm of terrorists, religious zealots, power-hungry dictators, and antisocials.

Susan had turned to research, where she had managed to find some instances. However, all of them had shown signs of violent intent long before they committed their heinous acts. Most had killed or tortured animals, either hunting, from spite, or both. All had spoken of hallucinations of murder or compulsions to kill. Payton did not fit the pattern. Just carrying the diagnosis of schizophrenia was not enough. Millions of people had it, but killing was rare. Though, Susan had to admit, a far higher percentage of murderers had schizophrenia than the general population, nonviolent psychotics did not become mass murderers overnight.

Something happened to Payton, and we need to know what. The same frustration that had assailed Susan for most of the morning returned to strike her now. The explosion had left little of Payton's remains and nothing of substance to examine. *Could the nanorobots have had anything to do with this? Anything whatsoever?* She had considered the idea several times before and always dismissed it. She understood how the nanorobots worked, at least in theory. If something went monumentally wrong, it could cause failure of the nanorobots to obtain data, headache, stroke, damage to brain tissue, or infection. Hijacking a bus required deliberate and cold calculation.

Susan's Vox buzzed. She stiffened suddenly, nearly wrenching several muscles. *Jumpier than I realized.* Susan glanced at the display as she activated the voice function. "This is Susan Calvin." The call came from Ari Goldman's private Vox.

"Susan, what happened?"

Peters' more mellow baritone cut in. "How are you, Susan? Are you all right?"

Susan smiled. "I'm fine, really. Just tired and a bit shaken. My date shielded me, and I'm not physically hurt at all."

"The neurosurgery resident at the scene?"

"That's the one."

"I thought those guys were all inconsiderate jerks."

Susan laughed. "This one missed his narcissism classes, I guess. He's a keeper."

"What happened?" Goldman said again, louder. "Did our patient really take a busload of people hostage, then blow it up?"

Susan nodded, though the men could not see her. She refused to activate visuals from bed. "He did. Luckily, he let us off first."

"Why?"

Surprised by the question, Susan hesitated.

Peters spoke first. "I think he means why did he bring a bomb onto a bus, not why didn't he murder you all. At least, I hope that's what he means."

"Sure," Goldman said.

Susan did not have an answer for either question, but

the second one had not intrigued her until that moment. Either way, she did not know exactly how to answer. "I imagine he was suffering some sort of schizophrenic break."

"Damn!" Ari Goldman said loudly.

Susan did not know what to make of that, either. She knew Dr. Goldman tended to get caught up in the research and not consider the human element, but he had a good heart.

Before anyone else could speak, he explained himself. "Can you imagine what we could have learned if we had those nanorobots from his brain? It could revolutionize psychiatry!"

Susan had to admit he had a valuable point. Readings on neuronal firing and neurotransmitters during an event this illogical and emotional could have brought the entire field of psychiatry an enormous leap into the future. "They're gone." Susan did not want to mislead him. There was no chance any of the nanorobots from Payton Flowers' head would ever be recovered. "But the good news is no one else was killed by the bomb blast. He gave us enough time to flee before setting off the explosion." *Barely.*

Susan's own words gave her more to think about.

Peters said softly, "Susan, who identified Payton Flowers as the bomber? It's way too soon for DNA or dental records."

"I did. I recognized him when he got on the bus. Remember, I followed him. I texted you, and you said to stay with him."

"Yes, yes, yes." Ari verbally waved off the explanation. "I remember the conversation; I haven't gone senile yet. But you didn't . . . happen to mention to the police . . . how you knew him?"

Susan thought back. A lot had happened in a small space of time. She had assisted several people until the paramedics arrived, patching open wounds, covering burns, keeping them calm. "I just said I knew him from the hospital, as a patient. I didn't mention the study."

Susan thought she heard two relieved sighs, and it bothered her. She could understand and forgive Dr. Goldman, but she trusted Peters to put the human side of everything first. "Good girl. We don't need that getting out."

Though it seemed callous to worry for the integrity of the study more than the lost life, Susan did now appreciate the information given on the first day of residency by Brentwood Locke: *"And, last but not least, stone tablet commandment number three is if you wind up involved with any medical studies, you do so with the explicit understanding the lead researchers' word is law and no information leaves the hospital grounds. After years of arduous research and expensive grants, no scientist wants his results leaked, or his ideas stolen, before publication. If you violate number three, you will likely disappear off the face of the planet. And rightly so."* Guess *I won't be disappearing any time soon.* The words rang hollow. Had Payton timed his explosion any earlier, she would have done so the previous day.

Susan had to ask, "Is our research really so secret that even a massive explosion, with lives lost, won't allow us to share it?"

"*Life* lost," Goldman corrected. "Only Payton's. You told us everyone else survived."

"More importantly," Peters added, "bringing up the study would only harm us, our patients, and psychiatry in general. Nothing good could come of it."

Susan found herself stating the obvious. "But the nanorobots had nothing to do with Payton's actions." She stopped herself from tacking on a "Did they?" Scientifically, logically, they could not possibly have played a role.

"Of course not!" Ari said in a tone that implied the mere suggestion was as much blasphemous as stupid.

Peters continued. "But that wouldn't stop the masses from believing they did. Look at the fuss people kicked up about genetically modified food. Like we hadn't been genetically modifying plants and animals for as long as humans have existed. Cavemen probably bred the fastest equid stallion to the fastest equid mare to produce even faster offspring. We created Chihuahuas from wolves. Yet, pull in a scientist and mention a lab, and the same process is . . ."

Remembering her dad's words, Susan finished, "Frankenstein's monster?"

"Yes!" Cody shouted. "That's it, exactly. We can pollinate and graft to make seedless grapes, but introduce a strand of fat carrot DNA into a skinny carrot and it's Frankenstein's freaking, green-haired, orange monster."

Despite her ordeal, Susan managed a chuckle.

When Cody Peters started sounding more like his laboratory partner, Susan knew he had a genuinely vital cause. "So I'm not to let people know the Manhattan bus bomber had nanorobots in his cerebrospinal fluid."

Ari confirmed, "Not on pain of death. I only wish someone had managed to stop him before—"

"The poor guy lost his life?" Peters tried.

"Yes, of course," Ari said gruffly. "That's precisely what I was going to say."

"I'll bet," Peters mumbled in the background.

Susan found herself smiling. She enjoyed the way the scientists interacted. "Well, I'm not talking, at least not to anyone who doesn't already know. But don't you think proper scientific procedure mandates we make absolutely certain our meddling didn't have anything to do with . . . what happened?"

Silence followed. Susan had the sudden feeling she had stepped into dangerous territory.

"Our . . . 'meddling'?" Ari finally said tentatively.

Having brought up the topic, Susan could not back down yet. "In science, we never say never."

Peters changed the subject. "Hey, we injected that patient you recommended yesterday. What a cutie."

Susan stiffened. "Sharicka Anson? *You* injected her?"

Goldman took over. "It was your day off, not ours. We didn't want to wait, so we dusted off our skills and did it ourselves."

"She's an absolute doll," Peters added. "Are you sure she's a mental patient?"

Susan rolled her eyes. "The worst kind, Dr. Peters. Antisocial personality. Manipulative, crafty, highly intelligent . . . and a vicious killer."

Dead silence followed. Clearly, her words shocked both men.

"Did I lose you?"

"No, just surprised us. Well, in a couple of weeks, we should know what makes her tick."

An explosive mechanism perhaps? Susan kept the sarcasm to herself. "Hopefully, we'll learn something that can save her. And what's left of her family."

"Yeah. So, when ya coming back?"

Susan stretched. "They told me I couldn't step on the unit for two weeks. They didn't say anything about the lab, though, so I may be able to sneak back sooner."

"Well, don't rush it," Peters said kindly. "We have enough mental patients in our studies. We don't need one working for us as well."

"I'm fine." Susan tried to reassure them. She did feel all right, rather like she'd had a near miss on the highway: a flash of adrenaline, a moment of terror, then back to normal. She doubted she would forget the ordeal soon, but she did not think it left some sort of terrible and lasting impression on her psyche.

"Good," Ari said gruffly, though he clearly meant it.

"We have three patients ready and waiting. Come back when you can. We'll see you then."

"All right." Susan prepared to disconnect. "Good-bye."

"Good-bye," Peters sang out before cutting off the connection.

Susan sat back. She had not slept well. Her head felt stuffy and her eyelids heavy. She was considering dropping back off to sleep, when a soft knock at the door roused her. "Come in, Dad."

John Calvin poked his head through the crack. "Were you awake?"

"Talking on Vox, in fact." Susan knew it would upset him to think he had bothered her. "Come on in."

John slid into the room with a warm smile that could not fully hide his concern. "Are you feeling all right?"

Susan sighed. "Why does everyone keep asking me that? I'm perfectly fine."

John cocked an eyebrow. "Perfectly?"

"All right, a bit shaken, but otherwise okay. I'm not a paper flower."

"No." John Calvin sat on the edge of Susan's bed. "But you're my baby, and you almost died. It's normal to feel rotten after something like that."

Susan grinned. "Thank you, Dr. Calvin. Would you like to write me a prescription for Muzon now?" She named a popular antianxiety drug.

John laughed. "Very funny."

"Seriously, Dad." Susan supposed she ought to feel worse than she did. She had always had a strong personality, but she knew near-death experiences could shake even the most stolid to their core. "I'm fine. I don't think I really internalized the danger until the actual explosion. By then, it was essentially over."

"Want to talk about it?"

Susan tipped her head. *Do I?* She did not feel strongly

one way or the other. "Dad, do you know much about the nanorobots your company makes?"

John Calvin's brows dropped, and his forehead furrowed. "Of course. Why do you ask?"

"Because, less than a week ago, I injected them into the bomber's cerebrospinal fluid. He had a head full of nanorobots when he hijacked that bus."

John Calvin stared. "What?" he finally said, though he had surely heard her. "You knew the hijacker? And he had USR nanorobots in him?"

As she had said exactly that, Susan saw no reason to confirm his questions. "Could there be a connection?"

John's brows knitted even further. His forehead became a mass of wrinkles. "I can't imagine one. But I also can't fathom the odds that the one man who goes utterly bonkers also happens to be one of three or four people with nanorobots in him."

To her own surprise, Susan took the opposite side. "Well, I'm not sure the odds are all that enormous. Remember, we picked the most hopelessly mentally ill patients in Manhattan for the study. When you realize how sick a man has to be to hijack a bus, I suppose the overlap is obvious."

"Yes," John said, but his brows remained in place, his forehead still lined. "How long has this hijacker been hopelessly mentally ill?"

"Years, now. Why?"

"And how many buses has he hijacked?"

Susan chuckled. "Just the one, Dad. It's tough to blow yourself up twice." Despite the joke, she recognized the significance of his questioning. She had spent hours researching the same information. "And, no, he had no history of committing prior acts of violence, except just before he got diagnosed. That time, he jumped off the roof of a building."

"To kill himself?"

Susan supposed confidentiality went by the wayside

when a man murdered himself in a public spectacle. "That's not clear. He claimed he thought he could fly, but he was also plagued by inexplicable hallucinations, worried he was going insane. In the hospital, he expressed the desire to escape, to end it all." She gave him the condensed version of a convoluted story. "About ten percent of people with . . . his diagnosis commit suicide."

"What percentage hijack buses?"

Susan shook her head. "I couldn't give you an exact figure, but I'm sure it's less than one in a million. On the other hand, nearly all unmedicated schizophrenics act irrationally, and quite a few are prone to violence."

"Was this man?"

"Schizophrenic?"

"Prone to violence."

Susan knew the answer. "Not according to his medical history, no." She sighed deeply. That had her flummoxed as well. "From what I know from the medical literature, and what I've read from the Net, schizophrenics who kill usually have a pattern: poor school performance, a cruel streak that starts even before the illness, compulsions to kill, and hallucinations of murder or voices commanding them to kill." She shook her head. "Schizophrenic killings are rarely premeditated, either. They're more likely to whirl around on a crowded street to strangle the woman they believe is beaming radio waves into their brain. Or run over a neighbor they're convinced puts thought-controlling poisons into their morning coffee. Schizophrenic murders are not thought out, at least not in the traditional manner. They're usually impulsive acts tied to personal delusions."

"So masterminding a hijacking and bombing . . . ?"

"Is unexpected, yes." Susan said. "I was scared on the bus; I knew we might all die. But I don't think my subconscious ever really accepted it. A fanatic with a bomb would have frightened me to the core, but a schizophrenic?" She shook her head. "Much more likely, he got a wild hair, snatched up a coil of wire and a garage door opener, then convinced himself he had a bomb."

"Except that he had a real bomb."

"Yes."

"Where do you suppose he got it? Did he have the knowledge and wherewithal to make it himself?"

Susan paused to think about it. "That's a great question, Dad. I imagine the police are asking the same thing." She considered longer. "According to his mother, he had a brilliant mind prior to his illness, which means he might understand a schematic. On the other hand, he was a prelaw student. That's not usually the realm of the bomb-building types. They're usually more math and science oriented." She shook her head. "He had never shown an interest in such things before. On his medications, I don't believe he would have any desire to build a bomb. Off them, I don't think he would have the concentration or focus."

John Calvin's face returned to normal, but he rubbed his chin with a thumbnail, clearly deep in thought himself. "So, in your professional opinion, someone gave him this bomb."

Susan had not considered it before, but it made sense. "I don't think he could have built it himself, and it's not like you can go to the downtown bomb store and purchase two or three." She raised her knees under the covers and drew them up to her neck. "Paranoid schizophrenics aren't known to be good judges of character. If he tried to hire someone to make it, he probably would have gone to someone perfectly innocent, someone who, in his mentally ill mind, could construct such a thing. I doubt whoever he asked wouldn't have reported it to someone: family, his doctor, the police."

"So, it's more likely someone recruited him. Gave him the bomb, showed him how to use it, and talked him into doing it."

Susan nodded. "Yeah."

John Calvin made a thoughtful noise.

"Do you think we should take our ideas to the police?"

"I don't think that's necessary." John studied his daughter. "You told them about him, didn't you?"

Susan raised and lowered one shoulder. "I gave them his name, told them I'm a psychiatry resident, and mentioned I knew him from the hospital. I didn't tell them his diagnosis, though. I could get in trouble for violating confidentiality." She repeated the movement. "Potentially, I could get in trouble for telling you." She doubted that would happen. Once the media got hold of Payton's name, every outlet would be blasting his diagnosis. Discussion groups would form, demanding to know why no one had recognized his illness, why he was not admitted to a hospital for treatment, why his doctors were to blame. Fingers would point in all directions. Then some new scandal would rock the city, and Payton's actions would be forgotten. Nothing would change; nothing ever seemed to change.

Once upon a time, people with serious psychiatric illnesses spent their days in facilities that could handle them, in a controlled and exquisitely structured environment. Their relatives visited them on a schedule that suited their individual needs. The patient with psychosis could live in a world that made sense to him, where his delusions could be safely indulged, where he could find some comfortable form of logic and security.

Then, in the 1970s, some good-hearted people decided it was cruel to keep people in asylums all their lives. It did not all turn out badly. As medical science advanced, the needs of those with emotional difficulties and neuroses, those with milder psychoses treatable with psychotherapy, with surgery, with ever-improving medications, thrived in their new and open environment.

But, for some, their psychoses remained incurable; and their needs were vastly different. They had functioned better within the confines of an institution, had relied on the structure and predictable routine for even a semblance of normalcy. For those patients with life-long, severe psychiatric disorders, the outside world was a dark and dangerous place. And so, they lashed out on occasion, leaving murder and mayhem in their wakes, or became crime victims themselves, or lived and died in grimy squalid conditions on the streets.

Doctors could hold patients only if they could prove imminent homicidal or suicidal intent, and then only for a maximum of two weeks' time. It required a perceptive psychiatrist with the luck of seeing his patient just before he committed a criminal act, as well as an honest patient in strong enough mind to admit his nefarious plans.

"Did you mention the nanorobots?" her father asked, not quite casually enough.

Susan groaned. "*Et tu*, Father?"

John Calvin looked at her curiously.

"I just got off Vox with Goldman and Peters. They wanted to make sure I didn't say anything about their study. Their concern is, if word got out, it would torpedo their research and set robotics back another century."

Susan expected her father to react more than he did. "They're right about that, Susan. Antirobot prejudice has held the field back more than any other. We have capabilities far beyond what we're using, and we're stuck in beta-testing land for most of them. We can access entertainment anytime, anywhere. There's a whole world of information at the touch of a Vox. But when it comes to robotics, the Jetsons have made more progress than we have."

Susan chuckled. "I know you're right. I've met Nate." A sudden thought derailed the conversation. "Dad, it's after ten on a Tuesday. Shouldn't you be at work?"

John Calvin flopped a leg across Susan's bed. "The explosion happened pretty close to the building. There was some minor structural damage. I've got the rest of the week off."

The explanation gripped Susan in a way it should not have. Something bothered her about it. A flash of memory returned, a man blocking her way into the building and warning her to stop working on the project. She dropped her knees to the bed. "Dad, do you think that might have been deliberate?"

"What?"

"That someone recruited a paranoid schizophrenic with nanorobots in his brain to blow up U.S. Robots and Mechanical Men?"

A light flickered through John Calvin's eyes, then disappeared. "Who would know enough about the project to do that?"

"I don't know." Susan studied her fingernails. She generally kept them short, as most doctors did. A small amount of white protruded above the pink; they needed clipping again. "But someone Goldman and Peters thought came from the Society for Humanity knew I was involved in the project, as well as the general gist of it. He warned me away from 'creating cyborgs.'"

"Hmm." John Calvin's discomfort became more apparent. He entwined his fingers and tapped the index ones together, a familiar, nervous gesture. "The study itself had to leave at least a small electronic trail. But confidentiality should have protected your patient's identity."

"Unless we have a mole of some kind. Either at USR or the hospital." Susan considered further. "Or, maybe, they didn't know. Maybe their recruiting our patient really is a coincidence." Even as she spoke, Susan found the connection too unlikely to believe it an accident.

Her father made another thoughtful noise. "If it was deliberate, we'll know soon enough. The SFH won't let it go without publicity." He shook his head, clearly flummoxed. "It's not their style to release potential victims before activating a bomb. They've murdered ruthlessly in the name of their cause before, and a busload of flying corpses would have generated a lot more publicity."

Susan shivered. The last comment struck too close to home. Hers would have been one of those flying corpses. "Maybe they instructed him to blow us up, but nonviolent Payton made the decision not to harm us all on his own. He might have been insane, but he still had a conscience."

"Maybe." John Calvin rose. "I'd like to make some inquiries and discuss this with some colleagues. I think you're right about too many coincidences: A formerly peaceful schizophrenic with nanorobots in his system hijacks a bus, takes it right in front of USR, and blows it and himself to kingdom come."

"In all fairness, he did it at one of the bus' regular stops."

John's head jerked toward her. "You mean he kept making the stops? Why didn't anyone get off?"

Susan laughed. "He drove past several stops before choosing that one." That only bolstered her father's theory. "I guess you're right; he could have been targeting something in that area. Quite possibly USR."

John Calvin twisted his lips thoughtfully. "Breakfast is in the microwave. Do you need anything before I go on Vox for some long conversations?"

Susan threw back the covers. "Nope. I'm going out myself."

"Out?" Her father returned to her side. "Are you sure that's wise? So soon after . . . what happened?"

"I'm fine," she reminded him.

"Where are you going?"

"To the hospital." Susan climbed out of bed and headed for her dressers.

"I thought you were forbidden—"

"From the unit, but not from the entire hospital. I have to visit Remy, and I'd like to talk to Goldman and Peters about our discussion."

"Remy?" Concern etched John Calvin's face. "Was he badly hurt?"

"Just a piece of . . . bus shrapnel in his shoulder, as far as I saw. But he shielded me from the explosion, and he may have taken some concussive forces. They wanted to observe him, at least overnight."

Opening the drawers, Susan tossed out a T-shirt and a pair of jeans.

John Calvin took the hint. "Good luck," he said. "I'll let you know if I find out anything."

"Same," Susan called out over her shoulder, closing the door behind him.

Chapter 20

Susan Calvin and Remington Hawthorn burst into the first-floor charting room to find Nate pouring through medical records, his fingers flying over the palm-pross. He looked up as they entered, and his face split into a friendly, all-too-human grin. "Where have you been?"

"Trying not to get too blown up," Remington answered facetiously. "And you?"

"I'm always somewhere in the hospital, here as often as not." Nate rose to give Susan a welcoming hug and Remington a short handshake–high five combination. "What do you mean 'trying not to get too blown up'?"

Remington pulled up his dress polo to reveal a wad of bandages enwrapping his shoulder. "I can show you the hole in my butt where they put the megacillin, too."

Susan knew he referred to the shot of long-acting antibiotics the nurses had injected to keep the wound from festering, but she shook her head at his word choice. "Remy, no one wants to see your butt right now, thank you very much."

Remington flushed. "It's a long story, Nate. But first, I promised Susan could ask you a question. She has a theory she won't share with me."

"Yet," Susan added. The idea had come to her while

they discussed the possibility that the SFH had had a hand in the drama. Remington had drawn similar conclusions as her father, but Susan's mind had taken it a step further. "Let's say someone put a bomb in your hands, told you to hijack a glide-bus full of people, take them to U.S. Robots, and blow it up. What would you do?"

Remington gave Susan an uncomfortable look. Clearly, he did not understand the need to involve Nate in such a direct fashion.

Nate took his hands off the keyboard and sat back. His brow furrowed. "I'd research the blast area of the bomb. I'd take it on the bus and hijack it to a spot near U.S. Robots, but not close enough to seriously damage the building or any others. I'd let the passengers off and make sure they moved a safe distance away." He shrugged. "Then I'd detonate the bomb."

Remington's face seemed to melt. He stared from Nate to Susan and back again. "No way. You guys worked this out in advance, didn't you?"

Nate turned his head to look directly at Remington. "What are you talking about?"

Susan sat on one of the couches, folding her arms across her chest and trying not to look too smug. "Nate, can you explain why you would do it the way you just described it?"

Nate shrugged. "Law Number One states, 'A robot may not injure a human being, or, through inaction, allow a human being to come to harm.' I'd have to make sure the passengers, bystanders, and anyone in the buildings did not become harmed by the blast. Law Number Two says, 'A robot must obey all orders given by human beings except where such orders would conflict with Law Number One.' So, I'd have to blow up the bus itself."

Remington sat up. "But doesn't the Third Law state you have to protect your own existence?"

"It does," Nate admitted, "except where doing so conflicts with the First and Second Laws. In this case, the directive to detonate the bomb would take priority over self-preservation, because the Second Law supersedes the Third Law."

Remington's head slowly moved to Susan. "Are you suggesting Payton Flowers released us from the bus because . . . he's a robot?"

Susan screwed up her features, then shook her head. "Nate, do nanorobots also have to follow the Three Laws?"

Nate went silent for far longer than Susan could ever previously remember. As he was clearly thinking, neither of the humans disturbed him until he finally managed words. "The Three Laws of Robotics are the basis from which all positronic brains are constructed. Without them, there is no positronic brain, no thinking robot. U. S. Robots has made the Three Laws so essential to production, that such cannot be undertaken without them."

"And the nanorobots?" Susan reminded him.

Nate shrugged. "I was not involved in their production."

Remington sighed.

Susan smiled. "No. But I know someone who was." She tapped her Vox to John Calvin's number and opened the connection to everyone in the room.

It took four beeps before he answered. "Susan? Is everything all right?"

"Fine, Dad. I just wanted to ask you a question."

"All right. But first, is Remy okay?"

Remington spoke up, "I'm fine, Dr. Calvin. Thank you for asking. I'm here with Susan."

"Glad to hear it." Calvin asked carefully, "Who else can hear us?"

Susan glanced around the room from habit, though she already knew the answer. "Just Nate, Dad. It's only the three of us in a closed room."

"Nate!" John Calvin said briskly. "How the hell are you?"

"Fine, Dr. Calvin." Nate looked sheepishly at the resident doctors, as if concerned John Calvin sounded more excited about him than the humans. "A bit bored. When these two visit, it's the best part of my day."

"I feel the same way, Nate," Susan's father said.

Susan smiled at Remington. Her father had not actually met the neurosurgery resident yet, but Susan had talked about him in glowing terms. "We're just wondering if the nanorobots have the Three Laws of Robotics embedded in them."

"The nanorobots?" John Calvin seemed surprised by the question. "Well, they do have a rudimentary positronic brain. We can't fit a whole lot of pathways in something that tiny, so we whittle it down to the basics."

"Do the basics include the Three Laws of Robotics?" Susan persisted.

"Well, of course." John Calvin sounded almost insulted by the question. "Nothing leaves U.S. Robots without those. Standard equipment." He hesitated, and a hint of suspicion entered his voice. "Why do you ask?"

Susan glanced at each of her companions in turn. She saw no reason not to include her father in their speculation, but she did not want to do so against anyone else's wishes. "We're thinking Payton's actions . . . seem to follow them. Parking near USR, but far enough to keep the explosion from collapsing the building. Letting off all the passengers . . ." Susan paused, expecting a reply.

John Calvin remained utterly silent.

Susan instinctively leaned closer to her Vox. "Dad? Did we lose you?"

The familiar voice issued from the device again. "No, I'm here. I'm just considering what you said."

Remington stepped closer. "What do you think, sir?"

"For starters, I think you should call me John."

Remington smiled. "All right, John. What do you think of the Three Laws theory?"

"I think . . . ," he said, pausing, "that it's an interesting idea, but it doesn't really pan out. While the nanorobots do have the Laws embedded, as every USR product does, they don't have the capacity to consider them."

Susan believed she understood. "You mean, because of their microscopic size, they have only a fraction of the computational capacity of, say, a man-sized robot."

John Calvin responded, "Exactly. The original wiring of the prototype positronic brain filled a large room. Over time, the brightest minds whittled it down to half, then a quarter, then an eighth. Nate's positronic brain is only half again the size of a human male's. We can get away with stuffing it into a normal-sized skull because he doesn't need cerebrospinal fluid, cisterns, direct blood supply, or as much cushioning. It's just skull, a thin layer of hair-growing skin, and the proper circuitry."

Susan could not help examining Nate as her father described him. He looked, for all the world, like a normal man. Had he not told her weeks ago, she never would have imagined he was composed of plastic, steel, and wires bundled into an all-too-human framework. He seemed so spectacularly normal.

John continued. "Obviously, with the nanorobots, we take out everything nonessential: emotion, calculation, reason. We leave only what's necessary for them to do their job, which consists of monitoring electronic activity and chemical composition of the cerebrospinal fluid and brain tissue. And, as you guessed, the Three Laws of Robotics. They remain embedded because our positronic brains cannot exist without them. It would violate the law, and our ethical code, to build even the most basic robot without them. It is the one and only process. All USR robotics begin and end with the Three Laws. It would be utterly impossible to build a positronic brain without the Three Laws or to remove them without permanently disabling the robot."

Susan tried to make sense of Payton's actions in the context of the current conversation. "So, what you're saying is the nanorobots have the Three Laws embedded. However, they don't have the capacity to act on them."

Remington took it a step further. "They don't have the capacity to act on anything except the task they were programmed to do. Even if they had the size, they don't have the hardware to do anything more substantial than swim through bodily fluids. And they don't have the intellectual capacity to . . ." There, his own knowledge ran short, so he finished by asking, "To what, sir?" Receiving no answer, he amended his question, "To what, John?"

Apparently satisfied, Susan's father deigned to answer. "They have some intellectual capacity, some ability to learn and make basic decisions, such as to focus in on a location in the patient's brain where neurons appear to be misfiring. But they're not programmed to act, just to record. Their encoding is extremely passive. They don't transmit; they only receive."

Susan sighed, disappointed. Her theory had seemed so plausible, and she could not help feeling as if a small piece of herself had died with it. "So, it's not possible to affect a person's thoughts and actions with injected nanorobots."

Nate finally spoke up. "Oh, it's possible."

All three humans fell silent. Susan could not help staring at the robot.

"Just not, as I am understanding it, with these particular nanorobots. I imagine a clever programmer could add a command and an interface to the human host."

"Conceivable," John Calvin said over the Vox, "but it would require someone with the knowledge of how to program them and the opportunity to tamper with them."

Susan felt a lump growing in her throat. "Do you . . . do you know . . . someone like that?"

"No." The answer came so swiftly, Susan did not believe he had had time to consider. "Alfred Lanning directly oversees this project. The company is the brainchild, the baby, of Alfred Lanning and Lawrence Robertson. Either one would sooner kill himself than put U.S. Robots at risk. At the other end, even if Goldman and Peters knew how to sabotage nanorobots, they'd never destroy their own reputations and careers. They've worked with us several times before; that's why USR picked them. And they're the primary force behind keeping Nate at the hospital."

Susan shook her head. She knew Goldman, especially, wanted more robots in medical use; and she could never imagine Peters doing anything so harmful. He did not have it in him. Their joint insistence on Susan not mentioning anything about the experiment to the police clinched their innocence. "So, if tampering occurred, it would have to have happened somewhere between USR and the lab."

"Susan, I like that you're thinking." Susan recognized the soothing, diplomatic tone John Calvin adopted when he tried to gently redirect her. "And I understand where you're going."

"But . . . ," Susan added, trying not to sound defensive.

"Well . . ." A note of discomfort entered her father's voice. He was a gentle man, not given to crushing ideas or dreams. "Some of the best minds in medicine and robotics have considered the situation, separately and together, and they have come to a conclusion."

"Yes," Susan coaxed.

"They strongly believe Payton acted in response to his very severe mental illness, his schizophrenia; and the nanorobots had nothing to do with it."

Susan had considered that possibility several times, and it made a lot of sense. Her mind just kept cycling back to the coincidence of his being a study patient and to the Three Laws of Robotics. Still, Susan knew that simply because things happened in proximity did not make them related. Such assumptions had caused many a scientific error and even more mass falsehoods and hysteria. Schizophrenics acted in schizotypical fashion; Payton did not need a reason beyond psychosis to act psychotically.

Susan sagged in her chair. It felt good to give up control this once, to allow wiser heads to prevail. "They're all in agreement? No doubts?"

"No doubts," her father returned. "And while that doesn't necessarily make them right, it's a good feeling when so many intelligent and experienced people agree."

Susan smiled. "Yeah. Thanks, Dad. Love you."

"Love you, too, kitten." John Calvin clicked off.

Susan rubbed her face, stopped in midmovement by a soft noise.

"Meow," Remington said.

Nate chuckled softly.

Susan's cheeks felt warm, and she turned man and robot a humorless glare. "Very funny. He's my dad; I'm his kitten. It's not like he called me 'snooky-ookums.'"

"Calm down, kitten." Remington looked sidelong at Nate. "What do you say we finally go on that date we keep postponing?"

To her surprise, Susan did not find the idea appealing. She wanted to do anything other than wander through the same city, reliving the experience, comparing everything to how it had looked before the bombing. "Can I take a rain check?"

"Ooo, another?" Remington pursed his lips and sucked air through his teeth. "Are you trying to tell me something?"

"I'm trying to tell you I'm not up for a repeat of two days ago, thank you very much. Also, Goldman and Peters said they had three more patients, and they dusted off their skills to handle Sharicka." Susan doubted the little girl's injection had gone smoothly. "If I were one of those three patients, I'd rather have me doing the procedure, wouldn't you?"

"Are you asking if I'd rather have a beautiful woman touching me or two male scientists?"

Susan could not help smiling. "Why don't you give me a hand? When I'm finished, I'll take you back to my place, and we can have a home-cooked meal à la Kentucky Roasted Chicken."

Remington bobbed his head. "Will your father be there?"

"Probably."

"Hmm." He pretended to consider. "I'll take you up on it anyway. At least you're not blowing me off this time."

"Or blowing you *up*," Nate reminded, proving a robot's sense of humor can be just as terrible as the next man's.

It also reminded Susan to say, "By the way, in case I forgot to say it before, thank you for saving my life."

A reddish tinge rose to Remington's face. "I'm not sure I actually saved your life. Maybe kept you from getting a hunk of bus embedded in your shoulder."

"Or my skull. Or my carotid artery." Susan knew all the ways a piece of flying metal could kill a person. "And I probably couldn't have handled the concussive forces as well as you did. I also appreciated that you went straight to work helping others, even though you were wounded and shaken yourself."

The new color drained from Remington's face, returning it to its natural hue. "I'm not sure whether to take that as a compliment or a backhanded insult."

The response startled Susan. She had not considered that he might perceive her words in a negative way. "What do you mean?"

"I'm just a bit miffed it even occurred to you I might not help in a crisis. You pitched right in, and I'm a doctor, too."

"Well, yes, but . . ." Susan finally paused to consider Remington's words. She had assisted the other victims of the bombing without any need for thought. She had the skills, and she used them. Why had she expected less from Remington? "You were hurt, and you took the full force of the explosion . . . and . . ."

"Just because I majored in biochemistry instead of construction doesn't make me a daisy."

"Of course it doesn't. I . . ." Susan finally looked directly at Remington.

Remington chuckled. "I was just going to say you were right about how to handle a dangerous schizophrenic. I shouldn't have pushed you to 'do something.'"

The words startled Susan. "I was just going to say *you* were right. I was the only one who knew his name and diagnosis, the only one who had a chance to successfully disarm him."

"The fact that we're here, alive, speaks otherwise."

Susan shook her head. "The fact that we're here, alive, is either luck or an echo of the Three Laws of Robotics. I didn't do anything because I think I never really believed he had a functioning bomb. I was obviously wrong."

Remington stared.

Uncomfortable under the sudden, intense scrutiny, Susan smoothed back her hair and worried about what might be sticking to her face or teeth. "What?"

"You just said you were wrong."

"So?"

"Dr. Susan Calvin was wrong about something?"

Susan did not wish to be reminded of her mistake with Sharicka. "Twice. In one week. And when I'm wrong, I do it in grand fashion. People die."

Remington intoned, "'People who think they know

everything are a great annoyance to those of us who do.'"

Susan blinked and repeated, "What?"

"A great man once said that. It's my favorite quotation. I use it whenever one of my peers gets too full of himself."

Susan did not like the sound of that. "Did I seem too full of myself?"

Remington took her hands. "Not at all. But if you get to thinking the world will end every time you make a mistake, you'll be afraid to do or say anything." He pulled her close. "The world needs you, Susan Calvin. With all your competence and your confidence. I'd hate to ever see you frozen in indecision."

"Never been accused of that," Susan admitted. "Though I can't say it's never happened." She wrapped her arms around him. He felt warm and strong, smelling of disinfectants and hospital bedding. "I'm sure you'll keep me . . . properly arrogant."

"I seem to manage it with my peers." Remington leaned in and kissed her.

A thrill of excitement swept through Susan, and she returned his kiss.

Nate feigned great interest in his palm-pross.

Remington proved invaluable as an assistant for Susan's first patient, Ronnie Bogart, a middle-aged man with bipolar illness who suffered from chronic depressive episodes. After his seventeenth suicide attempt, and his twentieth medication trial, it seemed unlikely any treatment would allow him to live outside of an institution. Alone in the world, he signed his own consent. The neurosurgery resident kept the patient still, as much with a steady patter of conversation as any type of physical restraint. When the vial of greenish liquid came out, Remington focused on it with grim fanaticism, running his fingers repeatedly over the rosy orange safety seal and, after its removal, studying the cap and the vial itself. Apparently satisfied, he tossed it in the biohazard can and proceeded to help Susan.

The second patient, Barack Balinsky, did not require anyone to hold him. Like Neal Fontaina, he was a catatonic schizophrenic, and he had not deliberately moved a muscle in nearly sixteen years. He had spent almost half his life in his mother's living room, a feeding tube dripping liquid food into his throat while he lay nestled into a mechanical bed that constantly shifted his position so he would not develop bedsores and contractures. Clearly long-suffering, his mother signed the consent form in silence, then left the residents alone to do their work. Susan supposed she appreciated the reprieve. She wondered if the mother hired babysitters to watch him while she went about her business or if she simply left him to his still and silent world.

When Susan injected the needle, the patient did not so much as stiffen in response. Susan waited for the clear drip of cerebrospinal fluid from the needle's barrel, only to get a disappointing wash of reddish liquid instead. "Damn it!" She gently removed the catheter, then held pressure over the tiny hole she had made.

Remington looked over the patient's body. "What's wrong?"

"Traumatic tap." Susan realized she must have nicked a small blood vessel on the way in. It happened fairly frequently, usually with a writhing pediatric patient and inexpert restraints. "I'm going to have to send this one home and try again tomorrow."

Remington stepped around Barack and examined Susan's work. She removed the gauze so he could look. The wound had already stopped bleeding. "I'm sure you know if you just let it drip a bit, it probably would have cleared."

"I'm aware of that." Susan hoped anyone performing a lumbar puncture was. "But it's protocol. Once we see blood, even if it's just peripheral, we have to redo the tap. We're not supposed to take a chance of injecting the nanorobots into the circulatory system. They're not programmed to function in that environment, and it doesn't help the patient, either."

"May I look?"

Susan stepped aside. Remington expertly palpated the area while the patient remained on his side. "You went in at L4/L5."

His words were not a question, and it was standard procedure, so Susan saw no reason to reply.

"We can still use L3/L4."

Susan did not know that. In her experience, bloody taps occurred for two reasons: Either the patient had a brain hemorrhage or the needle caught a blood vessel on insertion. In the first case, the tap should not be repeated because of serious danger of brain herniation. In the second, the fluid usually cleared in time, as Remington had stated. The technician could simply discard the first output and wait until the fluid became clear or use the bloody fluid for culture and the rest for cell studies.

If a nonurgent tap had blood, they either tried to work around it or repeated it the next day. If an urgent tap showed blood, they took the presence of the blood into account when performing tests. She had never heard of performing a second tap on the same day. "You can do that?"

"Sure, why not? It's upstream, so anything you might have nicked the first time shouldn't cause a problem."

Susan still hesitated. "And it's safe?"

"The spinal cord ends at L1 in adults." Remington pressed a finger into the indicated place in Barack's back. "It comes down a bit farther in kids, but L3/L4 should be safe for anyone." He indicated a spot one vertebral space up from Susan's tap. "Do you want me to do it?"

When Susan had offered to allow Remington to perform Fontaina's tap, she had not realized the irony of the situation. This time, she laughed out loud. "Isn't that rather like paging a cardiovascular surgeon to put in an IV?"

"Not exactly." Again, Remington examined the vial of greenish liquid, paying particular attention to the seal. "Unless you're planning to bring in Dr. Mandar."

Susan remembered when she had called on the neurosurgeon to reevaluate Starling Woodruff, and an involuntary shiver suffused her. "Not this time. A first-year neurosurgery resident is as expert as I'm willing to bother for a routine lumbar puncture."

Now, Remington had to laugh. "Could you imagine? After you gained his admiration, treating him like a scut puppy? He wouldn't know whether to jump at your command, in case you bested him again, or disarticulate your cervical vertebrae and show your body to your head."

Susan blushed, not wanting to be reminded of her earlier successes. She felt as if her recent blunders washed those away entirely. "If I paged him for this, I'd deserve the beheading."

Without further encouragement, or even a definitive answer, Remington set to work on the lumbar puncture. Usually, Susan enjoyed procedures. This time, she felt relieved to surrender it to Remington. He worked with a smooth and confident precision she did not have the experience to equal. In seconds, he had the stylet removed and clear fluid dripping from the barrel.

Removing the seal, Susan handed him the nanorobot vial. Using sterile technique, he attached it, manipulated the plunger, and patiently injected the fluid, a bit at a time.

Susan had done things slightly differently and wondered if Remington had a reason or simply another style.

"Is there an advantage to allowing that much CSF to drip out before you start? Also, the slower injection?"

Remington continued to inject the vial slowly. "There's an article in last month's *Oncology* that suggests making a bit of space before injecting intrathecally might decrease the risk for increased intracranial pressure."

That made sense to Susan. Emptying some air from a balloon prior to twisting it into a new shape did reduce the chances of popping it. What surprised her was discovering a neurosurgery resident who read cancer journals.

"Also, slower injections might minimize postinjection headaches."

"When did you start reading *Oncology*?"

Remington injected the last bit of nanorobots and fluid. "I don't usually. That article caught my eye." He stepped back, tossing the vial into the biohazard can. "There." He removed the needle and held a small piece of sterile gauze against the tiny hole it left.

"Wish I'd read it." Susan did read a lot of articles, about twenty percent of which were outside her field. She made a mental note to further broaden her research. "Do you want to do the last one?"

Remington snapped off his gloves and tossed them as well. "Why?" he asked suspiciously. "Is it an ill-tempered kangaroo?"

Susan cocked her head and turned him a searching look. "No, it's a paranoid schizophrenic. Why would you ask such a thing?"

Remington cleaned up his workstation, while Susan opened the door to admit the orderly who had brought Barack. The young man swept in, wheeling the patient away.

"Because that's one of the few reasons one of my colleagues would give up a procedure. I know you're not anticipating a call for an astrocytoma resection, so if you're giving away a procedure, it must have the fun factor of a digital bowel disimpaction."

Susan wrinkled her nose. "Actually, psychiatrists don't generally fight over medical procedures. We're more of the pensive variety." She recalled the joke she had contemplated a few days earlier, certain he knew it. "When a duck flies overhead, we're more interested in what it might be thinking and feeling than in blasting it out of the sky."

"Mmm." Remington accepted that explanation. "But then you miss out on the Muscovy à l'orange with shiitake mushrooms."

"I'm more of a barbecued chicken fan. I prefer my meat free of buckshot."

Remington chuckled. "Not to get technical, but you shoot big game, like deer, with buckshot; hence the name. You shoot ducks with birdshot."

"What's the difference?"

"About nine hundred pellets per cartridge."

Susan only nodded. She did not want to pursue a discussion about shotgun shells, especially with someone named after a gun. "Do you want to do the next LP, or not? Given the choice, the patients would probably prefer you." That made a better argument for her doing the procedure. The one who had less experience needed more practice, especially since she planned to keep working on this project. She thought of another issue. "I'll tell you what. Let's see how big and uncooperative the patient is. If we need more muscle to hold him still, I'll do the procedure. If he's even half as accommodating as our last patient, you'll do the procedure and I'll hold."

"Our last patient?" Remington glanced toward the door through which Barack had disappeared. "You mean, the statue?"

Susan knew he intended the words as a joke, but she did feel a flash of shame. "Hey, I managed a traumatic tap on that statue."

Remington blew off her concern with a dismissive noise. "Hell, I've seen guys get bloodier taps than that off people under anesthesia. On the surgery table, you get to see everything, move things around and out of your way, and everything's floppy and cooperative. When you blindly stab a needle into someone, you have no way of knowing where some tiny, feeder blood vessel might be sitting."

Susan appreciated Remington's earnest attempt to ease her conscience. Compared to the mistakes she had made with Sharicka and Payton, this barely showed up as a molehill in a mountain range. Susan shuffled away the paperwork for Barack Balinsky, pulling out a fresh sheaf on their next patient. She read aloud. " 'Cary English, sixty-four-year-old white male. Paranoid schizophrenic, refractory to treatment. Persistent delusions and hallucinations involving space aliens. Assaultive to staff and strangers; potentially dangerous.' "

Remington placed a fresh, wrapped tool tray on the portable stand. "Ah, sounds like you'll be doing this one, kitten. I'm no psychiatrist, but I have a feeling poking and prodding his body might just piss him off."

"Good thought, snooky-ookums. I'm just betting he comes with a couple of large nursing aides and maybe a son or two to assist."

Remington set the vial of nanorobots on the tray beside the sterile kit. "I hadn't considered that. I get most of my patients pre-anesthetized."

To Susan's relief, Cary did arrive with a burly nursing aide, as well as a middle-aged son who signed the consents. The two of them did a practiced job of holding the old man still, while he thrashed and howled about aliens stealing his thoughts and emotions through his bodily fluids. To her relief, Remington managed a swift, clean tap, followed by a slow injection. She wondered if she would have had the same result and supposed she might have managed it, although she could not have done it with the same speed and assuredness. She believed she had made the right choice.

The son and the nursing aide chatted baseball statistics while Remington held the gauze in place, then wheeled Cary English from the room with barely an acknowledgment. "Thanks," Susan said.

Remington tossed his gloves. "Thank *you*. It's not often I get to participate in research, especially this cutting edge. And I really like procedures, even relatively simple ones."

Susan smiled wanly. Whether he acknowledged it or not, she owed him. Without his assistance, she would have had to explain to Goldman and Peters why she had to come in another day and reinject Barack Balinsky. At worst, he had saved her the embarrassment and another day of work. She also would have had to find someone else to hold Ronnie Bogart. "I believe I owe you lunch and a trip to my place."

"I believe you do." Remington finished cleaning, put everything back in order, then took Susan's arm.

At his touch, a thrill tingled through Susan. It occurred to her, with abrupt and stunning suddenness, that she loved this man. And, though neither of them had yet spoken the words aloud, she believed he loved her, too.

Chapter 21

Doctors Susan Calvin and Remington Hawthorn sat on a bench in the park ten stories below the Calvins' apartment, their bellies full of John Calvin's special chicken-eggplant recipe, cobbled from the Kentucky Roasted they brought home and lots of fresh vegetables. The afternoon sun beamed down upon a horde of squealing preschoolers racing across machine-woven mats of recycled plant material and climbing ladders, tunnels, and bridges molded from shredded rubber. The softness of the ground and structures allowed them to push, shove, and plummet to their hearts' content. Their parents and nannies watched them from windows or benches, shouting encouragements.

Remington stretched his legs in front of him and placed an arm around Susan. Excitement flitted through her at his touch. She felt like a high schooler with her first crush. Everything he did that suggested he liked her seemed like a new and exhilarating experience. She loved the look of him: golden highlights glistening in the casual disarray of his blond curls, his physique a pleasant combination of slender and muscular, his features strong and regular, the very definition of chiseled. The natural scents of him enticed her in a way no human-created smell had before, bringing her thoughts back to childhood vacations and, inexplicably, stops for ice cream.

They had talked the entire trip and now sat in a comfortable silence Susan felt no particular drive to break. She could have sat like this all day, reveling in the warmth of his closeness, the thrill of his touch, a light breeze wafting the faint, sweet odors of toast and jam from the children. Then, her mouth opened, as if of its own volition, and words she had no chance to consider spewed forth. "Do you believe in love at first sight?"

Remington hesitated, his gaze tracking a toddler headed toward what appeared to be an older sibling, the toddler's steps tentative and bowlegged, his arms outstretched. "If you're asking do I believe it's possible to glance across a crowded room, meet someone's gaze, and instantly know you're soul mates, then no. I don't believe it's possible to love someone until you know what's in that person's heart and mind. Some of the most outwardly attractive people in the world are vain, prejudiced, or just plain stupid." He turned his gaze to Susan and raised his brows in quick succession. "On the other hand, I do believe in lust at first sight. You see someone exquisitely beautiful and can imagine making wild, passionate love for the rest of your born days." He smiled crookedly. "Usually, though, she opens her mouth before you can get her into bed and spoils everything."

Susan tried not to glare. She had asked an incredibly stupid question without giving it much thought, and he had simply responded in an appallingly forthright manner. She had always preferred people who spoke their minds.

Apparently sensing he had not given the answer Susan wanted, Remington continued floundering. "But if you mean do I think our first meeting might go down in the annals of history . . ." He paused thoughtfully, then shook his head. "I'd still have to say no. As I recall, one of us acted like a pompous ass." He grinned at her.

Susan knew how to play that game. "And the other one like a castrating bitch. Not exactly first-sight-love material."

To Susan's surprise, Remington further mulled a question that now seemed beaten to death. "However, I think I can firmly say that, with you, I did experience lust at first sight. And, over a relatively short period of time, I've grown to"—he looked at her, as if worried his next word might queer the deal—"love you."

The reply was startled from Susan. "You love me?" As soon as the words left her lips, Susan wanted to strangle herself. *Don't sound so surprised. You knew it. And you love him, too.*

Remington laughed. "Why else would I throw my body over yours to shield you from an explosion? Why would I give up my first day off to help you stab crazy people in the spine in the same setting I spend nearly every waking hour?" He shook his head. "Does reality have to strike you with a sledgehammer, you silly woman?"

Susan stared. "Well, when you put it in such a beautiful and romantic way, how could I not know it?" She snuggled against him. "And, by the way, I love you, too."

Remington's arms tightened around Susan. "Should I make you prove it?"

Susan forced herself not to flinch. "Right here and now?"

Remington glanced at the playground equipment, the running children, the parents ringed around them. "I'm game, but do you really think three- and four-year-olds are ready for a sex ed class?"

Susan felt her entire face warm, and that surprised her. She sighed before she could stop herself. "Remy, I need to tell you something."

He tensed but remained silent.

Susan got the idea he was bracing himself for whatever she might say. She looked up at him. He had his lower lip trapped between his teeth, and his eyes looked positively frantic.

Susan shook her head, laughing. The children's calls and shouts had drowned out their conversation thus far, but she lowered her voice further. Somehow, silence seemed to appear in the most unlikely places when a person said something inappropriate. "You think I'm about to tell you I'm a transvestite, don't you?"

Remington shifted in obvious discomfort. "Actually, I was thinking about an incurable venereal disease; but thanks for giving me something else to worry about."

"It's neither of those."

Remington guessed, "Lesbian?"

"Nope."

His voice became strained. "Cancer?"

Susan let him off the hook. "I'm a virgin."

Remington studied her face. He did not appear shocked, just more tightly braced, as if he waited for the other shoe to fall. Finally, he said in a strangely squeaky voice, "That's it?"

"That's it. I'm a genetic woman with all of the working parts." Susan swiftly amended her statement. "Well, they're working as far as cycling and all. To my knowledge, there's only one virgin who's ever given birth."

Remington cleared his throat, then spoke in his normal voice. "A virgin, huh? Well, that's nothing bad."

"In some circles, it's considered a major achievement. After all, I'm twenty-six years old." Susan did not want Remington to get the wrong idea. "Not that I haven't had opportunities, of course. I mean I started dating in high school. It's just I've always felt a person should be in love before making love."

"And," Remington started carefully, "you love me?"

"I do," Susan admitted, then wished she had phrased it any other way. She did not want him to think she was rushing him into marriage when they had barely even managed a second date.

Remington did not seem to notice. "And I love you?"

"Are you asking me? Or telling me?"

"Haven't I already told you?"

Susan recognized a pattern. "Why do we keep answering each other's questions with another question?"

Remington grinned and gave the obvious answer, "Why not?" Then the smile disappeared, and he drew her back to him. "Seriously, Susan. I'm a man; I'm always ready. But I'm not going to push you into anything. I can wait as long as you need."

"I'm ready," Susan said, then realized the folly of her words. She glanced around the park. "Well, not immediately, of course. Tonight, though. We'll barricade ourselves in my bedroom."

"Ooh-kay." Remington did not seem wholly comfortable with the suggestion. "But what about your father?"

"He can find his own date."

"Funny." Remington rolled his eyes. "I just mean, will he be all right with our spending the night together in his apartment?"

Though she had never tested him, Susan felt certain John Calvin could handle the situation. "He'll have to. When he asked me to stay with him, he knew I was a grown woman. And I pay my share of rent."

To Susan's surprise that did not put Remington at ease. When he did not explain why, she pressed. "What's wrong?"

"Well," he said softly, "I have a lot of respect for your dad, and I want him to like me."

"He does like you," Susan reassured him. "And he's aware that twentysomethings have . . ."

Remington remained quiet.

"What?" Susan demanded.

"Well, parents and kids are funny about that. I mean, I know my parents must have done it at least three times and probably a lot more, but I don't want to imagine it.

Or know it's happening. I'd rather just pretend they grew us in the cabbage patch; you know what I mean?"

Susan understood, though she did not share his sentiment. She wished her father would date rather than moon over a woman he had lost so long ago, even if she was Susan's own mother. "I know what you mean, but I don't see it as a problem. I'll talk to him first, if you want."

Remington's cheeks took on a reddish hue. "This may sound ridiculously old-fashioned, but do you mind if I talk to him?"

Susan gave him a pointed look. "You want to ask my father if you can . . . have sex with me?"

"Well, actually, I thought I'd phrase it more as you asked me to stay over, and I wanted to make sure he didn't have a problem with it before I agreed to do it."

"Oh," Susan said facetiously. "Make me look like the slut."

Remington did not rise to the bait. "By now, he surely knows you don't invite men to sleep over every day." He gave her a wide-eyed look. "You don't invite men to sleep over every day, do you?"

Susan put as much sarcasm into her voice as she could muster. "Sure, I do. Then I poison their toothpaste." She added, as if fielding the thought for the first time, "You don't suppose that might be why I'm still a virgin?"

"Could be." Remington rose. "No time like the present."

Susan also stood. "You're going to ask him right now?"

"No." Though he had gotten up with vigor, Remington seemed hesitant to take the next step. "But I do want to talk with him a bit. I think I'd like to get to know the man a little better before I ask if he minds terribly much if I steal his daughter's virginity."

"It's not stealing if I give it to you." Susan took Remington's hand and led him back toward the building.

*   *   *

When Susan and Remington returned to the Calvins' apartment, they discovered John Calvin striding from his bedroom in dress clothes, his fingers on his Vox. When he spotted the pair, he removed his hand, smiling. "Ah, there you are. I was just going to call you. I'm heading in to work."

"Work?" Susan paused halfway to the living room chair. "I thought you couldn't go. Structural damage."

"I'm not actually working. We're just having a short meeting, taking a look at the damage. That sort of thing."

It occurred to Susan that, with her father gone for hours, it might obviate the whole issue of Remington's needing to sleep over. She could feel her heart hammering against her ribs and a lump forming in her throat. A mixture of excitement, relief, and fear washed through her.

"Can we go with you, sir?" Remington said, then corrected himself. "John?"

"I'm not a knight of the realm," Susan's father said jokingly.

Susan might have grinned at the realization that her father did not kid with just anyone, so he must like Remington; but she found herself too surprised by the neurosurgeon's request to consider that long. "You want to go downtown? Near the bomb site?"

"I think it might do us both some good. Plus, I'd really like to see the place where Nate was built, and those nanorobots."

Susan could not help remembering she had initiated the exact same trip the day Payton had hijacked their bus. "I've been wanting to see where you work, too, Dad. I can't believe I've never gone before."

John Calvin toed his usual line. "Kitten, it's boring. There's nothing there but a bunch of middle-aged guys and some laboratory benches covered in tangles of wires."

No longer swayed by his words, Susan gave her father a stormy look. "Tangles of wires that bring plastic and steel and skin cells to life." She pictured Nate. "Come on, Dad. We almost got blown up along with your building. Can't you take us this once?"

John Calvin looked from one to the other. "You really want to go?"

Susan wondered if her father had gone stupid. "Of course, I want to go. You've worked there my whole life, and I've never even seen the outside of the building. Now that I'm actually involved in a USR project, I can't believe I haven't gone yet." Susan understood her own reasons, but she wasn't sure she understood Remington's. Obviously, the creation and animation of robots intrigued him, particularly since he had met Nate, and the nanorobot project seemed to fascinate him as well.

"All right," John Calvin said. The words emerged halfheartedly, and his smile seemed forced. "But don't get your expectations too high. There are places even I can't go, and a few things got unexpectedly shuffled after the damage to the building."

Remington held the door. "Lead the way, Sir John."

John Calvin gave him a look Susan knew well. "As you wish, Sir Remy." With a flourishing bow, he headed out the door.

Susan followed, and Remington took the rear, closing the door behind him.

A drab, grayish, rectangular building of insignificant size, U.S. Robots and Mechanical Men, Inc., did not stand out in any way from the offices and shops around it. Before the bomb explosion, it had displayed no sign or other identifying features; but, now, the front was marred by divots and patches of scorching. The front edge of the roof looked chaotically scalloped, as if some horror-movie monster had struck it with a claw. Otherwise, the building appeared to be intact.

Focused on the building with laserlike intensity, Susan nearly missed the other telltale signs of a recent catastrophe. Cued by her father's worried glance around, Susan opened her mind to the obvious details. Blinking police caution tape enclosed the area, and hazard blockades sat at either end of the street. The burnt, twisted, and sodden remains of the glide-bus still occupied part of the street, where a police forensics team conferred, taking myriad tiny samples. A tangled array of metal stood like a perverted piece of art, jutting from blackened concrete; and it took Susan a moment to recognize the remains of the bus stop. A dark pool of blood marred the sidewalk, connected to an erratic trail. Susan remembered its origin: She had eased a piece of glass from a woman's thigh, only to have her run in panic when it came free. Remington had had to tackle her to allow Susan to hold pressure on the injury.

The memory brought a deep frown to Susan's face. She had never understood why desperate circumstances brought out the best in some people and the worst in others. In emergencies, Susan had always noticed time seemed to slow down for her. When a driver swerved into her path, or a patient went into cardiac arrest, she felt as if she had all the time in the world to take evasive action or to recall the sequence of emergency procedures. Some other people seemed to freeze and grow desperately pale, or dithered wildly and purposelessly, and still more screamed and ran in some random direction, which usually only served to worsen the situation. She had even seen fellow students, male and female, faint dead away in a crisis.

Susan appreciated that one's reaction to disaster was a natural phenomenon, not under the control of the individual. Obviously, those prone to calm thought belonged in occupations such as law enforcement, military, traffic control, and medicine, where potentially life-threatening calamities arose often and required quick wits and action. She appreciated that Remington appeared to have nerves of steel. She could think of nothing more important for someone operating on people's brains and spinal cords, and she did not know if she could have respected a man who panicked in a crisis, no matter how natural and understandable the reaction.

A hand fell to Susan's shoulder. Startled from her thoughts, Susan looked up to her father, his face screwed up in pain.

Abruptly concerned, Susan grabbed his hand. "Are you all right?"

"Me?" Her father's features shifted instantly from discomfort to clear confusion. "I was worried about you. Are you okay coming here so soon?"

"I'm fine. I can't say it's not weird seeing it again, but I'm not suffering from post-traumatic anxiety or anything." Susan glanced past him at Remington, who seemed more interested in the USR building than in the wreckage. "Remy seems fine, too."

At the sound of his name, Remington looked at Susan. "Hmm?"

"I said you don't seem to be suffering from post-traumatic anxiety."

"No. Should I be?"

"I hope not," Susan said, "because I'm not, either."

Apparently intuiting the original source of concern, Remington addressed John Calvin. "If anyone should know, she should." He jerked a thumb toward Susan and whispered as if revealing a dangerous secret, "She's a headshrinker."

Susan's father chuckled. "Yes, indeed she is. And a good one, so I've heard."

Though merely banter, the words made Susan cringe. "Well, you didn't hear it from me. I sent a psychopath home to murder her sister and maim her brother, then couldn't talk a schizophrenic out of blowing up a bus." Those two enormous failures would weigh heavily on her conscience, she believed, for all eternity. She ground her teeth as guilt swam down upon her again. In her mind, the blood of Misty Anson would always stain her hands.

"Ah," Remington said. "So now we measure success and failure by whether or not crazy people act crazy?"

Susan turned him a withering look. "That is my job, Remy. To keep crazy people from doing crazy things."

"First of all," he reminded her, "Payton Flowers was never *your* patient. You didn't treat him, you didn't medicate him, and you didn't know him any better than I did. As for . . ." He paused, surely considering confidentiality. Payton Flowers had become a household name since the police had released his identity, but Sharicka and her family still had a reasonable expectation of privacy. "As for the girl, you took a calculated risk, and the worst happened. Learn from it and move on."

Susan wanted to do that; but, while awake and in her dreams, she found herself reliving the moment when Sharicka's mother had asked her opinion. "Who says I'm not moving on?"

"The person who watched you say nothing when a man announced his plans to blow us up."

Susan wanted to clobber both of the men in her life. "What are you saying? That I was afraid to try to dissuade Payton because I felt inadequate after allowing Sh—" She caught herself, then continued. "That little girl a deadly home visit?"

Both men only looked at her, brows raised like psychiatrists who have just tricked a patient into breakthrough self-analysis.

Susan shook her head so hard, her hair whipped her face. "I didn't act on the bus because I didn't know Payton well enough. I didn't know what would provoke or deter him. Besides, I didn't really believe he had a working bomb."

"Okay." Remington said in that aggravating tone men

use when they hand over a reluctant victory for the sole purpose of ending an argument.

Susan felt her limbs shaking. The whole ordeal seemed to crash down on her at once: the terror, the helplessness, and the realization she alone might have had the power to stop it.

Suddenly, Susan found herself enfolded in Remington's embrace. "I'm sorry," he whispered directly into her ear. "I'm sorry about what I said. I was wrong."

Susan trembled in his arms, cursing her weakness. Tears streamed down her face. "You're not wrong, Remy. I just didn't realize it before. I consider myself so strong; but, when it came to preventing a tragedy, I froze."

"You didn't freeze. You just didn't take a chance. As it turned out, your decision to say nothing wasn't wrong."

Susan had to admit the worst had not come to pass. "I might have stopped the whole process," she choked out. "I might have saved his life."

"Maybe." Remington squeezed her tightly and closed his eyes. "Or he might have freaked out and detonated the bomb with everyone on board. My point wasn't that it was in any way your fault. I'm just saying, if you start overquestioning your every decision because of one mishap, you deprive the world of your obvious and incredible brilliance."

John Calvin stepped aside, wisely allowing Remington to handle the situation, though his fatherly instincts had to ache.

Susan sank to the ground.

Remington squatted in front of her. "You're the one condemning both situations as personal failures and taking the burden of guilt on yourself. Medicine is an art, not a science. You use as much knowledge and thought as you can, but it reaches a point where you have to play the odds and intuition. A postsurg patient gets septic. Was it the glove that broke and had to be changed midprocedure? Was it the sneeze? Or was it simply inevitable? The Guzman procedure works best for sixty-two percent of people with early spinal cord separation. You use it on a patient, and he winds up quadriplegic. Could he have led a perfectly normal life had you gone with the Striker technique? Would the outcome have been exactly the same, or would he have died? Life has a lot of forks. Just because the consequences of choosing one was bad doesn't mean the others would have been any better."

Susan understood his point. "But had I not sent her home, her sister would still be alive. Her brother would not have had to undergo emergency neurosurgery. Her parents would not have been devastated."

"Her parents were already devastated," Remington said firmly. "Long before you came into the picture."

"Yes, but . . ." Susan forced back the tears, and a sob shuddered from her in its place. "But things would have been so much better. At least, the sister would be alive."

"Would she?"

The question seemed ludicrous. "Of course she would."

"Because, if you had not sent your patient on a home visit that particular day, no one else would have done so. Ever."

Susan finally managed to get control. "I'm sorry I'm blubbering like a baby. You'd never believe, just prior to this meltdown, I was thinking about how well I handle stress."

"Answer the question," John Calvin said quietly.

Susan's father did not issue commands often, and Susan always took them seriously. "Well, of course, she would have gone on a home visit eventually. When she was more stable."

"More stable than what?"

Susan flicked her gaze back to Remington, who had

asked the question. "More stable than she obviously was."

Remington released her, shook his head, and started to rise.

Susan wiped away the last of the tears. She felt ashamed of her weakness and hoped it would not drive Remington away. "Just ignore me. I got overwhelmed by the moment." She glanced around at the carnage. "I guess the whole ordeal hit me harder than I thought."

Remington smiled and offered his hand. "Ah, so the great Dr. Susan Calvin is . . . human, eh? Who'd have guessed it?"

Susan took his hand and forced her own weak smile. She hated the thought of appearing weak, promised herself not to let it happen again.

John Calvin waited patiently while they sorted themselves out before saying, "Ready?"

Back in full control, Susan said, "Ready."

Her father approached the door, scanning palm and retina simultaneously, a foolproof security system that required a person to stand in one precise spot and position. The door whisked open to reveal a stuffy, austere foyer containing only a large, semicircular desk. A woman wearing too much makeup sat behind it, partially obscured by a large computer console that clearly controlled more than the standard palm-pross. "Good afternoon, John," she said cheerfully. "They're meeting in Lawrence's office." She looked over Susan and Remington. "It appears you need a couple of guest passes."

John Calvin smiled at the woman. "Thank you, Amara. This is my daughter, Susan, and her boyfriend, Remy."

Amara winked. "I figured as much. Not only do you bear a resemblance, but I recognized Susan from the eight hundred pictures in your office." She tapped a couple of keys on her desktop, a printer beneath it hummed, and she pulled out two small, square pieces of paper. Stuffing each into a plastic holder with a thin lanyard, she handed them to John Calvin. Susan could now read the word VISITOR on each. She accepted one, slung it around her neck, then gave the other to Remington. He took his and put it on with the same deft flick of his hand.

"This way." John led Susan and Remington toward one of five doors, this one bearing the name LAWRENCE ROBERTSON. He knocked firmly, paused briefly, then opened it.

Apparently cued by the knock, three men in dress polos sat in silence, all looking at the opening door. One stood up behind an enormous mahogany desk that held a half dozen palm-prosses; two digital frames; a mass of books, mostly hard copies bound in large folders; an enormous printer combo; and a surprising amount of paper, most of which seemed to contain circuitry maps. Loose computational chips also floated through the mess. The other two men sat on comfortable-looking but mismatched chairs, while three more empty chairs were spaced around the room.

The man behind the desk said, "Hey, John!" He gave Susan a warm and genuine smile. "This must be the younger Dr. Calvin you're always talking about." He came around the desk and extended his hand. "I'm Lawrence Robertson."

From the reverent tone with which her father always spoke his name, Susan had pictured someone older, even though she knew they had been college roommates. He appeared to be about her father's age, with dark, wavy hair, a large mouth, and a rugged complexion. He carried a touch of gray at the temples that perfectly matched his pale, friendly eyes. Susan knew he had founded the company the year she was born. He must have done so in his early twenties, already the genius behind the positronic brain. She gripped his hand firmly. It was dry, solid, and powerful.

"And this is Susan's boyfriend, Remington Haw-thorn. He's a neurosurgeon."

Susan wished her father would stop referring to Remington as her boyfriend. It made her sound twelve years old.

Lawrence Robertson released her hand to reach for Remington's.

Remington clasped it. "You can call me Remy."

"Remy, it is. And you can call me Lawrence."

Susan did not feel any more comfortable referring to the founder of U.S. Robots and Mechanical Men by his first name than Remington did her father. She wondered if she could get away with "Sir Lawrence."

Lawrence continued the introductions by pointing to a frumpy-looking, balding man in wrinkled dress clothing. "This is my director of research, Alfred Lanning."

"How do?" Alfred mumbled when no one stepped close enough to shake hands.

"And one of our top roboticists, George Franklin." George did not wait for them to come to him. A tall, gangly youth, he crossed to the center of the room in a single step to shake hands with Susan and Remington. "Pleased to meet you."

Lawrence Robertson stepped back behind his desk, his gaze still on Susan. "So, young lady, when are you joining us on staff?"

"Me?" Susan could make no sense of the question. "I'm a psychiatry resident. I can't imagine you need one of those at a robot factory."

The men sniggered gently, except for Alfred Lanning, who gave the suggestion actual thought. "As complex as the positronic brain has become, I could see us putting a robot or two on the couch."

"Not to mention the staff," Lawrence added smoothly. "You have to be a bit nutty to work here."

Not to be outdone, Remington added his piece. "I could just picture a robot lying on his analyst's couch:

'Doc, I know my intelligence is artificial, but my problems are *real*.'"

Everyone chuckled, except Remington himself. As George retook his seat, Susan joined Alfred in giving the idea real thought, or at least appearing to do so. "I can't speak for the staff, but the robots shouldn't be too hard to analyze. Ethically, they have to conform to the Three Laws of Robotics, right? That doesn't leave a whole lot of wriggle room, really."

John Calvin took one of the chairs. "I think it's the general public who needs the help. We could hire a team of psychiatrists to eradicate the Frankenstein Complex, and people would still be worrying that robots are going to take their jobs, obliterate their privacy . . . and eat them."

George nodded grimly. "Well, I suppose the risk of having a psychiatrist on staff would be the further reaction of the public." He made a gesture toward the ceiling that Susan took to symbolize "the sky is the limit." "They'd be imagining a two-ton hunk of metal with the capacity to smash a girder running around clinically depressed."

Lawrence shook his head, still grinning. Clearly, he had asked Susan out of politeness, the kind of question all bosses address to a favored employee's children. "Well, John, we're still waiting for Javonte and Keagan. Why don't you give your guests a short tour?"

"That's all I can give them." John rose and ushered Susan and Remington toward the door. "We're not large to begin with, and we can't go most places."

"Sorry," Lawrence said, sounding honestly apologetic.

"No problem." Remington headed out the door, with Susan and John at his heels. "So long as we can get a glimpse of the nanorobot production, I don't mind. That's what Susan's working on, and it has me fascinated."

"Knock yourselves out," Lawrence said as the door shut behind them.

They found themselves back out in the foyer with the secretary and the assortment of doors.

"Nice people," Susan said.

"The best." John looked around thoughtfully, apparently figuring where to start. "Why do you think I've stayed so long?"

Amara piped up, "I thought it was my amazing coffee."

"Coffee?" John playacted exaggerated surprise. "You mean that stuff you give us in the morning is coffee? All these years, I thought it was motor oil."

It occurred to Susan that she had no idea how her father liked his coffee. She had never seen him drink any.

"Very funny." Amara returned to her work. "Next time, Dr. Calvin, you get a mug of gasoline. We'll see if you can tell the difference."

John Calvin pointed to one of the doors. "The other offices are through there, including mine. I'll take you there if we run out of places before Lawrence calls me back." He opened one of the other doors and ushered them into a laboratory.

Compared to Lawrence's office, the room looked positively germfree. The white walls gleamed, without a trace of stain or dirt. Long lab benches held racks of empty test tubes, and the sinks appeared brand-new. Small refrigeration units with old-fashioned key locks perched on each end of every bench. Each one also held a high-powered microscopic chamber. Hovering over the benches, clear Plexiglas shields could be lowered to create a soundproof or sterile environment. Only the chairs lay in disarray, apparently left where the workers had abandoned them.

"This is what you wanted to see, Remy." John Calvin waved a hand to encompass the entire room. "The skeletal forms of the nanorobots are produced in the micro-chambers." He led them to one of the boxes on the table. "You put your hands in here." He indicated cut-out areas on the sides, now locked down tight. "And the view screen magnifies the project and tools so our roboticists don't go blind."

Remington lowered his head until he looked directly into the screen. "How much magnification is there?"

"I can look up an exact figure, if you want to know." John Calvin hit a switch button on the back. Instantly, a brilliant light came on, demonstrating the contents: strange-looking pliers, guide wires, lasers, blades, screwdrivers, and even a tiny hammer. A sleek, pill-shaped body lay on a piece of cloth that looked like a chamois.

"Is that a nanorobot?" Remington asked, clearly awed.

"That's the shell of one, yes. And those are the tools we use."

Susan leaned in closer. "It looks so big."

"Magnification," John Calvin explained. "Put your hands in."

"May I?" Remington said breathlessly.

"Be my guest."

Remington looked at Susan, a stripe of red across his cheeks. "I'm sorry. Did you want to go first?"

Susan felt no particular need to have her own hands in the contraption. "Be my guest." She looked at her father. "Just promise me this isn't some sick practical joke that's going to mangle his surgeon hands."

John Calvin leaned in and unlocked the ports. He stepped back, gesturing at Remington.

Susan rolled over a chair so Remington did not have to crouch.

Without taking his attention from the magnification box, Remington settled his bottom on the chair and gently glided each hand into a side of the box.

They appeared instantly, wrapped in an opaque film.

They looked enormous, as if he could grip the entire room.

"Whoa," Susan said.

"Whoa," Remington and John agreed.

Remington tentatively touched one of the tools with his finger. "That's amazing. I didn't think glass this big could be ground that finely."

"It can't." John wore the expression of one accustomed to the impossible. "The glass is maximally magnified. Then we use an active system to multiply it another thousandfold."

Remington removed his hands and sat back. "I'm impressed." He rose and stepped aside. "Want to try it, Susan?"

Susan suspected, after a day of work, the nanorobot scientists walked around holding their arms spread far apart, afraid to knock over everything in their path with their gigantic hands. "No, thanks. I got the idea, and I'd just as soon not know if I have hair on my knuckles."

Remington reflexively examined his own hands. "What's the greenish fluid in the nanorobot concoction?"

"Normal saline." It was an extremely familiar product, one Remington ran through IV lines daily and Susan had used in her medical rotations as well. It consisted of a sterile 0.91 percent solution of sodium chloride in water, essentially the same composition as that of most bodily fluids. It was the safest solution known to man, one that could be injected or rinsed over any organ, vessel, or tissue in the body, even in relatively large amounts.

Susan asked the obvious follow-up question. "So, what makes it green?"

John relocked the magnification box and flipped off the switch. "As I understand it, it bleeds off the nanorobots' shell. Some kind of anti-infective, antirejection slime."

"Slime, huh? That must be the medicotechnical terminology," Susan said helpfully as her father reflexively restored every flap and detail of the magnifier box.

Remington seemed fascinated with the tiniest detail of the operation. He glanced around the room with slow thoroughness, then focused on the refrigeration units on the ends of the lab benches. "Is that where you store the vials?"

John Calvin followed Remington's gaze. "Yup. They're pretty basic units. You didn't want to see the inside of the fridges, too?"

"Please?"

"Seriously?"

"If you don't mind."

With a shrug and a glance that suggested he thought the neurosurgery resident had gone insane, John unlocked one of the refrigeration units. He opened the door to reveal thick walls and insulation. A test-tube stand held five of the familiar green vials with reddish seals. They seemed out of place to Susan, like running into an old friend from home while on vacation.

Remington leaned in so closely he blocked Susan's view. He studied the vials for several moments, while Susan and her father exchanged looks that expressed confusion, surprise, and, perhaps, a hint of suspicion. Susan had to ask. "What are you doing, Remy?"

Remington stiffened, as if awakening from a trance. "Sorry. It's just all so amazing."

At that moment, an alarm blared through the room, so sudden and loud that Susan let out an involuntary squeak. She turned to John Calvin for explanation, but he seemed as uncomfortable as she did. Remington stood up straight.

"Lock up, Susan," John Calvin said, heading for the door.

Susan reached to shut the refrigeration unit, but Remington caught her hand. "Wait," he whispered, pausing until John Calvin had fully exited. Only then, he whipped something from his pocket and held it up against the test tubes. Susan recognized it as one of the empty vials from when he had helped her inject her last few patients, along with the torn-off seal.

The alarm continued to shrill through the building, almost unbearable. She wanted to clap her hands over her ears and curl into a ball. Ventilator alarms made a similar noise, absolutely impossible to ignore, cuing medical staff to a life-threatening emergency requiring immediate attention.

"See?" Remington said.

"See what?" The words emerged more gruffly than Susan intended. Driven to find the source of the alarm, and fix it, she found concentration on anything else almost impossible.

"Look closely. At the seals."

Susan forced herself to study the removed seal, comparing it to the ones on the fresh vials. Now that Remington had pointed it out, she could see the previous seal had more of an orange hue, while the ones in the fridge were definitively red. "Do you think it faded a bit?"

Remington grimaced, then shook his head. "Don't be ridiculous. It came off yesterday, and it's been in my pocket since. Besides, you've seen the seals on the vials we're using."

The alarm seemed to explode in Susan's head, making original thought nearly impossible. "So . . . someone *is* tampering with them." The significance of her own words escaped her momentarily.

The alarm stopped abruptly, and realization smacked Susan so hard she nearly fell.

Remington closed and locked the refrigerator unit. "Exactly. And it's happening sometime after this step in the process."

The silence became nearly as overbearing as the alarm itself. Susan felt a shiver traverse her entire spine. "Let's go find my dad." She headed for the door, and Remington followed.

They wound their way swiftly back to Lawrence Robertson's office, where they found the door closed. Susan knocked politely before pushing it open. A screen blared the evening news. The same men they had met earlier, plus two more, leaned forward in their chairs, watching intently. At the back of the room, Susan's father appeared to be the only one who noticed them, and he ushered them inside with a gesture. The pair stepped in and closed the door behind them.

"Hell of a coincidence," someone muttered.

"But coincidence it must be," Alfred Lanning said emphatically. "There's no other explanation."

"What happened?" Susan whispered to her father.

John Calvin squirmed, clearly loath to tell her. "Valerie Aldrich just blew herself up in the Federal Building."

Susan felt as if a vice clamped onto her chest. "Valerie Aldrich? Princess Valerie? I injected her myself."

"Yes."

The situation seemed to require more. "Dad, that's the second person with circulating nanorobots who set off a bomb in Manhattan."

"Yes."

Susan made a wordless noise of frustration.

Remington took over the questioning. "Was anyone hurt?"

Lawrence Robertson shut off the news.

"From what they're saying, she ordered everyone to evacuate the room before detonation. Half the building went down, though, and some people got caught in the rubble. They've confirmed two deaths and a lot of injuries."

"We have to remember," Alfred Lanning continued, "we're working with the most psychotic patients in the city. Insanity is normal for them."

Susan blurted out, "But acting within the Three Laws of Robotics isn't."

Every eye, every head whipped toward Susan. Remington shook his head and unobtrusively took her hand in a quiet plea for silence.

But it was too late. Whatever damage he feared was already done.

Lawrence Robertson spoke first. "What do you mean, Susan?"

Susan had no idea why Remington wanted to silence her, but she had something to say and every intention of saying it. "Both of our bombers have had three things in common: They were injected with nanorobots, they somehow obtained functioning explosives, and they attempted to follow the Three Laws of Robotics."

An outburst of conversation followed Susan's pronouncement.

Lawrence Robertson raised a hand, restoring the quiet but not decreasing the intensity of the stares one iota. "How so? If they were operating under the Three Laws, they could not have injured anyone."

As Susan continued, Remington's grip on her hand grew stronger to the point of pain. "I think they tried to avoid it, but they had limited judgment and insight into the power of the explosives they carried. In both cases, they ordered people out of the blast area first." She gave Remington a questioning look and received a subtle cutting gesture at his throat. He wanted her to shut up.

Alfred Lanning screwed his features into a perfect depiction of disgust. "That's all very interesting, but entirely impossible. While it's true the nanorobots do carry the Three Laws by virtue of having positronic properties, they don't have the thinking capacity to contemplate and act on them. I think it's far more likely the functioning consciences of these psychiatric patients caused them to act in an ethical manner that simulates the patented Three Laws of Robotics."

"Except," Susan said, "that it's too far-fetched a coincidence to believe that, in a city of fifteen million, two of the seven patients injected with nanorobots, neither of whom had ever shown a violent propensity nor had any knowledge of explosives, independently decided to blow up prime Manhattan targets."

A handsome, fine-boned man of mixed race piped up next. "Are you saying the nanorobots caused these people to act this way?"

"Impossible," Alfred snapped. "I programmed those nanos myself. There's absolutely nothing in them that could induce someone to act in any fashion." He added emphatically, "Nothing!"

Remington released Susan. "Unless, Dr. Lanning, someone tampered with them."

The room fell into an even deeper silence than before, if possible. Susan suddenly understood why Remington had wanted to keep her from talking. He suspected someone at U.S. Robots and Mechanical Men, perhaps someone in the room, was a saboteur.

Apparently, Lawrence Robertson made the same connection. He addressed Remington directly. "With the exception of you, young stranger, I trust every person in this room not only with my business, but with my life itself. Not one has worked with me fewer than fifteen years, and all of them have invested a life work into this company. As to you, Remy, I'm assuming you don't have the knowledge to program nanorobots, and I know you haven't had the opportunity."

"No, sir." Remington rolled his eyes at the bare thought. "But I do have reason to believe this tampering is occurring, and not necessarily at your facility." He approached Lawrence Robertson with a hand in his pocket, pulled out the vial and seal, and placed them on the desk. "I compared the seals to the ones on the vials in your laboratory. They're not the same."

Alfred Lanning scooped it up before anyone else could take a closer look. "Where did you get this?"

"From one of the vials Susan injected into a patient."

Susan appreciated he did not mention he had taken over for her on two occasions. It might make her appear incompetent.

The scientist tossed the objects back onto the desk. "He's right. That seal is definitely more orange in color and not quite as thick as the ones we use." He shrugged a single shoulder. "Someone is tampering with our work." His eyes widened at the implications of his own words. "Someone sabotaged our nanorobots!"

A pallor seemed to overtake the room. Every face, the air in the room itself, seemed to grow white with strain. Susan watched them all carefully. She could read a lot from faces, from fidgeting, from words and movement. Everyone seemed genuinely shocked and dismayed. If a traitor stood among them, he was well trained at guarding his thoughts and emotions.

Lawrence Robertson took over immediately. "Javonte and George, start looking into whoever touches those vials once they leave the refrigerators: lower-level employees, delivery men, shipping companies. No one outside this room is above suspicion."

The handsome black man and the gangly roboticist rushed to obey. "Alfred, get Goldman and Peters up on the secure speaker. Susan—" Apparently suddenly realizing he was commanding someone not in his employ, he softened his tone. "Based on what you've seen so far, and your knowledge of the study patients, what can we expect?"

Susan had focused so intently on her theory about the Three Laws, she had not taken her ideas on the matter much further. Now, she thought aloud. "Since the nanorobots don't have the capacity to mull the Three Laws the way a full positronic brain does, we have to assume the patient's ethical considerations play a role here, filling in what the nanorobots can't." The idea was so stunning, Susan had to stop herself. The protestor, the one who had tried to talk her out of helping with the project, had a point. If she was right, they had created an odd and primitive form of cyborg, robot function interacting seamlessly with human thought and emotion. *Except we can hardly consider it seamless under the current circumstances.*

No one spoke, not even Alfred Lanning, who looked as if he had just rushed headlong into a train.

Susan had to continue, resorting to an exterior stony coldness to explain something shocking the instant it came to her mind, yet make it appear as if she had given it her full attention for an appropriate period of time to make it a viable theory. "The way I figure it, someone programmed the nanorobots to overtake the brains of their human hosts, each programmed to blow up a different target. But whoever did the programming either didn't know about, or didn't understand the overwhelming significance of, the Three Laws of Robotics."

To Susan's surprise, the silence persisted. Every man in the room kept staring directly at her, their expressions anticipatory, to a man. She wondered what more they expected. She felt as if she had thrown out more than enough ideas to contemplate for hours.

Remington gave her hand another squeeze, this one less insistent, more encouraging. "Susan, in your psychiatric opinion, will the Three Laws of Robotics hold? Can we be certain the other patients will also follow them when performing their . . . um . . . their, um . . . ?"

Susan did not wait for Remington to find the right word to describe the programmed missions of the saboteurs. Susan opened her mouth to answer, but the words did not come. She had no precedent on which to base her answer. She needed to think. "At this point, shouldn't we call the police with our suspicions? We need to prevent anything else terrible from happening."

Finally, murmurs swept the room, punctuated by Lawrence Robertson's loud sigh. He rose from his chair, walked around his desk, and came to Susan's side. He glanced at John Calvin before turning his attention fully to the daughter. "Susan, I'm not sure if I can explain this properly, but it's important I try." Again, he looked at John, as if trying to elicit help. "We can't go to the police."

Susan made no objections, wanting to hear him out first, but Lawrence raised a hand as if she had.

"Other than that, we will do everything in our power to prevent 'anything else terrible from happening.' "

Susan suppressed a horrific urge to laugh in his face. *Other than call the police? What else is there?*

Not entirely ignorant of her thoughts, Lawrence answered the unspoken question. "I know that sounds absurd, but it's true. If word gets out to the general public that the people causing these explosions had nanorobots injected into their brains, it would mean the end of U.S. Robots and Mechanical Men."

The words seemed irresponsible; yet Susan understood more from his eyes than from his explanation. The company was the life work of Lawrence Robertson, of Alfred Lanning, of John Calvin, of most of the men in this very room.

Lawrence leaned in closer. "Susan, you've met N8-C, right?"

Susan could not help smiling at the memory. "Nate, yes. Many times. He's absolutely amazing, brilliant."

"Yes." Lawrence glanced around the room, where so many men seemed to be holding their breath simultaneously. "And, if the population at large gets wind of this, Nate will be erased, along with all the other prototypes and working robots. Their positronic brains will be wiped out, the technology outlawed, robotics set back for at least another generation." His eyes grew moist; the thought was clear agony.

Susan bit her lips. She no longer thought of Nate as a robot, but as a living individual. The idea of allowing anyone to destroy him seemed as intolerable as killing her own father. "We don't know that will happen."

She was distracted by shaking heads all around the room, but managed to continue. "We could explain the truth. Give people some credit; they'd understand."

The combined force of those shaking heads stole Susan's concentration completely, especially when she realized her father's and Remington's were now among them. She considered all the things she knew, what Nate had told her about how few of the hospital staff felt comfortable using him, how many of the patients refused his assistance once they knew, how protestors demanded his immediate removal. "But we're talking about sabotage and spies. About homicide bombings, for Christ's sake. People have died, will die. Next time, it could be hundreds, thousands."

"Which is why we have to make sure there is no next time," Lawrence Robertson said with slow clarity.

As shocking as Susan's own revelations had seemed, the words spoken to her now flabbergasted her, mostly because they came from the lips of people she had always considered good and decent, upright and moral human beings. Her mouth and tongue felt numb, paralyzed.

John Calvin motioned for Lawrence to stand back, and he did so wordlessly. Susan's father looked down into her face. "I know what you're thinking, kitten. And, as smart as you are, you're wrong."

Susan's pale eyes flicked directly on his. They looked so like her own, the ones she saw in the mirror every day, and the sincerity deep within them seemed to penetrate her psyche. She did not know what she was thinking, so she found herself eager for her father's theory.

"U.S. Robots and Mechanical Men isn't some greedy monster of a corporation panicking over its profits. We're small, as you know, smaller than we ever should be. We deal with priceless concepts, with products that cost millions to build, yet 'making money,' at least in a significant sense, is a notion that hasn't reached us and may not for another century."

Susan could scarcely call her father rich. They had

both borrowed heavily to send her through college. The state covered medical school for all physicians. Had she had to make her own way, as in Bainbridge's day, she would have drowned in her own debt. Most of the men currently involved in the company's projects would never see the riches their hard work might eventually reap. They did it from a firm belief that, once accepted, robotics would make humans happier, healthier, and better.

John seemed to be trying to read his daughter's mind as he spoke, his scrutiny intense, his tone almost pleading. "People have imagined robots improving our lives since long before any of our births. The water clock was invented in 200 BC, for God's sake; and Leonardo da Vinci made a moving armored robot in 1495. Animatronics are commonplace at theme parks and as children's toys, and NASA has used robotic exploration and analysis units since at least the 1990s. General Motors had a functioning robotic arm on its assembly line in the 1960s. And that's all assuming you don't include computers in the robotics category. Yet, when it comes to an actual humanoid robot, one that can actually think and talk, one that has skin, muscles, and a functional skeleton, one that can actually *pass* for human, people panic." The disgust in his voice became palpable. "The Frankenstein Complex."

Susan had never heard her father denigrate anyone. He treated everyone kindly and had something nice to say about even the ones Susan would not miss if they fell off the earth. Although they argued about some things, she could never fault his knowledge or logic. He could make her see the other side of issues that did not seem to have one, and his love for humanity was unimpeachable. About this issue, he clearly felt passionate.

John cleared his throat. "Susan, the positronic brain will change the course of history. It's the greatest invention since"—he paused to consider—"the greatest invention ever, in my opinion."

Behind him, Susan could see Lawrence Robertson and Alfred Lanning exchanging glances, their cheeks flushed by the enormity of John Calvin's compliment.

"It will change the world as nothing else has since the Internet or the cellular phone. Society will improve a millionfold. Our lives will become easier, better in every way. Medicine will take a grand leap into the future. The possibilities are mind-boggling: prosthetics, transplants, fixing neural pathways, the intricacies of perfect surgery, even psychiatry itself, once we explore the relationship between human neural pathways and the positronic brain. Thousands of lives saved, millions in time." John Calvin's eyes held a gleam Susan had never seen before. It combined raw excitement with hope and joy and honest, innocent wonder.

Susan took a slow, deep breath. Her father had never steered her wrong. He had an uncanny memory, a keen mind, a gift for finding the best in everyone and everything. She understood the grandeur in his speech; yet she also saw why it might incite fear in some. What about the surgeons replaced by those robots who could perform those perfect surgeries? What about the mental status of those people fitted with wondrous, robotic prosthetics? Would a caste system develop: full humans versus cyborgs versus robots? Could fully sentient robots contemplate their superiority, their immortality, their precision, and program themselves to overcome the Three Laws of Robotics? She released the breath in a long sigh.

"Believe me, Susan." John Calvin had not finished. "I taught you to look at both sides of every issue, and I know you're doing that now, doing it with great intelligence and fervor." His gaze remained fully locked on her own. "Know this: I believe zealously in the Three Laws and in the process that governs their existence in each and every positronic brain. They cannot be removed or tampered with; the simple act of trying would utterly destroy the brain itself."

A shiver traversed Susan. She hated when people seemed to read her thoughts, even the father who knew her better than anyone else. "I think," she finally managed to say, "the world would be a far, far better place if all of us had to adhere to the Three Laws of Robotics." She knew they needed a definitive answer. "All right. No police." It amazed Susan how, this day, the men of USR seemed to do everything concurrently. Once again, to a man, the entire room appeared relieved by her promise.

Chapter 22

Susan could not scrub an image of "Princess" Valerie Aldrich from her mind. Seated beside Remington on the crosstown bus, Susan found her mind's eye filled with images of the elderly woman in the purple silk pants and cape, the tawdry tiara perched on perfectly coiffed white hair. Susan could still picture the put-upon husband, remembered only as a butler in the mind of his beloved after fifty-four blissful years of marriage. He had come to them with great desperation and hope that the nanorobots might rescue her from the fixed delusion spoiling their well-deserved happily-ever-after. If the nanorobots did their job, and Susan believed they would have, they could have salvaged the kind of rare and perfect love rarely seen anymore. Susan knew few enough marriages that had weathered two decades, let alone longer than half a century.

"Damn it!" Sorrow and impotent rage seized her. "Damn it, damn it, damn it."

Remington put his arm around her, drawing her closer.

"She deserved better, Remy. They both deserved better."

Remington's emerald eyes held Susan's gamely. "Which 'she' do you mean, Susan?"

"Valerie Aldrich and her husband," Susan said, then realized how ridiculous she sounded. "Well, I guess they all did. The victims of the explosion, and Payton Flowers, too. Not many people deserve to die." Susan huffed out a breath. "But she shouldn't have to leave this world as That Looney in the Princess Costume Who Blew up a Government Office."

"No," Remington admitted. He flipped his portable radiation detector over and over in his hands.

"They were married fifty-four years. Fifty-four *years*."

"Yes," Remington said unhelpfully, still playing with the object in his lap.

The true lunatics, Susan realized, were the ones who had reprogrammed the nanorobots, the ones willing to murder and defame. *For what?* She remembered Nate's definition of the Society for Humanity, verbatim to her surprise: *"a bipartisan political action group dedicated to 'rescuing' mankind from advanced intelligence, particularly the artificial type, and raising ethical challenges to several forms of robotic and medical technology." Can anyone who claims to "rescue mankind," can any group that calls itself the Society for Humanity, really be responsible for so much death and destruction?* Susan realized that without the Three Laws of Robotics, the devastation would have been a lot worse. She patted her pocket to assure herself she had not lost her own portable radiation detector.

Susan raised her Vox. Lawrence Robertson had demonstrated his leadership well enough by delegating responsibilities with the confidence of a general. As Susan and Remington rode toward Manhattan Hasbro, members of the USR team, including her father, had already traced the switch to the shipping company and were penetrating it, rooting out the perpetrators, and gathering the necessary evidence. Ari Goldman and Cody Peters were taking charge of the care of those patients still presumably at Hasbro on the psychiatric ward: Neal Fontaina, the catatonic schizophrenic in permanent residence; Ronnie Bogart, the middle-aged bipolar with chronic depression; and Cary English, the violent, aging paranoid schizophrenic known to be assaultive to staff and dangerous even without reprogrammed nanorobots in his brain.

It relieved Susan to know Sharicka Anson was also safely locked away on the Pediatric Inpatient Psychiatry Unit. And, surely, Barack Balinsky, the other catatonic, remained firmly ensconced on his mother's couch. That accounted for every patient, other than the two who had already blown themselves to bits. It should not take long to round those last five patients up, remove the nanorobots, and return them to their proper places. She and Remington would not need the portable devices they carried, except, perhaps, to make absolutely certain they had removed every single nanorobot from the patients' CSF.

Yet, despite the apparent ease of their part of the operation, Susan felt as if she had ridden roller coasters all day. Her stomach roiled, and her mind, once released from images of Valerie Aldrich, flit dizzily and without pattern. Unable to wait a moment longer, she tapped up Kendall Stevens' Vox.

The Vox buzzed twice before his image appeared, his ginger hair tousled and his dark eyes tired. "Ah, Susan. So you've heard."

Instantly, Susan's head began an incessant, internal buzzing as unignorable as the alarm at USR. "Heard what?"

A light flashed through Kendall's sleepy eyes. "Why did you call me?"

"I wanted to check on Sharicka. Wanted to make sure . . ."

As Susan spoke, Kendall's large-lipped face seemed to wilt before her eyes. "That's what I'm talking about, Susan. Sharicka's not here."

Susan's heart rate jumped a hundred beats. Sweat poured down her body. She suddenly understood what it felt like to suffer supraventricular tachycardia. "What do you mean"—her voice sounded strange, as if her throat had started to close off—"not there?" She tried to wet her mouth, with little success. "She has to be there. She's on a locked ward, for Christ's sake!"

"She's gone," Kendall said, articulating the impossible. "Last night, she got hold of a key and eloped from the unit."

"No." Instantly, images of Sharicka examining the locks filled Susan's head. When she had taken Sharicka and Monterey to visit Nate, the girl had shown a fascination for the unit's locks. Susan had worried that scrutiny would come back to haunt her. Now, she felt certain Sharicka had observed the disposition of the keys with the same fanatical intensity, from the moment of her arrival. The girl probably knew exactly which doctors and nurses carried them on every shift, in which pockets, and what diversion might gain her the opportunity to steal one. Susan wondered how long Sharicka had patiently waited to carry out the crime.

They know what she's capable of now. How could anyone be so stupid! Susan knew condemnation and finger-pointing were useless wastes of thought. Sharicka could not have used direct manipulation or trickery; no one had handed her that key. The key carriers let people in and out of those doors a hundred or more times a day. They had no choice but to keep the key in a pocket. And, amid innumerable distractions, pockets could be picked. Nothing mattered except the terrible knowledge that Sharicka Anson was free.

Susan could not think clearly enough to form coherent sentences. Young as she was, Sharicka was the most horrific danger Manhattan had faced since September 11, 2001. The Three Laws of Robotics were no match for a human being without morals, without a glimmer of conscience. The simple wisdom of a dog would serve them better. "No," she said louder. "No, no, no!"

Privy only to Susan's side of the conversation, Remington turned in his seat to look directly at her. "Sharicka's loose?"

Kendall watched Susan's reaction curiously. "She can't cause that much damage, can she? I mean, she's crazy, but she's small, only four years old. It's not like she can attack grown men or tear babies from their mothers' arms."

Susan looked helplessly at Remington and nodded. Then she turned her attention back to Kendall. "Get yourself excused for the rest of the day. If you can, grab two milligrams of IM Haldol. Meet us at the hospital entrance in ten minutes."

"What . . . ? How . . . ?" was all Kendall managed before Susan broke the contact.

Susan found herself wringing her hands and rocking like a stereotypical autistic child in the days before Arketamin. "She's loose," Susan confirmed. "Long enough to have armed herself and—" *And what? What's she going to do? Where's she going to do it?* The ten minutes it would take to reach Manhattan Hasbro seemed like an eternity.

Remington turned Susan a curious look. "What do you want with the Haldol?"

"Antipsychotic." Susan could not believe she had to explain something so obvious to another doctor, even one unaccustomed to violent psychiatric emergencies. "We use it for rapid tranquilization."

"Susan, I know what Haldol's for." Remington kept his voice low to exclude eavesdroppers. "I just don't see what good any chemical restraint will do ten to thirty minutes *after* she sets off the bomb."

Susan took a breath to reply, then realized Remington was right. The choice of medication did not matter: antipsychotic, neuroleptic, paralytic. It would take at least five minutes for anything to work its way into Sharicka's system by the IM route, long enough for her to detonate any kind of explosive. Susan supposed an intravenous injection might work quickly enough, but the most competent anesthesiologist in the world could never get a needle into a vein under duress in an unwilling, unrestrained patient. "Inhalational anesthetic?"

Remington's brows rose. "Got any?"

Susan had to admit she did not. "Who carries around sevoflurane?"

"Exactly my point."

"But you're a surgeon. Can't you get some?" The moment the words came out of her mouth, Susan realized how irrational they sounded. It was not as if she, as a psychiatrist, could grab a handful of schedule two narcotics on demand.

Remington gave a more straightforward answer than he needed to. Under the circumstances, Susan would have forgiven sarcasm. "Not without the time or authority to explain. Probably not with it. Even the anesthesiologists who work with the stuff can't just carry a tank home in a backpack. It's all locked up and monitored to the micromilliliter."

Apparently reading Susan's consternation as disappointment, he added, "Not that it would help. I mean, how would we administer it? If we loosed it blindly, it would take all of us out, including innocent bystanders. I don't think she'd stand still while we clamped a mask over her face. And how are we supposed to smuggle a tank, mask, and tubing through Manhattan without bringing every cop in the city down on our asses?"

Before Susan could reply, her Vox buzzed. Her first thought, that Kendall had called back to demand details she would not relay on a crowded bus, was dispelled when she glanced at her wrist. It was Lawrence Robertson. She opened the connection.

The head of U.S. Robots and Mechanical Men did not wait for her to speak. "Susan, Goldman and Peters report they've secured two patients."

Only two? Susan had expected them to haul down three from the adult psychiatric unit alone. "Who do they have?"

"Fontaina and Bogart. Bogart was trying to sign himself out Against Medical Advice, but he had a court order."

Susan ran their faces and diagnoses through her memory. She knew Fontaina, the hospitalized catatonic who had barely moved when she had injected him. Bogart was the chronic depressive who had attempted suicide on multiple occasions, which would ensure he had an unbreakable, legal commitment. "What about Cary English?" She worried about him nearly as much as about Sharicka, with his history of paranoid delusions and violent behavior.

"Gone," Lawrence said. "He attacked three medical staff who tried to stop him and put a security guard into intensive care." He shook his head. "He's armed now, too."

Susan bit back a swear word. "There are—"

"Oh shit!" Lawrence spat out the words Susan had suppressed. His face disappeared, replaced by moving flashes of walls and ceiling. The volume of a distant television grew louder, almost decipherable through the Vox connection.

Susan could make out the expressionless droning of a newscaster. "What's going on?" she demanded.

Lawrence told her in breathless bursts as he tried to talk and listen simultaneously. "A couple of my guys snagged a man headed into the airport." He paused. "Apparently, he had high-tech explosives on him." Another pause, with muffled television words. "Name's Balinsky. Barack Balinsky."

"Barack Balinsky?" Susan could scarcely believe it. "He's a catatonic. Hasn't moved a muscle voluntarily in sixteen years."

"Apparently, he was spry enough— Uh-oh!" Lawrence Robertson fell suddenly silent. His face remained on Susan's Vox screen, staring rigidly at something in front of him.

Susan waited patiently.

"They've made a connection, Susan. They've just announced that all three were mental patients with serious psychoses." He breathed out a long sigh. "That appears to be everything they've pieced together so far."

Susan could scarcely believe it. "Don't you think it's time to bring in the police?"

Lawrence Robertson put his head in his free hand and groaned. "Susan, the Society for Humanity, the SFH, is definitely involved. They've dedicated themselves to ending all robotic research and exploration, as well as several current and future medical techniques that have the potential to save and improve millions of lives. They don't just want to shut us down; they want to set science, medicine, space exploration, assistive devices, back to the 1900s."

Susan shook her head at what seemed like hyperbole. "That can't happen. Once a thing is out there, working, it's almost impossible to retract."

"Oh, is it?" Lawrence shook his head at what he clearly considered Susan's foolish naïveté. "Take a look at the abortion issue. In 1973, a woman's right to choose became the federal law of the land. Whether or not you agree with that decision, you have to admit it took half a century of all-out war for it to take effect, thanks to bureaucratic red tape, financial and physical blockages of facilities providing abortion services, parental consent laws, mandatory waiting periods, outlawing of selective procedures, intimidation and murder of abortion providers, and federal restrictions on funding.

"The government has already cracked down hard on robotics construction and research in ways you can't imagine. You already know we're the only company legally allowed to even involve ourselves in true artificial intelligence construction. But did you also know that it's illegal for positronic robots to be sold anywhere on planet Earth without explicit written permission from the federal government?"

Susan almost laughed at the wording. Did they expect Martians and Venusians to put in their orders?

"If positronic robots are tied, in any way, to these acts of terrorism, the SFH knows the technology itself, and everyone involved with it, will be blamed. USR, and its robots, will be put on trial, and the true killers, murderers who will stop at nothing to destroy us, will go free. We'll bring in law enforcement, Susan. I promise. But not until we have evidence to convict the true culprits."

Susan grimaced. She had asked the question because she worried USR had gotten in over its head, not because she intended to betray them. "I promise to let you decide when the right time is. I just want you to understand one thing: There are still two walking bombs in Manhattan, and neither of them has shown any compunction about committing murder, even before the reprogramming."

Lawrence's features pinched. "You mean . . . the four-year-old girl is . . ." He let Susan finish.

"The worst of the bunch, sir. The worst of the bunch."

And that was when Susan fully realized that nothing but three doctors, two psychiatry research scientists, and one tiny corporation stood between hundreds of Americans and their annihilation.

Susan guided Kendall away from the omnipresent protestors in front of Manhattan Hasbro Hospital to a secluded garden, where topiary in the shape of a Kuddly Kitten lorded over a landscape of flowers spelling out each letter of the Hasbro name. She thrust the portable radiation detector into his hands and demonstrated the proper setting. "So, we're looking for Sharicka and this man." She showed him a tiny image of Cary English on Vox display. "You'll know for sure because this"—she tapped the setting—"is set specifically for the nanorobot tags. It's not going to pick up someone's cancer-treating implant."

"Or a nuclear bomb, I presume."

Susan stared at him. "If someone with a nuclear device also happens to be running around plotting a homicide bombing, we're all screwed anyway." Panic settled over her momentarily, and she had to remind herself that, even if the SFH had leagued with international terrorists, they still had to get past the worldwide locks and regulations against illegal weapons.

Kendall looked over the device doubtfully. "And if I find one of them, is this going to help me catch him?"

"No," Susan admitted, unsure exactly what to do herself. "This will just locate the tags. After that, we're on our own."

"We?"

"You and Remy and I are not the only ones looking, if that's what you mean." She pulled out a list Lawrence Robertson had put together. "These are the places someone looking for publicity might target. They've already gone after USR, a government office, and an airport. We're thinking maybe a large, historical building next."

Kendall snapped his fingers. "Chrysler Building. It's not the tallest, but it's relatively close to the hospital. And it's currently ranked number three in the country as a must-see and number one in Manhattan."

Susan wondered why he had those statistics at his fingertips. "Good choice," she said, but it all seemed so futile, like looking for two lethal needles in a haystack the size of . . . Manhattan. "I'll meet up with Remy; he has the other portable. Keep in touch."

Kendall turned to leave, then stopped. "Where is Remy?"

"He said he needed to pick up a few necessities. Didn't specify. We're meeting up halfway between here and his place."

"Ah, so you know the location of his place."

Susan did not want to bandy jokes now. "Stop leering. He told me. I haven't actually been there." She could not help adding, "Yet." An image of their conversation on the bench slithered into her mind accompanied by a surge of rewarmed emotion. Though only hours earlier, it seemed more like weeks since they had had their talk and she had made the decision to relinquish her virginity to a man she had already come to love. *Once this is over, once we've saved Manhattan, nothing in the world is going to keep me away from him.*

Susan appreciated Kendall had no way of knowing her thoughts. He studied the device she had given him. "How useful is this thing, anyway? I mean, you can block alpha radiation with a sheet of paper and beta with aluminum foil. Is whatever's emitted by these things able to penetrate the human skull, let alone give off enough particles for me to find someone in a crowd?"

Although she probably had enough science background to understand the details, Susan had not taken the time to elicit them. "I didn't build the thing, Kendall. As best as I understand it, the radiation tags are nonionizing and biologically safe. Don't ask me to get into the molecular structure. I've always preferred biological sciences to chemistry and physics, and I honestly didn't ask." Worried for wasting even a second, Susan abbreviated the discussion. "Suffice it to say these are not your father's basic Geiger counters. They're incredibly complex machines that, when properly set and programmed, lock onto even minute amounts of a specialized radioactive tag, ignoring cosmic radiation, background radiation, microwaves, and whatever we transmit using Vox worldwide."

Kendall stared. "Thanks for the class, Calvin. What I really want to know is about how close do I need to get to Target A or B for it to start beeping . . . or whatever it does to get my attention?"

"Oh." Susan realized Kendall only wanted the exact same information the tech at USR had given them. "They're supposed to be exquisitely sensitive. So long as there're not a lot of obstacles, you can get a hint of vibration at about a hundred yards or so."

"Thanks." Kendall sounded almost giddy with relief. "That's actually doable." He started to turn, then whirled back. "Sorry, Susan. I couldn't get the Haldol. I needed a better explanation than 'I think it has something to do with Sharicka.'"

Susan winced. Given Remington's explanation, she doubted it would have done them any good, but she felt bad about putting Kendall in such an awkward situation. He had probably had nearly as much trouble getting himself off the unit. "It's all right. Just go."

Kendall headed off at once, his tread more stolid and serious than Susan had ever seen it.

Buoyed by Kendall's trust and optimism, Susan set off to find Remington.

The tram glided to a stop at Forty-second Street and Third Avenue, a block and a half east of the Chrysler Building. Kendall Stevens' gaze fixed on the massive, stainless-steel structure that seemed less to scrape the sky and more to directly pierce it. A seventy-seven-story rocket ship, it towered over the surrounding structures. It was an architectural masterpiece, slender and elegant, its proportions so much more eye pleasing than the

lumpish Bank of America Tower or even the blockier
Empire State Building. Its stainless-steel siding reflected
light all around it, as if to share its tremendous glory
with every one of its neighbors. His gaze fixed on it, Kendall headed down Forty-second Street.

Ahead of him, a glide-bus pulled up at a station that
still held the historical marker of Grand Central Terminal. Due to multiple attacks, security concerns, and major changes in New York's transportation systems, all
that clearly remained of the once-largest train station in
the world was a massive clock, the world's largest example of Tiffany glass. The people flowing from the bus'
doors filled the gamut, and nearly all of them stared at
the skyscraper as they emerged. Several tripped onto the
curb, and one nearly walked into a sidewalk tree.

Suddenly, the device in Kendall's pocket went crazy,
buzzing against his right thigh with a fervor usually reserved for electrocution. Startled, he bit his lips to keep
from shouting and hauled the device free, where it shook
with such fury his arms vibrated with it. *What the hell?*
Kendall glanced wildly around him. His heart slammed
against his ribs like a jackhammer.

Cary English had just stepped off the bus, looking
precisely like the picture Susan had showed Kendall. He
had a wild tangle of salt-and-pepper hair, several days'
growth of beard, and blue eyes that flitted upward and
sideways in random, nervous movements. A large man
with enormous hands, he stood at least half a foot taller
than Kendall's five feet eleven inches and outweighed
him by some eighty pounds. He wore an overlarge jacket
over his greasy jeans, big enough to hide any number of
explosives.

Shit! Kendall's usual defense mechanism, humor,
failed him now. He stood for a moment, trying not to
stare. The schizophrenic's gaze caught him, measured
him, then dismissed him to focus on something or someone else. *Now or never.* Knowing better than to give the

situation enough thought to keep him from doing something stupid, Kendall launched himself at Cary English.

As he flew through the air, Kendall's whole life flashed before his eyes. He relived an awkward childhood raised by a domineering single mother, school years filled with inexplicable desire and lonely uncertainty sublimated with jokes and clowning, college camaraderie and focused studying, then medical school, where he finally found his niche. Then, he crashed against Cary English with bruising force, and both men tumbled to the sidewalk.

A woman screamed. Cary shrieked and gibbered something about aliens stealing his liver, all the while pounding Kendall with hammerlike fists. Men rushed to the rescue, and Kendall found himself abruptly assaulted by more hands than he could count. The radiation detector clattered from his fingers, buzzing furiously against the concrete, and Kendall felt himself slipping.

"Bomb!" Kendall yelled, for the first time hoping he was right. "He's got a bomb!" Until that moment, he had worried Cary might panic and blow himself, Kendall, and the crowd to kingdom come. Now, Kendall worried more for getting beaten to a bloody pulp by would-be vigilantes. He caught the hem of Cary's jacket and clung with all his might. He no longer felt the blows. The myriad separate pains fused into one intense, indecipherable agony.

Rough hands jerked Kendall from Cary, who rolled free. Kendall's fingers ached and burned, and he felt battered in every part, but he doggedly refused to release the material. He heard a loud rip; something metal clanged against concrete; then a gasp erupted from the crowd.

The hands fell away from Kendall. He heard pounding footsteps, retreating, men and women screaming wildly, Voxes buzzing. Someone hauled Kendall gently to his feet while the mob fell upon Cary, pinning down his struggling hands, his flailing feet.

Breathing heavily from exertion, Kendall stepped away from the mass. Someone shoved the still-quaking radiation detector into his hands. "What the hell is this thing?"

"Bomb finder," Kendall lied. "Made it myself." He flicked off the switch, and it went quiet in his hands. "Did someone call the police?" he panted.

The man studied him in the reflected silver light of the Chrysler Building. He made a broad gesture to indicate the entire block. "I think everyone did. Who are you, anyway?"

Kendall had no intention of remaining to answer questions. "New superhero. Incredible-Guesser Man." With that, he headed back the way he had come, tapping up Susan Calvin on his Vox.

The three R-1s met up at a tram stop on the opposite end of the city. Kendall looked exhausted. His ginger hair, usually straight, now stuck up in random clumps. A bright red mark spread across his right cheek, clearly tender. His knuckles were abraded, his clothing torn, and his arms showed a parade of bruises just starting to turn from brilliant red to duller blue.

Apparently noticing Susan's stare, Kendall shrugged. "You should see the other guy."

As Susan and Remington already knew the story, they only smiled.

The tram pulled up, and they boarded quickly. "So," Kendall said as they squeezed into the same seat, Susan between them, "where are we going now, and what are the chances we're all going to die?"

Susan supposed Kendall needed to joke, but she wished he would use another defense mechanism to escape his anxiety. This time, his quip had struck too close to home. She and Remington had already surmised

Cary English had had enough morality left in his diseased brain not to immediately trigger his explosive charge when jumped on the street. Sharicka would require a whole different approach. The risk of all of them dying, along with hundreds of innocent people, was not remote.

Susan explained her choice of location. "We have ten different groups combing all the likely places. Then, it hit me. We can't think like an adult, or even like a normal child. We have to think like Sharicka."

Remington took over, "Obviously, she can't drive. The drivers of any type of public transportation will question an unaccompanied four-year-old. She can't pay for a cab. Lawrence believes there's no actual contact between the terrorists and the patients, that the bombs or components are left in a certain location and the means for using them is programmed. So, it's unlikely the masterminds even realize one of their victims is a child."

Susan found it difficult to think of Sharicka as a victim. "I got hold of her parents, and we brainstormed places she might go. Based on what they told me, and the location of the bomb materials uncovered by USR, we're almost certain she'll strike the Knickerbocker Mall."

Kendall rubbed his cheek, then winced in pain. "I presume you've told everyone to converge on the mall."

Susan made an uncomfortable face. "I've told Lawrence about my theory, but we can't put everyone in the same place without either alerting Sharicka or leaving too much unguarded. She's bright, Kendall, probably a genius. And, unlike those of the other patients, her mind isn't muddled; she's just . . . mean," she said, using Sharicka's grandmother's term.

Remington surreptitiously passed a pistol across Susan to Kendall. Kendall made no move to take it, only studying it through widened eyes.

"Take it," Susan whispered, not mentioning she had refused the same proffering. She knew doing so might prove foolish, might even cost her her life, but she doubted she could pull the trigger under any circumstances.

Kendall just stared at it, forcing Susan to cover it with her shirt. "Couldn't you get something . . . less lethal?"

Susan flinched. Remington had gone through all of this with her earlier, but his tone gave no indication of growing impatience. "There are no effective nonlethal alternatives." He said it with such authority, Susan believed him without question. "Those all take time to work and require us to get real close. Sharicka only needs a split second to trigger a bomb." He added something new. "We're just lucky the SFH, or whoever, didn't set them up with a deadman's switch."

Susan had to ask. "What's a deadman's switch?"

Remington didn't miss a beat. "It's a switch that's activated by releasing the button rather than pressing it."

Susan made a strangled noise. It made sense for a professional assassin to use such a thing. If someone took him down, it would initiate, rather than stop, the blast. "It's a good thing we're not dealing with that level of expertise."

Remington brought his full gaze to bear on her. "Susan, we're dealing with people who can reprogram nanorobots. How much more expertise do you need?"

Susan could feel the hairs on the nape of her neck rising and sweat trickling down her spine. She had understood the danger of their mission but never so much as at this moment.

"What about Tasers?" Kendall hissed.

Susan had not thought of that, but Remington still had an answer. "Private Tasers have been illegal since 2017; unlike guns, they're not protected by the Second Amendment. This isn't ideal, but it's better." He shook the pistol slightly, bumping it against Susan's leg. "I'd much rather have rifles, but I don't own any small enough to sneak through the city. At least, this gains us a little more distance."

Kendall wore a bemused expression. He did not look wholly convinced.

Remington glanced out the window, then back at Kendall. "Given Sharicka's size, a Taser is still technically a lethal weapon. They also have a high rate of failure used against psychiatric patients, and a stray Taser barb could theoretically set off the bomb itself."

Kendall's jaw set. He accepted the gun, shoving it into his pocket. "I don't have . . . much experience."

"You don't need much," Remington whispered matter-of-factly. "It has a red dot optical site, so you barely have to aim. Flip off the safety. Point. Pull the trigger."

Susan knew Remington carried a pistol as well. She did not know enough about firearms to guess the type. "Let's hope we don't need it."

"And thank God we have it, if we do," Remington added.

Chapter 23

By the time the tram drew up near Knickerbocker Mall, Remington had shoved the front of the radiation detector through the open window and was reporting on the strength of the signal. Driven to action, Susan glanced around restlessly, attuned to the change in the pitch of the brakes that would signal it was safe to leave the tram. "Are you sure she's close? She's definitely not there yet?"

Remington pulled the device back in the window. "Of course, I'm not sure. I've got no more experience with this thing than you do."

Although she could not feel the vibrations Remington did, Susan could hear the faint clicks suggesting someone with the proper radiation tags had come within range of detection.

"It's weak, but nothing else is supposed to set it off at all."

Susan caught sight of the mall, still standing, and relief flooded through her. *We're not too late.*

The brakes finally made the proper hissing tone. The seat belts clicked off. The doors flowed open automatically, and the three R-1s rushed out with the crowd. Once on the sidewalk, people scattered in all directions;

and the three headed directly for the mall, half a block north. Four stories high and completely brick, it squatted between smaller, thinner shops like an ancient castle. It had three entrances, but the Ansons had steered Susan to the one facing North Atlantic Street. It was the closest to the bus stop, and Sharicka had always liked the gargoyles overlooking it.

Remington grabbed Kendall's arm. "Find a way up on the roof and use your detector. You know what she looks like. If you see her headed for an entrance, shoot her." He released Kendall, leaving him sputtering, then took Susan's arm and guided her swiftly toward the building.

Only then, Susan could see the monitor going crazy. The clicks came fast and furiously, and the vibration of the thing shook Remington's arm. "She's here, Susan."

Susan's chest squeezed shut. She could feel her pulse hammering in her temples, and a lump formed in her throat. She craned her neck toward the gargoyle-decorated entrance, but she found no sign of Sharicka Anson. "I don't see her." She looked frantically through and around the passing people. It only made sense the girl would act in broad daylight, with the mall full of shoppers; but the crowds drove Susan wild. Having to see around them made it difficult enough, but Sharicka's small size only worsened the situation.

Remington broke into a run, and Susan chased him. She saw uniforms near the door, and relief flooded her. "There's security, Remy. They can intercept her. We just need to let them know—"

Remington's pace did not slow. "Let them know what? How are we going to convince them a four-year-old is armed and dangerous?"

Susan understood the problem, but it did not seem insurmountable. "Once they detain her, we can show them the bomb."

Remington shook her off. "By the time we tell them,

she's that much farther. By the time we convince them . . ." He threw up his hands suddenly. "Boom!"

Susan glared at him. "What the hell did you do that for?"

They skidded to a stop in front of the entrance. Susan cast about madly, looking for Sharicka. She saw no sign of the little girl, but her Vox shuddered. Nerves frayed, Susan jumped at the sudden touch, then stabbed the button to answer. "What?"

"It's Kendall. I'm in position. I think she's coming around the back."

Remington came to the same conclusion almost simultaneously. "She's around the other side!" The radiation detector had grown calm in his hands, blocked by the building and the layers of stores between them. "Go! Go! Go!"

Susan raced around a building that abruptly seemed enormously wide, hoping Kendall could stop Sharicka, by whatever means it took.

On the rooftop, Kendall reluctantly pulled the gun from his pocket. His hands trembled on the grip, and the sight jumped recklessly. Worried it would slip from his grasp, he wiped his hands on his tattered khakis, one at a time, his gaze trained fanatically on the entrance below him. People swept in and out, some in a city-hurry, others pausing to tie a shoe, blow a nose, or wait for a friend or family member coming in or out behind them. It all looked so serene, so incredibly normal. *This can't be really happening.*

Then, Sharicka Anson came into sight from around the corner of the building. She was alone, dressed in the same pink frilly dress she had worn the night of her escape, now covered by a bulky sweater. Her dark, wavy hair was pulled into a frazzled ponytail. Her pudgy body made her look even younger, like a toddler who must have escaped her mother's hand. Pressed against Kendall's side, the radiation detector went haywire, just as it had when he found Cary English. He could not spare a hand to silence it. He let it flop around while he aimed the gun at Sharicka's head and flipped off the safety.

Sharicka made a beeline for the mall entrance. Remington's suggestions on the tram flashed through Kendall's mind. *"Aim for the skull,"* the neurosurgeon had said with cold matter-of-factness. *"That's not standard procedure, of course. Head's too small a target compared with the body, but a random shot to the body might risk setting off the explosives. And, if you don't kill her instantly, she can set them off on purpose. A professional sniper with a rifle could sever the brain from the spinal cord, so the bomber can't press the button on a dying impulse. We're going to have to count on an untrained four-year-old not having that kind of instinct."*

An icy chill screwed through Kendall at the image. He could not believe a child, even one so horribly mentally ill, would have the wherewithal to set off an explosion with the agony of a bullet lodged in her abdomen.

Sharicka stepped into range.

Kendall hesitated, worried for a nearby shopper. He planted the red dot directly between her eyes, anxiety spearing through him. *What if I hit a bystander? What if I miss completely?* An image of splattered blood and brain filled his mind's eye. Bile crawled up his throat, sour as poison, as he envisioned a little girl's headless body flopping to the sidewalk.

Sharicka stepped away from the shopper. It was now or never.

Kendall's finger cramped on the trigger, unable to defy the pictures in his mind. He had dedicated his life to saving lives, to curing the sick, to making even the last moments of life peaceful for everyone. He had pithed frogs, trapped mice, but the idea of ending a human life refused to enter the realm of possibility. He tried to focus on the loss of life Sharicka would cause to so many others, to rely on the realization he had no choice but to exchange one life for hundreds of others. Still, his finger refused to obey him. Tears rolled down his cheeks.

Then, a rowdy gang of teenagers passed between him and his target, and Sharicka was out of range again.

Susan Calvin rounded the building at a gallop, Remington Hawthorn at her side. She caught a glimpse of a familiar dress in elegant primrose with a lacy hem and bulky sweater disappearing, with a crowd of teenagers, into the mall entrance. Susan knew the only hope for keeping everyone alive was to immobilize both of Sharicka's arms.

"Stop!" Susan shouted, lunging for the small, brown hands. She seized Sharicka's fingers with an abrupt violence that caught every eye in the vicinity, including the two security guards lounging near the entrance. Sharicka jerked in her grip, clearly startled. Susan's mind raced. She could yell "Bomb!" but doubted anyone would believe her. Instead, she went for a ploy that might buy her enough time to reveal the truth. "Sharicka, honey! You're too young to run off by yourself. You have to stay with Mommy."

Sharicka screamed and immediately started struggling.

Susan tried to look appropriately embarrassed by her offspring's behavior. Locking a death grip on Sharicka's hands, she attempted to reveal the telltale bulge beneath her sweater with a foot.

Sharicka twisted madly in Susan's grip, shrieking at the top of her lungs, "Let me go! Let me go!"

Susan felt her hold slipping.

A little hand squirmed free. Sharicka swung around

and glared into Susan's face with those same killer's eyes Susan had seen on the unit. "This is not my mommy!" Sharicka hollered. "Help me! Help!"

Susan lunged to recapture the hand as the guards moved in. Remington reached her first, seizing Sharicka's other arm and using an exasperated parental voice. "This isn't funny, Sharicka. Stop playing games with Mommy and Daddy."

Susan saw people staring. The teenagers had stopped, and the guards were coming closer. It occurred to Susan that Sharicka's biracial features bore out her claim that these were not her parents. *They're going to tear us apart, and we're all going to die.*

Kendall appeared suddenly, racing into the mall, attempting to herd the teenagers. "Bomb!" he shouted. "Run! Evacuate!" He thundered past, into the mall. "Run! Run! Run!"

All hell broke loose. Panicked people screamed and ran in all directions, some deeper into the stores, others out onto the roadways. Horns honked, brakes squealed, and the crash of collisions rang through the air. These sounded like distant background to Susan, lost beneath the ear-shattering shrieks of Sharicka Anson.

In the commotion, Sharicka ripped her other hand from Susan's hold and slammed it into the resident's face with enough force to stagger her. Pain spiked through Susan's skull accompanied by a flash of white light. For an instant, she thought the bomb had exploded. Then, Sharicka whipped her arm toward her own chest. *Detonator!* Susan realized she could not move fast enough to stop it.

Remington flung himself on top of Sharicka, driving her to the floor with enough force to foil the movement. Sharicka fought like a tiger. To Susan, she looked like a dark and desperate swirl of limbs and teeth. She saw one of the security guards shouting into his Vox. The other slammed into Remington, trying to thrust him off Sharicka. Tipped sideways, Remington lost his hold. Sharicka gathered her legs beneath her and squirted free. Again, her hand raced toward her chest.

"No!" Susan screamed again. She sprang for Sharicka, missing the girl but catching a handful of sweater. As the girl ran, the sweater slid down her arms, revealing the tangled coils of wires. Susan twisted, using the fabric to imprison Sharicka's arms. "Bomb!" she shouted, certain the guards would turn their attention to the appropriate target.

But, fully focused on wrestling Remington, the guards paid Sharicka no heed. She could see Remington fumbling for his gun, the guard pinioning his hand. Then, from the corner of her eye, she saw the second security guard pull his own weapon and swing it toward Remington.

"The girl!" Susan shrieked, clinging frantically to the sweater. "The girl has the bomb!" The fabric tore in Susan's grip. Abruptly released, Sharicka staggered wildly forward, tripped, and skidded across the floor. Her hand swung toward the button again, and Susan saw no possible way to stop her. Another scream ripped from her throat, this one without intention or direction.

Remington shouted, "Run, Susan!" Clearly fueled by adrenaline, he landed a desperate blow to the side of the guard's head that finally gained him his freedom. He flew toward Sharicka. Susan dove for the other guard, frantic to reach him before he pulled the trigger. She crashed into the man so hard, it rattled every tooth in her head. The blast of the gun deafened her left ear. Pain shocked through every part of her. For an instant, she thought he had shot her; then she realized it all stemmed from the force of the impact. The man toppled, and she tumbled over him, sprawling into the exit.

"Run!" Remington managed again.

Susan turned her wild momentum into long-strided running steps, charging out the exit. The pavement whirled in front of her, open. Everyone else had a head start, using it to take as many steps as possible away from Sharicka Anson. She listened for Remington's footsteps; and, when she didn't hear them, she dared to glance backward as she ran.

The guard Remington had struck lay still on the floor. The other was scrambling to his feet. Remington had wrapped himself around Sharicka, covering her like a carpet, using his own body to shield them all from the terrible might of the coming explosion.

"No!" Susan shouted again. She tried to turn, tripped, and sprawled, rolling across the concrete. She could feel the skin sloughing off her hands, the fabric of her pants abrading from her knees. Then, suddenly, a roar reverberated through her head. A wall of heat slammed her against the building with bruising force, and she could feel small, hard objects raining down around her. Fire washed over her. It felt as if it burned every part of her, through her clothing and skin, into her internal organs. The taste of gasoline filled her mouth like physical pain. Then, cold air gripped her, quenching the fire. She raised her head, bashing it against brick. Pain shot through her skull; then black oblivion descended upon her.

Susan Calvin awakened to the familiar sounds of a hospital room: the steady beep of a monitored bed, the rumble of the central air system, and the muffled sounds of distant conversation. She sat up too quickly. Dizziness swam down on her, and the room disappeared in a swirl of tiny black and white spots. She sank back to what she now recognized as a bed. Her vision gradually returned, first as a fine blur, then as distinct shapes. A screen traced her heart rate, breathing, and oxygenation. Someone tall slumped in a chair in a far corner of the room, his head clamped firmly between his hands.

"Dad?" Susan guessed, sitting up more carefully. "Is that you?"

The figure in the chair straightened. It was indeed John Calvin who rose to his full six feet eight inches and hurried to Susan's bedside. "You're awake."

"Only just," she admitted, pulling her hands from under the covers. They felt enormous and awkward, and she realized they were swathed in bandages. "How long have I been asleep?"

"Two days, in and out. We've had this conversation before. Don't you remember?" He tapped a button on his Vox.

Susan shook her head. I don't remember anything after—" Terror shot through her. "Remy?" She gave her father a desperate, hopeful look.

John Calvin shook his head with slow and weary sadness. He had that same, broken stance he assumed whenever the topic of Susan's mother arose. "He died a hero. If he hadn't thrown himself over the bomb, you certainly would have been killed. And, probably, several more innocents."

Susan felt as if the air had suddenly been sucked from the room. Instantly, tears filled her eyes, splashing down her cheeks, and sobs racked her mercilessly. She could not breathe, wasn't sure she wanted to ever again.

Gingerly, John wrapped his arms around his daughter.

Susan barely noticed. She felt cocooned in the depths of unbearable grief, an emotion that seemed destined to overwhelm her for eternity. No longer hearing the steady blips of the monitor, she was certain her heart had solidified into an unreachable boulder.

They remained enfolded together for what seemed like hours, until Susan's eyes felt on fire and her muscles became exhausted from the spasms. Lost and hopeless, she lay still in her father's strong arms and dared not contemplate the future.

John seemed to sense when she could hear him again. Either that, or she had simply missed everything he had said until that moment. "Susan, it wasn't supposed to go like this. The idea was to shield you and Remy from danger, to place the burden on the corporation."

The words seemed nonsensical to Susan, but she found herself unable to voice any opinion. Her throat felt raw with sorrow.

"When you suggested a smallish mall far from the downtown area, Lawrence deliberately sent you there to keep you busy and out of harm's way. None of us believed she would go there. We were sure the programming would send her to a larger, more newsworthy target."

Susan could only nod. The employees of USR had relied on logic and science. She alone had believed in the power of the psyche of a tiny sociopath; this time, she had not underestimated Sharicka Anson. Lawrence had done a stellar job convincing Susan he trusted her idea. She supposed the fact that he should have done so made the task simpler.

"I'm sorry, Susan." John's voice hoarsened. "I'm so very, very sorry."

Now, it was Susan's turn to comfort her father. She did not blame him for Remington's death. To fault anyone else was to belittle his sacrifice, to lessen the courage it had taken for him to forfeit his life to save so many others. "Dad, I'm not religious enough to believe everything happens for a reason, but I am scientific enough to know things that have happened cannot be undone." She remembered Remington's words at USR, the ones he used to soothe her while she blamed herself for Misty Anson's death. "Life is full of hard choices. When they're made intelligently and with all the best intentions, we must accept the results, whether or not they're what we expect, what we want, or something entirely different."

"But I feel responsible for Remy's death, for your suffering. If I hadn't convinced you not to call—"

Susan did not allow him to finish. "People still would have died, many more of them. I don't believe law enforcement could have acted any quicker than we did, and no one would have thought of going to Knickerbocker Mall. With the pressure off me and on the police, I know I wouldn't have. You'd probably be in jail, along with several other blameless scientists, and robotic technology would have been set back fifty years, a century, maybe indefinitely." Susan's words reached home, as comforting to her as to her father. "Nate would have been erased, and hundreds of people at the mall would have died needlessly instead of . . ." She paused. "What *was* the actual death count?"

"Three," John said. "Remy, a security guard, and the girl. A dozen in the hospital, but no one worse off than you."

Her father's words struck a note of terror that Susan would not have believed possible. If she still worried for her life and her future, then she would survive her grief, would find some way to limp through the rest of her life without the man she had come to love so absolutely, so quickly. "Dad, am I going to be okay?"

John Calvin managed an actual smile. "You're going to be just fine, kitten. Your hands are expected to heal fully. You have minor burns and bruises only. Nothing life threatening. They're already talking discharge."

Thanks to Remy. Pain seared Susan's heart. If she had believed in a higher power, her faith would have died in that moment. No superior being worth worshiping would bring a man like Remington Hawthorn into her life, only to place him in a situation where he had to die to save her. *If he hadn't done what he did, we would both be dead.* "And the people responsible? The ones who reprogrammed the nanorobots? Has anyone caught them?"

John Calvin turned Susan a wan smile, betrayed by the deep sigh he heaved at the same time. "We're still sorting it all out, but we're hopeful. The SFH has always been dangerous. Now, they've apparently managed to recruit accomplished scientists and experienced international terrorists. The men who made the physical switch worked for the delivery company. At least, they're in custody, and we hope they'll give up the others. Making the connection between them and the Society for Humanity will probably prove a lot more difficult."

Susan nodded grimly.

"We won't give up, though," John promised.

Nor will they. Susan guessed the Society for Humanity would have all the tenacity of most extremists. No matter how worthy the cause, those people who took it to irrational lengths always ruined it for the true and sanely passionate believers. Such were antiabortion extremists who murdered doctors and misrepresented beloved stillborn infants as aborted embryos; environmental extremists who slaughtered scientists, blew up corporations, and stole credit cards to finance their radical agendas; extremists on both sides of the political aisle who threatened federal buildings and workers, vandalized property, and fomented lies when elections did not go their way; radical Islamists who daily fired rockets into Israel, demonized civilization, demoralized women, and declared war on every religion not their own.

The Society for Humanity would not give up the fight until certain branches of science disappeared from existence. Individual victories would never suffice. They would not rest until the things of which they disapproved wholly perished from the earth, and they did not care whom they damaged, whom they murdered, to achieve that goal.

History had proven only one way to handle terrorists, Susan believed, and that was to defeat them. In the past, when one side wanted only peace and the other would settle for nothing less than total annihilation of the other, the side wishing for peace was the one that had to survive, the one that deserved to triumph. When extremists won, they did not quietly disappear; they did not embrace peace. They simply turned their might onto a new target. First, kill all the Israelis. Then, kill all the Jews. Then, kill all the gays, the Christians, the Hindus, the Buddhists, the gypsies and, eventually, even the gentler practitioners of their own religion. This was not a matter of dueling philosophies; to the Society for Humanity, this was all-out war.

Gradually, Susan became aware of more presences waiting patiently at the open door to her room. She glanced past her father to see Kendall Stevens standing at the entryway, the bare hint of a smile creeping onto his battered face despite two black eyes and multiple bruises. Beside him stood a middle-aged man Susan did not recognize.

Releasing Susan, John Calvin also turned to see the newcomers. "Ah, there you are. Did you get my signal?" He tipped his head toward the Vox on his wrist, and Susan remembered he had tapped a button when he first came to her bedside.

"I did." Kendall stepped fully into the room, gesturing for the other man to follow him.

Susan sat up in her bed. She knew she must look a fright. Besides having survived an explosion, she had spent what seemed like a lifetime crying. Her eyes felt swollen and sore. "Hi, Kendall. Hi . . ." She paused. Now that he stood closer, the man at Kendall's side did look familiar. "I'm sorry. I'm still a bit muddled. I can't remember your name."

"Ronnie," the man inserted in a cheerful voice. "Ronnie Bogart."

The name cued an image of his back, his body curled into a fetal position. Susan had injected Ronnie Bogart with nanorobots, but he little resembled the pitiful man who had come to her in desperation after seventeen suicide attempts. He seemed to have grown several inches, and he projected an aura of confidence wholly lacking the first time she had met him. His hair was still thinning, but now it was neatly combed and tended. "Ronnie Bogart?" Susan repeated incredulously. "You . . . you . . ." She did not know how to say it without sounding offensive. "You look wonderful!"

"I feel wonderful," Ronnie said, sounding wonderful. "After the docs analyzed the data from the nanorobots, they found an unusual chemical imbalance. I started on my new meds, and voilà!"

Susan could not help laughing. She turned her father a look that she hoped said, *The nanorobots still collected useful data despite the reprogramming.*

John Calvin pursed his lips and nodded.

Ronnie continued. "And you know that fellow, Fontaina? The one always on the unit whenever I got admitted? I used to sit and talk to him for hours, like I would a dog. I mean, he never spoke, never moved. Great sounding board, right?"

Susan wanted to rush him to the punch line. "Don't tell me he's walking around."

"Not yet," Ronnie admitted, "but he's sitting up and looking at people."

"The issues the nanorobots found are a bit more complicated," Kendall explained, clearly trying to maintain whatever confidentiality remained to Neal Fontaina. "And it's only been a couple of days."

"I can't remember the last time I had this much energy." Ronnie scooted back into a normal position. "I can't remember if I ever before felt . . . happy."

"Congratulations," Susan said. The nanorobots might just turn out to be the miracle treatment they had hoped for, at least for some refractory patients. She tried not to wonder if they might have helped Sharicka or if the Ansons were celebrating or mourning the loss of this particular child. Knowing them, she suspected they cried as hard as for her as Susan did for Remington. They truly had loved her, even after mental illness had turned their special child into something horrific and monstrous.

The conversations seemed to have come to a natural conclusion. Kendall scuffed his feet. "So, when do you think you'll be back at work?"

Susan looked at her father.

"The doctors say her wounds will heal in a couple of weeks." John Calvin made no real attempt to answer the question. They all knew shock and grief had more to do with her return than physical injuries.

"Sooner than later," Susan promised. She was not the type to wallow in sadness. She harbored no illusions she would handle the loss of Remington any better than her father had her mother's death. He had gone back to work, though, remained competent at it, resumed a mostly normal life with just a few quirks to prove he had become a different man. She suspected she would prefer leaping back into her residency rather than filling her days with nothing but thoughts of her loss and attempting to distract herself with inane movies and television shows. "I'll be back in time for our next rotation."

Kendall bobbed his head. "Well, it's not as if you left us a bunch of patients to clean up for you." He brightened. "By the way, I'm discharging . . . the teenager you helped me break through to." Confidentiality stopped him from speaking the name.

"Oh yeah?" Susan knew he meant Connor Marchik. No happy ending existed for the teen with refractory liver cancer; but, at least, he could spend his final months with friends and family in an environment more pleasant than the PIPU.

John Calvin took the hint. "You two look like you want to talk shop. Why don't I walk Mr. Bogart back to the unit, if that's okay with him?"

"I'm fine with that," Ronnie answered. "It's only a matter of days till discharge."

As the other men left the room, Kendall's smile faded. Even without the black eyes, the bruises, and abrasions, he would have looked more serious than she had ever seen him before. He paced the floor. Twice.

Barely recognizing him, Susan tried to break the silence. "So, what is our next rotation? The Violent Care Unit?"

Kendall resisted the joke, which surprised Susan in and of itself. "Outpatient psych," he answered distractedly. His smile returned, but it seemed forced. "You're already scheduled to see some old friends."

"Diesel," Susan guessed. "And Monterey. Maybe even Starling."

"Yup."

"And I imagine you'll see Connor."

"Almost certainly." Kendall dodged her stare.

Susan could not stand it any longer. Clearly, he was not going to raise the issue that bothered him on his own. "What's bugging you, Kendall? You look like a shark's eating you from the feet up."

"Susan?" Kendall attempted to look at her; then his gaze flitted away. "When I was up on the roof. With the gun. I had a perfect shot at . . . her."

Susan blinked, trying to understand the implications of what Kendall had just revealed.

"I could have prevented the explosion, Susan. Remy would still be alive." Kendall's eyes blurred behind pools of salt water. "No one would have gotten hurt. Not you. Not anyone."

Susan did not know how to feel. "Come here," she commanded.

As if in a trance, Kendall moved to her side. An uncharacteristic stiffness to his gait betrayed his own injuries, ones that ought to keep him out of residency, too, for at least a week or two.

Susan caught him into an embrace. "It's not your fault, Kendall." She spoke the truth the instant it came to her mind. "I couldn't have pulled the trigger, either."

"Remy could have. To save us. He—" Kendall choked on the words.

Susan did not know how he had intended to finish, so she used her own words. "He was a rare type of person. A true hero." It occurred to her the word was thrown about too casually, applied to inappropriate things. She had heard parents call their children heroes for winning a difficult race, had heard newscasters refer to random survivors of catastrophes as heroes, had heard hero bandied about the hospital to apply to patients who did nothing more than survive a dangerous procedure or let a dying loved one go. Surely, those things took courage and fortitude, but she wondered when hero had lost its meaning, when it had ceased to refer to someone who risked or sacrificed his own life to save the lives of others. Susan thought she had cried out all her tears, but new ones stung her eyes.

Kendall clung.

"We can't all be like that. If we were, it would take all the specialness, all the greatness from men and women like Remy." Susan clutched him tightly. He felt warm and comfortable in her arms. She had never seen him confront vulnerability with anything other than humor, and she liked this strange and different side of him. She whispered, "I couldn't have shot her, either."

Kendall pulled away far enough to look at her.

Susan explained. "That was why I refused to take the gun. Even knowing what she was. Even knowing she had murdered before and would eagerly do so again. Even knowing she would have shot me in a heartbeat, I couldn't have shot her." She looked directly into his eyes; and, when he avoided her gaze, she followed him until he had no choice but to stare back at her. "It's no dishonor to be incapable of killing a human being."

"But—," Kendall started.

Susan could not allow him to finish. "No 'buts.' Not ever."

Kendall clutched her again, and they both sobbed with raw and terrible grief, as if the world would end.

And when the embrace ended, Susan knew, there would be robots to construct and improve, diagnoses to make, and lives to save. Like a flower budding from a dormant stem, she would learn to laugh again, beginning, almost certainly, with a quip from Kendall Stevens.

"Nice going, Humpty Dumpty." He waved a hand to indicate the broken state of Susan's body. "Thanks to Major Medical and professional courtesy, your bill will only be eight hundred million instead of a cool billion."

Susan doubted all the king's horses and all the king's men had fully finished with Kendall, either. At least, they had salvaged his sense of humor, and she suspected they both would need it over the coming years.

Mickey Zucker Reichert is a working physician and author. She lives in Iowa with her husband and two of their children, and divides her time between taking care of her family, writing, practicing medicine, teaching at the local university, and tending the assorted livestock that roam her forty-acre farm.

National bestselling author

TAYLOR ANDERSON

IRON GRAY SEA
Destroyermen

War has engulfed the other earth. With every hard-won
victory and painful defeat, Matt Reddy and the Allies
encounter more friends—and more diabolical enemies.
Even in the arms of the woman he loves, there is little
peace for Reddy. The vast sea and scope of the conflict has
trapped him too far away to help on either front, but that
doesn't mean he and the *Walker* can rest—
and man and four-stacker must face a bigger ship.

Elsewhere, the long-awaited invasion of Grik "Indiaa" has
begun, and the Human-Lemurian Alliance is pushing
back against the twisted might of the Dominion. The
diplomatic waters seethe with treachery and a final,
terrible plot explodes in the Empire of New Britain Isles.

Also in the series:
*Rising Tides • Distant Thunders
Maelstrom • Crusade • Into the Storm*

Available wherever books are sold or at
penguin.com

facebook.com/acerocbooks

R012